Praise for *The Other Princess*

"*The Other Princess* is a poignant, intimate portrait of the extraordinary life of Sarah Forbes Bonetta. Bryce's sweeping novel is brimming with richly detailed history as she transports readers throughout Victorian England and West Africa in this unforgettable story. This is a must-read for historical fiction lovers!"

—Chanel Cleeton, *New York Times* and *USA Today* bestselling author of *The Cuban Heiress*

"Intricately researched and written with vivid detail, *The Other Princess* is a powerful, sweeping saga of resilience, of a young princess ripped from all she knows and thrust into a world not of her choosing. A must-read!"

—Eliza Knight, *USA Today* and internationally bestselling author of *Starring Adele Astaire*

"In *The Other Princess*, Denny S. Bryce brings to life the little-known story of Aina, the daughter of a chieftain in West Africa, who later becomes Queen Victoria's goddaughter, Sarah Forbes Bonetta, a real historical figure new to me. Engrossing, unique, *The Other Princess* vividly depicts Aina's intelligence and love for music and Western literature, as well as her destiny and dilemma as a Black princess in a Victorian court. A stunning saga of tragedies, trials, and triumphs, this is a remarkably told story of a remarkable woman!"

—Weina Dai Randel, *Wall Street Journal* bestselling author of *The Last Rose of Shanghai* and *Night Angels*

The *Other*
PRINCESS

The *Other* PRINCESS

a novel of QUEEN VICTORIA'S GODDAUGHTER

DENNY S. BRYCE

WILLIAM MORROW
An Imprint of HarperCollinsPublishers

THE OTHER PRINCESS. Copyright © 2023 by Denny S. Bryce, LLC. All rights reserved. Printed in the United States of America. No part of this book may be used or reproduced in any manner whatsoever without written permission except in the case of brief quotations embodied in critical articles and reviews. For information, address HarperCollins Publishers, 195 Broadway, New York, NY 10007.

HarperCollins books may be purchased for educational, business, or sales promotional use. For information, please email the Special Markets Department at SPsales@harpercollins.com.

FIRST EDITION

Designed by Diahann Sturge

Part opener illustration © AnyRama/Shutterstock

Library of Congress Cataloging-in-Publication Data has been applied for.

ISBN 978-0-06-314412-5

23 24 25 26 27 LBC 7 6 5 4 3

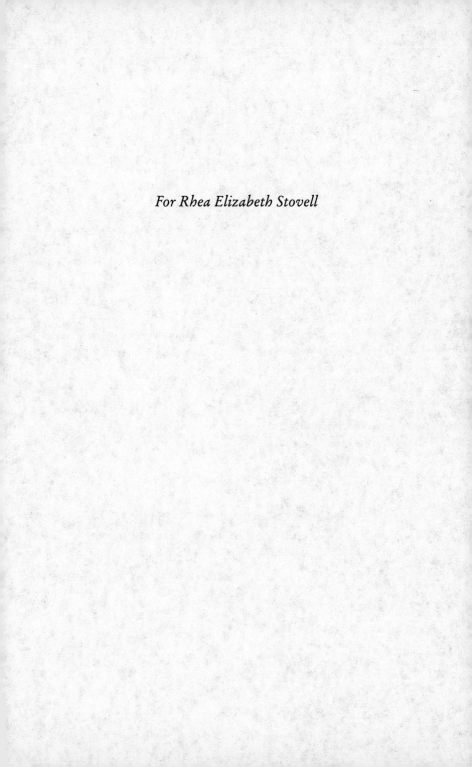

For Rhea Elizabeth Stovell

My mother's kiss, my mother's kiss,
I feel its impress now;
As in the bright and happy days
She pressed it on my brow.
You say it is a fancied thing
Within my memory fraught;
To me it has a sacred place—
The treasure house of thought.

—Francis E. W. Harper, excerpt from
"My Mother's Kiss" (1854)

Prologue

West Africa, 1843

The mother dipped a clay urn into the river's cool water and filled it to the rim. In her other hand, with strong fingers and a calloused palm, she balanced her newborn in the crook of her arm. Then lovingly, she poured the liquid over the child's body, rinsing away the blood, the birth, and the stench of new life. An odor that oddly smelled almost sweet in its foulness.

No other thoughts interfered with these early moments. There was only the cherished affinity between mother and child.

The mother's name was Kayin, which meant long-awaited one. Her child's large black eyes, having adjusted to the world's light, followed Kayin's every movement until the infant's and mother's gazes interlocked, sewn together with an unbreakable length of thread. Never too far away. Never too tightly bound.

The delivery had been long and torturous. A cord wrapped around the baby's throat had almost killed them both. Once the child's cries echoed into the dawn, the fear inside the mother's womb eased but didn't disappear.

A name defined a destiny for the Yoruba people, a map for the child's path in life, a path that followed her from infancy to childhood to adulthood and death. It was Kayin's duty and Yoruba tradition to name her little girl according to the circumstances of her birth. But she hesitated.

She wished to give her daughter a name other than Aina, the name of her birthright.

"Aina" meant born with her mother's life cord around her neck, born to a difficult life, born to an existence of heartbreak and hardship. The idea of burdening her child with such a name sickened Kayin.

Sitting cross-legged on the riverbank, she held her child to her breast, her heart at once full of love and heavy with sorrow.

What if she ignored tradition? Whom would it harm if she defied the gods and gave her daughter a chance at a joyful life?

Her name could be Oko Mi, which meant my darling and carried no curse. Kayin could call her Nothing, or Everything, or Why or Why Not—more names that didn't sentence an infant to a life of woe.

She'd take any risk and be brave enough to challenge the gods for her pure, innocent, beautiful child. But before facing the gods, she first had to convince her husband.

Kayin was a queen and wife to a king. She must seek his counsel before she dared defy the gods.

Kayin set out in search of him. Like the other men in their village, he was a warrior and stood guard over the town during the night and early morning.

The slave traders attacked when they believed the people of her town were the most unprepared. But her husband wasn't a man of chance. He and his men positioned themselves in the forest, where the moonlight allowed them to see into the darkness and through the shadows.

On a hillside overlooking the river, she found him.

"Why are you here?" he whispered as she approached. "Does the child continue to do well?" His voice was husky with concern.

"She is fine, but I worry about her future. Her birth was difficult and—"

"I know. What is on your mind?" he asked.

"I wish for you to grant me an act of opposition."

"Who do you wish to oppose?"

"I want to do something against everything we've ever believed in."

"Oh." The look in his eyes was more tempered indulgence than concern. "All right, I am listening. Proceed."

"We have six children, whom I love dearly, but our seventh child is unique."

"Each of our children holds our hearts in their hands."

"But my heart is full of worry and regret for this little girl." She rocked the baby in her arms. "How can I saddle her with a lifetime of sorrow and sadness?"

He didn't respond, only stared at the child she held.

Kayin took a deep breath. "I want no part of the naming tradition if it means cursing her with a legacy of hardship."

"You've had seven children. Not all the births have been easy. What makes this child different?"

"She is the last one I'll bear."

He hadn't moved since they'd begun speaking. But now, his weight shifted backward as he peered down at her. "You know this. How? Why?"

"My body will no longer make children." She kept her gaze on his chest until she dared look into his eyes, praying she'd find them understanding and not filled with hatred for her betrayal.

"I didn't expect this decision from you," he said. "No matter how difficult the birth."

"My love for you is as strong as when we first met. But I am older now, my husband, and my womb is exhausted. We've had seven children. I can bear no more."

Sunlight streamed through the tree leaves, drawing Kayin's attention to the sky. With the dawn, the clouds changed from black to gray to orange and yellow and blue and green everywhere else—the colors of a rainbow after a morning shower.

The first time they lay together, there had been a rainbow.

"Do as you wish," her husband finally said.

Had she heard him correctly? He wasn't looking at her, but his voice had been distinct, unmistakable. Yes, she'd heard him correctly. "Are you certain, my husband? You will allow me this?"

"Today, I learned I cannot stop you from doing as you see fit. My arguments fall on ears that refuse to hear me."

Her stomach clenched. His tone was a snarl. His words chewed and pushed out of his throat like chips of wood. She had hoped not to hear her king's anger, but she accepted that his ire wasn't because of her desire to abandon the tradition of the naming ceremony. She had left his bed. "I am sorry, but I can't take back what I know to be true. I thank you, my husband, for loving me and understanding this decision."

She leaned forward, baby in her arms, to kiss her husband's cheek, but he turned away, avoiding her touch.

"I will not stop you from giving our daughter whatever name you choose," he said. "But I will call her Aina. An Egbado princess born with a cord around her neck. Aina, the last child of my wife, who is Kayin, which means the long-awaited one."

With those words, he left her and returned to his post, although he did not need to guard the road. The slave traders didn't attack the villages after the sun rose above the treetops.

Kayin stood, unable to draw a breath. The hopefulness that had flooded her chest had seeped away.

A day later, she prepared for the ritual, which had been delayed as long as she dared. After she built a fire that blazed toward the sky, she was joined by the town's wives, mothers, daughters, sisters, aunts. All the women of Okeadon came to bear witness.

Kayin's first act was to make two small incisions with a sharp instrument in her daughter's cheeks. The wounds proved to whoever saw them that Aina was royalty, a princess among the Egbado.

Then the ceremony began, and Kayin hesitated only once and only for an instant when she met her daughter's gaze. Kayin had accepted tradition. There was no escaping it or her husband's will.

She announced her daughter's name with trembling lips, but her words were clear as thunder and bold as the lightning of a summer storm: "Princess Aina. Born with a cord around her throat, child of a difficult birth. This is your name, and this is your destiny."

PART ONE

The Watering of
the Graves

Chapter One

West Africa, 1848

$\mathcal{B}$y the time I was five years old, I had a reputation.

All because of a game played on the riverbank with sticks and stones and lines drawn in the dirt.

They called it Mancala. An amusement of placement. The board, small holes dug in the sand, started empty, and the players chose to add a new piece or move an existing one. The game pieces were black, gray, and smooth white stones. All found on the rocky ground a few minutes from Okeadon.

I played against my brother, Kola, and two of my sisters—but there were seven of us. The oldest ones didn't play. I always won.

I credited these victories to my physical speed—I had small, quick hands—and mental acuity. My recognition of patterns, whether in sounds or figures etched in stone, filled my mind with ideas from which I created melodies. I had such a strong sense of catch. I could grab anything thrown at me before it struck its target, which in many cases was me (my siblings loved to tease). I could also decipher any puzzle, written or spoken, if it wasn't too complicated—I was only five. But even then, I believed my five-year-old talents would serve me well until the end of my days.

It was late one afternoon, and the river was full of women cleaning and washing tunics, long cloths, cooking vessels, and infants. Kola, my sisters, and I had knelt in the dirt nearby, our stones in place, our hearts happy, especially mine, since I expected to win. But the very next moment marked the beginning of the end of my innocence.

Not only had I lost the game for the first time in my life, but also my temper. Something I hadn't realized I had or could lose.

Disbelief erupted from my throat, and I started kicking and scratching like a horned goat trapped in a briar.

One of my sisters grabbed my shoulders and shook me, hoping to calm me. "Stop making so much noise. It's a silly game. Hush up. Someone might think you're weak-minded."

This sister was only two years my senior and had never raised her voice toward me before. No one in the family had, for that matter, including my father and mother.

Confused, I cried harder. I didn't understand. "Why are you mad at me? I was the one who lost. You won the game! Why are you yelling at me?"

Despair was building a nest of thorns behind my eyes. I had a right to be upset, cry, and stomp, but why were Kola and my sisters staring at me? Did they think me ridiculous? Had they forgotten I was the youngest child of Kayin—and her last-born? I eyed them with five-year-old ferocity.

Desperate, I asked, "Why didn't I win today? I always win."

"Your life has been too easy," said one of the sisters. "You needed to learn a lesson."

"It's time we stopped coddling you," said the other. "At five years old, you are not a baby, and we—"

"Almost six," I interrupted her.

"That's right," added Kola, who was almost old enough to join our father's army. "And you must face your destiny like the rest of us."

"What destiny?" I asked. "I don't understand. Please."

"You want an explanation," my brother said. Then he glanced at my sisters. "Should I tell her?"

"No, don't tell her. Mother should talk to her."

"The way she's been treated is because of Mother," Kola said. "Mother never wants her to feel bad about anything because she's her darling."

The way his voice hardened gave me chills.

"It might be difficult to hear," he said. "But at almost six, it is time you learned the truth."

"What do you mean—truth? What truth?" I looked from Kola to my sisters, hoping one of them would contribute something that made sense.

"We let you win. We've always let you win because you've never been good at games—and our mother insisted you win."

For a child who believed she was the luckiest girl in Okeadon, his words were like a fist striking me in the gut. But I ignored the sickness rolling in my stomach.

"You are liars!" I kicked the ground, sending the stone game pieces flying. "And I don't have to listen to liars!"

My three siblings only stared at me. I stared back. I'd feel better if one of them reached out to me, offered to wipe my tears, and apologized for their mean words and harsh expressions. But instead, they turned away and started to play another game without me.

My heart skipped a beat. I needed a hug. My mother was knee-deep in the river a few feet away, washing my father's tunics. Kayin loved me, but when I cried, she cried, too, and I had shed enough tears for both of us.

So I ran.

Forbidden or not, I headed for the forest to find Dayo, my second-eldest brother. He would hug me.

Poju, the eldest brother, had a family, and I rarely saw him. He came by sometimes to join my father and the other brothers to exchange stories of our ancestors and play musical instruments, such as the balafon or the bata drums, or my father's favorite, the ubo aka. But these times were few.

So it was Dayo whom I sought. He was fifteen and tall and wide-bodied. He was the son my father counted on. The son my mother doted on. The brother I loved the most.

A soldier in the king's army (our father's army), he wielded a sword and sometimes carried a musket and planned to marry a girl named Bimpe the following spring.

Dayo would hug me.

The field on the other side of the river was where my mother and the other women pulled root vegetables from beneath the ground. Once I reached the open area, it took a few more minutes before I entered the forest, where the day only existed in chunks of shadow and light beneath the leaves of a million trees. I couldn't see more than a foot in front of me, and the possibility of getting lost or eaten by a wily beast finally crossed my mind.

But I had to believe I'd find my brother before danger found me.

"What are you doing out here?"

I covered my mouth with my hand to silence the scream Dayo's sudden appearance had pulled from my throat. He had leaped from the treetops and glared at me with a scowl on his face.

"Looking for you," I said in my smallest voice.

"Whatever for? You know better than to come into the forest by yourself. You know better than to come into the forest at all."

"I had to talk to you." But that was as much as I said before the tears started again. And I had thought I was done crying.

"Whatever has happened must be serious." He patted the top of my head, then knelt in front of me and wiped my tears with his fingertips. "You are not one to sob so loudly or so much without cause. Have you been injured? Did something happen to one of our brothers or sisters? To our mother?"

"No, that's not it." I swallowed. "I lost a game, and they told me that I'd only won the games before because everyone let me win—they said mother made them, but now that I'm almost six, they decided to stop letting me win."

"Don't worry about the game. It was never as important as you seemed to think," he said. "You should not have come into the forest. It's not safe, and you should stop crying. It makes too much noise, and you'll frighten the creatures I'd rather not see."

Then he gave me the hug I'd come into the woods for, and I melted in his embrace.

"I love you, Dayo."

"I love you." He released me and stood. "Now, I'll walk you back to the riverbank. Then I must return to my watch."

Feeling better, I asked, "What are you watching for?"

"Slave traders." He pushed aside low-hanging branches with his sword. "The Dahomey warriors, mostly."

"What is a slave trader, and who are the Dahomey?"

"Our enemy."

"They are people like us?" I asked.

He shrugged. "Yes and no, not exactly."

He sounded as bewildered as I felt. "Is that why you are in the forest every day?" It was a question I'd asked him before. "To watch out for our enemies?"

He nodded.

I exhaled slowly, still puzzled. "Why are they our enemies?"

"We used to be one nation, all part of the Oyo Empire, until a brutal civil war broke out long ago. The Egba, our people, joined with several other Oyo states and ended up enemies of Dahomey and the Porto Novo, who had banded together. Bitter rivalries, opposing views on trade goods, and other things led to more fighting, and the land of the Egbado nation was caught in the middle—between the two great halves of the once all-powerful Oyo.

"Many battles were fought and continue to be fought, but Dahomey does not want only to win a war. Their business, their trade, is the capture and selling of people—they are slave hunters in the slave trade." His voice sounded as if it had been stretched so thin it might break. "That is why we guard the road. We can't be surprised by Dahomey warriors. For them, winning a battle means murdering as many people as they enslave."

The story frightened me, but not for the reason Dayo might have imagined. "Am I like the Dahomey warriors because I want to win?"

He laughed softly. "No, you are not Dahomey. You misunderstand." He picked me up in his arms and cradled me under my bottom as if his forearm were a stool I sat on. "Father says that the difference between war and savagery is Dahomey—you are no savage." He patted my head. "You are a sweet little girl."

Thoroughly satisfied by his compliment, I circled my arms around his neck. But as I hugged him tightly, I looked closer at the bluestone neckpiece he wore. I had admired it when I first saw it around my father's throat. It was the most beautiful shade of blue I'd ever seen, the only such-colored stone in all Okeadon.

"I thought Father promised the necklace to Poju. Why did he give it to you, Dayo?"

"It's a long story," he said solemnly. "I'll tell you tomorrow. But now, let's get you home where you can apologize to your brother and sisters, and I can return to my post."

I pouted. "I don't want to."

"Don't want to what? Apologize?" He shook his head, and his eyes clouded with concern. "If you don't say I'm sorry, you won't sleep when you go to bed tonight. You will have no rest if you are still angry."

Why should I say I'm sorry? Why should I be the one to bow my head in shame? But Dayo had sounded so severe. I had to tell him the truth. "I don't want to say I'm sorry if I don't mean it."

He adjusted me in his arms. "Aina. Aina. You're almost six. You're old enough to know better."

Of course I knew better, but that didn't guarantee I'd make the decision he wanted me to make. "Oh. Oh. I know what I'll do." I grinned proudly. "I just won't sleep."

* * *

As SOON AS we reached fallow ground, I began pestering Dayo about the necklace with the bluestone pendant.

The questions ran in circles in my mind. How had he convinced our father to give it to him? A family heirloom passed down from father to eldest son for generations was never meant for the second oldest. And me? I only dreamed of wearing it.

But if Dayo wore it, I could also wear it, even if I wasn't a boy. Father had made an exception to the rule by not giving it to his oldest son. He could do it again for his youngest daughter.

But after I admitted to preferring a sleepless night over an apology, Dayo stopped speaking to me. He still carried me in his arms, but no matter how many questions I asked or how heartfelt my pleas for a reply, he didn't say a word until the stranger appeared.

Dayo put me down and fisted the handle of his sword. "Your trade, mister?" he asked, his tone none too friendly.

The stranger had stepped from between two tamarind trees and blocked our path. He was strangely thin, like a weed in the tall grass. A stiff breeze would send him deep into the forest where the anthills were high and the lions hungry. I wondered why he didn't eat his meals. Perhaps Dayo would invite him to dinner. I nudged Dayo's leg to tell him, but my brother held me behind him with the hand he hadn't wrapped around his sword.

"I am a merchant who travels between Abomey and Abeokuta. I come to Okeadon to speak to your king."

Dayo pointed his sword at the stranger's throat but didn't extend his arm. So the blade's tip didn't touch the man's skin, only threatened. "How are you traveling these roads between the Dahomey palace in Abomey and the Egba kingdom in Abeokuta? Those states are at war."

The man tilted his head as if surprised by Dayo's knowledge.

"I should speak with Okeadon's king," the stranger said.

"You can speak with me. I am his son."

"The eldest son?"

"The second eldest."

"The king or his firstborn male child must hear the news I have sworn to deliver."

Dayo moved his sword closer to the man's throat. "What is your name, merchant?"

The stranger hopped from one foot to the other as if a horde of bug-a-bugs chewed on his ankles. "My name is unimportant, but if you must know, it is Simeon Olayinka, and I am a courier of the king of Kuta—whom your father knows. My king instructed me to speak only with your father or his eldest son, and I must obey my king."

The man ended his speech with a crooked smile, as if he'd said something magical. I looked at Dayo and wondered what he might do next. He gave little indication of his thinking, but his eyes were narrow and darker. Was he worried about what the man had said, even though he was holding the sword?

My height wasn't much to speak of—I came to Dayo's waist if I held my head high—but I had strong lungs. And I wanted the worry on my brother's face to disappear.

"Dayo. Dayo." I tugged at the sash of his tunic. "Father will be home. He's always home for dinner." I pointed at Simeon Olayinka. "He looks hungry and should come home with us and eat dinner, and after, he can talk to Father."

Dayo squeezed my shoulder.

Then he poked Simeon Olayinka in the side with his sword and gestured for him to walk in front of us. "Head straight. My sister's right. You should join us for dinner and tell my father about your message from the king of Kuta."

Chapter Two

A forest flanked Okeadon to the east and west, and a rapid river flowed to the north. It was not a small town. Thousands of people—families, soldiers, wives, sisters, and brothers—inhabited Okeadon. So having a father as king meant we were known, our faces recognized. My mother claimed that the townspeople watched our family, studied us, and pointed to us as examples of what was excellent, but that would change if we behaved poorly in front of others.

I didn't know anyone other than my parents and my siblings. I didn't play with other children. I didn't need to seek care, affection, or love outside my home. We had everything I needed inside. I never needed to look elsewhere for more.

When Dayo and I entered our home with Simeon Olayinka, the family was preparing for dinner, but everything stopped at the sight of us.

Father gestured for my brothers to stand in specific spots, as if they were on guard. They faced the doorway but angled their bodies to shield our mother and sisters, who had backpedaled toward the rear of the house, but not before my eldest sister snatched me from Dayo's grip and pulled me to her side.

When Father spoke, he looked only at Dayo. "Son, who is this you have brought into our home?"

"He is Simeon Olayinka, but he introduced himself as a courier from the king of Kuta."

"There is no king of Kuta. A chieftain, yes. But not a king." Father turned to Olayinka and his gaze swept over the thin man from head to toe. If my father had ever looked at me in such a way, I would've melted into the dirt, but Olayinka didn't shrink away.

Dayo made a noise in his throat. "That's why I brought him to you, Father. Because I knew it was either a lie or something else."

"You chose correctly, my son." Father folded his arms over his chest. "The chief of Abeokuta would only send a courier with a message for a king about a danger coming to my village. Have you come with a warning?"

Suddenly bold, Olayinka stepped from the entryway to the middle of the room and stopped squarely in front of my father. "Yes, I have," he said earnestly. "King Gezo and the Dahomey warriors will attack Okeadon tomorrow before the sun reaches the middle of the sky. Your town should prepare for battle immediately, or the Agojie will overrun it and butcher those they do not enslave."

My mother gasped, and my sisters hugged each other around her waist and shoulders. I was left without anyone to hold on to, but I also didn't understand why everyone was afraid.

"How does he intend to break through our walls, get past our guards?" Father asked without looking at the horror-filled faces of his wife and daughters.

"One of the Egba chieftains is a traitor and will betray your borders at dawn."

"Do you know the traitor's name?"

"My chieftain only gave me the message," said Olayinka. "The traitor's name and face are unknown to me."

Father unfolded his arms and nodded at my mother, but he didn't give her a reassuring glance. Instead, hard lines circled his mouth and the skin around his eyes. An uneasiness filled the room and hung in the air as thick as molasses.

"Father, do you know King Gezo?" asked Dayo, who, like me, had noticed our father's strange behavior. "Have you met him? The way you—I thought—"

"Yes, I did, but before the war broke out," Father said. "Our states were part of one empire. We fought side by side in battle but eventually ended up enemies." He rubbed his brow, but the wrinkles in his skin only deepened. "The rest of the story is too long to tell. We have to prepare for an attack, which we will discuss after dinner. Will you join us, Simeon?"

The courier nodded vigorously. "Yes, thank you, Sovereign. I haven't eaten in days."

I listened with pride and grinned at Dayo, although he had no idea what had made me so happy—I'd been right to encourage Dayo to invite Simeon Olayinka to dinner. He was hungry. From then on, I'd never doubt any thought, idea, or bone to pick that came into my mind. There was always a chance I'd be right.

* * *

DURING DINNER AND most of the evening, I avoided my brother and two sisters, the trio who had thought to break my spirit by telling me my winning days were a lie. However, I need not have bothered ignoring them. Talk of King Gezo and battle had stolen their tongues, and my family ate a meal in silence for the first time in my memory.

After dinner was when the commotion began.

Everyone had a task, a place to be, a musket to clean, meal pouches to fill, and urns to carry to the river. Everyone was busy except for me.

My mother said a battle was coming, but I was too little to help. I should stay out of harm's way. Okeadon had to be ready, and its king and his family led by example.

As Simeon Olayinka had warned, Dahomey attacked at dawn. But Gezo's Agojie, the female soldiers who fought fiercely and brutally, weren't a match for the bravery of Okeadon's warriors.

When Dayo returned home after the battle, excitement gleamed in his eyes. "We were better fighters, stronger, smarter, and Father had us positioned so that not one Agojie broke through the barricade." He placed a hand over his heart. "And we are grateful to Simeon Olayinka of Abeokuta and his warning. I hate to think what might have occurred if the Agojie had surprised us."

The town rejoiced following the victory, but Father forbade prolonged merrymaking and, after a short celebration, ordered the people to return home. I was sad we had to stop dancing and singing, because everyone was smiling, laughing, and hugging.

We had conquered Dayo's enemy.

Our family went to bed exhausted, and victory made for a deep sleep. A dreamless, peaceful rest, until the noise of a thousand warriors stampeding our barricades awoke us.

My sister lifted me into her arms with the moonlight shining behind her head. She placed me firmly on my feet. "Wake up. You must wake up. Now."

Her breath felt strange against my cheek, not warm and

gentle but brittle and cold. I looked up, and the fear in her eyes stopped my heart. "What's wrong? What is happening?"

"Don't worry. Just do as I say." Unfortunately, her lie did not calm me. Fear couldn't be replaced by a soothing touch or whispered words. I tried to swallow, but there was nothing to taste but dread.

Another roar of sound moved toward us. Soldiers approached with clanging swords and thunderous strides. I tried to listen and judge the distance, but the dundun drums and brass bells grew louder as the warriors surrounded Okeadon.

"What is that? Who is making the noise?" My small hand twisted the edges of my sister's tunic.

"King Gezo and his butchers have returned in the middle of the night."

It had been a ruse: the daylight battle, a pretense to take Okeadon off guard.

Father appeared in the entranceway. "They have killed the guards. No attempt to take prisoners." He hurried through the house, flinging items over his shoulder, searching for something he'd never find, I feared.

"Easier to butcher us, cut our throats, and end our lives," he ranted. "Next, they'll set fires and make more noise." Empty-handed, he stared at Mother, his face contorted with the same expression I'd seen in my sister's eyes. "It's the cackle of their murderous laughter I hate the most." He rubbed his forehead. "Chaos leads to panic, and indecision prompts inaction." Again, he looked at Mother. "Run. It's the only thing to do. Take the children to the forest. Disappear. I will find you when I can."

"No," she replied, her voice wild. "We can fight with you and my sons—their brothers."

Father grabbed her shoulders. "You will do as I say and run. Gezo will have no mercy for our family. I know him, and there is no time to explain further. Go."

My father and his sons reloaded their muskets and grabbed long knives. Even Kola, the youngest brother, would fight. Dayo was the first one ready and raced from the house for the battleground without saying goodbye. I would've run after him and called him back to hug me, but he disappeared before I opened my mouth.

My mother gathered her girls, but I had drifted toward the door through which Dayo had raced and wasn't close enough to cling to her.

"Aina, come here. Hurry. We must run. Hurry, my darling." My mother held out her hand, but my legs were heavy. I couldn't reach her. Then the enemy, the Dahomey warriors, filled the house.

How had they gotten inside so quickly? I spun around and around, looking for a place to hide.

"Agojie! Agojie!" my mother wailed.

At first, I thought these women, who held muskets and swords like my father and brothers, hid their faces behind masks. But the closer they came to me, I saw hollow eyes and smooth skin, untouched by emotions but drenched in sweat.

The noise grew louder and louder and blurred into screams and pleas for mercy. My mother was too far away now, and I hated the noise so much that I stood like a statue and covered my ears.

Then, silence surrounded me like a large black shadow. It covered every corner, every ounce of air, and shut every door until it was so quiet I heard my breath catch in my lungs.

The warriors held my father by his arms and around his

throat, apart from my mother. They had corralled my sisters and brothers, except for Dayo (nowhere in sight), into a tight circle. The Agojie cut off my mother's, sisters', and brothers' heads. It's not so easy to separate a head from a body with a sword. Sometimes it dangles, as with the youngest of my brothers. He stubbornly attempted to hang on to his head, but the Agojie refused to allow it. They kept at him until it fell. The sisters weren't as tricky. Their narrow necks popped clean with one slice. As horrible as these images were, the silent screams devastated me, filling my ears, tearing away my heart and soul, and leaving my throat dry and useless. Nothing came out of my mouth. I stared wide-eyed and curious, like a mad dog, mesmerized by the color of blood and how it came in so many shades of red.

All the while, the women warriors chopped, chopped, and chopped.

Father screamed. The sound broke through the silence in my head, and I turned to look at him. His face was twisted and tormented.

He was crying, not for himself but for those he loved and cared for more than his own life.

"Father!" I called.

"Don't look," he begged. "Close your eyes, Aina. Close them tight."

An obedient daughter, I fell to my knees, closed my eyes, and covered my head with my hands. I would not see the weapon that ended my life, and during that instant before the sword's blade landed, I'd find my mother whole, and fall into her arms, loved and safe in her eternal embrace.

Chapter Three

Abomey, West Africa, 1848

Jagged strips of memory filled my head.

I walked in darkness, in daylight, in filth, over rough ground and pools of mud, through swamps with swarming mosquitoes, my body shivering one moment, covered with sweat the next.

With each step, the memories came. Memories I had hoped were my imagination, memories that played horrible, vicious games with my heart. But none of it was a dream. It was real, except I had no idea where I was. All I knew was that I had to keep putting one foot in front of the other.

Horses galloped toward me, and warriors sat in their saddles, carrying muskets and wielding long swords. My eyes widened. They were chopping off heads. The wails of the dying were thunder and lightning bolts, and I wanted to run, flee, move from harm's way, but someone shoved me in the back, and I fell to the ground.

After a second on my knees, I was once more on my feet. The warriors had missed taking my head off again. I prayed they would not make a point of correcting their mistake.

I closed my eyes.

A chant echoed: "Hail King Gezo. Hail King Gezo."

The name. It was familiar. I had heard it before. I opened my eyes.

A wall of death surrounded me, and people were moving everywhere, marching over hard ground. Stiff rope and brass chains bound us; the same rope tied around my naked waist tethered me to them.

I was not dead but captured. Caught. Enslaved.

An elder ahead of me stumbled and fell. A long line of men, women, and children dropped to their knees, unable to move because of the fallen man's weight.

I hid behind another man and watched and listened. The warriors ordered the elder to rise, but when he didn't move, they jabbed him in his side with the tip of a sword. He rolled onto his back and groaned. A third warrior poked him in the rib cage. The elder didn't cry out. He was too exhausted to scream. He'd gone as far as he could go.

An Agojie in a short skirt that barely covered her bottom stepped away from the others and made an awful sound, a screech, a cackle, and then she lifted her sword above her head and buried it in the elder's hollow chest. Then she withdrew the blade and killed a few more people for no apparent reason other than that they'd been within arm's reach. Other warriors dismounted from their horses, untied the dead from the rest of us and, using long spears, shoved the bodies to the side of the road into the marsh.

I would not let my knees touch the ground again.

The days went slowly. Minutes were hours and passed in a haze of pain and fatigue. The soles of my feet swelled like the bellies of the frogs at the riverbed. Each breath was like swallowing a handful of sand.

Still, we marched. So many deaths and lives I loved lost, but after a long while, I remembered Dayo. I hadn't seen Dayo die. He'd left before the Agojie attacked our home. He had escaped, run into the forest, as Father had taught us, and now he was somewhere in the long line of people. I wasn't alone.

I turned my head, but there were too many tall bodies, and I couldn't find him. My stomach cramped, and I wrapped my arms around my middle and squeezed, calming myself with my embrace. It took a few minutes, but soon, I was fine, because in my heart Dayo was alive, and the very thought of him made everything all right.

I, Aina, an Egbado princess, had felt joy. My spirit had reentered my body to help me find my brother. Once I found him, we'd return home to bury the souls of the dead and start anew. It was possible with him. Just him and me. Dayo and me. Always and forever. My second-eldest brother, whom I loved more than anyone. I'd find him, and together, we'd go back home.

* * *

I WAS THROWN into a tent with a hundred other townspeople from Okeadon. Fear was a cord around my neck those first days, but then the smell and monotony were a prison. The only way to tell one day from the next was by who was missing from the tent the following morning.

Each day, another man, woman, or child was gone but replaced every other day by a new man, woman, or child.

Some of the missing hurt my heart more than others. Like the ones I'd curled up next to or shivered alongside when my nightmares were at their worst.

An elder, a woman who knew my mother and grandmother, told stories and fables—the Lion and the Jackal, the Tortoise and the Daughter. I loved those stories, and when she disappeared, I tried to cry, but I'd used up all my tears by then.

I had yet to find Dayo. I'd hardly looked, because I was trapped in one spot, in one tent. I was sad and lonely. I missed my family, my mother and sisters. Still, to find Dayo, I needed help, which meant asking questions, but my voice sounded the same as theirs, and I hated hearing them coming only from me.

So I stopped talking. I didn't say a word to anyone until I met Monife. There was no keeping quiet around her.

The morning I first saw her, she walked toward me, muttering to herself with this incredible bounce to her step. It was how I used to walk when I played on the riverbank with my youngest sisters and brother.

She didn't look much older than me and was slightly taller. Her slim body had spidery limbs and stringy muscles, as if she ran with gazelles and never tired. Then I noticed she wasn't tied to anyone. Why? I was tethered to an elder, a gray-haired woman who moaned in her sleep.

Where was the rope around this girl's waist? Then I saw what she was hiding.

Oh, she was clever. She held the rope in her hand to appear bound, but she wasn't attached to anyone or anything. More remarkable was the smile on her face. No one smiled in King Gezo's slave tents. The old woman who told stories had laughed at her own joke once, but no one except the girl walking toward me ever looked happy.

She was all smiles.

I never thought a smile could hurt. The pain in my stomach spread to every muscle and bone in my body. But I couldn't let her smile alone. So, when she reached me, I gave it a go.

My smile pleased her; she took my hands, held them in hers, and squeezed. Not hard, but with warmth and kindness. I prayed she'd never let me go.

"Tell me your name," she said.

Having not used my voice in a while, I worried how I might sound—or worse, if by talking I somehow would betray the memory of my mother and sisters. Would I hear their voices in mine? Would the sound make me miss them more?

"Are you going to answer me?" she asked with a tilt of her head, but the smile remained.

I felt a chill from a nonexistent breeze and shivered. I had to do something, say something, or she might leave—walk away with her smile and never see me again.

One word. That was all I needed.

She squatted in front of me. "How old are you?"

I pressed my lips together. The silence in my throat made no sense, but I couldn't speak. I raised a hand, spread my fingers, and with the other hand, wiggled only one finger.

"Six, huh," she said. "I'm twelve but small for my age, a stroke of good fortune, I believe. I think that's one of the reasons I'm alive. The Agojie don't know I'm no baby."

I took offense. Was she calling me an infant because I was only six? I was scarcely a child after what I'd seen and been through.

"My name is Monife," she said casually, as if unconcerned that I hadn't spoken.

"Those markings—" She leaned forward, studying my face. "You're from a royal family, aren't you?"

I nodded.

"I've been looking for you." She licked her lips. "With your scars and my abilities, we could get out of here."

My heart pounded. "Yes, I was royalty."

She sighed. "I hoped you weren't mute."

"I chose to stop talking. I had nothing to say." I swallowed the knot in my throat. "No one to say it to."

She wrapped an arm around my shoulders. "Don't fret. You've got someone to talk to now—me. And you and I are going to escape."

A sudden tightness in my chest made it difficult to breathe. "We can't escape." My fingers tingled. "The guards are everywhere."

She frowned. "How would you know? You've been inside this tent for weeks and weeks, and I have ways of doing things."

"What do you mean?"

"I'm a thief." She smiled. "I know how to steal things, take them, and I learn what I need to know to stay alive."

I had trouble following some of her words, but I understood staying alive. I had a reason to live, too.

"I should confess," she said. "I didn't need to ask your name. It's Aina. Right? Your father was the chieftain of Okeadon."

"He was king." I looked down, surprised by the strength in my voice. Then I noticed our fingers were intertwined. "But he's dead." I let her go.

"Sorry. I knew that." She puckered her lips. "When we escape, you can come to my village if you have no place to go. You and I will make a team."

I stared at her curiously. She'd already decided so much about us, from escaping to teams. She also talked as if we were about to play a game right in front of the guards.

"Don't you ever wonder why you're still alive?" she asked, sitting cross-legged on the ground. "I'll tell you why. It's your scars. King Gezo's warriors were told not to kill you. He likes to save the last living member of a royal family to sacrifice during one of his big celebrations."

She spoke in such a cheerful, happy voice that I hated to disappoint her, but I had to tell the truth. "I don't want to escape."

Her smile vanished. "Why say that?"

"My brother is here."

"Your brother? But your family was murdered by the Agojie, throats cut in their beds."

"That's not true. We were in the middle of the house, and the warriors killed my other brothers and sisters by chopping off their heads." I swallowed a dry lump in my throat. "I don't know why they didn't kill me, though."

"I just told you why. You were spared to be sacrificed at the palace."

I didn't want to believe what she was saying and didn't want to talk about death or sacrifices. "Can you show me how to get out of these ropes?"

"I'll do it." She reached into the folds of her sash and removed a small smooth stone, sharpened to a point. "When I cut you free, hold the rope to your waist and stay close to the old woman. It won't be as obvious that you aren't tied."

She worked quickly, and when the rope loosened, I held it to my body and glanced at the elder to whom I was no longer roped. The woman had noticed but made no sound, only closed her eyes.

"Thank you," I whispered to Monife.

Then the guards entered the tent, carrying pots of what looked like the leftover stew my mother threw out for the wild pigs and dogs.

They deposited the food bins near the tent opening. Monife and I glanced at each other and rose from our crouched positions. We'd have to move fast or deal with scraping the bottom of the pot.

Staying close to each other as if we were tied, we moved forward, taking small steps to avoid drawing attention. But a very wrinkled man with very black skin shoved me in the backside, and I bumped into Monife hard.

"Be careful," she grumbled and, with a swift hand, checked her sash for the stone, I imagined, and whatever else was hidden there. "Hold your footing."

The old man pushed harder, punching people and creating havoc.

"Stay still," warned one of the women from Okeadon. "You'll get us all lashed."

I went to shove back but dropped my hands. Someone might notice I'd been cut free.

Inhaling deeply, I kept my head down and accepted the blows from the others, rushing toward the food. Eventually, Monife and I grabbed whatever was within reach and returned to my spot in the tent.

"I will help you find your brother," Monife said after we'd finished our meal. "It won't be easy. Everyone here looks the same. Dirty. Black. Afraid."

"He'll be wearing a bluestone necklace, or if he's not wearing it, he'll have hidden it somewhere, but he'd never part with it."

"There are lots of necklaces."

"No one has this shade of blue stone. It's the bluest of blues. If someone has seen it, they won't forget it."

"The warriors probably took it from him."

That wouldn't happen. Dayo would die first. "No. He'd hide it from the Agojie. But he'd show it in his tent to others from Okeadon to prove he was the king's son."

She nodded thoughtfully. "That could help us find him, but you've got to do something for me." She leaned forward, her voice low. "I want you to cut my face."

I scratched my ear, not sure I'd heard her correctly. "Why would I do that?"

"The scars on your face are why the Agojie won't snatch you up without orders from King Gezo himself. So if I have scars like yours, they'll think I'm royalty, and princesses don't end up on slave ships. They are kept for sacrifice during special celebrations. And can remain captive for years."

"Is that what happens to the people missing in the morning?" I asked, sitting on the ground facing Monife.

"They've either been taken to a slave ship or sacrificed or gotten themselves killed by Dahomey warriors because the Agojie are good at killing. But the king sacrifices royalty during his celebrations."

I didn't understand. It didn't make sense. King Gezo's warriors had killed my parents, sisters, and most of my brothers, all royalty. I was the only one spared. How could a scar prolong my life but not theirs? Also, I wouldn't say I liked the thought of slicing her face. "Why don't you do it yourself?"

"I don't want to do it wrong, and I figured you'd know how."

I took the stone from her. "I should tell you that I may be five, not six. I lost count of the days and weeks."

"You're smart. I trust you. Besides, you look almost seven."

I rose from my cross-legged position and squatted in front of her. I held the stone with a steady hand and touched the scars on my face with the other, checking their shape, the depth of the wounds, and the position.

I took hold of Monife's chin. "Don't move. All right. Ready?"

She bowed her head and smiled. "Yes, Princess Aina. I am ready."

Chapter Four

Abomey, West Africa, 1848–1849

With Monife by my side, I didn't feel lonely, and my grief wasn't as sharp. I had her. At least, I thought I had her. But she had an awful habit of disappearing, leaving for long periods and suddenly reappearing as if she'd never left—and that brought back the hurt. How could I trust her? There was no logic to it, but I did trust her. I needed to trust someone.

She stayed away from me for more than a week after I cut her face—and I was a wreck. It was another loss, and I was as heartbroken as the night the Dahomey warriors killed my family and forced me to march from Okeadon to Abomey, a hopeless, helpless, grieving mess with no end in sight to my pain.

When she finally showed up in my tent, she told me why she'd left. It seemed she thought I'd hurt her deliberately.

"You asked me to cut the scars on your cheek."

"I did, but how was I to know how much it hurt and how long it would take to heal?"

I considered her concern and confessed. "I'm not sure it was my fault, but I admit, I'd forgotten to mention that I was only a few days old when my mother made the marks on my face. I can't remember if it hurt or not. I was a baby."

When I'd cut her, I knew how much pain she was in. She hollered and barked like a hyena, and the waterfall of blood gushing from her wounds didn't help.

Honestly, I thought she'd die. I'd even said so. I'd seen so much death, it had become part of my nature to expect it. I think that made her mad—how swiftly I'd put her in the grave. She had a temper like a hippo during mating season, too. That's what my mother had said about one of my sisters. I figured Monife was like her in that way. So I followed my mother's advice and left her alone when she stalked off. I didn't even wave goodbye, for I never imagined she'd be gone so long.

But as soon as she returned, I forgot about my fears, and we started where we'd left off.

"You were an infant when you were scarred. Right," Monife reasoned. "So I have forgotten my rage about it."

"The scars are healing, though," I said softly.

She touched her face. "Now I am protected from the Ago-jie until the king orders us to be sacrificed. So, enough talk of scars. Are you ready to begin the search for your brother?"

"Yes." I nodded fiercely.

We immediately started searching for my second-eldest brother, but it didn't go as I had imagined. Monife had her way of doing things, I learned quickly.

Crossing a field behind a row of tents at the edge of the camp, Monife insisted I learn everything there was to know about chewing the stems of green leafy plants for water and hunting wild pigs and rabbits for their skin and meat. There was more, but I was antsy to find Dayo and not have a lesson on how to survive in the jungle.

She explained that this knowledge would be very useful when we ran. She laid a hand on my shoulder. "Remember our bargain. We find your brother, and we escape from Da-homey."

I half listened, mainly because I could only keep so many

missions in my head. I was almost six—and my devotion to finding my brother owned my thoughts.

Monife continued her lectures, and despite my lack of interest, some of what she said seeped into my brain. I learned how to skin animals with sharp-edged stones and why we didn't use knives. It seemed they were impossible to conceal beneath our loosely fitting tunics.

"I'll teach you how to catch and scale fish later," she said. "You need time to let these lessons sink in."

She reminded me of Dayo and my sisters. Always teaching me how to do one thing or another when all I wanted to do was eat, sleep, and play.

"When will we go into the tents to look for Dayo?" I asked, bored and making no effort to hide it, between rolling my eyes and sighing like the roar of a lion. But there was no stopping her.

"The slave camps aren't too far from Abomey and King Gezo's palace." Monife pointed toward the city. "You can make it there before the sun reaches the middle of the sky, even if you leave long after sunrise."

"Will we go into the city to look for Dayo?"

"No. If he's in the city, he's about to be sacrificed for one of King Gezo's holidays. The Agojie are even more frightening in the palace. They are the king's guards."

My disappointment had to show on my face. She was talking about all these other things but not about finding Dayo.

"We also have to study the guards. Where they sleep and eat, where they go when they disappear from one post to another."

"All right." I peeked into a tent where a guard had stepped out.

"Pay attention, Aina. We must know as much about the guards as they know about themselves."

"Why? They killed my family, and they cut off the heads of

slaves to celebrate their holidays. I don't want to know any-thing more about any of them."

"If they are chasing us, we'll need to know where to hide so they won't find us."

I pouted, having never liked a scolding, but Monife made sense. I should listen. "I want to go inside the tents and look for him. We haven't been inside one tent yet, other than mine. And Dayo—well, I can't find him without you." My lips quivered with frustration. "We've got to find him. He might be sick—or alone."

Monife took hold of my shoulders. "He could be dead, too, Aina."

"Wh-why say something like that? That was mean."

"I'm not mean. I'm worried that if we don't find him, you'll be so sad, you won't want to escape."

I turned away from her, unable to face her because—how did she know? I'd already thought that if we didn't find Dayo, I wouldn't want to do anything other than lie in a corner, like so many others did, barely breathing, barely alive, waiting for an Agojie sword to fall on my neck.

"Not finding Dayo doesn't mean he's dead," I said. "I'd know if he was gone. I'd feel it inside me." I placed a hand over my heart. "You must believe me—he's alive."

Monife's sigh was long and breathy. "There are thousands of slaves in this camp. Too many to count. Finding Dayo will take time. Especially if we visit every tent."

"I think you lied to me. You don't want to look for my brother."

"What will we do after we find him? Take him to your tent? Take him to mine?" She tugged me by the hand. "No. When we find him, we will run."

"Escape?"

"It won't be easy, even if we know every corner of the camp and where every guard is standing, sleeping, or eating."

I clapped my mouth shut. She was right, and arguing with her made little sense. She might be small, but she was thirteen by then and less willowy. I had to follow her to find Dayo, and I didn't wish to be alone.

Another month passed before Monife changed her approach. It was a large camp and Abomey a big town, and I swear we visited every inch, twice. We stopped pretending to be tied up. The Agojie had lost interest in roping children together. They let us travel freely, within the camp. This allowed Monife and I to meet new people—including other children who weren't roped or chained to anyone—and everywhere we went, we asked about Dayo and his necklace.

Did I mention it was a big camp and Abomey a large city? More months went by, season after season, then a year, which neither of us noticed, not even me. After a while, we weren't looking for Dayo. Instead, we began to do what children do, even in horrible circumstances.

We played.

We skipped, jumped, and hopped. We formed groups, hiders and seekers—even warriors and enslaved. After all, we were children in a smelly, deadly slave camp.

We were resilient, however, and turned the search into a game. The camp and the tents were our game board, the bound people and the guards our game pieces. We stole food, clothing, jewels, and gold from the Agojie. Whatever we put our hands on and could hide before the Dahomey guards caught us, we took. Weeks passed, and I scarcely thought of my brother.

A child's mind can only hold on to tragedy for so long.

* * *

DRY SEASON. WET season. Dry season again. Our search for Dayo had its ups and downs—unfortunately, mostly downs. Luck was not with us. Our efforts to find him consistently fell short. I was on the verge of giving up. Hope drifted away, hid in corners, and protested when I asked it to remain by my side. Of course, I would never admit such a thing to Monife, especially since she behaved as if nothing dared stop her from doing whatever she wanted, no matter how dangerous.

I swear she was possessed by Elegbara, the trickster, the god of chance, and rejoiced in taking unreasonable risks. But I kept those thoughts to myself, even after she nearly got us killed.

One day, we were strolling through the campgrounds, taking a break from the search for Dayo, when Monife stopped to stare at an Agojie. Her gaze held such contempt that I thought we'd be drawn and quartered then and there.

"Do you want us to get a lashing, Monife?"

She frowned at me as if I'd said something wild. "We're not here to fight with Gezo's warriors," I said, reminding her of the lessons she'd taught me. "We avoid them until we need something. Then we approach only when desperate and with a good lie in mind."

"Hush," she said, staring at the warrior.

"Monife." I ignored her rebuff. "We have a plan. We steal what we need and sneak around danger, not into it. So don't stare so forcefully at a warrior."

I had to speak boldly. Monife was not following her own rules. I was worried. She'd also started to disappear again, which she hadn't done since I cut her face after we'd first met.

She took risks, but this risk seemed unlike her. Why did this warrior mesmerize her? A woman who held no physical distinction. She was dressed in a tunic with a sash, weapons on a belt, and jewelry like any other. However, her gleaming gold hoop earrings were beautiful.

"I love her jewelry," I said with reverence.

"Do you want those earrings?"

I reached up and tugged on Monife's ear. "My sister pierced my ears. How about yours? Are they pierced?"

"No." Monife narrowed her eyes. "Do you want the earrings?"

"I can pierce them if you like."

She shook her head and didn't stop for several seconds. "No. I will never let you near me with a sharp stone again. My cheeks are burning."

"Many seasons have passed since I cut you." I touched her face. "Your scars have healed perfectly, and you look like me, a princess."

She pulled away. "Yes, they did heal, but I won't go through that again. You're not very good with sharp things."

"I'm older now. I can do better," I objected, but she wasn't paying attention to me. Her gaze had returned to the warrior. I changed the subject. "I'm hungry," I said. "Let's get some food."

"I'm not hungry." She kept staring at the warrior. Through our travels over the seasons, we attracted the attention of many warriors throughout the camp. Whatever was bothering Monife was making her careless.

"Wait here," she said suddenly. "I'll be back."

I went to grab Monife's hand in case she planned to leave me alone again without warning. But she had scampered off, disappearing behind a group of young men chained together with iron cuffs on their wrists and ankles. I'd never seen anyone shackled that way before. Their dark bare flesh was caked with dirt and patches of mud because their wet skin was covered with sweat, which, mixed with the soil, made mud.

Some had on tunics, others only a sash covering their bottom halves. Some were crying, but their tears looked more angry than sad. The sight of these men harnessed together like animals should have frightened me, but what made me tremble were the men who weren't chained.

They were pale-skinned, almost the color of clouds, except they had long hairs on their faces and necks, and long pants covering their legs. They also wore jackets, shirts, boots, and so much clothing I thought their skin must be boiling like my mother's stew. I didn't understand their language, except I recognized three words, having heard them often in the camp: Slaves. Traders. Ships.

The men grabbed the chained dark-skinned men, opening their mouths with rough fingers and pulling on their arms and legs. I stared at them with more curiosity than heartsickness. Then Monife reappeared.

She held out her hand. "Look what I've got."

She had a pair of earrings in her hands, but she was limping, and blood dripped from a nasty scrape on her knee. "What happened?" I asked nervously. "How'd you get hurt?"

"I was clumsy, and a guard stabbed me. But that's no matter. It will heal." She held the earrings up. "But I got them."

"Are you sure?" I glanced at her leg.

She widened her eyes with anger as she shoved the earrings at me. "These are what is important. Not my leg."

I didn't want to argue. I also didn't understand why she didn't care about her injury. But her stubborn glare was a thing I didn't wish to mess with. I also believed that my fears weren't imagined. She was growing tired of being around me. During the past dry season, we hadn't spent nearly as much time together as we once had. "All right, then. I won't ask about your leg. How did you steal the earrings?"

She grinned, but her eyes were sad. "I'm a good thief."

Her reply didn't answer my question. "The Agojie had them in her ears, and you stole them while she was walking about?"

"No." She chuckled. "These aren't the same earrings. I took them from one of the warriors taking a nap near the fruit trees."

"The one that stabbed you?"

She closed one eye, and the other shot me between mine. "Let it alone."

"Did you change your mind about getting your ears pierced?"

"No. Never." She shook her head, but not as intensely as before. "The earrings aren't for me. I stole them for you."

"Really? Oh, my." I took the earrings and held them over my heart. I couldn't wear them. I'd hide them in the safest place I could find in my tent. "Thank you. Thank you. They are lovely, but why?"

Her gaze shifted from the forest to the camp, and a faraway look settled in her eyes.

"What do you have to tell me?" I asked with great concern, a feeling conveyed by my unsteady voice.

"I've been trying to escape—without you."

"I don't understand."

"I hate it here."

"We all do."

"No, I hate it here so much, I'd rather die. I tried to drown myself in the river, but a boy came along and pulled me out." Her eyes didn't stare off into the distance but at her empty hands. "When I'm not with you, I am with that boy."

Tears poured from my eyes. My throat ached. Had I lost my friend? "You lied to me." Her story made no sense. "But why not keep the lie going? Why tell me about this boy today?"

"Last night, they took him away, the boy I loved, and I wanted to die, but an elder walked up to me. I thought she intended to console me, but she had another message. She had heard we were looking for a young man with a bluestone necklace. A boy from Okeadon."

A shudder went through me, and everything around me, inside me, stopped, including my ability to breathe. What more was she about to tell me? It had to be about Dayo. God. What if he was dead? What if all this time I'd been looking for a ghost?

"The elder told me she knew of Dayo—she's seen him. Talked to him. He's here in the camp, Aina. He isn't dead."

A herd of elephants stampeding across the savannah made less noise than my heart pounding.

I took a deep breath and closed my eyes tight.

I'd been right. All along, I'd been right. He was alive. My brother Dayo was alive.

Chapter Five

*H*e had survived.

I could breathe without breaking into pieces—and search for him with hope in my heart and a smile on my face. And Monife and I did precisely that.

We traveled from tent to tent each morning, from slave pen to slave pen each afternoon, and each day we came closer to Dayo. We missed him by a week on the east side of Abomey—and by a day at a tent in the lowlands. A group of the enslaved had seen him near the river one morning, and we arrived at the spot that afternoon. But he was gone.

We were two little girls on the hunt for a young man, sixteen or seventeen, and everyone in the camp knew him, not by name but by the bluestone necklace in his possession.

I was a jumping bean of excitement, and the thought of keeping still made my stomach tumble. All day, all night, I wanted to look for him. I needed to see him again, hug him again, and have him hug me.

My spirits had lifted and soared into the Orun, the afterlife. But I should've known something not good was coming.

It began with a disagreement. Monife and I had returned to my tent and curled up in an open spot on the ground. I was frustrated. We had ended another day empty-handed. No new luck finding Dayo.

"We should take a break." Monife sat with her feet folded beneath her bottom. "Go to the river tomorrow for a swim. There's a spring on the other side of Abomey the guards don't bother with. We can cool off."

"It will take most of the daylight to get there and most of the evening to return," I said.

"I know," Monife sighed. She had changed. When I met her, her bony body resembled a little boy's, but now she looked like a young woman. "We can afford a day away from the hunt."

"We took a day away three days ago. And three days before that."

"We can take another one tomorrow."

That broke me. I'd been stewing about our half-hearted search for a while and should've said something sooner. "Did you ever care about my brother?"

"What are you accusing me of?"

"You weren't excited to learn he was alive. Did you ever believe me?"

"I helped you look for him—I am helping you look for him now."

"You always want to play instead of search. Why?" I asked angrily, as upset with her as I was with myself for agreeing to take those days off. "You never believed me about Dayo," I accused. "You never had faith. I saw it in your eyes." And the doubt was still there and covered her body like a fresh layer of skin.

"Whether I did or not doesn't matter anymore. He's alive and probably looking for you, too." She picked at the dirt. Something more was on her mind. "So what if I didn't believe as much as you believed? You're a kid. I'm fourteen years old. Small for my age, but a woman, taking care of you and your imagination."

Everything in me wanted to yell at her. Make her take back her words. But whenever I was hurt or injured, I struck back. "I never needed you. When I cut your cheeks, I was the one who helped you. Those scars are the only reason you're alive. The Agojie think you're a princess—like me. But I am the only real princess. You are a liar."

Monife raised her hand, and I thought she'd hit me. I winced before the blow—but she didn't strike me. She punched the air.

"Oh! You make me so mad. You are a child, and I don't know why I bother with you." Monife stormed off, and I was glad to see her go this time.

Gulping down my anger, I waited before stepping outside the tent, giving her plenty of time to disappear.

To my frustration, I wasn't upset with Monife for long. After a few hours, I realized that her company and friendship were more important than my anger. So I looked for her. But instead of her, I stumbled into a warrior different from any other.

Dressed in jewels, sashes, and belts, her hair piled on her head, she was a mesh of ringlets and braids, her throat adorned with bands of silver necklaces, one on top of the other, elongating her neck. Her bare breasts glistened, and her skin was free of battle scars. She was as beautiful and elegant as a butterfly. I didn't see her as a killer at that moment. All I saw was a stunning creature.

Unable to look away, I studied every inch of her, but then I saw it, and my breath cut across my chest and tore into my heart.

The realization poured over me like rainwater.

Dangling from her sash, hanging limply from her belt: the bluestone necklace, my family's heirloom, the one my brother Dayo had worn around his neck.

Sound disappeared, and silence swallowed me whole. It was the most dreadful place for me, where silence was the only thing to be heard—silence and loneliness were a deafening pair.

I let it sink in until it reached the bottom of my feet.

Dayo never allowed anyone to take the necklace from around his throat or remove it from wherever he might have hidden it. Nor would he hand it over to anyone other than Father or our eldest brother—but there it was, hanging from the warrior's waist. Our family keepsake—the necklace with the bluestone pendant. There was no mistaking it.

But how could she have it unless my Dayo was dead? Hurt and anger surrounded my heart, and a numbing chill covered the rest of me. I held my hand over my mouth. He was dead, but I had to have my necklace.

What if I ran to the warrior, grabbed my property, dropped to my knees, and waited for her sword? Would I reach the pendant? Of that, I was unsure. I'd die empty-handed. No. No.

My mind cleared. The necklace was all I had left—getting the necklace back was all that mattered.

* * *

MONIFE AND I sat on a large rock near the river. Our feet dangled over the edge, toes dancing in and out of the cool water as our eyes gazed upward, lost in the blueness of the sky.

She had returned a few days after I found Dayo's necklace on the warrior's sash. I hadn't told her what had happened. I needed time to gather myself. It was hard to think about anything while grieving for my dead brother.

Besides, I hadn't said he was dead out loud yet. I hadn't told anyone. It was buried in that unreliable place deep inside me, where, maybe, if a thing was never said, it wasn't true.

But if Monife was to help me, I had to tell her the truth. Didn't I?

So as we sat on a rock near the river, splashing our feet and legs and making waves, I summoned the courage to embrace my grief and widen the hole in my chest and—Just. Say. The. Words.

Dayo was dead.

"I need your help to fetch something stolen that belongs to me." I turned to Monife, my feet still dangling. "One of the warriors has it, and I must get it back." My voice broke. "It's something she can't be allowed to keep."

"What is this something you are rambling about, Aina? Why are you this upset? What do you need to get back?"

"The necklace with the bluestone pendant." The words exploded from my mouth. "My brother's necklace. An Agojie has it tied to her sash."

Monife lifted her feet from the water. "Your brother isn't wearing the necklace anymore?" She sighed woefully. "That will make him harder to find."

"Will you help me get it back?" I implored. "Will you steal it for me?"

Monife looked confused. "You said the necklace hangs from the sash of an Agojie?" She leaned back, her arms extended behind her, palms planted on the rock. "I can't steal that."

"You stole the earrings."

"Yes, but this is more dangerous. The Agojie I took the earrings from was asleep and had drunk a large amount of Brazilian rum. Nothing would've awoken her that day. Not even if I'd danced on her head."

"So what if this is dangerous? Everything we've done has

been dangerous, but we've survived." I pulled my feet from the water and my knees into my chest. "Will you help me get back Dayo's necklace?"

"I don't know if I can, Aina."

A fish splashed in the river, sending slow waves toward the rock. I watched for a long moment, hoping to see another fish leaping into the air and landing, tail wiggling before it vanished. But there was only one.

What had Monife said? Had she refused me? Did she think I'd give up? "Then I'll steal it myself. Just tell me how, and I'll do it as you say. Exactly the way you tell me."

"Aina, neither one of us can do such a thing. Why not keep looking for Dayo? It will be a bit harder but not impossible." She paused, looking at me oddly. "Don't you want to find your brother?"

I leaped to my feet. "Don't you understand? He's dead. He would never give up that necklace unless he was dead. I don't even know how long he's been dead. What if everyone who claimed to have seen Dayo had told us such things to be kind to a pair of little girls? What if he was killed in Okeadon the day the others were murdered? What if I have been alone all this time?" The sob rose from my chest like a lion's roar, and I shook like a twig in a storm. "He's dead," I cried. "Everyone is dead—my family's necklace is mine, and I must have it returned to me."

"Stop wailing and look at me," she ordered, standing in front of me, the weight of her hand on my shoulder.

I wiped my eyes and face and swiped my wet nose with both hands. Then I blinked my eyelids until my eyes cleared, and I saw her.

"Aina. Poor Aina." Monife touched my cheek. "I am sorry if he is dead, so very sorry. But if he is, there's no reason for us to stay here." She wiped the remaining tears from my face. Her movements were jerky with excitement. "We can leave—we can escape. We can run away from here."

I stared at her, my surprise an ache in my side. "No. No!" I said, balling my fingers into a fist. "I won't leave without the necklace."

Monife glared at me with so much anger that I leaned away. "Then you'll never leave," she said. "I have stayed here season after season, watching over you, helping you search for your brother, helping you survive from one day to the next, and now that we can leave, you won't go with me?" Her chest heaved, and her dark eyes glistened.

Then abruptly, she turned and walked away.

"Monife," I called after her. "Monife," I whispered, but it didn't matter if I shouted or screamed her name, she was gone, and I was alone.

I sat on the rock, staring at the river, dipping my feet in the water again. I stayed there for a long while, too exhausted to think, cry, or mourn. Then I slid from the rock into the river and lay on my stomach, my face covered by the water, and I waited. Then, just before my breath gave way, my temper broke. I kicked and splashed, and kicked and splashed, forcing the pain and anger from my body.

But it didn't work. My body was on fire. A flame ignited by rage and hate and loneliness.

Monife had abandoned me, and my brother was dead. Nothing was left of the king of Okeadon. Other than me, and a bluestone necklace in possession of an Agojie, the murderers of my family.

* * *

I LOOKED FOR Monife everywhere, boldly asking everyone if they'd seen her, including the Agojie guards.

"The girl with scars on her cheeks—scars like mine? Have you come across her this morning, afternoon, or last night?"

No was the reply. No. Each and every time. No. And we do not know where she might be.

Had she escaped without me? If so, I should be happy that she'd found safe passage, but I was not. I needed her help, and she'd gotten angry at me for reasons I didn't understand. Why was she upset with me? I had not stopped her from leaving Abomey. It was not my fault she hadn't run before.

A day passed, and Monife had yet to return. Stubbornly, foolishly, desperately, I had convinced myself she would reappear as if she'd never left, as she had done many times before. Then she'd show up in my tent and scold me for my wet eyes and broken heart.

So I waited—one more hour, one more afternoon, one more night, for her to come back to me.

The next day rumors spread like a firestorm. Soldiers were coming from England for a meeting with the king. By midday, what had been a scorching whisper from hollow tongues was shouted with fear and certainty. The British were heading to Abomey, and King Gezo proudly announced a celebration with dance, music, food, and sacrifices upon their arrival.

With some trepidation, I ignored the talk and set out on my morning journey around the grounds, hoping for news of Monife and keeping an eye out for the Agojie with my brother's necklace hanging from her tunic's sash.

I was stopped by a woman from Okeadon. I had seen her by the river, talking to my mother occasionally. I did not know her name and had never asked, but I recognized her, as did most of us in the camp. She had many moles on her face and neck, and a permanently broken leg.

As she approached, my anxious feet longed to move on, but the memory of my mother's words calmed me—the people of Okeadon were watching me. Set a good example.

"Your friend Monife," she said, beckoning me closer. "Are you still looking for her?"

"Yes, I am," I said excitedly, with my chest suddenly full of hope. "Do you know where she is? Will she return today?"

"You won't find her," the woman said sharply. "She's been taken to a slave ship. She's on her way across the Atlantic to work in cotton fields, clean white women's houses, and wash their clothes."

"I don't believe you," I snapped. "You're just saying things to smash my spirit. Being enslaved has made you mean and hateful."

"And what has it made you? A foolish dreamer?"

"They don't take princesses on the ships—and Monife is a princess."

The woman laughed. "Who told you that nonsense? Slave hunters don't care about markings on a black face. They care about money and robbing the free of their freedom."

I heard what she said but it didn't matter. I refused to give up what I chose to believe. "It's not true. Monife is here. Somewhere. And I'll find her, or she'll find me."

She grabbed my arm, her strong fingers digging into my flesh. "You silly child. Do you think the Agojie didn't notice you weren't roped to one another? They grew tired of crying children and ignored them when they untied themselves to run and play. But it never meant they wouldn't sell you to slave merchants or cut off your head when they wanted."

I squirmed out of her grasp. "Why are you telling me such lies?"

"Because the English are coming, and you, and I, and many others, will die in a few days. Meanwhile, you are wasting the last hours of your life searching for a girl who is nowhere to be found. A girl like her, of her age, can bring a slave trader plenty of grain and gunpowder when she is sold."

"Liar. She is too smart and will never be caught."

The woman shook her head, and the moles moved with it. They were affixed to her flesh like the skin of a bitter gourd.

"I performed a kindness by telling you about your friend. If you don't believe me, your stubbornness is your problem."

She walked away, moving more sprightly than she had approached on her twisted leg.

I ended my search early that day. The camp was too full of fear and stories of British soldiers and white queens.

The hurt in my body was too deep for something as shallow as tears. Sadness was so thick in my chest that I could have been stone. Looking skyward through an opening in the tent, I watched the stars twinkle against the blackness of the night and closed my eyes.

The English would arrive soon, and from the whispers I had tried not to hear, I would be tied up and taken to King Gezo's palace and thrown into the pits where he sacrificed the chosen.

I smiled thinly but bravely. Facing death with courage was possible, entirely imaginable. The next day, I would think upon it even more, but that night, exhaustion's arms embraced me, and I lay in my spot in the dirt. Sleep came swiftly.

Chapter Six

Abomey, West Africa, 1850

I opened my eyes to a bright blue and orange sky with fluffy white clouds floating like lilies in still waters. Peace filled my spirit, and I lay thinking of nothing but sky for a very long time.

A muffled moan, a loud yawn, and the rustling of limbs awakening to the dawn brought a halt to my reverie. I no longer roamed the sky, free as a bird, and a sadness came over me that could fill a desert with my tears.

I had a lost friend to find and a necklace to retrieve.

Rolling onto my side, I prepared to rise, but something hard jabbed into my rib cage. I propped myself up on an elbow and searched the ground, pushing aside loose earth to find what I thought I'd felt, what I prayed I'd felt hidden beneath me.

Finally, after a few desperate seconds and just before I gave up thinking I'd dreamed it, I lifted the edge of my tunic and gasped.

There it was. There it was—my bluestone necklace.

I clutched it to my chest, tucked my feet beneath my bottom, and rocked back and forth, eyes closed, heart pounding. It had to be her. It had to be Monife. She had slipped into the tent between the moonlight and the dawn, and while I slept, she had returned my family keepsake to me.

How long ago had this happened? Was she still near? I

leaped to my feet and hurried outside the tent, hoping to catch a glimpse of her.

I spun toward the river, toward the palace, toward the tents, but she wasn't there. Had she taken off to freedom? Had she deliberately delayed her escape to return my necklace to me? Or had she been taken to a slave ship?

I hoped not.

But I would never know, because she was gone, and this time she wouldn't reappear. I could only hope that wherever she went next, it would be her decision—not that of some slave merchant or careless god.

Holding the bluestone necklace to my chest, I began to tremble. My hands were too small. I could lose it or have it taken from me. I had to keep it safe, but how? Where could I hide it?

My breath came in short bursts. I eyed the people around me, but they weren't interested in a child. I had to solve my own puzzles. Thankfully, I was good at games and went to work once I figured out what was necessary.

I removed the pendant from the woven cord and threaded the cord into the cloth of my sash. But where could I hide the stone?

The idea came to me like a cool breeze during the dry season. I closed my eyes and thanked the stars.

I would hide the pendant in my mouth, where it would be safely hidden as long as I remained mute—an easy path. No one left for me to talk to anyway, not with Dayo dead and Monife gone.

* * *

THE DAY BEFORE the soldiers from England arrived, the watering of the ancestral graves, or See-que-ah-hee, as the Dahomey called it, was upon us. According to the elders, it was the beginning of the end, and it began with the cackles of the Agojie.

They stormed the tent with swords drawn, barking orders, their yelps as murderous as their weapons.

My backside managed to escape the pointy end of a blade. I rolled away from the jabs, grabbed my sash, and tied it around my loose-fitting tunic. All the while, I held the bluestone in my cheek and obeyed the warriors' commands without uttering a sound—no yelps when a whip ripped across my back and no sobs when I was tied to another person. My mouth would remain shut until a sword took my head.

Herded like cattle toward the palace, we were corralled in a holding pen close to the king's throne. Pressed against the ropes and wedged between a white-haired male elder and a girl a bit older than me, I had a clear view of the courtyard. It was full of people moving to take seats near the throne while others remained on the edges.

Out of the corner of my eye, I glimpsed a white man on horseback in the distance. He was dressed in festive, brilliant colors, straddling a sizable black horse and leading a line of brown-skinned men (slave merchants, I overheard) also finely attired. However, they lay in hammocks carried by Black men in chains, holding umbrellas over the slave merchants' heads, umbrellas decorated with skulls instead of fringe.

Following them were rows of uniformed soldiers in high boots and carrying long rifles. These white men had to be the British and looked wilted and red-faced from the heat, with sweat-streaked empty gazes and parted lips catching flies.

I wanted to learn more about these white men. It was the only way to lessen my fear and keep me from constantly thinking about when they would join King Gezo to hurt me. All I knew of them was what the elders had said about their brutality. Still, my curiosity was sometimes more insistent than my fear. Discreetly, I removed the pendant from my mouth, held it in my palm, and poked the girl tied to me. "Who is that?" I pointed at the man on horseback.

She looked at me crossly.

"I'm sorry. I didn't mean to bother you."

Her cold stare pulled at my skin, but then her gaze softened. "I know you," she said. "I am the one who is sorry. I didn't recognize you until now. My name is Sade. You are Aina, daughter of the king of Okeadon. I am from Okeadon."

"Sade," I said softly. I very much wanted to hug her, but the ropes prevented it. So, instead, we touched our foreheads together in greeting.

"You wish to know about him? He is the chacha." She nodded toward the white man on horseback. "He is the king's consul who escorts visitors, like the soldiers from England and the slave traders, to the palace and tells them how to greet the king and request King Gezo's attention."

Her voice quieted when she said the king's name. I glanced around, but the guards appeared enchanted by the arriving guests and had lost interest in us.

"Why is this on your mind? Are you worried about dying?"

Since Dayo's death and Monife's disappearance, I expected no less than to die. So I replied with conviction. "No, I am not worried."

She looked toward King Gezo's throne. "Do you see him? The white soldier seated to the king's right. He talks for his queen, who wants to stop slave hunters, and met King Gezo at the palace a year ago."

I frowned. "I don't remember seeing a British soldier in Abomey."

"No matter, he failed then as he will fail now."

I eyed the commotion at the throne with great interest. The queen's soldier had fire-colored hair and a stern brow but a nonetheless round, pleasant face with large white teeth. But I lost all interest in his appearance when he began to speak. He spoke in King Gezo's language, a language I understood.

"Did you hear that?" I said to Sade.

"Yes, of course," she replied with a chuckle.

"Why is he funny?"

"He says that King Gezo must obey the laws of his white queen." She held her stomach. "Gezo only obeys Gezo."

The king drank from a large cup and waved to his servants, who quickly brought him more drink.

I pointed at the soldier. "The British leader? Does he have a name?"

She moved close to the roped fence and cupped her ear. After a few moments, she spoke. "He is the commander. I think it means the same as king."

A group of load-bearers paraded into the arena. They carried open crates and large baskets filled with muskets, silks, and other goods.

King Gezo nodded his appreciation for the gifts the commander had presented. But the guards had regained interest in those of us locked in the nearby pen. A gesture by the king had reminded them of the holding pen full of men, women, and children, including me, waiting to be sacrificed.

* * *

IT WAS OUR turn.

A sharp pain shot into my chest and plunged downward. My legs just about collapsed beneath me. I struggled to remain on my feet but sank into a well of fear so deep and wide I couldn't breathe. I was going to die a coward, shaking and trembling. I had thought I'd be brave. I had thought I wouldn't mind.

Strong fingers squeezed my hand. I blinked, and once the panic cleared my eyes, Sade's sweet face and gentle smile appeared. I placed the pendant back in my mouth.

"You and I should think about something other than the chopping block," she said. "Something else altogether. How about if I tell you a story? Do you like fables?"

I exhaled the breath that had been trapped in my lungs forever.

She touched my cheek. "Do you know about the Lion and the Jackal?"

I nodded.

Her dark eyes brightened. "It is a good fable. It is a story worth telling and hearing as often as it needs to be told. Do you agree?"

Her voice was calm and low, smooth and warm. And somehow, through luck, coincidence, or inspiration, the story was one my mother used to tell me. I almost heard the voice I'd missed for so long. I clutched at the fabric covering my breast, pressed my lips together, and held back a deep sigh. I had to remember the pendant in my mouth.

"You don't talk as much as I recall. But no matter." Then she started the story.

I listened, paying heed to every word as well as I could, but the Agojie were on the move, shoving us out of the pen and whipping us into long lines. Some of the enslaved did not fuss. No whimpering or pleading, only acceptance, and hope for a painless passage into the afterlife. Others cowered, falling to their knees, trembling like wild dogs dropped in a cold river at dawn. I hated cowards, though my fear made me no better.

"You should not be ashamed. We each choose how we will face death, Aina. Do not judge," said Sade, interrupting the story to chastise me.

I hoped for such a death, but I was shaking like a leaf in a windstorm.

"What happens next, Aina?"

"Huh?" I had forgotten about Sade.

"To the Lion and the Jackal?"

I removed the blue stone from my mouth, cleared my dry throat, and said, "After the Jackal saved the Lion from the mud, they were friends."

Sade raised an eyebrow at the pendant I held in my hand, but she didn't ask about it. "Yes. The Lion and the Jackal were together until the end of their days."

"It's a story with many different beginnings and endings but always a story well told."

I popped the blue stone back into my mouth. It was not the same story my mother recited, but it didn't matter. Sade and I had been herded to the front of the line, but for me, the strangling fear had lessened thanks to the Lion, the Jackal, and Sade.

* * *

"Your Highness, I am honored." The commander's voice jolted me from my reverie. He was yelling but not angrily; his voice was loud enough to ensure everyone nearby heard what he was saying to the king. I believe that was what he had in mind.

As he spoke, he strode by the bodies already sacrificed. He didn't linger on the dead; he looked at those next to die.

A chill ran through me. Again, I popped the blue stone from my mouth. "Is he looking at us, Sade?"

"I believe so," she whispered.

"By your invitation," the commander went on. The Yoruba language he spoke was easily understood. "My battalion and I have joined you in this important tradition—celebrating the watering of the ancestral graves. We are honored," he said, but his tone and the paleness of his skin betrayed him. He looked ill. So the sight of the sacrifices had bothered him. However, he regained his composure and pointed at the many crates from the queen, paraded by King Gezo earlier. "And in response to your generosity, I have brought you many gifts from the white queen of England." He paused, finger pressed to his temple somewhat dramatically. "Perhaps, however, you might consider another token, something unique, from a Black king to a white sovereign."

Gezo eyed the commander as one might examine a trickster. What magic could he produce? I, too, wondered what he could mean. What was his purpose?

"What do you mean by unique?" the king asked.

"One of a kind. A gift that has never been given by any king to Her Majesty and will never be given again."

"And that would be?"

"One of your enslaved people. An irrefutable statement to show your righteous intentions toward ending slave-hunting and slave ships in your region."

King Gezo lurched backward with a snarl. "Again, you

suggest I am a slave hunter, but I am a merchant with many products for trade, including palm oil. Do not think of me as only capable of one thing, Commander. It would be ill-advised."

The commander wiped his mouth, but his fingers trembled, his nerves exposed. "My apologies, but if you do this, the queen of England and the entire world will praise your greatness."

King Gezo summoned one of his servants and drank slowly from a large vessel. He took several more swallows before he replied. "I'm not a fool, Commander. Your queen signed laws against buying and selling humans as property many seasons ago, but those are Britain's laws. They do not govern Dahomey. We signed a treaty of friendship, and as a friend, your queen will appreciate the leathers, furs, and jewels I have provided in those crates."

"King Gezo, I am only suggesting you offer one of the children set to be sacrificed as a gift to Her Majesty. It will mark an unforgettable moment in history. You will be a legend."

"A legend, you say?"

"Yes." The commander bowed, and the pitch of his voice hummed with humility. "A king among kings—you will defy and pay homage to the queen of England in one gesture. No one else will compare—not in this century."

"Which one would you take, Commander? It is your choice."

So many faces had turned in our direction, staring and wondering *whom will he choose*. Sade squeezed my arm. Hope was a rock tossed in the river that floated. Anything was possible.

"What do the markings on her face mean?"

Sade's fingers dug into my flesh, and I thought I might choke on my next breath.

The king huffed. "She's a princess, and her name is Aina. Her father was a chieftain of a village I conquered. He also was a soldier who once fought at my side. When we conquered his small town, I had him and his family beheaded because he had betrayed me. I saved his youngest to sacrifice her but kept forgetting she was even here." He laughed but not for long. "I think you strike a good deal, Commander. She is yours."

King Gezo flicked his wrist, and a guard reached into the pen, untied the rope, and pulled me out by my shoulders.

"Make sure your queen understands. A Black king to a white queen, I am gifting this child to her, and she represents a bond, uniting the queen of England and the king of Dahomey in history for an eternity."

"Of course, Your Highness." The commander leaned forward in his deepest bow. "On behalf of Her Majesty, I extend my gratitude."

He took my trembling hand but didn't hold on to it for long. A boy, Dayo's age, with black hair and the same wiry limbs and lean features, but white skin with many red blotches, came to him.

Leaning forward, the commander spoke to me so I could see his face. "This is my cabin boy, William Bartholomew. He speaks your language. You will stay with him until I have completed my duties on behalf of Her Majesty."

The cabin boy took my hand as the commander had instructed him. He didn't speak. He pulled me to a spot behind the men seated close to King Gezo and released my hand, only to place his hands on my shoulders. If the thought had crossed my mind to run, I would not have gotten far.

Elation mingled with fear, gratitude, and a large slice of curiosity. What intentions did the queen and her commander have for a Black child who had spent several long seasons enslaved by the king of Dahomey? Had I been saved? Or traded into another camp of enslavement, except this one designed by white soldiers and their queen? I felt sick, my body ravaged by the need to expel whatever lined my stomach onto the dirt, especially once the king had ordered the next girl in line to be sacrificed.

Was it Sade?

My head snapped in the commander's direction. He had to save this girl; whoever she was, she must be saved. He had soldiers, not as many warriors as King Gezo, and not as sturdy in appearance, but if he had me removed from the pen, he could do the same for the next girl—and if it was Sade, he had to rescue her.

I waited with my lips parted, my breathing shallow. He had to act. Prance in front of the king as he'd done before and demand the girl's life be spared. But he remained straight-faced, his lips sealed. He didn't blink an eye when the Agojie chopped off the girl's head. I couldn't look. If it was Sade, I didn't want to see it.

Instead, I screamed, or I thought I had. But the cabin boy's sweaty palm had covered my mouth; his grip held me firmly in place. I attempted to struggle, but it was pointless. The law, according to King Gezo, must be upheld. Sacrifices had to be made.

I went limp. Why bother protesting? I was a stone in a game played in pools of blood.

Chapter Seven

Badagry, West Africa, 1850

The language had no meaning, only a rush of sounds. I watched the British soldiers' faces, attempting to pick up what they meant by how they looked, but wide eyes, flashing dull smiles, and eyebrows that came together and broke apart told me nothing.

* * *

Footsteps. Boots. Uniforms. Heat.

I had been on this road before.

Everything was open and wide and large, the leaves the size of an elephant's ears and the rocks like boulders. The greenest pastures. The blackest dirt and the bluest skies. The beauty of our land was in its extremes. Plants grew to the size of mountains. Mosquitoes traveled in packs, and swamps made fevers to burn souls alive.

It was a very different march from Abomey than the trek to the king's palace after the Agojie murdered my family. I did not know where the commander was taking me, but my feet didn't hurt. When I was too tired, the cabin boy lifted me onto his back, but then he must have tired, too, and now I was on horseback. He sat behind me, his hands on my shoulders, always holding me in place.

We'd been hiking through the jungle in scalding heat for

hours, sweat pouring from our brows and those of the nearby soldiers, soaking their clothing. They were so wet they appeared to have taken a swim in a river. They should wear tunics, I thought. Or march naked, but I imagined the insects and the sun would ravish and burn their pink flesh, turning it into leather.

After a while, the cabin boy pulled up on the horse's rope, and the animal stopped. The other soldiers paused, too, whether on horseback or foot. We were in a small clearing, and they pulled pouches of water from sacks carried with a strap looped over a shoulder. The men gulped down as much water as their stomachs allowed. The cabin boy helped me from the horse onto my feet, handed me his pouch, and gestured for me to drink. I leaned away from him, covering my mouth with my hand. I still held the pendant in my jaw.

"Why do your cheeks look like they are full of porridge?" He had asked the question in Yoruba, pointing at my face. Then he knelt in front of me. I tried to wiggle away, but, of course, his hand was on my shoulder.

"You have something in your mouth. What is it?" He opened his hand and held it in front of my mouth, waiting.

I reared farther away, but not too far, not with his grip on me. Panicking, I pressed my lips into a thin, frightened line. He would not take my pendant.

"Mmm. So you are refusing to open it. That's a bloody shame. I'll have to force it out of you then." He smiled as he spoke, but I didn't consider him a friend. And why did he keep using a word I didn't understand? What was bloody? Did he intend to slice my mouth open?

My eyes must've grown to the size of a lily pad floating in a lagoon.

"Don't be afraid. I won't harm you. It's a trick I used on my little sister in the East End. She loved to eat dirt, and I came up with a method of coaxing her mouth open."

He reached for me, and I shook from head to toe. My fears were rightly placed. I couldn't trust these men any more than the Agojie or King Gezo, whether they spoke my language or not. His hand came closer and closer, and I shut my eyes. When his fingers landed on my cheeks, I felt like I was spinning.

He squeezed my cheeks, not hard, but somehow, I could not keep my lips pressed together, and when he squeezed again, my mouth opened. The pendant fell into his palm.

"Oh, my. What a lovely shade of blue."

I reached for my heirloom. "No. No. It's mine."

"You shouldn't keep this in your mouth." He tapped his lips. "Mouth. Do you understand? Not safe. You could swallow it, and it would get lodged in your throat." He pointed at his neck and coughed. "You'd gag. Understand."

"No." My eyes flooded with tears. How could I lose the pendant now? "No!"

"Don't worry. I'm not a thief. I'll return it to you. But how about if I keep this in my pocket? Pocket." He patted his pants on the hip. "I'll give it back to you when we board the *Bonetta*. How does that sound?"

I blinked, wanting to believe him but knowing I couldn't trust him. So I cried when the pendant disappeared into his pocket, sobbed, and the tears wouldn't stop.

"Bloody hell."

There was that word (or was it words?) again.

His face had distorted as if he were the one in pain. "Why are you crying? Don't you understand me? The commander taught me to speak your language, and I speak it well." He touched the top of my head the way Dayo used to do when I cried. "Do not worry. I'll watch over your blue stone, and no one will get their hands on it. I promise."

* * *

THE LAST TIME I'd seen the commander was at King Gezo's palace; since then, a day and a night had passed. While camped in the jungle, William brought me to the commander's tent the morning after he'd taken my stone, and I had only one thing on my mind.

"He took my pendant," I said in Yoruba, pointing at William with his wide-mouth grin and missing teeth. There was nothing to laugh about in my mind. The years at Gezo's slave camp had taught me to mistrust. And although William, the commander, and his soldiers hadn't harmed me, I didn't trust any one of them.

Where were they taking me? To a ship to be shackled, tormented, and sold on an auction block? William's grin only set fire to these beliefs.

"Whatever he took, he'll give it back. Do not be concerned."

"How do I know that?" I shot back.

"You should trust him," the commander said with a smile of his own. "He's not a perfect lad, but I've never known him to lie or steal."

Then why does he smile so much without a full mouth of teeth? This, I thought but didn't ask.

"Thank you, sir," William said sternly, but I spotted the humor in his eyes. "I attempted to explain this, but she doesn't listen to me."

"Is it his accent, Aina?" the commander asked. "Does it make him difficult to understand?"

I didn't know what he meant by accent. I understood William perfectly when he spoke in my language. The problem was I didn't trust him with my blue stone, but I didn't say it.

"You'll need to learn English anyway. So William will teach you."

William's eyes grew as large as the eggs of a giant bird. He didn't seem pleased.

"Of course, I will help, too, Aina," said the commander. "But I have many duties on board the *Bonetta*. So I am making it William's responsibility to teach you English, and by the time we reach England, you will greet the queen in her language." He glanced at William. "That's an order."

William nodded. "Yes, sir. Of course, sir."

The two men spoke in English for the rest of the morning meal. I didn't attempt to memorize any words. I ate as much of the food as my stomach could handle. Most of it was too salty and hard to chew, and I wondered if that explained William's missing teeth.

Curiosity filled my mind, and compulsively, I stared at every morsel of food William put in his mouth. Then I ended up hearing a familiar word. "Atlantic." The mole-faced woman said Monife had been taken to a slave ship that sailed across the Atlantic.

"Have you seen the ocean before, Aina?" the commander asked.

I looked at him, trying to recall, but my memory failed me.

"Never mind." He smiled. "I'll explain."

The commander went on to tell me about the ocean called the Atlantic. A large body of water, broader and deeper than a river. We were headed to Badagry, a harbor town on the sea's coast where his ship was anchored. It was busy with many people and ships from Her Majesty's Navy, as well as Brazilian, Portuguese, French, and British merchants. Some of the vessels sold merchandise that was against British law to sell. He wanted to encourage the owners of these ships and African tribal leaders who were slave hunters to stop conducting this form of trade.

"When we arrive in Badagry, we will visit the church missionary school. Before we board the *Bonetta,* you will need things like clothing that I'm sure they'll have. So we're off to Badagry."

"Bad-angry," I said slowly.

"Almost. Almost." He nodded happily. "Badagry." He turned to William. "See, boy. She's a bright girl." He smiled. "You'll learn our language and learn it quickly."

* * *

THE FOLLOWING DAY we arrived in Badagry. A sharp and sour smell wrinkled my nose. Indeed, there were many unfamiliar and unpleasant scents. However, the most noticeable thing about the town wasn't the odors. It was a tree.

An enormous tree with roots shaped like boulders and a trunk like a towering stone beast stood in front of me. I tugged on William's arm and pointed, furrowing my brow, hoping he knew what it was called—this tree the size of nothing I'd seen before.

"Oh, it is the Agia tree. A-gi-a, a sacred tree." William gestured skyward. "It is a hundred and sixty feet high and thirty feet wide—and the African gods planted it with their own hands."

I nodded. "The A-gi-a tree."

"Yes. Very good."

Groups of African women surrounded the tree and most of the open space nearby. The women sat making straw chairs and baskets or selling other goods like fruits and vegetables. It must be a marketplace like the one in Okeadon.

As I watched, loss and longing struck me like an Agojie whip. The memory of home was so vivid I felt faint. A heaviness spread into my legs and chest, and I struggled to stand. A woman put down her basket and called out to the soldiers to help me.

"She is ill," I heard her say. "She is ill. She's falling."

I swayed and stumbled. Suddenly, I couldn't see anything, including the gigantic Agia tree. But I never hit the ground. William reached me, and I was in his arms.

His red-skinned face was redder than ever. "I think you fainted, but you're just tired. You need to sleep and eat something better than the hardtack we've been feeding you, I'd wager."

I was hungry, but my dizziness had little to do with food. It was the memory of Okeadon that threatened to bring me to my knees.

Chapter Eight

Badagry, West Africa, 1850

William carried me through the gate into the courtyard of the Church Missionary Society station at Badagry. The commander had whispered the name of the cluster of small buildings and pointed roofs to me as he walked by us into the compound.

"You're all right." William placed me on my feet. He then quickly positioned himself behind the commander, who greeted the two white women standing in front of a building with a pointed roof.

I stayed next to William and stared.

It was my first time seeing a white woman, and there were two of them. The paleness of their complexions struck me, of course. It was a very different shade of white from the men. However, it was their dress that made me gape.

Layers of clothing. Long billowy skirts that nearly touched the ground. Thick-waisted blouses ballooning from their bodies, and their shoes roped up to their ankles. Everything about them seemed sweaty and uncomfortable. I'd refuse to wear so much with the sun blazing down on me.

The commander spoke to the women in their language but frequently looked over his shoulder at me. Then he talked to me in Yoruba, letting me know what was being said about me.

He had introduced me as Aina, an Egbado princess. The women were Mrs. Vidal and Mrs. De Graft, wives of men who preached God's words. I wondered which gods they preached for, but there was no time for my questions.

He told me that the men of God and their wives were in charge of the mission and the school we were visiting. He pointed at the buildings in front of us. The couples had come from England to Africa on behalf of the Church of England to evangelize, educate, and civilize the barbarian Africans.

I understood almost everything, but not the word "barbarian," spoken in his tongue.

There was more conversation, plenty more, but I couldn't keep up, and my thoughts drifted. We had been standing in the courtyard for a while, and I felt unwell again. William was beside me, his hand on my shoulder, but his grip felt less firm. I started to sit on the ground, but he wouldn't allow it. So I stood, feeling very near to keeling over.

Finally, as if they read my mind, the women walked toward one of the smaller dwellings and beckoned us to follow them.

Inside, Mrs. De Graft and Mrs. Vidal led us to a room with a round table and chairs. A distinct aroma of cooked food and rich spices reminded me of my mother and the meals she'd cook in the firepit. But there was no fireplace for preparing food in this room.

* * *

THE WOMEN AND the commander sat at the table, but the invitation didn't appear to include William and me. So we stood behind the commander's chair.

They talked in English for a lengthy period, leaving me

clueless about what was going on until William bent forward and whispered in my ear. "They want to give you a bath and cover your body with decent clothes."

I frowned at him. Why were my clothes not decent? Did the two women not like me? Or was it just Mrs. De Graft, who looked at me with the most unkind expression in her eyes? William must have seen it, too, and pulled me closer. I was thankful. I didn't wish to be gobbled up by her.

"Jinjin," Mrs. Vidal called suddenly.

A moment later, an African woman appeared in the entrance-way. She was ordered to do something, and William again whispered, "They are bringing us tea and fixing your bath."

My bath seemed terribly important to them but not as critical to the commander and William. I'd been with them from Abomey to Badagry, a fifty-mile trek, and neither of them once mentioned a bath.

When Mrs. Vidal spoke again, I was momentarily stunned. I could understand her. She was speaking in my language.

"You say, Commander, that she's a princess because of the scars on her face," said Mrs. De Graft, her eyes narrowed as she studied me.

Mrs. De Graft not only didn't like me, judging from her snarling tone, she also didn't like to hear the Yoruba language spoken in her presence. I don't know what she said, but Mrs. Vidal seemed willing to ignore it.

"Sorry, dear," Mrs. Vidal said to me. "Mrs. De Graft has only been in Africa for a few months and hasn't picked up the language. But she objects to your scars. She is unaware that they are a sign of status, showing you are a member of a royal family. I explained you wear these scars with pride."

She was right. "Yes, I do."

Jinjin returned, carrying a large tray with food and drink and pretty cups and plates etched with flowers and green leaves. She placed it on a table and stepped backward toward the entranceway, but before she could withdraw, another flood of angry words erupted between Mrs. De Graft and Mrs. Vidal.

When they'd finished, Mrs. Vidal clenched her hands together and placed them carefully in her lap. Then she took a slow, deep breath. When she spoke again, it was in Yoruba. However, she wasn't speaking directly to me.

"Let's not dwell on the things we can't change," Mrs. Vidal said to the commander. "Our husbands, Reverend Dr. Vidal and Mr. De Graft, are on an expedition to the Niger River. They will be disappointed they missed you."

She smiled at me, and a soft sparkle filled her eyes, which were a color that reminded me of my pendant. "Come here so that I can see you better, child." She glanced at the commander. "I think she has developed a fondness for you and your cabin boy." She turned back to me. "Come closer."

That's when I noticed I was half-hidden behind William and the commander's chair. I stepped out from their shadows but didn't move too far away from them.

"It's all right, child. I speak several Yoruba dialects. I will understand when you talk to me—just like you understand William and the commander. What is your name again? Do you know what it means?"

My nerves were tangled rope, knotting my tongue and preventing me from speaking until I forced my mind to behave. "My name is Aina," I said in a small voice. Then I shook my head. "I don't know what Aina means."

"It means difficult birth and thus difficult life." She glanced at the commander, her eyes softening. "However, I believe the commander has tossed your destiny over the bow. You are now the African child gifted to Her Majesty."

The room had become quiet and still, but that ended shortly. Mrs. Vidal had more questions for me. "How old are you?"

I stepped farther away from William and the commander and closer to Mrs. Vidal. "I am seven or eight years old."

"Yes, that is what the commander told us as well," Mrs. Vidal replied.

Mrs. De Graft cocked her head and shot a string of words toward Mrs. Vidal. William didn't like what was said. I could tell by the jerk in his body and his effort to remain calm.

The discussion between Mrs. Vidal and Mrs. De Graft sounded like the argument of two women with very different opinions about a subject equally important to them. I heard the word "princess" more than once and concentrated on remembering to ask the commander or William, when I learned the English language, what had been said.

"Barbarians," Mrs. De Graft snorted.

I recognized the word. I had committed it to memory after the first time I'd heard it and didn't like how it sounded.

Mrs. Vidal side-eyed Mrs. De Graft before she said in Yoruba, "I agree with Mrs. De Graft. You should have a Christian name."

I must have looked surprised, but Mrs. Vidal pushed on.

"What do you think of the name Sarah?" Mrs. Vidal asked me. "It's from the King James Bible and means exceedingly beautiful. It also means princess." She took my hand and squeezed it. "Say it after me. My name is Sarah."

The commander cleared his throat. "Sarah Forbes Bonetta."

Mrs. De Graft put down her cup and clapped. What she said next was a mystery to me, but her unkind feelings toward me remained unmistakable. I wondered how many women I'd meet in the queen's England like her.

"Jinjin, please take the child and bathe her," said Mrs. Vidal. "You'll find some clothes that should fit her in a box on the shelf in my closet."

"Go along, Sarah," said the commander. "Everything will be all right."

* * *

JINJIN BROUGHT ME to a room that wasn't like the one with the table and chairs and the smell of food and spices. Instead, this was a much larger space with only a few places to sit, one of which was a tall stool with three legs—other items in the room I'd never seen before.

Jinjin, noticing my confusion, spoke to me in the Yoruba language, replying to my unasked questions. "It is an artist's studio, and these are the artist's tools. Canvases and easels, paintbrushes, jars of paint," she said, pointing. "And paintings, too many paintings. But Mrs. Vidal loves to paint and draw. So we pile her work in corners or mount them on the walls."

Then I followed the African woman to another room. This one featured a large basin, which she called a tub, full of water.

"It's a copper tub, imported from England," she said, but those words seemingly had exhausted the chatty side of her personality. They were the last spoken to me as she stripped off my tunic and guided me into the tub. She washed and scrubbed me in the cold water. I shivered and endured being poked and soaped.

After a brisk drying off with a piece of coarse fabric, I had to put on clothing similar to what the white women wore, except the other garment, which Jinjin called a dress, was one piece.

She did take the time to name each item as she put it on me, which included a pinafore, white stockings, shoes with laces, and a straw bonnet with a wide brim. She also put ribbons in my hair. "Mrs. De Graft insisted you have ribbons and take off your earrings."

I had never felt so hot and sweaty with the layers of cloth trapped against my skin. I looked around for my tunic and the sash in which I'd threaded the neckpiece of my family heirloom. "Where are my things?"

"These are your things now," she said with finality. "Come along. Mrs. Vidal wants to see you in the artist's studio."

I started to object, to beg her to give me back my belongings, but we were already in the hallway. A few steps later, we entered the artist's studio.

"Stand over there, Sarah." Mrs. Vidal indicated a spot between two large leafy plants in tall white and blue vases. "Don't look so frightened, dear. I'm painting a picture of you. Commander Forbes will return shortly, and you'll be on your way to his ship and England. This painting will commemorate your visit to the CMS School in Badagry at the beginning of your journey to an exciting life, one of privilege you should be very thankful for. This image will help you remember this day and your indoctrination into civilization. Also, you look lovely dressed in such a pretty frock and hat."

Mrs. Vidal's Yoruba sounded different from the language I'd grown up speaking. Although I understood her, some phrases didn't make sense. But I had a sharp mind and strove to commit to memory as many words Mrs. Vidal used as I could—England. Badagry. The commander.

Like my new name, I'd get used to it soon enough. Since

my family's murder, I guess I'd grown accustomed to making adjustments.

Standing with the small brush in her hand, looking at me with a wide grin, Mrs. Vidal said happily, "I am so pleased, Sarah. You look like a proper British girl in a pretty dress, a lovely bonnet, and a Christian name—Sarah Forbes Bonetta. You can forget all about Aina and the horrors that poor child experienced. You are a new girl, and let's say Sarah doesn't have a horrible past—she only has a future. Beginning with your voyage to England on board the HMS *Bonetta*. It'll take a couple of months, maybe three, to reach London. Commander Forbes has a few stops along the coast before setting sail for England. But that's good for you. You'll have time to learn English, and the cabin boy, William Bartholomew, seems to be an attentive lad, although raised in the East End. Hopefully, you won't pick up his accent. Nonetheless, you'll learn manners and enough English between him and the commander to greet the queen properly."

As Mrs. Vidal talked, she moved confidently from the canvas to her jars of paint, adding colors to the canvas. She paused a couple of times, walked over to me, adjusted my hat, straightened the skirt of my dress, and asked me to smile, which was hard, and a thing I'd forgotten how to do.

I hadn't smiled since that day in the camp when I thought I'd found Dayo alive.

"You will love the ocean, Sarah, and the commander has sworn to read to you regularly from the King James Bible, too. It will be the beginning of your faith training and a good start on missionary work." She looked at her canvas. "You are a fortunate child, Sarah."

Mrs. De Graft suddenly appeared in the archway of Mrs. Vidal's studio. She looked as if the doorway was as far as she ever ventured into the studio. She spoke in English, and whatever she said appeared to make Mrs. Vidal angry. It was as if the two women disagreed about how they felt about me. My guess was Mrs. De Graft didn't like having me around.

Mrs. Vidal spoke to me in hushed tones. "You are a bright girl. I can see that in your eyes. My friend Catherine," she said, glancing at Mrs. De Graft, "will learn to respect the African people one day, once she's spent more time here. So don't mind her."

I would never mind her, I thought. She wasn't a woman I had to obey. Neither of them would ever be.

Mrs. De Graft continued speaking in English to Mrs. Vidal, and I felt sure she was saying things she didn't like about me. But the only reaction Mrs. Vidal had was to roll her eyes when Mrs. De Graft used that awful word I'd heard her use several times before, "barbarian."

The next moment, Mrs. De Graft stomped her foot, her face changing from white to bright red. She was behaving as one of my sisters had when our mother scolded her. Then, with skirts rustling, she stormed from the room. Mrs. Vidal giggled.

"I'm almost done," she said after Mrs. De Graft's departure. Then she pointed her paintbrush at me. "Sarah, lift your chin and smile. You look lovely when you smile. Just like a princess."

* * *

WHEN THE COMMANDER and William returned to the mission and entered the artist's studio, I was shedding tears by the barrel.

"The painting is beautiful, Sarah," the commander said, his gaze locked on my tear-streaked face. "Why are you upset?"

Mrs. Vidal shrugged when he looked at her. But William came close to me and said, "Tell us what we can do?"

After a few seconds of stammering and whimpering, I explained. "My clothes, my sash, the neckpiece for my pendant." I gulped out the words between sobs. "Jinjin is burning my things."

Still speaking Yoruba, so I understood him, William's voice was forceful. "Commander, she wants her belongings. The African girl has threatened to burn them." He turned to Mrs. Vidal. "Where is she?"

Later, after a few weeks on board the *Bonetta*, when my English improved, William told me how he had raced from the studio and found Mrs. De Graft and Jinjin at a bonfire, preparing to drop my clothing into the flames. Unable to save the tunic, he snatched the sash from Jinjin's hands, using formidable speed and agility. He proudly recited this tale to me more than once, perhaps a half dozen times. But I knew by then that he could be a braggart. Although relief filled me, I swore to repay him for his kindness each time he told the story.

The following morning, we bid farewell to the mission in Badagry, Mrs. Vidal, Mrs. De Graft, and Jinjin. We took with us the painting Mrs. Vidal had completed, which the commander kept, and a steamer trunk full of clothing, shoes, stockings, pinafores, dresses, face creams—even notebooks and pencils. By then, William had given me my necklace and expressed excitement at the many beautiful items the missionaries had selected for me. "And just imagine the riches that await you in London when you are the queen's godchild."

I might have shared his enthusiasm if I hadn't been forced

to change my name, clothing, and gods. I was also to become a gift to a queen I'd only heard of a few days before.

The bright light in the din was my necklace, with its blue-stone pendant. In Badagry, they had made me someone other than myself. If I had known this, I might've fought against the changes and never taken a bath in a tub, worn a dress, or brushed my hair.

I didn't plan on losing the original me, the other me, who I thoroughly believed would be lost and forgotten if not for my heirloom. It belonged to my family. I had to believe that as long as I could wear it around my neck, I was Aina, an Egbado princess, daughter of a king.

Chapter Nine

The Sea, 1850

Sarah Forbes Bonetta was no different from me at first.

She had terrible nightmares, found it difficult to sleep, worried about what had happened to Monife, and wished Dayo had lived. Tears came to us often and too quickly, and we hated crying. Like me, Sarah also loved to learn, play games, and discover secrets about the people around us.

This was how my voyage to England began—with a thirst for knowledge and determination to embrace the new me.

However, a shadow loomed, creeping over the side of the ship, tragically unexpected but unavoidable.

When we boarded the HMS *Bonetta*, the first thing William did was show me to my stateroom. Or the makeshift cabin he and members of the crew had assembled just for me. He explained the *Bonetta* was a battleship in the Royal Navy, and accommodations for guests, especially females, weren't readily available.

My stateroom was two flights of stairs down into the belly of the boat. With each step, my body trembled violently as I thought about the elders' stories of the ships that had crossed the Atlantic with the enslaved shackled to the bottom of the boats. The fear ate my bones, for the day hadn't come when I completely trusted William or the commander. They were

white men, and all I'd ever been taught about them had to do
with pain, suffering, and enslavement.

However, being a good teacher seemed a matter of pride to
William. On the first day, in my stateroom, he showed me everything: the bed, the desk, where I would practice my handwriting and work on my studies, the space for the trunk with
my clothing and other items the women at the Badagry had
given me. My bucket for my body's waste, which had to be
emptied daily at the ship's bow—a location that had no meaning
to me at the time, but I would learn.

He continued, touching the furniture, porthole, and beams,
saying their names slowly in English, pointing and repeating,
and then pointing and repeating again.

Afterward, I followed him up the stairs to the deck for a
tour of the ship. I barely spent time in my stateroom for an
entire week, except when I slept. There was so much to see and
remember.

"A ship runs on a schedule," William said the second morning on board. "And you need to know it, but first you must
gain knowledge of the alphabet and how to count. Of course,
I'll teach you about the ship, too, but counting and your letters
come first."

He then started singing in a voice not unpleasant to my ears.
"A, B, C, D, E, F, G . . ."

He kept going, too. It was a bouncy tune with the same
rhythm from beginning to end, except in the middle, when it
sped up. "H, I, J, K, LMNOP."

We traveled from one end of the ship to the other. All the
while, William repeated that same song while showing me the
different sections of the boat. Honestly, I couldn't keep much
in my head except for that tune. I began to hum along with him

and attempted to repeat the letters he sang. By the end of that day, he was pleased.

We were on the top deck in the evening, enjoying the calm seas. I wore my pendant around my neck and held it up, comparing the blue color in the moonlight to the dark sea.

"The first step to conquering the English language, Sarah, is letters and numbers," William said, always teaching.

I listened, fingering my pendant, until the loudest sound I'd ever heard set my ears on fire, and I screamed.

William jumped. "Bloody hell, Sarah."

The noise rattled again, even louder. I let loose another squeal, and William pressed a palm over my mouth. His eyes were wide with astonishment until the next noisy gong sent a mighty shudder through my body. From that, he figured out what had made me panic.

"It's the watch, the bell announcing the time. Nothing to fear." He removed his hand from my mouth. "Loud noises. You'll hear them when something bad has happened. Like a fire in the hull, man or woman overboard, or a storm is upon us."

I grabbed his sleeve, taking deep breaths to calm down. He was speaking in Yoruba, but it was still too much for me to take in.

He continued his effort to explain and stop my shivers. "It's the bell sounding the time, or what we sailors call the watches." He rubbed his chin thoughtfully. "At sea, we ring bells to mark time passing. The sun reaches the middle of the sky and then dissolves into the sea. But since the sun is not always shining at sea, we have a ship's boy who strikes the bell."

His explanation calmed me; my shaking felt controllable. "Oh. It is like a musical instrument, the gangkogui bell, which is not as loud and scary as your ship's bell."

From sunrise to the smoldering midday to nightfall, when the sun sizzled as it sank into the sea, I followed William, learning about letters, numbers, time, and the ship's parts and pieces, and not having a fit at the sound of the bells. Soon I could count and tell the time by the strike of the bells, and I sang the alphabet song as loudly as William.

"You have a beautiful voice, Sarah," he said as we stood on the deck, watching the waves jump up from the sea.

I looked at him sideways, adding my usual I-don't-understand-what-you-mean glance. He reached out and lightly touched my throat and then his ear. "You sound lovely when you sing."

I understood and smiled.

* * *

THREE WEEKS LATER, I was told I was a quick study. The commander and William said I was a wizard in English. I wasn't familiar with the word "wizard" but didn't ask for an explanation. They were so pleased. I didn't want to interrupt their excitement. I also didn't want the moment to turn into another lesson.

I had accomplished a lot in a few weeks. I bested the alphabet song and could count numbers up to ten. I refused to leap out of my skin when the ship's bell rang for the watches, and once a week I dined with the commander, who read me lengthy passages from the Bible, first in Yoruba and then in English—and then expected me to have memorized a verse or ten.

The wizard was exhausted.

"We'll reach Britain in July," the commander said. "You must prepare to meet the queen sometime after the *Bonetta* arrives in England. I'm not sure when, but eventually."

I had so much to learn, but one afternoon, I discovered that not every member of the crew liked having an Egbado princess on board.

"What are you doing there, Bartholomew?" It was the ship's doctor, a man named Benjamin I had been introduced to once before. "What is it you are trying to do with this child?"

William and I stood on the deck. He was teaching me about sails.

"She should stay in the storage room." The doctor stared at me with his hairy lips twisted. "She could get injured, out and about so much. If something happens to his prize, Forbes will have your knickers tied in a knot."

William's body went rigid, and when he attempted to swallow, I thought he'd choke on the knot in his throat. "She's not a prize, sir. She's a gift to Her Majesty from the Dahomey king."

The doctor rolled his eyes. "If that's what you want to call it." He reached down and touched the pendant but then wouldn't let go. "What kind of necklace is this?"

"A family heirloom, a keepsake," William said.

"Oh." The man's eyes lit up as he removed his hand from my throat. "What a gorgeous shade of blue. A lazuli stone, isn't it? I am surprised to see such a valuable stone around her neck."

"Why is that, sir?" William asked, gently moving me closer to him with a hand on my shoulder.

The doctor's eyebrow rose. Something about William's remark displeased him. "Well, boy, they are mined in Afghanistan. I have no idea how she'd have gotten hold of it in Africa unless her people stole it from a British soldier who grabbed a handful in the Afghan War." The doctor licked his lips. "You should let me hold it. When we get to our next port, I can check on its value."

I didn't understand everything the doctor said, but I had an idea he wanted my pendant. I grabbed William's pant leg so hard he stumbled. "I am sorry, sir, but the commander asked me to keep an eye on her and her property. If I hand it over to anyone, I must speak to him first. Sorry, sir."

The doctor frowned; apparently he didn't like what he'd been told. I stuck close to William and wrapped my fingers around my pendant.

"Well, you may wish to have Forbes keep it safe in his cabin. It looks valuable, and some of our crew aren't honorable men." His smile was as thin as a piece of string.

The doctor walked away, and William exhaled.

"I think of him as Uriah Heep," he said in Yoruba with a chuckle. "That's a character in a novel by Dickens. The doctor is just like him, a villainous, vain man."

"What's a novel?"

"It's a book," he replied with a deeply furrowed brow. "You do know what a book is?"

"Yes. The King James Bible is a book. The commander reads it to me when I have dinner in his cabin."

"A novel is different from the Bible," he said. "I love novels."

He took my hand and we took the stairs down to my cabin.

"You know what? I'm going to add novels to our lessons," William said when we reached my stateroom. "If the commander reads to you from the Bible, I'll read to you from my novels. How's that sound?"

Another lesson, I thought, with a sigh. "I would enjoy listening to you read novels very much."

* * *

WILLIAM ENTERED MY cabin shortly after sunrise carrying a tray of food. "Good day. I have your breakfast. Salted beef, dried peas, hardtack, cheese, and coffee. Eat it all and get dressed. I'll be back for you at six bells."

My slumber interrupted, I rolled over, hearing some of what he'd said, but in what felt like a second later, he was nudging me in the shoulder. I must've fallen back asleep.

"Get up, eat, and get dressed," William said forcibly, jarring me out of my bed. "Today, I want to introduce you to some of the other members of the crew."

He left, and I ate what I could stomach, then tossed on a dress, heavy stockings, and a pair of lace-up leather shoes.

William returned as promised and led me to the upper deck.

"I've already gone over some of this, but let's do it again. Stay close and stay sharp."

We went toward what William called the front of the ship, except it had another name. "This part of the ship is the bow."

He repeated this information twice before spinning toward the other end of the ship. Except we stopped halfway. "This is midship." He waved his hand. "Starboard is the right-hand side, and port is the left-hand side."

I had just learned left and right hand, so my face must have shown my disappointment.

"It's all right. You'll get the hang of it." He next discussed the sails, the masts, the fire buckets, and the ship's wheel. He went on and on about that thing and this name until the sun was in the middle of the sky.

"I'm hungry," I exclaimed. I wasn't, but I thought I had to do something to stop him from teaching me One. More. Thing.

He raised his head. "Right, let's go to the galley. There's someone I want you to meet."

"What's the . . . galley?"

"Where our meals are prepared."

I followed him to a stairwell toward the stern of the ship—which he pointed out again. We then moved through passageways and down more stairs until we reached the place he called the galley.

It was a warm—no, scalding-hot room with a huge iron stove, fueled by wood. Beads of sweat coated my skin within seconds. The heat and the smell of cooked meat and stews thickened the air to the point where I could taste what was boiling in the pots on top of the metal box.

I lingered in the doorway, wary of entering such an overheated, smelly room.

"Don't worry," William said. "There's nothing here that can harm you, Sarah. Unless you get too close to the flames."

There was a man peeling potatoes with a floppy hat on his head. "He's our cook from America, and he reads all American novels. I've only read British fiction, but I thought you should know about American novels, too."

"William, my boy, don't tell the child such fibs. You are the one who wants to hear me talk about American novels. You're just using the princess to get to me." He dropped a peeled potato into a bucket. "My dear. So you're Princess Sarah. My name is Tennessee, and I'm the commander's cook on this vessel. But I'm sure William told you that already."

William hadn't mentioned anything other than that he was a cook. But Tennessee was colored, the shade of dry grass in the heat of summer—more brown, not black-skinned like me. Also skinny, and not much taller than me, he had to stand on crates to reach the stove and the shelves where some cooking supplies were stored. I glanced at William. There had to be more about Tennessee than his ability to read American novels, because William had brought me to the galley. Or could it be he wanted me to know there was someone other than me on the ship who wasn't white?

I turned to Tennessee again.

"Tell her where you've lived, Tennessee."

"I'm from the Carolinas by way of New York City—and don't ask me how I ended up with the name Tennessee, where I've never been, 'cause I don't know." He grinned.

William nudged me. "It is because his name is a state in the United States."

"Sure 'nuff," said Tennessee.

He sounded so different from William, too, and I was already struggling with how William spoke English compared to Commander Forbes. William had grown up in a part of London called the East End. They spoke with a funny accent there. And another accent in Tennessee.

"Tell her, quick. How'd you get here on this ship?"

"I was born a free man. I have never been a slave, but I made the mistake of visiting some family in the Carolinas, and white men tried to arrest me for being a runaway. So I sneaked onto a boat, leaving the harbor that day, and hightailed it across the Atlantic to London. Found a captain who didn't mind having a nonmilitary man in the kitchen and joined a crew."

"Tell her about the books. One story, at least."

"Sure, sure. How about 'The Legend of Sleepy Hollow'?"

"The story is a good one."

"It's my favorite. Somewhat scary, but memorable." Tennessee returned to peeling potatoes, and William found a stool to sit on and lifted me into his lap. It was the first time I'd heard the story of Ichabod Crane. Although I didn't understand much of what Tennessee said, he had a way of using his voice and his eyes I liked very much. We spent half a day in the galley, listening to stories.

Chapter Ten

The Sea, 1850

I wasn't always with William. Once a week, I had dinner with Commander Forbes in his chamber. These were special evenings, and I would wear the fanciest dress from my trunk and always the bluestone pendant around my neck.

We'd been at sea for four weeks and had recently departed from one of several coastal ports the commander visited on Her Majesty's business. Those stops always added quite a bit of variety to my meals.

There were no dried peas, hardtack, or salted beef. Instead, when I had dinner with the commander, there was freshly baked bread and meat from chickens and pigs, and Tennessee seasoned the food with spices, flour, sugar, butter, canned milk, and alcohol—and served it as well.

So I saw him often, too.

I believe he thought of himself as my kinsman because of our skin's dark hues. His interest turned to kindness, and he watched out for me. He even brought meals to my cabin when William wasn't around (rarely), and served me fresh fruit he'd purchased while the HMS *Bonetta* was docked at a port, to make sure I didn't end up with something called scurvy. These frequent stops, where Commander Forbes negotiated treaties with African tribes, always ended with the best meals upon departure.

In the evening, after supper, the commander taught me board games. The first was chess. Soldiers, kings, queens, castles, and black and white pawns arranged on a lined board reminded me of something I'd played with my brothers and sisters on the riverbank. But my memory had become waterlogged, and I couldn't recall the game's name. We had played with stones, not carved ivory statues.

The commander also taught me checkers, a pointless game, but my favorite was backgammon. He loved it, too. We'd play for hours with the pieces made of pinewood, natural and stained dark brown with rounded edges. I always wanted to know the materials that made the game pieces and, if possible, the history, until we put games aside and he'd read to me from the King James Bible.

"Christianity is the path to God," the commander said. "And in Africa, missionaries are saving your people from themselves. You are an incredibly bright child, Sarah. The way you've picked up English and your mathematics skills are impressive. You will make a fine missionary."

I blinked at him, unsure if there was something I should say. The way he spoke, I believed he thought missionary work was as exciting as being captain of a ship.

"What if I don't wish to be a missionary, sir?"

His hand jerked and almost knocked the game board from its table. "What do you mean, Sarah? Of course you'll be a missionary, or I should say, you'll be whatever the queen has in mind for you. But I think she'll agree with me and Reverend Venn, one of her advisers, that you weren't saved to lead a purposeless life. Missionary work will give you purpose, peace, and a connection to your people and God that you will find very satisfying when you grow up, young lady."

"Yes, sir." I didn't want to be a missionary, but I did hear him say that the queen of England would decide what to make of me. My future was her decision, not his. That meant I had to learn what she liked most about princesses and little girls, and then I had to make sure I became whatever that was. Because I never wanted to return to Africa. Never.

* * *

AFTER ALMOST TWO months on board the *Bonetta,* I had grown more than a little accustomed to William. I looked forward to the time I spent with him, and my lessons became the highlight of my day. Although I wasn't about to admit it or let on how much I enjoyed his company.

Part of that joy had to do with William's novels. He read to me frequently from British popular fiction, as he called it. He kept his books in a box beneath his bunk. After a while, he would leave a copy or two in my cabin. I couldn't read them yet, but I liked thumbing through the pages, thinking about how the words he'd read to me sounded.

Jane Austen's books were the best. William had several of them: *Sense and Sensibility, Pride and Prejudice, Emma,* and *Persuasion* (my favorite).

The words flowed from the pages, and I fell in love with the sound of the language as much as the stories. I was seven or eight years old, so I didn't understand much, but I asked William a thousand questions, many of which he answered.

One evening, he'd finished reading *Persuasion* and had started *David Copperfield.* But after a few chapters, he closed the book for the evening and we went to the upper deck. The moon was full, and thousands of stars were in the sky, making the night as bright as day.

"I don't believe I like Mr. Dickens's serials as much as I enjoy Miss Austen's books."

William scratched his ear. "How can you say such a thing? I've told you Dickens is my favorite author. I think you're trying to rile me up."

I looked at him curiously. "Not at all. I was only letting you know my thoughts on the authors and their stories."

"Of course, Austen is different from Dickens," William said flatly. "He writes thrilling stories with great drama. His books are meaty, while Austen, well, some call her work bland. I enjoy it for its simplicity and because her female characters are women I'll never meet. And she writes about relationships and emotions."

"Emotions?"

"Feelings. Passions. Anger. Hate. Love. Emotions." He made a different face as he pronounced each word. It was something Dayo would do to make me laugh, but William was teaching. I nodded with understanding and a wide grin.

"Things like that." He smiled.

"Do all writers write about emotions? In the Bible Commander Forbes reads to me, there are emotions."

"The Bible has different rules than novels." William gripped the railing, his gaze on the sea.

"Do you like the Bible?"

He looked at me as if I were someone other than me. "What a question from a little girl." He scratched one of his eyebrows. "When I return to London, I return to the East End. I don't think much of God there. But don't mention that to the commander. He is a man of God."

"Yes, he told me. He also said I would grow up to be a minister of God's word for my people." I grabbed the railing, imitating William's stance. "I'd rather be Jane Austen."

He laughed. "Aww, Princess Sarah. You might well become a writer, singer, or whatever you want to be. Nothing would surprise me."

* * *

"WE MUSTN'T HIDE from the sunlight. A warm breeze and a calm blue sea are not daily occurrences in the British Navy," William said, walking along the deck. "These times are to be respected and enjoyed."

It was a perspective I didn't appreciate until my first rough sea. But that didn't come until later.

We were ten days from England, and I could finally admit I'd fallen in love with the ocean and sailing. Never once had I suffered from the rocking of the boat, even when the waves rose against the side of the hull and the *Bonetta* tilted and swayed. I thought it was a game the sea was playing. *Will you get sick or laugh at the excitement you're feeling inside?*

It was another night of calm seas, and I wanted a lesson in the stars. It fascinated me how the tiny lights in the night sky clustered together into shapes of animals.

"Why is that?" I asked William.

"I don't know. But they are called constellations. And some of them are shaped like birds, cranes, even sea creatures such as flying fish or swordfish."

"No giant whales in the stars?"

"I've never seen one."

"How do you know about these animal-shaped stars, which you called con—"

"Constellations? The commander. When I came on board as a wee lad, he said I needed to read, write, and study. So he taught me."

"Like you're teaching me?"

"Yes."

I stared at the sky, marveling at the brightness of the night. But there had been nights when I could see nothing but blackness so thick I could slice it into pieces.

"When the clouds cover the sky, and there isn't any light, how does the ship know which direction to sail?"

He smiled. "Excellent question." He reached into his pocket. "This is a seaman's compass, a gift from the commander."

It was square and brass with a glass face. "What does it do?"

"This arrow, here, always points north."

I rose onto my tiptoes and peered at the device. "Is that all?"

He nodded. "It replaces the moon in the sky and the stars—all things that help the sailor get from one place to another. The sun and the stars and the moon help us navigate."

"It looks too small to replace the moon," I said thoughtfully. "I wonder if the queen of England has a compass."

"Why?" He sounded irritated, but then he apologized. "Sorry, I forgot you will meet Her Majesty when we arrive in England, and you'll want to impress her with your knowledge." He sighed. "The queen has a fleet of ships with thousands of British naval officers who make sure she's always headed in the right direction. She doesn't need a compass." He shoved it back into his pocket, but there was so much anger in his voice.

"William, what's wrong?"

"I would like to meet Her Majesty and go with you to Windsor Castle. I want her to fix the East End. It's overcrowded.

Every hovel must hold no less than six people. There are more thieves, murderers, and drunks in the East End than in all London—and more starving children, too."

"Oh," I said softly. "Then I guess you should come with me and tell her. Since you helped me learn English, read books to me, and watched over me, you should come with me to meet the queen. We can meet her together."

He laughed. "Sarah, you have a kind heart, but I lost my head for a moment. I won't meet the queen. I'll never see you again when I leave this ship unless you return to the *Bonetta*. I'll go home to the East End until the *Bonetta* sets sail again or I join another ship's crew. It doesn't even matter where it's heading."

He sounded very sad, which made me sad. "No, you're wrong. I'll ask the commander if he can arrange for you to join us. He likes you. He'll do that if we ask him."

"I don't think so, Princess."

"No, William. You must be wrong, but it doesn't hurt to ask. I'll do it tomorrow."

The following day, I had intended to bring up the subject with the commander. Still, with the *Bonetta*'s arrival in England only days away, everyone on board the ship was very busy, even me (although I don't recall the task I was given), and William never mentioned it again.

So I was off the hook, except whenever I saw him, he seemed sadder and less talkative and hadn't opened a book in days. He wasn't happy about returning to his life in the East End of London. He'd made that clear to me, whether he meant to or not.

The brightest cabin boy in all of England was what Commander Forbes said about him.

I had neglected to mention the commander's praise to William. Not on purpose, I don't believe. Or I wanted to believe it wasn't on purpose. I was a princess, and almost everyone except for the doctor and a few others on board the *Bonetta* treated me well enough. They praised me for learning English so fast and for my skill and tenacity in playing games.

I was special and heading to England to meet with the queen.

In hindsight, however, I wished I had asked the commander if William could join me. Even if it was impossible, at least I should have asked.

* * *

THEN THE NIGHT came when everything William and the commander had taught me was forgotten, and I was convinced I wouldn't make it to England at all.

There was a storm, a very bad storm.

I put my fingers in my ears and squeezed my eyes shut. What I couldn't see or hear couldn't hurt me. It was childish to believe, but I was a child, and it helped. Soon, though, there was nothing any of us could do but survive the storm.

It began in the middle of the night: the howling wind, the screaming whales, and sailors yelling orders. A gale had found us, a raging beast, swirling across the waves, but William made light of it.

"Do not worry. You'll be fine. We've seen stronger winds." He'd come to my cabin, knowing I'd be cowering in a corner, frightened.

The tilting and swaying of a giant ship weren't as horrifying as the sound of the storm. And then it got worse. The ship plunged downward, then leaped toward the sky, bow and stern dipping in and out of the sea, the hull straining against the pressure of the water. But it was the noise that stole any courage I might have possessed.

"I don't believe you," I said. "The storm is worse than the last and the one before that." We'd been at sea or anchor for close to three months. I had experienced bad weather and rough tides, but the gale blowing against my porthole was different. It had a mouth and tentacles and reached out of the ocean, snatching pieces of the boat and breaking them apart. "I saw a barrel fall from the upper deck and plunge into the sea."

"So you haven't spent the entire storm hiding beneath your bed."

"I wasn't hiding," I said defensively. "There is no place to hide in this cabin unless I can fit into the trunk." I had tried but couldn't fit, so I didn't mention it.

"We'll go below and head toward the middle of the ship, where we won't feel the boat's rocking as much."

"It's the noise that frightens me."

"We won't hear as much, either."

Rocking from side to side, I spread my arms to keep my balance, but a loud crash practically knocked me under the bed. The porthole had exploded, shooting glass shards everywhere.

"What in the bloody hell." William was a wave of movement. He instantly pulled me to him, shielding me from the wind and water pouring through the broken porthole. "Are you all right, Sarah?"

I nodded, my face buried against his chest. He lifted me into his arms. "Are we going to drown?"

"Don't be foolish, Sarah. You won't drown, but we can't stay here."

Water splashed our faces and drenched our clothes. Glass

had cut William's forehead, and blood covered his hands when he wiped his face.

"Where will we go?"

"We'll go to the galley, where it's safe."

Another loud noise shook me. Waves crashed against the hull, seamen shouted orders, and some screamed in pain. "Safe?"

"It means no harm will come to you."

The ocean poured in from everywhere, and men rushed by us sightlessly, eyes bright with fear.

"I've got you." He shoved seamen aside and held me tight with strong, thin arms.

I yelled into his ear. "I do not wish to drown!"

Without breaking stride, he barked orders at the seamen flailing around, telling them what to do next. Many knew, but William sounded like an officer, instructing them to grab the rope, barricade portholes, and stay calm. "Do your job, man," he shouted. "Gather your strength and courage."

"Yes, sir." I heard a sailor reply, probably blinded by the water and everything happening at once. He didn't care that William wasn't in charge of anything other than me.

"Where is the commander?" I asked, suddenly worried about him.

"He's where he should be, steering the ship."

Somehow we made it to the galley. Tennessee might well have been kin. I realized this when I spotted him hiding in a corner.

"You won't be safe there, Cook." William was insistent and brave. He searched the space with keen eyes. "There. You two will go inside the storage room."

"It's very small, sir."

"You'll be fine, Tennessee—and when did you start calling me sir?" William grinned. "Now, let's be about it, eh?"

He guided us into the room he'd picked, checked on the top shelves, and removed items that might fall onto our heads and injure us.

The ship lurched, and Tennessee grabbed on to me. Although, of course, his small stature made holding on to me difficult for him. I swallowed hard and tried to stop shaking.

"You're right, William," I said.

"How's that, Sarah?" He held on to the wall and stayed on his feet as the ship swayed violently up and down, hitch left, spin right.

"It's not as noisy here."

He patted me on the head. "I've got to go and check on the commander."

"He's steering the ship, you said."

He squinted at me. "He is that."

"Then he doesn't need your help," Tennessee said. "You should sit down next to us, boy."

"I've got to get something."

"Aren't we safe here? You should stick close and keep an eye on the girl." Tennessee looked at me.

"You'll take care of her for a few minutes."

"Where are you going, William?" I asked with the weightiness of fear in my voice.

"If you must know, I'm going to my bunk."

"You're going to get your books, aren't you?"

"Your bunk is in the seaman's quarters near the bow. We're closer to the stern." Tennessee sounded concerned. "Your books will be fine. And if they aren't, you can buy new ones in London."

"Don't worry. I'll be fine," he said, and then he was gone.

The ship bounced up and down, but the wind wasn't as loud.

So, again, William was right. And indeed, I would have a fabulous story to tell about my third storm at sea if it hadn't ended badly.

William never made it back with his books. He was taken overboard by a huge wave, and more than one seaman witnessed it. They also swore he was empty-handed. That meant he hadn't made it to his bunk. Sailors said he was grabbing ropes, helping men secure the ship. Had he lied to us?

He had helped save Tennessee and me, but William was the one who was lost. He died helping to protect the *Bonetta*.

At least that was the tale Tennessee told Commander Forbes when asked how William perished. I wasn't old enough to tell the other story of how William went back to his bunk to save his books after putting Tennessee and me in a storage room in the galley. He had patted my head and smiled as he left, with no more care in his step than a man walking across a rose garden.

I wasn't surprised to learn he'd drowned. I had come to care for him, and as had been the case for the past few years of my young life, caring about a thing and losing it walked hand in hand.

Death had numbed my heart, and I couldn't even mourn the loss of the best cabin boy I'd ever know.

PART TWO

Hurrying Feet and Groping Hearts

Chapter Eleven

The Sea and Winkfield Place, Berkshire, England, 1850

What was a forest without trees? A sky without heaven? A lion without a roar? Sticks in a bundle were unbreakable. A man or woman alone had little power, but sticking together made them strong.

As HMS *Bonetta* closed in on the shores of Britain, I was thinking about stories. The ones my mother had told me. They had a moral or spiritual center, imparted peace of mind, and taught lessons about life and living, even if most of those precious things had been taken from me.

Around William, I was whole. When he read books to me, I was transported. Now he was gone, and I missed him terribly. I'd thought I'd been broken as thoroughly as anyone could be, but his death had torn me in half.

Could I survive if any more of me was sliced away? Perhaps my attention should be on things, rather than people, like the new home I'd live in with Commander Forbes and his family and my meeting with the queen of England. Things and places caused less pain than people. That sounded smarter to me.

At dinner that night in the commander's cabin, where I had resided since the storm, he announced, "The HMS *Bonetta* will arrive at the Gravesend port in Britain tomorrow. Organize your things for departure before noon." He started to leave but hesitated. "God save the queen."

I walked down the plank holding the commander's hand with trembling fingers and barely catching my breath. I was searching for a glimpse of Queen Victoria. I had expected to see Her Majesty in the crowd, waiting for me. How William had spoken about her was how I imagined her—regal and larger than life. A head above the masses.

I pictured her stepping from her carriage and opening her arms to greet me.

But the sea of people made picking her out impossible. There were so many people. My gaze shifted from one end of the pier to the other and from bow to stern.

People were everywhere, all shades of people, black, white, brown, tall, short, wide, thin, dressed in full skirts and blouses, trousers and shirts. Merchants hawked their wares with loud voices, sang songs, or played music with instruments I'd never heard before. Other men carried large barrels or nets full of fish, buckets full of foul-smelling liquids, like the whiskey I had sipped from Tennessee's hidden jug.

The sky was full of gray clouds, and the air was moist, chilly, and rotten. It was the vilest-smelling place ever to punish my nostrils.

I tugged Commander Forbes's sleeve. "Is this London? Does the queen of England live here?" I asked, hoping she didn't live anywhere near the place. I hated the noise, and—"Why does it stink so bad?"

"No, it's not London. It's Gravesend," he replied. "The stench is the River Thames." Beyond that, he did not elaborate. Probably there was no more to say to a young girl like me. However, nothing should smell that awful without explanation.

Commander Forbes said we were taking a carriage to my

new home. A steward would send our luggage and other items to the house later.

I was disappointed the queen hadn't been waiting for me at the pier, but other things captured my thoughts. My first ride in a carriage wasn't memorable. I mostly looked at the scenery. I was overwhelmed by the number of people in the streets and the noise.

Occasionally, I'd point out to William a group of fishermen, nuns, or Blacks carrying books and dressed in frocks until I remembered he was dead, buried at the bottom of the sea. Then my chest tightened as I attempted to breathe through the memory and reach the other side so the thought of him wouldn't feel so bad.

"Do you have them?" The commander had been silent and startled me when he finally spoke.

He had instructed me to retrieve William's books from their hiding place beneath his bedding, but I had taken only Jane Austen's *Persuasion*, not any others.

"No, sir, I left them behind." I felt strangely satisfied, as when I refused to apologize to my sisters and brother. I had dared disobey one of the commander's orders and then had the nerve to confess. I wondered if William would be proud of me. "They are beneath his bunk," I replied, figuring the quicker I spoke, the quicker God would forgive me for my small lie.

"I wanted to give them to his mother, Sarah." He sounded unhappy, but that wouldn't have changed my actions. I wanted William to be happy, and returning to the East End of London would make him sad no matter the length of time.

"I believe that on a future voyage of the HMS *Bonetta*, William will return from the sea and rest in his old bunk. While there, he may wish to reread some of his old books."

The commander snorted, but a smile came quickly.

"Should I be sorry, sir?"

"That William is dead? I would hope so. He cared for you and was devoted to teaching you English and everything he knew about ships. Which was plentiful." He said this with the saddest look in his eyes.

"I wish he weren't dead, but most of the people I've known have died, so I expect death to come more often than not." My voice didn't catch. It frightened me how calm I sounded, as if he hadn't mattered, as if nothing could hurt me, when every loss had the power to crush me.

"Dear God, child. I am so sorry. You have endured so much grief in your life. But those horrible days are behind you. Trust me. You will thrive in England."

"The missionary woman said that my other name, Aina, means difficult." I looked at my hands folded in my lap. "Does that mean I will be a difficult child? A difficult woman when I grow up? Will the queen not like me because she will be able to tell I'm difficult?"

"No. No. No," he said, shaking his head, frowning, then smiling. "You must not worry about such things, I say. When we get you settled at Winkfield Place, my home, my wife will ensure that you spend plenty of time with our children, and we will dedicate ourselves to reminding you how to be a child." He touched my hand. "Did I mention I have four children?"

He had never mentioned his wife or children while we were at sea, but before I could open my mouth to tell him this, he said, "I want you to feel safe, Sarah. To play. To learn. To enjoy the miracle that is your life." He took one of my hands in my lap and held it between his two giant hands. "You are going to meet the queen of England. That is not a difficult girl's life but a brilliant child's future. One whose journey will continue to be blessed. Trust me, Sarah. Your life will be the best of times."

And I chose to believe him.

* * *

COURAGE LOOKED DIFFERENT from the outside than it did from the inside.

The commander was courageous. He'd saved me from King Gezo. Dayo and Monife were also brave, but they were dead or had vanished.

The courage inside me was different.

Knowing what I wanted and doing my best sounded like courage now that I was in England.

So I paid close attention to what I liked. I fancied being called princess and having a room like my cabin on board the *Bonetta*. I wanted Mrs. Forbes to treat me the same as she did her children or almost the same, and if not, I would have to find the courage to get my way.

A few hours by carriage from Windsor Castle, Winkfield Place was a mansion, according to Commander Forbes. "I am proud of my home. My family lives well, and we have plenty of room for you to join us. There are four floors, with bedrooms on the top two levels, a library filled with books, and the *Encyclopedia Britannica*. I've mentioned the volumes. You'll enjoy them." He sighed. "There's also a dining room, a morning room, a garden, stables, and two drawing rooms on the first floor, one with a piano."

His excitement continued to flow as we left the carriage and began the walk to the front door, tall doors that reached toward the sky.

"Don't be alarmed. I expect the house staff will be waiting to greet us."

The foyer was larger than my stateroom on the *Bonetta*, and as the commander had indicated, many people were waiting for us. At least fifteen, I counted. However, I couldn't tell the difference between his family and the maids, butlers, housekeepers, and nursery maids he mentioned until a woman with bright eyes and yellow hair smothered him with hugs, kisses, and tears, two small children hanging on to the folds of her skirt. Two others had hold of the commander's pant leg.

I tried not to feel lonely or forgotten. It had been two years since they'd seen him, and I had to allow the commander these moments where I wasn't the recipient of his full attention. But I had never shared him with anyone other than William and the seamen on board the ship.

Watching them, I felt something change inside me. It had likely begun on the HMS *Bonetta*, but it didn't come to me entirely until I saw Commander Forbes's wife.

I blamed Jane Austen's *Pride and Prejudice* for my opinion of women in England. Whether I understood everything about the story (and at the time, I did not), I had learned about a side of British society, fictional or factual, that I would hold on to for a long time.

A bold woman eventually gets her way.

I decided I would not fear people who looked like Mrs. Forbes. Of course, they were curious, but I had to learn to be bold around them, like Elizabeth Bennet in Jane Austen's *Pride and Prejudice*. So I grabbed his pant leg and pulled forcibly. It still took him a moment to look at me.

"Everyone," he said, gently touching my shoulder, "this is

Sarah Forbes Bonetta. She will be living with us for a while. And I want her to feel that our home is her home."

A wave of surprise swept over the faces of those in the foyer, except for the children, two of whom hadn't let go of the commander's other pant leg.

"Aren't you an unusual-looking girl?" Those were the first words I recall hearing from Commander Forbes's wife.

I didn't take offense, although the longer I thought about it, I wasn't sure if I shouldn't. I had nothing to compare her to, other than the two white women at the Badagry mission.

But she wasn't either one of them.

She had a pleasant face and pretty yellow-colored hair and smiled at me, with moist eyes the color of the sea. No deep lines were cutting into her brow, no dark circles beneath her eyes, but she wasn't looking at me so much as at Commander Forbes.

"Jessie, take the children into the nursery. I'll show Sarah to her room."

"Yes, my lady." Jessie had the same full skirt as Mrs. Forbes, reaching the floor like Mrs. Forbes's skirt. But Jessie's dress was drab, black or brown, hard to tell, and she wore a long apron. Mrs. Forbes's dress was bluish-green and matched her eyes.

"I will have my room, eh?" I said, smiling happily.

"Yes, you will, Sarah. Now, follow me," Mrs. Forbes said, pulling her gaze away from her husband. "I will show you where you will sleep, and when your trunk arrives, where to put the rest of your clothing." She made a gesture toward Jessie. "She is one of our house servants but will serve as your lady's maid to help you. Your luggage will be here soon, but let's get you cleaned up and settled best we can, so you can get to know the children."

"As soon as we docked, I sent a courier to Her Majesty's secretary to advise of our arrival and desire to meet with the queen," the commander said. "The maid advises that a response was hand-delivered, and Her Majesty is interested in meeting you but didn't mention when. So, until then, you'll join my children in their daily routine. But we will be ready when the messenger arrives."

Mrs. Forbes lifted her hand to touch me, but I pulled away. We weren't friends yet, and I didn't know if we would be.

She smiled shyly. "I hope Her Majesty won't send for you this week or next, because we won't be ready."

Commander Forbes looked at his wife with an expression of gratitude. He then patted me on top of my head. "It's time I reacquainted myself with my home. I will leave you ladies to do the same." He smiled warmly and left. Mrs. Forbes headed in the opposite direction.

I followed her out of the foyer. I wasn't sure where the commander went off to, but I was alone with his wife, whom I imagined I should trust. After all, the commander hadn't hesitated to leave me with her.

We climbed a hillside of stairs until we reached the top floor of the house. She flung open a door, and I stepped into a room with wall coverings and rugs and a dresser and something else. It captured my image but much clearer than my reflection in river water on a sunny day: "What is that?"

"The mirror?"

"That's me in the mirror, yes?"

"You haven't seen yourself before?"

"We could see our image in the river in the sunlight. But there was no mirror in my room on the ship or at the mission. I once saw a painting of myself—I believe the commander has it."

"You look nice, dear, but we will need to find you some better clothes. Those are old and not the latest fashions," Mrs. Forbes said. "When you meet the queen of England, you must be fashionable."

I kept staring in the mirror as she walked around the room.

"Everything seems to be in order here. Now I will leave you to explore without my eyes following your every move." She paused. "Oh, the bath is two doors to the right." She had moved to the archway, her hand on the doorknob. "Jessie will be right up and show you what to do there." She sighed. "You understand me?"

"Yes, ma'am, I understand—I'll wait for Jessie."

She seemed relieved, as if she'd done as much as possible for me. "I'm sure you're tired after your voyage. Dinner will be served soon, but you have time for a brief nap." She started to close the door, but her head bobbed back in. "We're delighted to have you with us, Sarah. Please do believe that."

She closed the door behind her. I continued to stare at myself in the mirror. I was black compared to Mrs. Forbes, her children, and her maids and butler. Indeed, no one around looked like me. And that was a blessing, I figured. I would be the most notable girl in the room—the most sought after. I wasn't positive I was the only African princess in England, but it made sense that I would be one of only a few.

After a while, I was tired of looking at myself. I thought briefly about exploring my new bedroom, but exhaustion struck me like a hammer.

I sat on the edge of the bed, one much larger and softer than the one on the HMS *Bonetta*. I curled up in the middle, fully dressed, shoes on my feet, bonnet on my head, and fell into a perfect, dreamless sleep.

Chapter Twelve

Winkfield Place, Berkshire, England, 1850

I had been a member of the Forbes household for about three weeks, and my English had improved during that time. I also took dance lessons (and showed talent) and started lessons on the piano, a musical instrument that became an instant obsession. I'd also had a severe coughing jag that kept me in bed for a day and a night. But I got well and, late one evening, left my room, anxious to practice on the piano.

The drawing room at Winkfield Place with the piano had the most eye-catching colors, fabrics, and portraits. Gold-leafed framed paintings hung on the walls. Exquisite red, blue, and yellow fabrics covered the seat cushions of the chairs and settees. Carpet from China (one of many places I'd never heard of) was made of plush wool and beautiful patterns and colors. I hated to step on it, but it was the room with the square grand piano.

The instrument had an ivory and ebony keyboard, maple wood outer casing, copper strings, and a soundboard crafted from spruce wood. All of which Mrs. Forbes had lovingly explained.

She was the first person I'd heard play the piano. It took only a few notes for me to be in rapture. The sound made by the keys, when struck by fingers and thumbs, captivated me from the first time I heard it.

It also jarred a memory.

My father had played a musical instrument with his thumbs that made a similar sound. It took me a week to make my mind remember the name of it, but I did—the *ubo aka,* a thumb piano.

So I had no choice but to master it, and I was as persistent as a starving fruit fly. I demanded to learn everything about the piano.

Luckily, Mrs. Forbes agreed that a proper young lady should be able to play the classics, but she had other children and wasn't always around when I needed her. So I decided to practice on my own.

One evening, I slipped into the drawing room, which I'd thought was empty.

"Why aren't you with the commander and Henry playing backgammon?" Mrs. Forbes was seated in the shadows. Henry was the oldest of the Forbes children.

"Oh, ma'am. I was unaware you were here—but I can play backgammon tomorrow," I said, staring at the piano.

"Oh, yes. Go ahead and practice your scales." She stood as I moved to the piano bench.

I sat and waited for her to lift the lid. The instrument wouldn't play until she'd done so. But she didn't come.

She was standing in front of the fireplace, staring at the painting of her husband above the mantel.

"Mrs. Forbes, ma'am."

I was impatient. Why hadn't she moved toward me and the piano? I was waiting to play. Then she turned, raised a hand to her face, and wiped her eyes. Had she been crying?

"I'll be right there, dear." Her voice trembled. "I can count my husband's loyalties on three fingers." She raised a fist and then one finger at a time. "Her Majesty, the Church of England, and his wife. In that order."

Why was she saying these things to me? I hoped she didn't expect me to respond.

I had interrupted her when she thought she was alone, but I didn't want to leave. I wanted to play the piano and needed her to lift the lid.

"He trusts me to care for his children, but they are not often in his thoughts." Her voice was hoarse. "He does not concern himself with their day-to-day lives. He has to deal with Africa, the nightmare visits to King Gezo's camp, the insects, the swamp fever."

She looked at me with sad eyes. "I found the journal he is writing about his adventures in Africa and read some of it." She raised a hand and covered her mouth, stifling a gasp. "My husband loves both Africa *and* his family. That is what I believed. But he returned home only days ago and already plans another journey to Africa as soon as possible." She walked over to me and lifted the lid. "Tell me, Sarah, why is Africa so important to him? What makes him suffer through its horrors only to leave his family again for another two or three years?"

I gulped down the unpleasantness in my throat. How would I know why he chose to do what he did? He was the man who had taken me from King Gezo, the butcher who murdered my father and mother, brothers and sisters, and hopefully not, but likely, sold Monife to slave merchants.

Maybe the commander planned to return to Africa and save another girl from the kingdom of Dahomey. That would make her stop crying, I thought. But I couldn't be sure.

"Sarah, why is it so hard for him to let go of Africa? What keeps drawing him back?"

"I'm not sure, ma'am. I thought Commander Forbes loved

the ocean as much as he loved Africa, and if he had to choose, he would choose the sea."

"So he wouldn't choose his family or his home? It would be Africa or the sea, you say?"

She clasped her hands together and squeezed her fingers until they turned a whiter shade of white. I had said something wrong.

"He loves his family," I added hastily, although he'd never mentioned a wife or children while we were at sea.

She sat next to me on the piano bench. "My apologies for my behavior. I have a slight headache. That makes me needlessly melancholy."

"Ma'am, I don't know what to say."

"Of course you don't." Mary Forbes dragged her fingers across her brow. "You came to practice your scales. How about if we begin and you do just that, dear."

"Yes, ma'am."

At least she had stopped crying.

* * *

MRS. FORBES AVOIDED me for several days following the incident in the drawing room. But if I were to become an essential part of the Forbes family, she had to like me.

Commander Forbes had negotiated my escape from King Gezo's camp, but I hadn't trusted him or William immediately. For a while, I suspected he was a slave merchant like the other white (and brown) men I'd seen in Abomey.

Now I was in England, living in his home, and one day soon, he'd take me to meet Queen Victoria. He had proved trustworthy enough and showed how much he cared about my well-being. But a husband and wife—don't they think as one?

If Mrs. Forbes hated me because she blamed me for her husband's love of Africa, might she convince him to abandon his feelings and plans for me?

Perhaps not the most rational thinking, but I had to make certain that Mrs. Forbes liked me—or better, loved me enough to never turn against me.

So how would I go about gaining this love?

I didn't have to think about it long. Frankly, it came to me one afternoon. In my younger years, whenever I was ill, no matter how much I misbehaved or how sweet I might be, my mother would wrap her arms around me and hug me close. A sick child draws a mother's attention and sympathy.

I wandered downstairs before dawn. Mrs. Forbes spent her mornings in the dining room with a cup of Arabian coffee (I learned this by eavesdropping on Jessie). Mrs. Forbes's husband had introduced her to the coffee beans after a fellow British naval officer brought some back to England. Of course, she served it with scones, jam, and clotted cream.

"Mrs. Forbes, I don't feel well," I said, strolling into the room with a pinched expression.

She placed her coffee cup on the table. "You don't look well. Are you warm?"

"Yes, ma'am. My face is on fire." I wiped a finger beneath my nostrils and coughed.

"Oh, dear, you should've stayed in bed."

"No, I want to take my lessons today."

"And have all of my children catch whatever you've got? No, you hurry upstairs to bed, and I'll bring you a tray of warm milk, tea, honey, and lemon. A glass of hot wine will come next if that isn't a cure. Now, off with you."

I was right, I thought, rushing up the staircase to my bedroom. She enjoyed the opportunity to take care of me while I was ill. But, within hours, I was really sick—a punishment from God for feigning illness. I had a fever and severe cough, and my vision played tricks on me. Or I was having nightmares, something I hadn't experienced since the *Bonetta*. Dead people came to my room, Dayo and William mostly, scolding me for something I hadn't done or should've done, but what I hadn't done was never clear.

My sickness lasted for a week, and I spent most days in bed and alone in my room, except for Jessie, who delivered my meals. One afternoon, there was a knock on the door shortly after lunch. I sat upright, hopeful the lady of the house had come to visit me. I hadn't seen her since I'd interrupted her morning coffee.

As the door cracked open, I called out, "Mrs. Forbes, I am feeling much better."

But it wasn't her. "Miss Sarah, half the household are in their beds with your cold." Jessie had brought a tray with my afternoon tea, including honey and biscuits.

"The next time you have a cough, tell me right away. We'll confine you to your room, to save me from running from sick bed to sick bed to tend to ill children and their parents."

"What do you mean?"

"Haven't you wondered why Mrs. Forbes hasn't visited you? She's ill, too, along with her husband and children."

"I am sorry they aren't well, but I won't be sick that often."

She looked at me oddly. "You can't help but cough and sneeze."

I shook my head in bewilderment.

"Every other night since you arrived, you've coughed the night away. You are so accustomed to your hacking that you sleep right through it. Why do you think I always keep a fire in your room? Hoping the heat will keep your body warm like it's accustomed to in Africa."

"I am not aware of coughing all night," I said.

"They say Negroes don't fare well in English weather. Your constitution can't handle the chill and the dampness." She prepared me a cup of tea, adding plenty of honey and lemon.

Then Jessie was gone.

I pondered her words but forgot them once I was well. Whatever she'd implied didn't matter. I wasn't sick anymore. I had schoolwork and piano lessons. However, Mrs. Forbes was spending less time teaching. The governess, a broad-bodied woman who liked me about as much as Jessie, didn't have the same flair for instruction as Mrs. Forbes. I became bored.

But Mrs. Forbes did extend my practice time on the square piano. Before long, I believed I'd been born with musical fingers.

She praised my skills, too. "I love teaching someone as naturally talented as you, dear Sarah."

* * *

In late October, four months after I arrived at Winkfield Place, I thought of myself as part of the Forbes family, and meeting with Her Majesty was no longer the end-all to me.

One morning Mrs. Forbes was teaching her son Henry and me about the Roman Empire while her three younger children were with their governess. It wasn't a special day, but it was perfect for me. Family. Laughter. Joy. Learning. Then a message from Windsor Castle interrupted us.

Not a letter from the queen directly, but from Prince Albert's private secretary Sir Charles Beaumont Phipps, a member of the royal household.

Commander Forbes accepted the envelope and responded to the invitation, confirming our attendance at Windsor Castle to meet with the queen of England on November 9, 1850, at eleven thirty.

Everyone was pleased except me. I wanted to cry. After such a long wait, did I really need to meet the queen of England?

* * *

As THE GRAY mare clip-clopped over the winding road to the main gate of Windsor Castle, I sat in the carriage, growing faint with apprehension.

Except for the occasional slip when some of William's East End accent came through, my English had improved. Mrs. Forbes had worked tirelessly on my manners. She had taught me much (and quickly) about what to say, how to say it, how to move, and when to bow or not. Since we'd waited so many months, I also had a fashionable wardrobe. When I met Her Majesty, I would be flawless.

I thought Winkfield Place was huge, but it was one building. Nothing had prepared me for Windsor Castle. It had two courts and a massive round tower visible from kilometers away. Commander Forbes pointed it out as we approached from the surrounding flatland.

When I fearfully asked how many rooms were in the castle, he laughed, perhaps hearing my panic.

"A thousand rooms and three hundred fireplaces," he said with a grin.

My confidence fled like a fox outrunning the hounds.

"That many," I replied shakily.

We were met by two servants dressed in fancy costumes as we descended from the carriage. They looked nothing like the maids at Winkfield Place, who wore white aprons and caps but had dresses that didn't match. These did, and the fabric resembled taffeta. Even though I'd learned taffeta was for evening gowns, that was how these servants looked—elegantly well-groomed.

As I walked through the massive hallways with sky-high ceilings, reams of wallpaper, and gold-framed paintings, much larger than those at Winkfield, I carried the burden of perfection on my shoulders and the commander's look of pride on my back.

After all the waiting, I had hoped to take the meeting in stride, but I couldn't pull a full breath into my lungs. Instead, I hung on to the commander's hand so tightly, I imagined that was why he stopped to look at me and pat me on my head.

"Everything is all right." He smiled and loosened my grip with a slight shake of his fingers. "You are more prepared for this moment than any child in England. Do not fret. She will love and cherish you as much as I do."

His eyes beamed, and I believed. He was right. I was ready to meet her. I was prepared to meet the world with my chin up and a smile on my seven- or eight-year-old face.

Then we were escorted into a waiting room. It was as big as the two drawing rooms on the ground floor of Winkfield Place.

We were seated when someone new entered.

"Good day, Commander Forbes. I am Lady Margaret Phipps, wife of Sir Charles Beaumont Phipps, secretary to Prince Albert and keeper of the privy purse for the queen. I am in charge of day-to-day activities at Windsor Castle on behalf of the queen and will keep you apprised of the queen's appointments scheduled with Sarah."

It was a long introduction for our first meeting with Lady Margaret Phipps, but at least we knew everything about her. Why else say so much if she hadn't expressed everything we needed to know?

"I will escort the child to the Waterloo Chamber, but I must ensure she is suitably prepared to meet the queen."

"Oh, of course, yes, Lady Margaret." The commander seemed flustered.

"However, Her Majesty wishes to meet with you now, Commander."

He turned to me. "I believe she wants to discuss my trip to Africa. It won't take too long."

Another gentleman entered the waiting room and bowed. The commander smiled and followed the man out of the room, leaving me alone with Lady Margaret Phipps.

"Stay here and keep still. I will return shortly, Sarah."

She left me sitting on the edge of the chair, my feet dangling, swinging more than slightly because she was as gruff in appearance as Old Martin, the grizzly bear in London Zoo, which I'd seen drawings of during a lesson about wild animals.

I watched the giant doors close and folded my hands in my lap, but the skin beneath my petticoats was itching me. I could barely keep still.

Then a noise came from behind one of the oversized chairs. I drew my knees into my chest, planted my feet on the chair's cushion, and waited for whatever creature might attack me from the shadows. I didn't have a voice to scream and wolfed down as much air as possible because I believed it would be my last breath.

Chapter Thirteen

Windsor Castle, 1850

My name is Alice. Are you the Black slave girl who is a princess and was almost murdered by an African slave hunter and his Amazon warrior women?"

Emerging from the shadows wasn't a beast but a child, a girl my age and not my skin color.

"I am not a slave. My name is Sarah Forbes Bonetta." I wondered how no one had seen her. Where had she been hiding? I would have expected Mrs. Phipps or a servant to have noticed her (even if I hadn't).

"I am a princess, and I'm from Africa," I continued to explain. "It is a place full of people like me, and not all Africans are bad people. Some are kings with kind hearts, like my father."

The girl stepped from behind the chair and walked into the middle of the room. She wore a pink dress with white pantaloons, the bottoms trimmed with lace that showed from beneath the skirt's hem. She also had on black lace-up shoes like mine. Her dress was similar to mine, but my blue dress was prettier than her pink one and matched my bluestone necklace.

She swayed as she held the edges of her skirt. "I'm a princess, too," she said. "My mother is Her Majesty, Queen Victoria, the queen of England. I am her—" She paused and counted her fingers. "Her third child. But she had her"—another pause to count—"seventh, a son, Prince Arthur, this past May. She's not having another baby anytime soon. I don't think." She smiled brightly, more pleased with getting the number of children right than the chances of a new brother or sister.

I didn't comment on the part about her being a princess because she had no scars on her face to prove it.

"How old are you?" she asked.

"Almost eight."

"I'm almost eight, too."

She didn't look it. "You're small for your age."

"You are small, too."

Not that small, I thought, keeping an eye on her. How was I to know if she was who she said she was?

"My father is Prince Albert." She stopped swinging and took one step toward me. "He told me size isn't something to brag about or be bothered by. Doing your best is what matters."

"My father and mother are dead."

"I'm sorry. My—" She glanced at the ceiling, looking distressed momentarily. "Condolences. Yes, my condolences. I'm sorry they are dead."

"I am, too."

"Are you visiting my mother, Her Majesty, the queen of England, today?"

"Yes, I am."

She shrugged. "Mothers are extra . . ." Her eyes rolled up toward the ceiling again. "Ordinary. Yes, extraordinary. That's what my older sister said. And they are best tolerated from a distance, especially if they are the queen of England. That's why we children spend so much time with our governesses."

"You have more than one governess?"

"You don't?"

"I don't have any, but the family I live with has one, and two servant girls."

"I thought you might have several since you don't have a mother."

"I do have a mother now," I said. "My mother in England is Mrs. Forbes. She's the commander's wife."

"I don't know the Forbes family. They aren't a part of the royal household, are they?"

"I wouldn't know." I may have growled. I wasn't sure I liked her. She talked too much about things I knew nothing about, like royal households. "Mrs. Phipps could return any moment," I warned. "You may want to go back to your hiding place."

"You're right. But you can hear her coming from across the courtyard. She's always shouting orders." She moved closer.

I inched backward in the chair, using my hands to pull me over the cushion. "Will you get in trouble if you are caught?"

"Not sure. I've never been caught."

I kept looking at the doors, waiting for them to fly open.

"The only person I fear is my mother, Her Majesty, the queen of England, but she won't come into this room."

"Why do you add Her Majesty, the queen of England, every time you say 'mother'?"

"My little sister Louise says that, and I think it's funny."

"How will you get out of here if Mrs. Phipps suddenly opens the doors?"

"I'll leave the way I came. I know all the secret passageways."

I leaned forward. Our faces were a few inches apart. "I had a friend once, she was like a sister, and we were good at getting in and out of places we shouldn't be in, too."

Alice grinned. "When you come back, I'll show you some of the better hiding places in Windsor Castle." She smiled. "There are also places in Buckingham Palace and Kensington Palace, but mostly, I know Windsor."

A voice on the other side of the large doors startled me. It was Mrs. Phipps.

Alice laughed. "I told you. She's always barking orders. I'd better go." Then she waved and slipped behind one of the thick drapes that hung from the ceiling to the floor—and was gone.

* * *

AFTER THE PRINCESS left, I had an attack of doubt. What if my meeting with Her Majesty, the queen of England, went badly? I was a spirited girl with a curious mind, but I had a horrific past. What if bad memories slipped into my mind and made me melancholy? What if I forgot how to speak English and made mistakes in etiquette, for example, which made light of the hard work Mrs. Forbes had done to teach me?

I inhaled. It was difficult to shake off the craziness crawling through my thoughts, but I had a fierce sense of competition and an adventurous soul.

I will not forget why I am in Windsor Castle.

I was there to impress Her Majesty, the queen of England.

When we met, she would like me. After we met, she would want to see me every week. We'd become friends. Not like Monife or William, whom I counted as friends, but like my mother or oldest sister. Or Mrs. Forbes.

I liked living in England, living with the Forbes family, studying piano, and meeting princesses who hid behind walls.

I needed the queen on my side. To accomplish that, I had to be perfect.

It was to be the greatest moment of my young life. An un-precedented occurrence that would never happen again, no matter if I met with the queen of England every day for the rest of my days. The first meeting, the first time we set eyes upon each other, could never be repeated. A daunting thought, but at almost eight years old, I was less introspective and more interested in the moment at hand.

Mrs. Phipps returned to the room and examined me head to toe. She went as far as to put on her nose spectacles to study my fingernails and stockings. She then instructed me to keep on my bonnet.

"It suits you."

I nodded but decided to save my words. A conversation with Mrs. Phipps had little benefit now. I needed to hold on to whatever words I could muster for my meeting with the queen.

"We're ready," Mrs. Phipps said, finally appearing to be satisfied with me. "Now we can proceed to the Queen's Drawing Room."

I glanced at the long curtain Alice had stepped behind and noticed one of her lace-up shoes sneaking from beneath the hem. It was as if she was waving goodbye. I did not react but smiled on the inside. And then Mrs. Phipps took my hand and led me out of the room.

* * *

"WE WILL MEET Her Majesty in the Queen's Drawing Room," Mrs. Phipps said as we trotted down a very long corridor. "She will be seated in an open armchair in the middle of the room in front of the bay windows. Commander Forbes will be in the room and seated or standing nearby. I believe he was standing when I left them. You will remain standing until she gestures for you to sit. If you have any confusion about what to do, look at me. I will point you in the right direction."

We entered the room, and everything was exactly as Mrs. Phipps had described. My first thought, however, upon seeing Queen Victoria was that she wasn't much taller than me, even seated, but she was sharp-eyed. The way she looked at me, although not a glare of dislike, was a thorough examination of my appearance and demeanor. However, she offered no immediate sign of approval or disapproval, which pleased me tremendously. It made me think she wasn't quick to judge. I would try and be the same.

Some things were undeniable, however. She resembled Princess Alice, but only around the mouth and nose. She had a round figure and kind eyes.

I curtsied as Mrs. Forbes had taught me, bowing my head only slightly as part of the gesture, but didn't fan my skirt. The queen smiled, increasing my confidence in my performance.

"Your Majesty," I said, waiting for her to take the lead.

"Sarah Forbes Bonetta. I have heard much about you and your tragedies. Commander Forbes was quite clever, saving your life by inviting the Dahomey king to allow him to give you to me as a gift." She tilted her head, her eyes widening. "A person cannot be given to another, but it was still clever of him."

"Yes, ma'am," I answered.

"I understand you are living with the Forbes family."

"Yes, ma'am. They have been very kind to me. I am taking piano lessons, studying history and English, and reading the King James Bible daily."

She looked at me with a hint of admiration. "When did you begin learning English? It is exceptional."

"I began learning after I met Commander Forbes," I said, holding her gaze. "He is an excellent teacher, as was his cabin boy, who helped me, too."

"Your dress is lovely," the queen said. "You look like any other English child, I dare say. Other than your skin." She leaned forward, narrowing her eyes. "Mrs. Phipps, please remove her bonnet."

Mrs. Phipps, who had practically disappeared into the wallpaper, stepped forward. Then, with deft fingers, she untied the bow beneath my chin and removed the bonnet. She returned to her spot against the wall as soon as she finished.

"Look at your woolly black hair and those big earrings," the queen said. "Now you look like what I expected of a Negro."

I smiled, but I didn't understand how she couldn't tell by looking at my Black face that I was Negro.

The queen settled in her seat. "Tell me your story, what you remember of those days before the Dahomey king—" She looked at Commander Forbes. "What is his name?"

"King Gezo."

She nodded. "Gezo murdered your family."

"Yes, ma'am. It was horrible." That was how I began, and I told the story from bow to stern, leaving out nothing about the slave camp, even the story of the bluestone necklace, the search for Dayo, and the disappearance of my friend Monife.

"My scars helped keep me from the sacrifice pit for two years," I said as I prepared to end my story. "They are a symbol of my royal family."

A respectful silence settled over the room as we waited for the queen's response to my story. It took a moment for her to speak, but there was a sigh of relief from Commander Forbes and Mrs. Phipps when she did. So I guessed I had done well.

"I will arrange for Sarah to return to Windsor Castle next week if that is agreeable to you, Commander. Mrs. Phipps will coordinate arrangements with your household."

Commander Forbes beamed. "Yes, ma'am. That will be just fine."

He grinned at me, which made me smile, too. He was proud of me, and I was proud of myself.

"You have an amazing appearance about you, child," the queen stated. "You may not be what we're accustomed to think of as attractive, but you are striking." She turned to Mrs. Phipps. "I would like her to be photographed. I am impressed by the American photographer with a studio in England. Will you make the arrangements?" She stood. "I enjoyed your visit, dear. And thank you, Lieutenant Commander, for your courage and quick thinking."

Then she stepped from her chair and walked across the room to the double doors, which two servants opened for her. Next, she stepped into the hallway, but she turned and called over Mrs. Phipps before she disappeared. They whispered for a few minutes and then the queen departed.

Mrs. Phipps walked up to the commander and me. I had taken hold of his hand again while we watched the queen give Mrs. Phipps instructions.

"Her Majesty has informed me that she has approved of Commander Forbes's request that Winkfield Place be the official home of Sarah Forbes Bonetta, and the Forbes family will manage her daily affairs unrelated to the royal family."

The commander's relief was apparent. He bowed in gratitude.

Mrs. Phipps cleared her throat and continued. "Her Majesty also will pay for Sarah's education and clothing and provide a stipend to cover any expenses the Forbes family might incur."

"Her Majesty is taking on the role of guardian for Sarah, then?" Commander Forbes said, gently squeezing my hand.

"Yes, Commander. That is correct, but your family will implement Sarah's education. We expect you to include a rigorous Bible study—which the queen will question her about, including her other studies, during her trips to the castle and Buckingham Palace when the family resides there," Mrs. Phipps said. "If Sarah is to become a missionary, the profession the queen agrees is best suited for her, she must be as knowledgeable in the Church of England and the King James Bible as any subject. Frankly, even more so, wouldn't you agree, Commander?"

"Yes, ma'am. Absolutely. I completely agree."

Chapter Fourteen

A few nights after my first visit with the queen, I was in bed, having just pulled the homespun wool blanket up to my chin, when there was a knock on my bedroom door. Groggy, I thought it could only be Jessie or Mrs. Forbes. They were the only two members of the household to enter my bedroom.

Candlelight flickered, casting shadows on the wall as I struggled upright in the bed. The door opened, and Mrs. Forbes entered.

"Yes, ma'am," I said, half-asleep.

She moved toward the bed, and I shoved aside the blanket and sat up, unexpectedly nervous. She was taking too long to speak, and I panicked, thinking I was dreaming. What if she wasn't there at all?

I gasped. "Is someone there?"

"Oh, no, dear. Don't be upset. There is no need."

"I am not upset, Mama. But I thought you might be a dream." I had started calling Mrs. Forbes Mama after meeting Alice and her mother, the queen. Mrs. Forbes didn't seem to mind, so I kept it up.

"I heard you coughing and came to check on you."

"I don't remember coughing. Did I sound very sick?"

"No, you sounded better than you have in weeks."

My cough had been a worry. With winter and the cold weather came drafty hallways and white rain, as I called snow the first time I saw it. And no matter how many fireplaces or how brightly they burned, I was always cold and surprised I didn't cough all day and night.

Mama walked in circles, not quickly but steadily, as if she had something on her mind and had to figure it out before she said a word. I watched and waited. It was something I wanted to learn, too. Taking a moment to think before blurting out the first thought that came to mind.

A proper English lady was polite and thoughtful, and even at my young age, I had decided to be a proper English lady when I grew up.

"You made quite the impression on the queen, Sarah." Mrs. Forbes had stopped pacing. "She has invited you to return—as soon as next week."

"Oh," I said glumly. "I am so pleased." Of course, I wasn't as pleased as I would've been if the queen hadn't mentioned Bible studies and missionary work. But I lived in a Christian household in a Christian country governed by a God-fearing queen and Parliament. And being a clever girl, I didn't speak that thought aloud.

"You don't sound pleased," Mrs. Forbes said warily, picking up on my hesitation.

"Are *you* pleased, Mama?"

She folded her arms over her stomach. "Mr. Phipps, Prince Albert's private secretary, will provide us with an allowance to support you, courtesy of the queen. But this allowance requires a schedule and attention to detail. So we must keep records of every penny spent. There must never be a question about how we use the money provided by Her Majesty for your education, clothing, and board."

"Yes, ma'am." I couldn't add anything useful, especially about money. "I will keep up with my studies. I promise." I thought those words might ease her concerns.

"I know you will. I can't even explain why I'm mentioning this, except it was on my mind when I checked on you and your cough."

Mrs. Forbes sat on the edge of the bed. "Commander Forbes will be leaving us for a few weeks."

"He is returning to Africa?" I sat cross-legged on top of my blankets.

"No, not yet. He must travel to his home in Scotland to visit his parents. His father is ill."

"I thought his home was England."

"Don't forget your studies, dear. Scotland is part of Great Britain and ruled by the queen of England."

"Oh, yes, that's right. Since 1707."

"Yes. But that means he won't be here to accompany you on your visits to Windsor Castle." She paused to take a deep breath. "Mrs. Phipps, you recall meeting her?"

"Yes."

"She will become your escort for all visits with the queen. She will also coordinate all your encounters with the queen and her children, including, I was told, Princess Alice."

"Alice." The pitch of my voice changed. "Why do you mention her?"

"Because Mrs. Phipps informed us that you two met the other day when Princess Alice's governess lost track of her. Mrs. Phipps also recalled seeing a pair of girl's shoes behind one of the drapes in the waiting room when she spoke with you."

"Oh." It was the only reply I could summon. My surprise was too great. Alice wasn't as good at hiding as she thought. She'd been unmasked.

Mrs. Forbes rose from the bed. "You go back to sleep. We'll prepare for Mrs. Phipps's visit tomorrow."

"She's coming here tomorrow?" My voice shook.

"Not tomorrow. Day after. But it will take an entire day to prepare. She is a member of the royal household and must be received accordingly."

"Yes, ma'am."

Mrs. Forbes was at the door. "Many changes ahead during the next few weeks. You stay focused on your studies, and everything will be fine, Sarah. Just fine."

"Thank you, Mama. Good night, Mama."

"Good night, dear."

* * *

AFTER SEVERAL VISITS with the queen, I prepared a surprise for Her Majesty for my next trip to Windsor Castle.

I was incredibly proud of myself, too. I had managed to do this despite Mrs. Phipps's habit of looking over my shoulder, watching me as if I were a jackal come to steal the chickens.

Mrs. Forbes had told me of Her Majesty's love of music and the piano, and I had nagged Mrs. Phipps about practicing my scales to play for the queen. However, she didn't say I could until we were in the carriage outside the castle entrance. We met in the Queen's Sitting Room, where there was a piano.

"I am thrilled you were able to return so promptly," the queen said after we had completed the greeting formalities, which were more complicated than before. We weren't alone, as we'd been in the first meeting. The room was full of the queen's children, in dresses and sailor outfits, and governesses and servants. Prince Albert was there, too.

My hands didn't feel as steady with so many people in the room. But I refused to abandon my surprise.

"I am happy you wanted to see me again so soon."

"Tell me about what you are reading. I am interested in how your English has progressed and what areas of study Mrs. Forbes and her governess have focused upon."

"The novel by Jane Austen, *Pride and Prejudice,*" I said.

"Who allowed you to read such a book?"

All eyes in the room turned on me, the cause of the queen's indignant tone.

I had said the wrong thing and stammered for a few seconds, trying to come up with a reply that would not cause further anger for Her Majesty.

My lips moved, but no words came. Why had I mentioned Jane Austen? I had read plenty of children's stories with Mrs. Forbes. What had brought a book read to me on board the HMS *Bonetta* to mind?

Then I looked at the child in the sailor's suit. It was his fault. He'd conjured William Bartholomew into my thoughts.

I turned to the queen, words flying from my mouth. "A cabin boy read it to me on board the HMS *Bonetta*. He helped teach me English. His name was William Bartholomew. He was raised in the East End of London and desperately wanted to meet Your Majesty, but then he drowned at sea."

The room had quieted during my speech. By the end, I couldn't even hear an infant's cries, although there were so many babies in the Queen's Sitting Room.

"What brought that story to mind, Sarah?" Her Majesty asked.

I glanced at the sailor's suit but chose not to mention it. "William wanted to meet you very much, Your Majesty. He had wanted to join me when I visited you." I exhaled. "He was my friend and is often on my mind."

She smiled. "It is good to have an unforgettable friend, Sarah. Never be shy about admitting a kindred spirit." She cleared her throat. "By telling me his story, in a way, you have brought him to me. I suggest that his spirit is in this room with us now. Wouldn't you say?"

"Yes, ma'am." A warmth came over me. To have the queen understand me in such a kind manner. "That's exactly right."

We continued to talk about books for some time. Prince Albert joined in the conversation, as did the Princess Royal, the queen's eldest daughter, Victoria, and others, including the occasional remark by Princess Alice.

Then I remembered my surprise.

I whispered in Mrs. Phipps's ear. "Can I play now?"

She frowned, of course, but she announced that I would play my piano scales a moment later.

I grinned and rushed over to the piano. On my way, I had to collect myself and calm my fingers. Then I corrected Mrs. Phipps before I began.

"I hope you won't mind, ma'am, but I will not play scales today. I will perform a piece by Johann Pachelbel. It is called Canon in D."

"I love surprises, Sarah. Of course, please do."

I glanced at Mrs. Phipps. Her expression showed no indication that she felt the same about surprises. I expected a scolding, but fortunately, my surprise was a triumph.

By showing off my talent and love of the piano, I further endeared myself to the queen. The piano was her favorite musical instrument. She invited me to return the next week to take piano lessons with Princess Alice and her piano teacher.

I was ecstatic. I imagined I would be invited to move into Windsor Castle, staying weeks or months at a time. I would miss the Forbes family, but they would also come to visit and have guest rooms in their names. Why not? Commander Forbes told me there were one thousand rooms in the castle. So there was plenty of space for whatever daydream I imagined.

How could my life in England be so divinely perfect?

* * *

Mrs. Phipps had arranged for Princess Alice and me to spend time together in the playroom. Of course, Alice wanted to sneak away, and now we were running through Windsor Castle corridors I'd never seen before.

"I want to go to a different part of the castle today." Alice's curls bounced wildly as she ran down the corridor. "Someplace enormous where I've never been before."

It was my third or fourth trip to Windsor Castle, a week before the Christmas holiday, and Princess Alice was in the mood for adventure. Even though I had given her a warning— her disappearances from her governess weren't a secret. Eyes were everywhere, watching her—watching us.

She shouted, "So what!" It was so emphatic I was stunned. "As long as they don't stop me, I can pretend I am getting away with things."

It was an exciting perspective—pretending one had snared freedom when one hadn't—but I followed her lead. I thought it was how a princess should behave, the same way Elizabeth

Bennet in *Pride and Prejudice* was such a proper British lady
and bold. A princess should act boldly, too—and that was Alice
and me.

"The castle is enormous," I said. "What more about it can
be that large?"

She turned, making sure I was behind her, I suspect. I
wasn't moving fast. I was not as sure-footed running on thick-
threaded carpeting or slick wood floors.

"It is the biggest structure of its kind in the world. Well, except for Buckingham Palace. But I wouldn't say I like that place
as much as this one. I prefer Windsor Castle."

She'd stopped skipping as we reached a stairwell. "We must
go down into the depths of Windsor."

"The dungeons?"

"No, not the dungeons. Next time you come, we should find
them and see what they look like. I've never been," Alice said.
"But now, we are heading to the Royal Kitchen."

I was still contemplating what a dungeon might look like
since Jessie, the Forbeses' nursemaid, had mumbled the word.
"Don't you have servants who will bring you whatever you
want to eat from the kitchen? So why do we need to go there?"

"Have you been to a kitchen in a castle before?"

"No, I have not. I've only been to one castle."

"So there were no castles where you grew up? I thought all
princesses lived in a castle."

I tilted my head, thinking. "There were no castles in Okeadon,
but all princesses had scars on their faces to prove they were royalty."

Alice touched her cheeks. "I'd rather a castle than a scar, but
your scars are interesting and not unattractive."

"Thank you. Now, about the trip to the kitchen."

Alice giggled but composed herself a moment later. "The kitchen is the size of a small town, according to the Princess Royal—and I've never been, but today we are going."

At first, every stairwell was cold. A thin white cloud appeared every time I took a breath. Then, when the chill disappeared, I stopped my descent and thought my nose was on fire. "Are you sure we're allowed in this part of the castle?"

"I am a future queen who will marry a future king. I can go wherever I want—when Mrs. Phipps is not around."

"Why is it suddenly so warm?"

"The cooking fires. It's a kitchen. The cooks are cooking. And the fireplaces are always stoked."

We had reached the kitchen, a room of full skirts and trousers, the bottom of cabinets, shelves, and the cooking fires.

Suddenly Alice took off. She dodged between servants, cooks, and load-bearers, maneuvering with practiced skill to avoid a collision.

I didn't want to be left behind, so I moved recklessly and fearlessly as she had.

"We're here." She stopped in front of a door. We were in one of the less crowded halls.

"Where is here?"

"You want to know what's inside?" She pushed open the door.

"My goodness," I said.

The room had four walls lined with shelves stacked to the ceiling with sweets, sugary desserts, and more lollies than I had ever seen.

"What room is this?" I asked, twirling slowly around in the middle of the space.

"I call it the chocolate and sugar room."

"Oh, my," I exclaimed. "Sweets!"

"Yes, and yes, and I told a fib. I've been here before. The cooks and servants let me explore without tattling on me. At least so far."

I was still spinning in a circle, taking in the shelves of bonbons and chocolate bars. "I want one of them." I pointed at the chocolate. "And one of these—what are all these creations?"

"We have truffles, lemon drops, and biscuits with chocolatey fruit and marzipan centers."

"What is marzipan?"

"It's almond flavored, has sugar, and is soft enough to spread over chocolate-covered biscuits."

"I don't believe you."

"Try one."

"Only if you do, too."

"Don't mind if I do." Princess Alice smiled.

"I wish we could stay here forever."

Chapter Fifteen

Between January and April 1851, I spent every other day at Windsor Castle or Buckingham Palace.

After my morning lessons with Mrs. Forbes and the governess at Winkfield Place, I'd be put in a carriage and escorted to the Queen's Sitting Room. There, I would show off my English, arithmetic, and geography. When the queen didn't wish to discuss my studies, I'd play the piano before joining Princess Alice, Prince Albert Edward (whom everyone called Bertie), and Princess Royal Victoria (Vicky) for all sorts of activities.

From riding in the royal pony cart to backgammon to playing in the garden when it snowed—my least favorite activity. The white flakes falling from the sky made me too cold. However, the queen enjoyed my company so much that she started to think of me as one of them.

I even imagined that the queen preferred spending time with me to time with her children.

Soon, I was the talk of the castle and most of England, too. An article in the London *Times* told how I'd come to England, why I was a frequent guest at Windsor Castle, and about my relationship with Queen Victoria. Before we knew what had happened, there was more than one article in more than one newspaper about the Negro princess from West Africa the queen had adopted. But I was never adopted. I was the queen's ward.

It didn't matter what I was called. Before long, I started to notice the muttering among the household staff. Their raised eyebrows and loose tongues judged me for my *good fortune* of being Negro and socializing with royalty. I had overheard nasty comments about my character in the Forbeses' kitchen. From the cook, maids, and governess. They were accustomed to speaking freely among themselves and didn't pay attention to the small Negro child, who had slipped into a hiding place to hear better what was being said about her.

The British citizens, they claimed, were unhappy that the queen's latest "project" was an African child.

Before, I had never paid much mind to the hawkeyed looks I'd get from the servants or members of the royal household. But after those newspaper articles, I couldn't ignore them. During my visits, the servants gave me hard, angry glares whenever they spotted me in the queen's chamber or the castle's massive hallways playing and laughing with Alice or any of the royal children. It was as if I'd stolen the family crest and carried it in my little hands.

So, yes, I noticed the stares, but there were too many new things to discover to be worried about people who weren't the royal family.

And I certainly didn't care once I set my eyes on the pony. I'd never seen one before until Alice insisted we go for a ride.

Commander Forbes's gray horses were giant animals with great long manes, powerful legs, and broad hoofs. A pony was a baby horse with a long, cute nose and big pointy ears. I could touch the pony's nose or ears without losing a finger—the gray horses had huge teeth.

So, we rode in the royal pony cart for hours, circling the castle's courtyard.

"I told you it would be fun," Alice insisted.

Vicky and Bertie were with us, and we were as happy with the ride as Alice.

"I love the pony ride and bouncing over the road," I said. It was my favorite thing to do.

"Are you warm enough, Sarah?" Vicky sat on the low bench and stuffed her hands into a fur muff.

We were bundled up in heavy wool coats with scarves around our necks, and in case we needed blankets, the servants had stacked them in the cart.

Bertie pointed at me and laughed. "You have icicles in your hair."

"I do not. That's not true."

Vicky wiped her nose with the back of her gloved hand. "I am afraid that's true, Sarah. We'd better head back inside. The queen warned me if you caught a cold, Bertie and I would be punished." Vicky rolled her eyes. "Not the servants, Mrs. Phipps, not even you, Sarah. The fault would be ours—no one other than you and me, Bertie."

"Why? That's not fair."

"We're the oldest and must be the most responsible."

"I don't wish to be responsible," Bertie whined. "Let someone else be in charge."

"Can I be responsible for myself?" I asked, impatient with the back-and-forth. "If I catch a cold, I will tell everyone it was my fault."

* * *

OF COURSE, I caught a cold.

The weather in England was my enemy. It was almost as cruel as King Gezo, especially on those mornings when the fireplaces hadn't been lit, or I'd kicked my quilt to the floor, or a strong wind had found its way through the cracks in the window frame. I was always cold.

One morning, Mrs. Phipps canceled my trip to Buckingham Palace. She claimed my cough was too severe, and later that afternoon, Winkfield Place received an unexpected visitor from the royal household.

"He is the queen's doctor," Mrs. Forbes whispered. "See the crest on his carriage. Right there." Her fingers trembled as she pointed. "One of the most important men in England, other than Prince Albert—and he's come to our home."

"It must be about you," Jessie said. "None of us warrant such attention from Her Majesty." Her poisonous words were always delivered in a rush, followed by scurrying feet.

There were more whispers and shocked gasps as I realized Jessie had been correct: the queen's doctor was there to see me.

With Mrs. Phipps leading the way, we arrived in my bedroom, where the doctor asked me to unfasten my dress so that he could listen to the sounds inside my chest and lungs.

I turned frightened eyes to Mrs. Phipps. What was the man about to do to me? Cut me open? I hurried away from him and hid behind my bed.

Mrs. Phipps's soft laugh forced me to lift my head to see what she had found humorous.

"Dear," she said, smiling, "he will listen to your heart with a stethoscope. It is a medical instrument a doctor invented a few decades ago so that they can hear the air in your lungs."

Her voice carried a kindness I hadn't heard from Mrs. Phipps before, not directed toward me or anyone, as I thought about it.

I left my hiding place and went back to the doctor for the examination, happy for Mrs. Phipps's reassurance.

"This climate is not good for such a child," the queen's doctor said. "She needs constant warmth and more sunlight than our winter months offer." He placed his medical instruments in a leather bag, and by then, Mrs. Forbes was also in the room. "The cold, wet, rainy seasons and the near-frozen winters can kill dark-skinned people. They require warmer weather to survive. This has been proven."

"What do you prescribe?" Mrs. Forbes asked, not attempting to disguise the worry in her voice or eyes. "What can we do to treat her?"

The doctor looked taken aback. "I am the queen's physician and will discuss with Her Majesty what should be done with the child."

And then he left, and I heard nothing more about his visit for several months.

* * *

IN APRIL, AFTER what felt like ages, Commander Forbes returned from Scotland, and he made a surprising announcement during his first night home.

"I will be setting sail soon for Africa."

Mrs. Forbes looked as if she'd been struck. "When?"

"Late summer or early fall."

"I thought you didn't have to return to Africa."

"I said I'd try, but a lot is going on there," he said. "Last month, Dahomey soldiers attacked Abeokuta."

"Abeokuta," I whispered.

"You know the name, Sarah?"

I didn't want to remember, so I lied. "No, ma'am. Only the word is Yoruba, yes?"

"That is correct, Sarah." The commander looked at his wife,

his gaze filled with sadness. "The Egba chiefs fought back, but the Dahomey soldiers—"

"The Amazon warriors," I said, using the British term for Agojie.

Mrs. Forbes looked at me oddly. "Frederick, perhaps we shouldn't discuss this in front of the children."

"You're right, Mary." He sighed. "I'm sorry to have brought it up."

"It's all right," I said. "I want to understand—did the Egba win?"

"No. Chieftains Balogun Ogunbona, of Ikjia, and Sokenu, the seriki of Abeokuta, led brave armies to defend Abeokuta, but the Egba warriors were pushed back."

"They lost," I said.

"Yes. And the attack occurred while the British were in a battle at Lagos." Then, leaning forward, he looked solemnly at his wife. "I must return to Africa as soon as plans are finalized and the queen and admirals agree upon the mission."

Mrs. Forbes hadn't spoken and didn't look at her husband. I seized the opening to ask, "Is King Gezo dead?"

"No, he is alive and still king."

* * *

IT WAS THE first of May, and England was green—a thousand shades of green and a rainbow of flowers blessed every garden, every patch of land, every corner. The countryside smelled of peonies, hollyhocks, lavender, herbs, and primrose. Sweet and pretty. Even the sky was free of clouds.

The English gardener created beauty with dirt beneath his fingernails and a tanned face, weathered by the summer sun.

For a while, I believed I could survive any winter as long as May came at the end of the cold, dark months.

The warmer nights were blissful, but soon even that was spoiled for me—my nightmares returned. I'd thought they'd left me for good, but no.

I'd fall asleep only to awake drowning in sweat and damp sheets.

It was the same dream night after night. My brothers' and sisters' sad faces and frightened screams yelled a warning. It was so loud I thought I'd lose my hearing: Don't come back. Not safe. It will never be safe for you.

For days, I was convinced my nightmares were a prophecy. I'd read about prophecies in the King James Bible. It was all I could think about. It preoccupied my thoughts so much that I forgot about the queen's doctor—but I was the only one who had.

The first week in May, we received a message from Sir Charles Beaumont Phipps, the "man of many titles," as I sometimes thought of him. He had booked my passage on a steamer, the *Bathurst*, to Freetown, Sierra Leone, departing on the seventeenth of May, leaving little time to prepare. My chaperone would be the honorable Reverend Henry Venn, the head of missions in Africa.

For these past months, I'd stayed awake all night to study and learn as much as possible about England, the royal family, and the royal household. I'd go over my music and hum the songs I wanted to memorize to sing to the queen. But then I received the news that I was heading back to Africa.

My nightmares stopped, because instead of sleeping, I wept. And I made no apologies for those tears. I had earned every drop.

Mrs. Forbes came to me one night when the nightmares had slipped back into my sleep. "Why don't you tell me what happened? Sometimes talking about what you see in your dreams can be less horrifying if someone else knows. I can be that someone else, Sarah."

"You know what happened to me. Why do I have to tell it again?"

"What happens in your dreams is what I want you to tell me. I am as aware of the facts of your tragic life, as you. But a nightmare wants to make us weep and scream and shiver. It tortures us with an uglier version of the truth."

"The truth is ugly."

* * *

As the household prepared for my departure, I was an English racehorse on some days. Time sped by. I couldn't catch my breath. The other days dragged on, and I was a garden snail in a muddy pond. And it hurt to move. Then the very next thing, I was on board the steamer, heading back to Africa, a continent I had never wanted to set foot upon again—a place that held more pain and harm than my young life deserved. But what I wanted didn't matter.

Somehow, I had to accept that what happened to me would never be my choice. There would always be someone, something, waiting to make decisions for me.

* * *

In thirty-three days on board the *Bathurst,* I hadn't opened my mouth to speak more than a handful of words. Why would I? I had nothing to say. The queen and her doctor had killed my voice.

I had believed I was Princess Sarah, on the path to becoming a proper English lady. But no. I was an African girl with a cough who needed to be sent back to her country because people who looked like me couldn't thrive in cold, damp weather.

But I read the newspaper headlines. Half the people in England were sick. They were all sick—white, black, and brown—sick of Parliament, poverty, and the stench of the River Thames. And sick and tired of how their dreams were tossed aside because they weren't the class of people allowed to dream. That luxury belonged to the British elite, and I thought I was included in that better class—indeed, I was a member of the best class. The royal family had taken me in as their own.

I'd been full of hope. But I was chopped in half by a doctor wielding a royal ax.

Maybe Africa was where I should be—the continent where I was born, where my family and friends had died or abandoned me. There would be no royal pony cart rides, pretty dollies, grand meals in the Waterloo Chamber at Windsor Castle, or breakfasts at Buckingham Palace. I would not play on Her Majesty's grand piano, or sing beautiful songs in harmony with the queen and the royal children.

All because I was an African with a bad cough.

I thought about Okeadon, where I'd had a family I trusted. I'd helped my older sisters prepare for dinner while our mother stirred a pot of stewed root vegetables—a pleasant memory as long as I stopped there. As long as I didn't think beyond that moment, I had to put aside anything that happened after that. I would do the same with England. Forget everything except Africa before the night the Dahomey warriors attacked.

If I tried hard enough, nothing and no one could make me

remember what I wanted to forget. I was a quick learner. I could learn to forget as fast as I remembered. All I needed was time and a miracle.

Commander Forbes could be that miracle. According to how many stops he and his ship had to make before Freetown, I could see him within a few weeks. If he could save me from King Gezo, he could convince a doctor and a queen to allow him to bring me home.

I believed in him. I believed in him completely.

And when he learned of my predicament, he would come for me, sail the seas and take me back to England, my home, his home, and Mrs. Forbes, Mama, and Windsor Castle. Home, where I deserved to be.

Chapter Sixteen

Freetown, Sierra Leone, 1851

The *Bathurst* docked in Freetown Harbor on June 19, and Reverend Henry Venn and I stepped off the steamer minutes after the anchor sank to the bottom of the bay. Such a vessel did not require hours of preparation by the crew or its passengers to disembark. It pulled into the harbor, and Reverend Venn and I got off. No fond farewells to the captain or crew. I left the vessel as I had come aboard, sullen and silent.

Freetown's harbor was different from the one at England's Gravesend. It stretched as far as the eye could see. According to Reverend Venn, a natural harbor is a body of water deep enough to allow anchorage. A gift from God, he said, for Africa.

But it was scarcely populated. Freetown was not a destination for big ships like the HMS *Bonetta*. Most of the vessels were fishing boats, but nothing of a size to hold more than a few fishermen.

Formerly enslaved people from Britain and North America had fled to Freetown after the 1807 Abolition of the Slave Trade Act and were responsible for building up the town. The rest of the population were Africans who had escaped from slavers. Freetown was a safe harbor for the formerly enslaved, and the ships of slave traders were unwanted. The British Navy helped ensure that; since the law of 1834 that forbade the trade of humans as property, slave traders had learned to avoid this harbor and others along the coast.

I learned these things from Reverend Venn. I did not say much on board the *Bathurst,* but he never stopped talking.

We walked away from the ship and had traveled only a few yards when the reverend stopped. A thin white woman with rough, ruby-colored cheeks and thick spectacles had stepped in our path.

"Reverend Henry Venn, I presume." She spoke with a British accent.

He removed his hat and bowed. "Miss Julia Sass."

"No, Reverend. She sent me in her stead. I am Mary Wilkerson, a teacher at the Female Institution and assistant to the headmistress. I have worked with Julia since she joined us three years ago." She glanced at me. "And this must be the child."

I curtsied, but Miss Wilkerson was bothered by my manners.

"So, she has had British society training. She won't need that behavior at our school. A polite nod is sufficient."

"I would agree, but this young lady is special." Reverend Venn touched my shoulder. "May I introduce Princess Sarah Forbes Bonetta? She is Egba royalty and Her Majesty's ward."

"Sarah. It is good to meet you," Miss Wilkerson said with an eyebrow raised to her hairline. "I am pleased you will be joining us, but unburden yourself. Titles aren't used here. We don't recognize such things. Our mission is to evangelize, educate, and civilize the Africans under our tutelage. We teach what is taught to British girls from modest homes, not a royal household."

The way her gaze settled on me, I felt as if I were something she needed to tame instead of teach. I wouldn't say I liked how she called me a child, as if that was all she needed to know

about me. She reminded me of Mrs. De Graft, the more unpleasant of the two women I'd met at Badagry.

"I think you should discuss Sarah's schooling and other
matters with Miss Sass," Reverend Venn said firmly. "I sent
her the letter from Sir Charles Beaumont Phipps, Mrs. Phipps's
husband, the keeper of the privy purse for the queen. His correspondence provided Miss Sass with the details regarding
Miss Sarah's tuition, school supplies, and boarding."

We had started toward several carriages lined up on the dirt
street. I only half listened, but Miss Wilkerson made no effort
to disguise her agitation.

"What do you mean, details, Reverend? All the girls at the
Female Institution are treated fairly. We will also handle her
anxiety as a formerly enslaved child. Here she will be treated
like any African child at our school—fairly but equally."

Her voice dropped on the last word, and Reverend Venn's
eyes darkened. A lecture from a schoolteacher on the mission
of the Church of England's missionaries was unexpected. He
was in charge of all CMS missions throughout Africa. He, better than anyone, knew how the mission schools operated.

"You are aware, Miss Wilkerson, that Her Majesty handles
Sarah's expenses, including her education, clothing, and other
expenditures. She is the queen of England's ward. And Her
Majesty insists upon regular reports from the headmistress
on her studies and activities." He exhaled through his nose. A
man of God was allowed to show a temper, I hoped, because
he wasn't hiding his.

"Julia shared the note with me. I have seen what was written,"
Miss Wilkerson said. "However, the queen has entrusted the
child's education, health, and welfare to the Female Institution
in Sierra Leone—not a private boarding school in England,

which would have been her prerogative. Her Majesty is a five-week voyage away. And no one from the royal household will be in Freetown to look after the child. We then must assume the queen trusts our judgment regarding the child's care. I am confident Her Majesty wouldn't tie our hands by requiring we wait weeks for approvals on day-to-day matters. Don't you agree, Reverend Venn?"

He didn't look as if he agreed. "This is a debate that can wait, Miss Wilkerson. I will discuss the details of Sarah's care and schooling with the school's headmistress."

Miss Wilkerson sauntered toward the nearest carriage. "Oh, dear. I'm sorry." Miss Wilkerson, of course, didn't sound very sorry. "You wouldn't know, having just disembarked from the *Bathurst,* but Miss Sass and I share the headmistress role. The previous headmistress, poor Miss Smith, is ill with swamp fever and had to be taken to the hospital in Lagos."

"Oh, I am sorry to hear she's ill, but as mentioned, we'd sent Miss Sass the correspondence."

That silenced Miss Wilkerson for the moment. I was thankful, too, having grown tired of listening to her bickering. She didn't like me at first sight, and her unattractive demeanor had been proof of it.

We climbed into the carriage, and no one spoke as Reverend Venn helped me settle into the seat next to him. "It will be a bit of a ride to the Female Institution. You'll want to rest."

I folded my hands in my lap and rested my head on his arm. Perhaps I could sleep, but Miss Wilkerson sat across from me, and I didn't trust her. So instead of sleeping, I watched her.

"If you don't mind, Reverend," she sparked, making conversation, "why are you here in Africa?"

He adjusted his shoulder.

"I am continuing my work with the missions. Unfortunately, some of them sadly have lost sight of our goals. I'm here to help remind our brethren of those goals and the agreed-upon methods for achieving them." He looked out the carriage window at the afternoon sky. "I fear some of us have lost the way."

Something in Miss Wilkerson's voice made me think she'd only asked in order to remind me the reverend wouldn't be around forever. That meant he wouldn't be around to interfere with her methods.

"Where is your next stop?" she asked.

"Abomey, and then Abeokuta."

Miss Wilkerson gasped. "I trust you'll hire load-bearers with long guns. There has been some trouble in Abomey and Abeokuta. Again, Dahomey warriors are raiding villages, attacking both cities."

I sat upright at the mention of Gezo's murderous kingdom. My interest in their conversation went from mild to feeling as if a gnarled hand were reaching into my chest and squeezing so hard my rib cage snapped. Fear and memories had me close to tears.

"The Dahomey warriors are killing Egba people." My voice cracked as the words came from my dry lips. I turned frightened eyes toward Reverend Venn. "How far away is Abeokuta?"

"Don't worry, Sarah," he said. "It's thousands of kilometers from Freetown, and Dahomey would never attack a church missionary school."

"We would hope not," Miss Wilkerson said with a huff. "On second thought, they wouldn't dare. The heathens wouldn't want to incur the wrath of the British Navy." She grinned at Reverend Venn. "Aren't I right, sir? We are all perfectly safe at the Female Institution. Perfectly safe."

* * *

"Miss Sass, this is Princess Sarah." The reverend gave me a gentle shove so I was within arm's reach of the woman.

We had arrived an hour earlier at the mission, a large wooden building with two floors, and received a tour. We saw the classrooms on the first floor and the dormitory on the second floor. A chapel with a rectory was next to the school. We met Miss Sass in that room, and I stood a few feet from her, staring at her outstretched hand.

"It's a pleasure to meet you," she said, shaking my hand before sitting behind a large desk. "The queen has arranged for you to have private accommodations. It is not our policy to separate the girls, but we made arrangements as specified for your private room in the rectory."

Reverend Venn had taken a seat on a wooden bench near the door. "Her luggage will arrive shortly and be sent directly to this room. Will someone help her unpack?"

"Yes, Reverend," replied Miss Sass with what I would learn was a perpetual cheerfulness in appearance and tone, quite the opposite of Miss Wilkerson's furrowed brow and gravel voice.

"The girls don't have servants," Miss Wilkerson said. "This is not a British boarding school, as I mentioned before."

"I will ask one of the older girls to help her," Miss Sass said, covering for her co-worker's rudeness, something she seemed accustomed to doing. "I'm sure Abigail won't mind."

"Perfect choice, Julia," Miss Wilkerson grumbled. "Of course she wouldn't mind."

"Miss Wilkerson believes a private room may cause trouble between you and the other girls at the school. She is not entirely wrong." Miss Sass looked at the reverend, who nodded for her to continue.

"We believe you might prefer the opportunity to get to know the other girls by living in the dormitory. You'd have a bed in the dormitory, a shared bathtub, and a chance to develop friendships through proximity."

Miss Sass glanced at Miss Wilkerson. "This is Miss Wilkerson's recommendation, and she is in charge of the day-to-day activities of our students outside the classroom. She is looking out for your best interest. But we are bound by Her Majesty's instructions, unless you prefer the dormitory. So what would you like to do?"

I didn't want to meet new people. I wanted to board the next ship back to England. I understood that Miss Sass strove to be kind by making it seem as if Miss Wilkerson had suggested this change out of the goodness of her heart. She preferred I lived in a dwelling with the other girls. Period.

"I do not wish to stay in the dormitory. I wish to follow Her Majesty's instructions. I want a separate room."

Miss Wilkerson couldn't hold her tongue. "Why are we allowing the child to choose? We should make a stand now regarding her lodging and studies, or we will be haggling over one thing or another as long as she's a student here."

Miss Sass sighed heavily. Then she faced Miss Wilkerson. "We can manage the other girls if we explain with reverence and kindness why Sarah merits a private room, Mary."

"Thank you, Miss Sass," I said, shooting a warning glance at Miss Wilkerson. She was not on my side and would never be someone I relied on. Perhaps Miss Sass could be that someone one day, but for now, I wanted to be alone.

* * *

I said goodbye to Reverend Venn without fanfare. Miss Wilkerson then led me to my room. She didn't say anything once we arrived other than to point out the room's furniture, a bed, a desk, a chair, and a dresser.

I felt like I existed on a bed of pins and needles, however, waiting for her to say something to make me feel all wrong. There was a difference between the other girls and me, and I was proud of that difference. Indeed, I might have told her so if given a chance. So I was lucky we both knew enough to keep our mouths shut.

Once she was gone, I explored my new home. It wasn't as small as the cramped space on the *Bathurst* nor as large as my bedroom at Winkfield Place.

There was a painting on the wall above the bed. I recognized the man from my Bible studies. He was white, with long yellow hair and a halo surrounding his head, wearing a blue robe, and holding a spear with an English cross. Next to it was the flag of England. The picture was of Jesus Christ.

Was he there to watch over me?

I preferred a portrait of Queen Victoria, which I would insist upon having on my wall. Jesus could stay. I didn't mind having him for company.

An hour later, my luggage arrived, and after the load-bearers departed, there was another knock on the door. Before I could say come in, the door was flung open.

"Miss. I'm Abigail." She burst into the room. Her thick black hair, pulled away from her face, touched her shoulders, and her smooth black skin glistened as if she'd run from the other side of the compound.

Catching her breath and panting, she was much taller than

me, but I was short and small for my age. She was long-legged and had to be fourteen or fifteen. She had round breasts and round hips. I could tell from how her dull brown dress fit her body and cinched her waist.

She held something in her hands. "Your name is Sarah."

I leaned forward to see what she was holding. It was a notebook.

"You are a lovely little girl, Sarah. This is for you. It lists your classes and the start time of each. Also, since you've missed some of the courses, you'll need to catch up."

They had a library. I hoped it had the same books as the one at Winkfield Place. "My name is Aina."

She shook her head and smiled. "No, it is Sarah. We use our Christian names at the Female Institution, not Yoruba." She glided across the room and stopped in front of my steamer trunk. "Now, how can I help you unpack?"

Why had I told her my name was Aina? Perhaps to see what she'd say. Well, now I knew. But for a moment, since I was in Africa, I felt the pull of the girl I used to be, and her name was Aina.

Abigail moved toward the trunk, but there was one thing inside I had to protect. The bluestone necklace was wrapped in a silk chemise nightgown Mrs. Forbes had bought me.

"I must keep this safe. Where can I hide it?" I asked Abigail.

She seemed startled by my question. "Everything is safe here."

"All right, but turn your back. I will feel better if I hide this," I said, and placed it beneath the pillow on my bed.

"Are you done?"

"Yes."

Abigail started going through my trunk, working swiftly, moving items aside or gathering them in her arms.

Next, she filled each drawer with items like petticoats, bloomers, underskirts, and stockings. When she reached the dresses, she lifted a blue day outfit with fringe and velvet bands and shook it. The queen had sent this dress to me in a beautifully wrapped box.

"Careful. That's one of my favorites."

"My goodness. Where do you think you'd wear such a fancy dress?" She removed another dress from the trunk and squealed like a startled mouse. "The skirt on this one is hard as a . . ."

"It's whalebone. That's what gives it shape."

"Oh, my goodness. Don't you have any plain dresses?"

"These are clothes the queen of England bought for me. I can think of no better attire."

"I don't want to argue, but you may need to think about what you wear here—not only because of the heat, but because you don't want to stand out too much. It's a good town, but like most villages, the people outside the missionary and the British camps are poor."

"Don't worry about me. Can we hurry, please? I am tired after my journey and would like to sleep."

The sharp look she had given me dissolved into sympathy. "I can't imagine what you are feeling. Miss Sass told me some of your story. I am sorry you've had so much hardship. But this is a good place. You'll find friends here and make adjustments. But it will take time."

"Don't worry," I said. "I won't be here long enough to make friends."

"I don't believe you understand, or perhaps you're too tired. I'll come back tomorrow and finish helping you unpack. I'll also find another dress for you to wear to the classes. I'm afraid you'll boil in these outfits."

"All right."

"Sarah. No one here is your enemy. You don't have to avoid making friends. On the contrary, you may find that you like it here."

"Do you like living here?"

She shrugged. "I don't exactly live here year-round. Most of the time, I'm traveling with my father."

"Who is he?"

"His name is Samuel Ajayi Crowther. He's a clergyman and a linguist. Do you know what that is?"

I shook my head, trying to keep my eyes open. I was exhausted.

"He's translating the Bible into Yoruba." She sounded so excited and proud, but I didn't understand.

"I thought the missionaries and their schools, like this one, were in Africa to teach English to the Africans."

"Yes and no. Not all Africans will attend the mission schools. Spreading the word of God must happen through whatever means possible. It is critical for the survival of Africa that Christianity reach every corner of the continent."

"You sound like a minister yourself."

She looked at the floor. "I'm sorry. I love my father's sermons, and I memorize them."

I yawned.

"Oh, I am sorry. I said I'd leave so you can rest." She backed toward the door. "I'll return tomorrow." She put her hand on the doorknob. "You know, we could be friends."

I looked at her and thought she was a nice girl. Pretty, thoughtful, and pleasant. "I told you, I won't be here long enough to make friends. And even if I am here long enough, I don't believe I'll need friends."

She started to object. I could see her thoughts as if written across her forehead. But instead of trying to change my mind, she said, "Very well. I'll see you tomorrow."

I lay on the bed, fully clothed, curled into a ball, and fell asleep.

Chapter Seventeen

Freetown, Sierra Leone, 1851

I overheard a girl claim that a spirit inhabited something called the Iroko tree, located on the edge of town. The spirit was kind, welcomed strangers, and granted wishes in exchange for a promise. What kind of promise? I had asked the girl. Her reply: It was a secret. And the only way to learn the secret was to go to the Iroko tree when the moon shone full and bright in the night sky. Then the spirit would appear.

I listened intently. If my plan to escape Africa didn't work out, I thought I might visit the tree one day.

For now, I had to put up with Abigail Crowther.

She came to my room every day or stopped me in the hallway between the classrooms to say good day or introduce me to African girls with English names like Rose, Louise, Catherine, Emily, and Winifred. Of course, once introduced, I avoided them. Why would I bother to get to know other girls? Why did Abigail keep pestering me, even when I told her I didn't need new friends?

But she wasn't aware of my secret.

I had received a letter from Mrs. Forbes that made me gasp with joy. Commander Forbes was sailing closer to Freetown. And as soon as he saw how miserable I was and I told him, a small exaggeration, about how poorly I was treated by teachers and students alike, he'd pack my bags and load them and me onto the next ship to England. I didn't need friends when I would soon return to my family and friends in Windsor Castle and Winkfield Place.

But my excitement was tempered. It could take more than a month for the commander to complete the queen's business during his voyage from London to Freetown. Meantime, Miss Wilkerson made every moment in her presence miserable.

Many days were warm, with abundant sunshine and heat. And like the other girls, I had worn a straw bonnet to protect my face from the sun, except my hat was store-bought, not handmade, and the bow at my throat was a blue silk ribbon, not twine.

I loved the hat and never thought it was a thing to be jealous of. Indeed, I would never be ashamed of a gift from Her Majesty. But it had caused a stir. I wasn't aware of it until Miss Wilkerson made it clear.

On my way to my morning lesson, I was daydreaming, thinking of the commander's face when he learned of my woes. It slowed me down, and I entered the classroom after Miss Wilkerson had shut the doors.

"You are late, Sarah," Miss Wilkerson called from the front of the class. She was scribbling on the blackboard with her back to the students.

"I am sorry, ma'am." I sat in my seat and placed my notebook and pencil on the desk.

She turned around, showing me a fierce expression. "And why do you have on that hat?"

I touched the hat's floppy brim. "Oh, bloody hell," I muttered. We weren't allowed to wear our hats inside the classroom. Unfortunately, I had forgotten to remove it in my haste to sit. "I'm sorry, ma'am."

I started to untie the bow, but my fingers trembled. Not only because of Miss Wilkerson's harsh words, but because every girl in the class was watching me. And between them and Miss Wilkerson's glare, my cheeks were on fire.

"Take off the hat, or I will cut the bow with these scissors," Miss Wilkerson said.

I stopped moving. Her threat astonished me. "I'm trying, ma'am." I pulled one end of the ribbon before realizing I'd turned the pretty bow into an awful knot.

Miss Wilkerson stalked across the room. I spotted the scissors in her hand and couldn't stop my mouth from flopping open. "My hat is a gift from Queen Victoria. You wouldn't dare cut the bow—or I will tell."

"Are you threatening me?" Miss Wilkerson grabbed my head, pressed her palm into my skull, and held me motionless with her giant palm and fingers. Then she jerked me backward at an angle, exposing my throat. "Hold still and take hold of that ribbon tie."

I believed she'd harm me. So I obeyed, staring at the scissors coming toward me.

"Now, steady," she said. Then she cut the bow, snatched the hat from my head, and stalked back to the front of the class, depositing the hat on the desk like it was trash.

"How could you?" I gasped. "You ruined it."

"And if you don't stop talking, you will remain in that seat until nightfall, missing lunch and dinner."

"I don't care. I will sit here until tomorrow, but I will tell."

"And sully the reputation of the Female Institution with the queen of England." She looked around the class, capturing the gaze of every student, it seemed. "Just because your instructor reprimanded you for being late to class."

I don't remember exactly how I felt. Too many pairs of dark-skinned eyes had narrowed in my direction. I expected their mistrust and jealousy. I was different from them and wasn't interested in making friends, because that risk ended with pain.

I sincerely thought that the kind of trouble Miss Wilkerson caused me was better than my caring about someone or something and losing it. Furious, I glared at her, but I didn't care. She didn't know about the commander. He would come for me. I knew it. Until then, I could stomach Miss Wilkerson's hurtful words, her destruction of my gift from the queen, and the side-eyed glances of my fellow students.

But I was hungry.

"I'm sorry, ma'am. I won't do it again."

She went on with the class. I returned to my room later and found a letter on the desk from Mrs. Forbes.

Excited, I ripped it open. Her handwriting was excellent. I could read every word perfectly. And every word tore a hole in my belly. It didn't matter that I hadn't made any new friends or that Miss Wilkerson hated me. I could still be gutted.

He was dead.

Commander Frederick Forbes, thirty-two years old, had died of malaria on board the HMS *Bonetta* before he reached Sierra Leone.

My legs collapsed beneath me. I fell to the floor and lay there on my stomach, too broken to move or cry.

* * *

No one was coming to my rescue.

It took months for me to accept that Commander Forbes was dead. I kept dreaming about him and the crew of the HMS *Bonetta,* marching into the courtyard of the Female Institution, shouting my name. I would run from the rectory into the commander's arms, and seconds later, we would be home—in England at Winkfield Place.

But that was never going to happen.

I did take solace in my bluestone necklace. Looking at it, I felt love, generations of love, and connection. Commander Forbes's journals were another story.

Published in England a year after his death, *Dahomey and the Dahomans* was two volumes about his travels in Africa between 1843 and 1845, when he met King Gezo at his palace in Abomey. The second volume was about me. It included the painting Mrs. Vidal had made of me. I didn't have the volumes. I read about them in a letter Mrs. Forbes sent me. I never could bring myself to read them. They were too close to my heart. And what would they teach I didn't already know? That danger was ever-present, and love was never guaranteed? I didn't need to read the commander's words to know that.

King Gezo was a thousand kilometers away, but I would never feel safe in Africa. So I buried myself in my studies.

My favorite courses were cartography, arithmetic, grammar, geography, and studying Earth and its people. I had a talent for knitting, sewing, darning, and mending. However, I struggled through the morning sessions, the prayers, and the scripture lessons. Anything to do with the King James Bible had become difficult.

I was too angry to hear anything God had to say.

Chapter Eighteen

Freetown, Sierra Leone, 1852

The girl who had talked about the Iroko tree on the edge of town talked about it again, except this time, I didn't have to eavesdrop. She spoke loudly for anyone who wanted to listen during lunch one afternoon. She even gave an example of the tree's power.

I bent over my food tray, my meal of yams, okra, and rice, and listened intently.

She said a girl had left school and returned to her village the week before—a day before her father died—after visiting the magical tree. It was what she'd wanted, to be with her mother and sisters, and the tree had granted her wish, and she'd kept her promise.

"What was the promise?" a wide-eyed girl had asked.

The answer had been the same as before. "It was a secret."

The next time the girl mentioned the Iroko tree within earshot of me, I'd ask her where I could find that tree. If it was magical, it should be able to help me return to England. I wanted that more than ever. But I'd have to wait until Abigail wasn't around. It was apparent she didn't believe in the spirit in the Iroko tree. Her advice was always to pray for the strength to see beyond earthly things.

"You should not have to sit alone in the dining room, Sarah."

I didn't look up. I recognized Abigail's voice, having heard it every day, sometimes ten times a day, since I arrived. She sought me out, lurking in the shadows, pushing me to be friends. I was so accustomed to "running into her" that I began to look forward to our awkward exchanges.

"They're shy about talking to you." Abigail placed her dinner tray on the table and sat on the bench opposite me. "You've met the queen of England. She sends you packages from Windsor Castle, and your mail has the royal seal."

I still didn't speak. I had been doing well without company. I had gone as far as to remove the painting of Jesus Christ above my bed, replacing it with a portrait of Her Majesty.

It had been almost a year since I'd been forced to leave England, but I was steadfast in my decision not to make friends with these girls. It would feel like I was trying to replace Monife, even the Forbes children, or William and Dayo. I couldn't keep finding and losing family. I hated and feared my schoolmates almost as much as I hated and feared Dahomey and its king, Gezo.

"Are you going to stay quiet through our entire meal?" Abigail held a fork of mashed potato in front of her mouth. She waited for me to answer but placed her fork on the edge of her plate when I didn't.

"Miss Sass agreed you can join me this weekend when I go on a few missionary visits, delivering the King James Bible in Freetown after morning prayers."

"What?"

"Good, you'll go."

"I didn't say that."

"You didn't say no. In my book, that means yes." She gobbled down a few more forkfuls of food. "I've got to go now.

Miss Sass has asked me to join her to meet with some local chieftains. She may need me to translate."

I was grudgingly impressed. "How many languages do you know?" She'd already told me her father was translating the King James Bible into Yoruba.

"Four African languages and three others."

"How old are you?"

"Fifteen." She grinned. "I'll graduate in another year."

"That soon." The lump in my throat came on without warning. I coughed.

"Are you all right?"

I nodded.

"We will have an excellent weekend."

"I do not wish to go," I said.

Abigail frowned. "Miss Sass worries about you, not wanting to be around the other girls. So she asked me to watch over you. But we can talk about this at dinner. Then we can have a long conversation."

"About what?"

"Whatever crosses your mind."

"What if all I want to talk about is England and the friends I made there?"

"Did you not hear me? Whatever crosses your mind means what we discuss will be your choice."

I chuckled.

"What's funny?"

"You wouldn't understand."

That evening I met Abigail for dinner. We sat at a table with three other girls—Rose, Louise, and Catherine, a name ruined for me. All I could think about was Mrs. Catherine De Graft of the mission in Badagry. To this day, thinking of her sharp tongue pulls a shudder down my spine.

"Where were you from before you went to England?" Louise wore a colorful scarf wrapped to cover her hair and large hoop earrings, similar to the jewelry of the Dahomey Amazons.

"A town in Egba called Okeadon."

"I've heard of that town," Rose said, eyeing the yams and boiled fish on her plate. "A couple of the girls here last year were from there. They were homesick and left for Abeokuta."

I bristled. "Why would they go there? It's in the middle of Dahomey."

"They couldn't go back to Okeadon. It was burnt to the ground three years ago."

"Almost four years ago."

Louise disagreed. "No, Rose is right. Three years."

"No." I slammed my fist on the table. "I know because I was there."

Abigail patted my hand. "You didn't hurt yourself, did you?"

I only glared at her.

"We all have stories, Sarah. Several girls here are from villages and towns attacked by Dahomey warriors. But they are far away from here. We are safe in Freetown."

"I will never be safe in Africa." I stood. The dining hall had turned into a place I didn't want to be. It was too crowded and full of things, making it difficult for me to breathe.

"I need to go outside," I said, and left.

* * *

THE FOLLOWING DAY was Saturday, and for the first time in weeks, I had eluded Abigail Crowther—for an entire morning.

I hoped she'd forgotten about our trip to Freetown, but when I returned to my room after prayers and the weekend scripture lesson, there was a knock on my door.

"Are you ready?" It was Abigail.

I wore a blue cotton dress with pink flowers with small egg-shaped white centers. The skirt billowed from the waist-fitting bodice, and the puff sleeves tied just below my elbows. I even remembered my petticoat with the lace hem and my stockings. The African sun was a volcano in the sky, and I wore enough clothing for six girls. But I didn't care. My dress was beautiful.

"Yes, ma'am," I said, wiping the sweat from my brow with a handkerchief. "I'm ready."

"Now, none of that yes-ma'am business. It's just Abigail, and I've told you that a million times." She looked at me sternly, then smiled. "And we're going on an adventure." She frowned. "Take off those stockings. It's blazing outside." She lifted her skirt slightly. "I'm bare-legged. That way, we won't boil."

"Thank you." I started to add that we'd boil anyway, but instead, I undid my shoelaces and stepped out of the stockings. The warm air felt cool when it hit my legs, and I sighed with relief. "That's better."

"Good," she said. "Now let's go."

The streets of Freetown were one huge marketplace with a thousand voices speaking a thousand different languages, but the words didn't matter. It was the expression in people's eyes that told me their story. The arch of an eyebrow. A sweet toothy grin or a sly toothless smile. I hadn't seen so many dark-skinned people so happy since Okeadon—before Dahomey. The streets were filled with merchants, male and female, carrying baskets of corn, okra, and yams, and buckets of water with live fish, sea urchins, and shrimp.

During my year in England, I'd not seen or smelled a pot of slow-cooked mutton with vegetables from any kitchen, at Windsor Castle or Winkfield Place. I was happy I remembered the smell. I'd been away from the food my mother used to cook for so long that I should've forgotten it. But I hadn't. Just as I hadn't forgotten how much I missed my mother.

I swallowed the sudden lump in my throat. Thinking about her was not allowed. Not while I stood in Africa.

"Do you understand what these people are saying?" I asked Abigail.

"Most of the languages are Yoruba, so I do understand quite a bit." She twisted her lips to the side. "You should, too. If you were raised in Okeadon."

"I've forgotten everything I once knew about Okeadon."

"Sarah. Come now, you didn't forget. You choose what and when to remember."

"Is that from one of your father's sermons, too?"

She giggled. "Caught me, huh?" She skipped ahead a few feet but then turned, her skirt swinging. "I love his sermons. I wanted to be a minister one day." She tossed the words over her shoulder as she moved along. "But he said it wasn't a job for a woman."

"Abigail, why did you want to show me this?"

"This town and its history are important to many people. I wanted you to see something other than school and meet some of the Africans, free people who were once enslaved."

I stayed close to her as we turned down a dirt road with a row of huts.

"Take my hand. I want you to meet someone."

We still took our time, strolling by the different homes, occasionally stopping to deliver a translated Bible. In exchange, we might receive fruit, seeds, and yams. Abigail had a large cloth bag she had filled after a handful of stops. We only had a half dozen Bibles left.

"It's getting late. We should return to school. I would not like to be here at night."

"Remember, I want you to meet a friend of mine. You will enjoy meeting her, I promise."

We walked until we came to the last hut on the road, at the bottom of a small hill next to a smaller lake. It must be part of the harbor. I could smell the sea even as we entered the hut.

"Aina, this is Tiwa."

Hearing my old name, my other name, the one I'd almost forgotten, jangled my nerves and set my skin on fire. That girl hadn't been with me in a long while. The name sounded strange and out of place.

"She is from Oshun and practices the Yoruba religion," Abigail said. "I thought it would be good for you to learn more about the Yoruba religious traditions. That way, when you become a missionary and talk to native Africans anywhere in Yorubaland, you will better communicate the Church of England's God versus the Yoruba gods and goddesses."

Abigail pointed at me to sit on the mat next to Tiwa. "She also has lived in Freetown for more than fifty years. Isn't that right?"

The woman nodded. She looked older than any person I'd ever seen. Her skin was deeply wrinkled around her eyes and mouth, but her cheeks and throat were smooth and shiny and black like the polished ebony on a piano's keyboard.

"You are all right?"

"Ma'am." I was staring quietly, but she had my attention now, and I bowed. She was an elder, and I was respectful.

"Your name is Aina, born with a cord around your neck. A difficult birth. A difficult life."

"Yes, ma'am."

"You can change your destiny. Did you know that?"

I didn't know if I understood the word then. "No, ma'am."

"It is possible, but you must set a course for where you're going and why you need to get there. For example, Abigail tells me you do not wish to talk to the other girls at the school. Why is that?"

"I do not need new friends. My friends are in England and one day I will return to them. So making friends here is not important, since I'll leave soon."

"You are wrong." Tiwa sat cross-legged on a woven mat with the most beautiful design, like the side of a mountain covered with trees and bright orange leaves. "You are a child but have survived losses few elders could withstand."

I glared at Abigail. "Did you tell her about me? Why? It is not her concern."

Abigail's eyes were wide. "No, I told her nothing."

"I don't believe you."

"Aina, I do not need to be told your story. I can see it in your eyes." She rocked back and forth and side to side. "Do you know Oshun?"

I shook my head.

"Best to answer her, Sarah," said Abigail. "The tone of your voice helps her."

"Helps her to do what?"

"You'll see."

"Oshun was my home. It is also a river and a goddess. And Oshun can mean many things, but mostly water, purity, fertility, love, and sensuality."

"Why does this matter to me?" I asked.

"You are a river, Sarah, and meant to flow. A river is always moving, except sometimes life will try and stop you."

I stared at Abigail. "What does she mean?" I was frustrated and felt warm tears pool in the corners of my eyes.

"Look at me," the elder woman said roughly. "A river stops flowing because of the dams, the walls put up by man or creature. So don't separate yourself from others. It will only make it more difficult to love again."

"I don't wish to speak about love, rivers, or goddesses."

"Oshun is a protector, savior, and nurturer of humanity and maintains spiritual balance."

"You are telling me things so I'll make friends with the girls at school?"

Abigail smiled. "Is that what you think? I'd bring you all this way to meet someone like Tiwa so you could be friends with the girls at school? I would never bring them here. They don't know her. I brought you to meet her. Not them."

Abigail hadn't moved from the hut entrance but came over and sat next to me on Tiwa's mat. "I want to be your friend. So I brought you to Tiwa because she has a gift. Something in her words calms angry hearts. You don't have to be friends with everyone. Just with me."

"Why do you want to be friends with me so badly? I'm younger than you. And I told you and everyone how I feel about being in Africa." Then an ugly thought entered my mind. "Do you want to be friends because I know the queen?"

"I am not interested in the queen of England. I am a loyal British subject. But everyone needs a stubborn friend. Someone who is not easy to like."

"And that's me?"

Tiwa chuckled.

Abigail shot her a warning glance. "Yes, Sarah. That's you."

Because it was always in the back of my mind, I asked Tiwa if she had ever met the king of Dahomey, King Gezo. Had she ever been to Abomey?

"I know of Dahomey. But fifty years ago, when I was caught, the leader of Dahomey was King Agonglo." We stopped talking about Yoruba goddesses and friendship. Instead, she spoke of her village and how she was captured by slave hunters and shipped to the Americas. But she ran away and made it to Freetown and freedom.

Abigail wanted her stubborn friend to hear this, too.

Chapter Nineteen

Freetown, Sierra Leone, 1852–1853

$\mathcal{I}$ was around ten years old (my age was always a question mark) and precocious, incredibly well-read, and my vocabulary as an English speaker had mushroomed. Then, sometime in the spring of 1852, I had a brilliant idea. It would bring me closer to the queen and might convince her how lonely I was without her and my British family.

"I want to throw a party, Miss Sass."

"A party, Sarah? What kind of party?"

"A birthday party." I was sitting in her office in the rectory, down the hall from my room. "It's something I've been planning, and I'm very excited about it."

Miss Sass's eyes sparkled as if I'd given her a gift. "You do seem happy about whatever plan this is. I am glad to see you with a smile."

Why did she and Abigail think to comment about my smile as if I never smiled? Lately, I felt as if I had smiled all the time. "After sending many letters to Queen Victoria, I finally received a reply, and I had to talk to you about it right away."

"Don't leave me in suspense. What is the queen of England's response, or better yet, what did you ask her for?"

"A birthday party."

"You want a birthday party, and you had to ask the queen?"

"Oh, no, it's not for me." I shook my head and smiled. "I'd

never want such a thing for me. I want to throw a birthday party for Queen Victoria, and she has agreed."

Miss Sass looked faint. "The queen is coming here?"

"No, ma'am. But her birthday is May 24, a little over a month from now, and she'll be thirty-three, and I thought it would be splendid to host a tea party in her honor to celebrate."

"For all the girls in the school?"

I looked down at my hands and intertwined my fingers. I hadn't thought about inviting every girl in the school. There were at least a hundred. I hadn't asked for a hundred tea sets. I'd asked for thirty-three, because I thought it was clever. After hearing from the queen, my next step was to get Miss Sass to say yes, and then I'd worry about who. I should have told her the truth, but instead, I said, "As many as are interested in attending the party. So, I guess, yes."

I squeezed my hands so hard my fingers ached. I'd been at the Female Institution almost a year but hadn't spoken to Miss Sass that often. She had to say yes. She just had to.

"I would love to agree, Sarah, but I am not sure we have the money."

I was prepared for the money concern. "Her Majesty will pay for everything. She will ship the teacups and saucers and add the money for the cakes and chocolate bars to my monthly expenses."

Nothing was left to make her say no, but waiting for her to speak made my stomach hurt. Then she took another ten minutes and asked a dozen more questions—then she said yes. Finally.

I burst into the hall outside her office, bubbling with excitement.

"Did she say yes?" Abigail had been waiting for me.

"Yes." We clutched hands and spun each other in a circle of joy. "I am throwing a birthday party for the queen."

"I am so happy you are happy."

We stopped dancing and inhaled deeply, catching our breaths. "She did misunderstand one thing," I confessed.

"Which was?"

"She thought all the girls in the school were invited." We started walking toward my room at the end of the hall. I hung my head, concerned that I should've told her I only asked for thirty-three teacups.

"You don't have to worry," Abigail said with a pat on my back. "Miss Sass will sort through the particulars."

A smile of relief spread over my face. Abigail was right. Miss Sass could explain that only a portion of the Female Institution's students would be invited. And I had a week or two before I'd send out invitations.

By the first week of May, everything I requested arrived on time, from china teacups to linen tablecloths, to ingredients and instructions for making the most fabulous birthday cake—all I needed for Queen Victoria's birthday party.

Of course, Rose was the one to make a fuss.

"What do we wear? Besides you, none of the girls have petticoats with fancy hems or bonnets with silk ribbons. And a proper royal birthday party requires fancy dresses."

Louise was next. "The queen won't be here. Can it be a proper party for the queen if she isn't here? When has she ever been to Africa, anyway?"

"I never said she'd be here. She permitted me to host the party."

Typically, Catherine had heard only parts of the conversation. "As if she'd come from England to attend a party thrown by a student at the Female Institution."

I hadn't liked Catherine from the day I met her, and with good reason.

"She'd come to Africa for me." My mouth had a mind of its own. I hadn't meant to say any of it. "I am her ward, but she is celebrating in Buckingham Palace with Prince Albert, and she is with child, and the queen's doctor doesn't recommend a sea voyage."

"So she is not coming?" Rose asked.

Have you ever felt trapped but had nowhere to run? Heat surged through my body, making my skin feel too close to a fire. Why didn't I walk away before pride's flames caught me?

Then I remembered the Iroko tree. I could use help from a magical tree if things became difficult.

"She might come," I said, hating my arrogant soul. "I made it from London on a steamer in thirty-three days, and the ships in Her Majesty's Navy are much faster."

"Isn't that something," Rose said, giggling. "The queen could travel from London for her thirty-third birthday in thirty-three days."

"It would have to be less," I said with unbridled enthusiasm.

"That isn't very funny, also impossible." Abigail strolled to the group, greeting us with a hand planted on either hip. "What is going on here?"

"The birthday party," Rose, Louise, and Catherine chimed in together.

I hoped Abigail saw the expression on my face, which begged for her assistance. I needed her help to fix the mess I'd stepped into.

"The queen isn't coming to the Female Institution," she said when we were finally alone. "Why would you imply that she was?"

"I didn't mean for this to happen, Abigail. I didn't mean it."

We had left the dormitory and walked hand in hand across the courtyard, Abigail tugging me close to her side.

"So what should I do about the birthday party?" I asked her.

"Tell the truth. The queen is not coming, and not all the girls are invited. And Miss Sass says you must explain why."

"They'll be mad at me."

"Yes, but you shouldn't have lied."

"I didn't mean to, but everyone got excited, and so did I."

Abigail squeezed my hand. "That is not an excuse."

I almost said it felt like a reason. "I have an idea. The queen insisted that only thirty-three girls celebrate her thirty-third birthday. They will be disappointed, but they can't be angry with me. It's the queen's mandate, not mine."

She released my hand, and her jaw tightened unattractively. "Such a clever tale, Sarah. Almost too clever."

"It is almost the truth. And it makes sense, yes?"

* * *

THE BIRTHDAY PARTY wasn't the smashing success I had hoped for. Of the uninvited, several girls didn't speak to me for the next two years. But I had never strived to be the most popular girl at the Institution, so instead of feeling poorly, I felt brave— the queen had noticed me and sent me almost everything I had asked for, except a ticket home. When I told some of the other girls as much, they stopped talking to me, too. They didn't like bold, confident girls like me. They were jealous of an African princess and Queen Victoria's ward, a girl who spoke her mind.

I didn't rejoice at making so many enemies, mind you. But I didn't cry. On the other hand, though, I wondered if I should be less of a provocateur—a word Abigail had taught me. She said that it described me perfectly. Or rather, the ups and downs of my personality.

Anyway, the incident caused me to think seriously one more time about a trip to the magical tree. It was overdue. I needed to test its skills and learn the secret behind the promise.

I didn't do it, however, at least not that year.

* * *

By the end of 1853, England was at war with Russia, and according to the letters I received from Princess Alice, the most exciting news in London was about the Crimean War. She called the subject quite intriguing, and her letters brimmed with whatever gossip she gathered from articles in the London *Times* or overheard in Buckingham Palace.

In Freetown, things weren't as exciting. Indeed, two and a half years since I arrived, nothing had changed.

I continued to avoid most of the girls, except with Abigail having graduated, I spent more time with Louise. Abigail often visited, though, and at times it felt like she was still a student at the school. And I liked seeing her. But I didn't feel the same about her as I had Monife or William. She and I were friends, and we got along most of the time, but I never minded the times when we disagreed. Life was easier to handle if I cared less about other people and they cared less about me.

When I wasn't studying, I buried my face in the most recent novel I'd received from Mrs. Phipps or Mrs. Forbes. The books at the CMS school weren't novels. They had good stories, and I enjoyed the King James Bible. The Old Testament, in particular, included some of my favorite tales. But I'd read the Bible from stem to stern twice a year for the entire time I'd been in Freetown.

My other favorite thing was learning Yoruba and the other African languages Abigail could teach me. That included the Egba language I'd grown up speaking but had started to forget. Thankfully, I was a quick study of new languages, as with the piano lessons in England. I became proficient in two Yoruba dialects in only a year: Egba and Oyo.

However, my interests outside of my scripture and knitting and sewing weren't looked upon kindly by Miss Wilkerson.

My trouble with her began in earnest during my third year at the Institution.

Rose was at the blackboard finishing an arithmetic problem. Catherine sat staring out the window, daydreams clouding her gaze. Louise and I passed a note back and forth about one of the new girls from Oshun we didn't like.

"Some of you will not be receiving new workbooks this month," Miss Wilkerson said in her stiff voice. "We are experiencing delays with shipments from England. It should be rectified in a month or so. Until then, we will share." Miss Wilkerson eyed the class over the bridge of her spectacles. "Scoot together two by two. I will hand out the books to pairs."

Suddenly, Rose was next to me, although I knew she had a seat in the back of the class while I sat in the front row.

I looked at her with a furrowed brow. "What do you want?"

"We should share."

The other girls had already partnered up, leaving me no choice but to share with Rose.

Miss Wilkerson held the last book in her hand, peering down her nose at Rose and me. "How fortunate are you to pair up with Sarah. It means you'll receive your workbook. A special courier ships Sarah's school supplies, and her books have arrived." A corner of her mouth raised. "Sarah doesn't need to share. Indeed, I'm sure she'd prefer not to."

A series of oohs and aahs swept the classroom. Rose looked dejected. "We could let someone else have the extra workbook," she said, looking at me with fretful eyes. "I would like very much to share with you."

I hadn't thought of Rose as being a nice girl. I hadn't thought of her much at all. I learned later that she was the daughter of one of the Africans who had been on board the schooner *Amistad* when it ended up in America. Her family was famous, but she'd never met the queen of England.

"Would you like to share?" Strangely, I felt obligated to at least ask her.

"I would like that very much," she said.

"Then make me a promise."

Suspicion made her sit taller. "What kind of promise?"

I whispered in her ear. "It has to do with the magical tree on the edge of town."

Her eyes widened with curiosity.

"What are you talking about?" Miss Wilkerson tapped the table with her pointer stick.

"A magical tree," Rose said, and I kicked her in the shin. "Ouch." She rubbed her leg.

"Are you out of your mind?" Miss Wilkerson was annoyed. "That voodoo nonsense is blasphemy. If I ever hear of you, Miss Sarah Forbes Bonetta, going anywhere near that ridiculous tree, you will spend the rest of the school year in your room."

I glared at Rose but aimed my best sad, apologetic eyes at Miss Wilkerson. "I would never, ma'am." I even changed my voice, sounding less British and like someone who spoke the Yoruba language.

But I think Miss Wilkerson didn't buy my story.

"Enough of your tomfoolery, Sarah. Just stay away from that Iroko tree." She walked away, but before she reached her desk, she turned. "You two share."

She held on to the extra copy. "I'll keep this if someone loses a book."

Chapter Twenty

Miss Wilkerson had finally gotten her way, but of course, at my expense. I had an unwanted roommate.

After three years of fretting with Miss Sass, she had convinced the headmistress I had spent too much time alone. I wasn't developing the way a girl like me should, and I needed company. She pointed out that I hadn't made friends because I refused to socialize with the other girls—I claimed I was a princess, after all (I didn't recall having said this aloud, by the way). Furthermore, I had a difficult personality and would never be a helpful missionary with such a temperament.

The last part sealed my fate with Miss Sass.

"There's nothing wrong with me," I said when brought to Miss Sass's office for a talk. "I don't need to be friends with all the girls in the school. I excel at my studies. The queen takes care of me. That's all that you should be concerned with." This I said directly to Miss Wilkerson as she stood opposite Miss Sass. "There is nothing wrong with me. I prefer my own company. I shouldn't be forced to make friends. I had a friend before she graduated—Abigail Crowther."

I lost that argument, and Miss Wilkerson moved a cot into my room for Rose the next day.

Rose Orji—her last name had something to do with trees— was like a cloud, sometimes bright and cheery, a fluffy ball of fun, other times a dark, crackling storm of thunder and light-ning. Two-sided and unpredictable. That was Rose, the girl I had to live with.

At first, I didn't begrudge our time together too much. We spent the nights reading novels and playing backgammon and chess. One night, I even showed her what was in my trunk.

"Everything is so pretty." She held up one of my silk dresses and, a moment later, waved a lace-hemmed petticoat. "Why don't you wear these?"

"They are for tea parties, dinners with members of the royal household. There is nothing like that in Freetown."

I folded the items she had tossed on the bed and placed them back into the trunk. Then she opened my jewelry box.

"This is gorgeous."

"It is a family heirloom." I took the bluestone pendant from her and put it back in the box. An hour later, we were in our beds, curled up, eyes fluttering shut, sleep coming as fast as possible after such an exhausting day.

The next day, Rose acted strangely, avoiding me all day.

We usually met following knitting class and worked on our projects together, but she never showed up. We also usually had breakfast and lunch together, but I didn't see her anywhere. I felt as if she was avoiding me. Then that night, exhausted, I collapsed into bed, falling asleep as soon as my head hit the pil-low. In the morning, I overslept and was running late. That's when I saw that Rose's cot hadn't been slept in. She'd been out all night.

* * *

I DIDN'T PANIC. I reasoned that she might've gotten permis-sion to stay in one of the communal sleeping rooms for the night, or she went home to visit her parents. Her family lived in Freetown, and she stayed with them on Saturdays. But this was Tuesday.

I debated what to do. I had to get to class. I couldn't risk being late for Miss Wilkerson's morning session. She enjoyed terrorizing me for the slightest infraction.

So I chose a mad dash into my clothes, out of our room, and over to the cafeteria. I had to eat fast, but I nonetheless joined the group of girls that I'd been having meals with and told them about Rose.

"I haven't seen her since yesterday afternoon. Has anybody seen her?"

Eyes darted left and right. Heads bent, staring at the wood tabletop, deep in thought. I found the same expression on each girl's face suspicious. What did they know that they weren't telling me?

"Louise, do you have anything to say about Rose?"

She gulped down a mouthful of porridge. "I am just having my breakfast without getting into trouble."

"What kind of trouble? Catherine, do you know what she is referring to?" I demanded. "Emily? Winifred? All of you know something. I'm just asking one of you to tell me. What happened to Rose?"

It was Winifred who spoke up. "I heard that her brother was badly injured."

"No, he was killed," Emily interrupted.

I swallowed the brick in my throat. "He was killed? By whom? Was it an attack?" My heart felt like it was a rock thrown into a well. I had to put a question to my fear. "Was it King Gezo? Did Dahomey attack? Were the Agojie in Freetown?"

Catherine punched Emily in the arm. "Stop making things

up. We don't know what happened to Rose. We did hear this morning before you came to breakfast that she disappeared."

Winifred shook her head. "You should go to Miss Sass and ask her what happened. She'll have answers you can believe. These girls want to scare you."

"She's right," said Catherine. "She's probably at home with her brother, who hurt his leg fishing."

I felt my heart begin to beat normally, not with the worry of Dahomey holding on to it. "I'll do that. I'll go see Miss Sass after class."

I could not meet Miss Sass until after lunch, but by then, I wasn't so much worried about Rose as curious about what she'd done and why she'd left.

Miss Sass sighed heavily. "That is a good question, Sarah," she said. "We have no idea where she is, and I don't mean to alarm you, but we think she may have run away. Her parents were here this morning beside themselves with worry. And they already have trouble with their son. He's very sick."

"I just wish someone would have told me she was gone."

"We were focused on a missing student, and there was a lot of excitement as we tried to figure out what happened and prayed she was found safe. I'm sorry. I should've told you."

I left her office with a thousand pounds of dread on my shoulders. Something told me none of us had the whole story. The truth of why Rose had vanished was unknown. Or was it?

Suddenly I had to run. I had to get back to my room. The feeling that had hummed into my bones was now a trio of banging drums beating a warning into my flesh.

I burst through the bedroom door and ran to my trunk. I opened it and started rifling through the contents, searching and searching. The box with my pendant would be near the bottom.

I never left it on top of the clothing. I heaved the clothes and other possessions over my shoulder. Soon, dresses, stockings, petticoats, shoes, books, and papers were everywhere except in the trunk. It was empty. There was nothing left. She'd taken the most important thing in the world to me. I don't know why. I just knew she had it.

Rose had stolen my blue pendant necklace.

* * *

I THOUGHT I'D lose my mind. The necklace meant everything to me. Without it, I'd lost them. All the people who had worn it around their necks, helped me find it when it was lost, and kept it safe for me when I couldn't.

That necklace was love, tears, Dayo, Monife, William, the commander, and now Rose, except she was the devil who stole it.

That weekend, Abigail returned to Freetown from Abeokuta to visit me (and, of course, to see several other families in town). But she spent the late afternoon with me. First, she and I went for a walk through the Freetown marketplace. Then I invited her to join me while I dropped off Bibles at some African homes. She thought that was all I had in mind to fill our afternoon, but I was on the hunt and needed her assistance.

"I know Rose stole my necklace. Why else would she suddenly disappear? But I think she went home. Her family came here teary-eyed, looking for her a few days ago, but haven't returned since. I bet she's at home now. Wherever that home is."

"I thought there was a death in her family, Sarah."

"I don't believe that, but I must find out for myself. Do you know where she lives?"

"I'm not sure, but maybe—Tiwa knows everybody in town. She might. Or whether there has been a death in Rose's family."

"Can we go and see her? I'm sure she'll help us."

Abigail looked unsure. "I don't want to bother Tiwa with this, Sarah. I know the necklace is important, but—"

I looked at her with doe-shaped eyes. "Please. The necklace means everything to me. It's the last object touched by my father and brother Dayo. It connects me to them, to my entire family."

She smoothed her hands over her hair and huffed loudly. "You are persistent and persuasive." Then she turned down the road that led to Tiwa's hut.

"Good afternoon," Abigail said as we stepped into Tiwa's home.

"What are you girls doing here on such a lovely day? You should be outdoors."

I had barely made my way through the entrance. "Rose Orji stole my necklace, and I need to get it back."

Abigail leaned against the wall. "She doesn't know if Rose has her necklace for certain."

"Believe me. She stole it."

"You are bold to make such a serious accusation." Tiwa sat on the green mat and stretched her gnarled legs in front of her. "The girls at the Female Institution are good, Sarah. Have you talked to Miss Sass? Perhaps your necklace was lost and returned."

Tiwa was frustrating me. "If you are Oshun, you should be able to tell me how to find Rose and my necklace."

Abigail reached me with two long strides. "You are being

rude, Sarah." She squeezed my shoulder. "We came here to ask Tiwa if she knows where Rose's family lives."

"Rose Orji." Tiwa drew her eyebrows together. "I know where they once lived, but Rose returned home a day or so ago. She and her family packed up and left for Lagos immediately. They won't be back."

* * *

"How come no one at the Female Institution knew she'd left town?" I asked, with an anxious glance toward Louise. "I want to go to the Iroko tree tonight," I said, rising from my seat at dinner. "Will you go with me?"

"Why? To ask for help to search for your necklace?" She shook her head. "You've been looking for that necklace for weeks."

"It's the only thing I own that belonged to my family, and I'd do anything, believe in anything, to get it back."

"The tree is nothing to play with."

"I am not playing."

The sky was blue, streaked yellow from the sun's blazing rays. I couldn't see for the briefest moment, blinded by the daylight. "I'm not sure I know enough to believe or not believe in any of the gods."

"Then why do you want to go to the Iroko tree?"

"I prayed to the Christian God for my necklace to return, and I don't have it yet, so what is the harm in making a promise to Oshima, too?"

"The necklace is essential to you?" Louise sighed.

"Without it, I feel I've lost them again." I brushed a hand over my face. I didn't want her to see my tears. "Will you come with me, please?"

"Will there be a full moon tonight?"

"Yes, there was last night. And so it should be plenty bright."

Louise came with me. I had not been outside the Female Institution compound after dusk, but the moonlight helped us to find our way. It was a long hike, and my feet ached when we arrived.

The Iroko tree wasn't as large as the Agia tree in Badagry, but it was impressive, with fat, swollen roots the size of an elephant's legs tied in knots but lying on top of the ground.

I needed the spirit inside the tree to grant my wish and help me find my necklace. I needed its magic. But did I believe in magic? Did I believe in anything other than despair and loss?

Chapter Twenty-one

Days after my visit to the Iroko tree with Louise, with no reappearance of my necklace, unexpected visitors to the Female Institution created a commotion that garnered everyone's attention, students' and teachers' alike, including mine.

Abigail and I entered the rectory after being summoned by Miss Sass. Her father, Reverend Crowther, and Reverend Venn, whom I hadn't seen since my arrival at the school, were in the rectory with another man I'd never seen before.

But what disturbed me was how they all shared the same expression of worry and significant strain. If I could smell bad news, they reeked of it. My knees weakened, and my heart kicked at my rib cage. What had caused them to look this way?

"Reverend, what has happened?" Abigail asked, holding my hand.

"The Dahomey warriors have attacked Abeokuta," responded Reverend Crowther.

"Dear God, they are hunting again," Miss Sass said shakily.

I stood frozen, fearful the slightest movement would result in my collapse. Rose had said King Gezo hunted the children of the African chiefs he'd conquered if they survived his raids. What would they do to her? An Egbado princess who had escaped his sacrificial pit but dared return to Africa to mock him?

Would Gezo reach Freetown and steal me from my bed?

"I can't stay here." My voice was shrill with terror. "I must go home to England. Please send me home."

The tallest of the men, dark-skinned and dressed like one of the lords I'd seen at Windsor Castle, stepped forward and knelt in front of me. I didn't know him, but he looked into my eyes, and his voice was gentle and kind when he spoke. "You should not worry, Princess. Gezo will be stopped before he and the Agojie reach the coast, let alone Freetown. Trust me. They are a thousand kilometers from here. Very far away. So rest easy."

Miss Sass moved toward us. "Thank you, Captain Davies. Sarah has had some tragic experiences with King Gezo and Dahomey. Please excuse her outburst. I hope you don't mind."

"Not at all."

"He would never be bothered by a child." It was Abigail's father, his arms wrapped around his daughter's shoulders.

"Your kind words are appreciated, gentlemen." Miss Sass glanced at me with a furrowed brow, but my chest was about to burst, and my tears flowed. Couldn't Miss Sass see I was snapping in two like a dried twig?

But no. Instead of caring for me, she was busy flattering the captain. "A man of such wealth and influence being so generous to our school—your donation is a blessing, sir."

"I just hope it will buy the supplies you require." He touched the top of my head. "But how about this child? She is so distraught. Is there nothing to be done to calm her? Can she return to England?"

Miss Sass heaved a sigh. "I—I will see what we can do. But you say Dahomey warriors won't reach us."

"They won't, but her fear is so strong. I'm sure you don't wish to break her spirit if a note to Her Majesty might be well received."

I sniffled, drying my tears as I watched Miss Sass stiffen. She looked as if her spine was pressed against the wall.

"You are quite right, Captain Davies," she said. "Quite right, indeed."

* * *

LATER THAT EVENING, I couldn't let go of the day's events. How could I forget what I'd heard? After four years at the Female Institution, I had to write Mrs. Phipps about the Dahomey king and his Amazon warriors. And I didn't trust Miss Sass to write to England, no matter what she had said.

Hopefully, she would understand how fearful I was and convince the queen to bring me home to Mrs. Forbes, my family at Winkfield Place, and my friends at Windsor Castle.

When I returned to my room that evening, I quickly grabbed paper and a pencil.

Dear Mrs. Phipps,

Dahomey attacked the ancient town of Abeokuta and nearly overturned it. Others say they hunt for the children of the chieftains they've conquered.

The conditions at the school are appalling. I am an outcast because I am the only one receiving the support and kindness of the queen of England. I fear for my safety on so many fronts.

Please bring me home. Please.

Yours with love and affection.
S. F. Bonetta

* * *

I HAD A reply two months later, in early May, just enough time for a letter to be carried on board a ship to England and one to be sent from England to Africa. Queen Victoria had summoned me home.

The following month another letter from England came to Miss Sass from Mr. Phipps, advising her to prepare to return me to England. Accordingly, I was scheduled to depart on June 23 under the care of Reverend E. Dicker.

I was happy. I'd gotten what I'd hoped for, but without my bluestone necklace, I was also sad. It held the memories of my African family and friends—those I had loved first.

Death and loneliness were what I understood best. Why did the brutality of my family's deaths rule over the memories of their lives? No matter how I tried, I couldn't remember my mother's smile, my father's laugh, or the warmth of my brother's hand on the back of my neck. None of the beautiful times remained in my thoughts. And without the bluestone pendant, I felt only the horrible. Only the disturbing memories survived.

At twelve years old, I'd lived a hundred years and died a thousand deaths.

I was mistrustful and angry, lonely and sad. But deep down, I knew what I had to do. All I could do was put one foot in front of the other, as I'd done during any march I'd survived, be it the trek to Dahomey and Abomey or the march to Badagry with Commander Forbes and William. I must stay alive one day, then the next, and another—and survive.

But would that be enough?

What happened to joy? To love? To laughter?

I honestly didn't know, but at least I'd be in England and not close to the Dahomey leader I called the devil.

* * *

"When you return to the land of castles and carriages, fireplaces, and dining room tables the length of a room, don't forget what you planted here." Abigail took my hand. She had come into Freetown to see me off.

"You will always be with me in my heart, mind, and memories. But keep your soul safe." She held my hand to her breast. "It is important you don't allow hate or fear to rule your spirit. Trust in God and yourself."

Her eyes welled with tears, but I didn't feel the same sadness or loss at leaving Freetown or her. But I didn't wish to hurt her feelings. Saying goodbye to her didn't hurt. It barely touched my heart.

"Do you think I would ever forget you?" I said, trusting that my voice had held steady. "You have been my friend, and I will never forget a friend."

She let go of my hand, and we stood staring at each other. But she looked at me as if I were going off to battle, not home to London.

"Yes, you are right. We are friends, and perhaps I am making too much of this, but I don't want you to forget Africa. This is your home. One day you'll remember the places you've been, the people you've met, and those who are like you."

"I'll never forget Africa." I wrapped my arms around her waist, rested my head on her chest, and pulled her to me as tightly as possible. Of course, I didn't explain why I'd never forget Africa. The place of death and loss and hate. She was part of it, even if she'd done nothing but try and be a friend to me.

I let her go and touched her cheek with my open palm, rubbing my thumb over the tear she'd shed. Then I whispered goodbye, turned, and walked away.

I had a ship to board.

Part Three

Piano and Drums

Chapter Twenty-two

Palm Cottage, Gillingham, England, 1855

My British mama, Mrs. Forbes, and her family had moved to Scotland after the death of the commander, and of course, I was not permitted to join them. That option was not made available to me. My new residence, assigned to me by the queen through Mrs. Phipps, was the home of Reverend James Frederick Schon and his wife, Elizabeth.

During the voyage from Freetown to England, I learned about my new family from my chaperone, the Reverend Dicker. He was a talkative chap with endless stories of African missionaries and the wealthy African merchants who supported the crown and the Church of England. He seemingly shared everything there was to know about my new home.

Palm Cottage, on Canterbury Road in Gillingham, was an hour by train to London and Buckingham Palace, a half-day carriage ride to Windsor Castle, and even farther to Winkfield Place. I blinked back tears as I listened. I had loved Winkfield Place, and Palm Cottage sounded too far away from the London I adored.

The head of the household, Reverend Schon, was a German missionary and renowned linguist who had spent much of his career in Sierra Leone, learning African languages as part of his missionary work. He had published multiple journals and served as an interpreter on the Niger Expedition in 1841.

Abigail's father, Reverend Samuel Ajayi Crowther, was also one of the men on that mission.

Reverend Dicker kept repeating how honored I should feel to live with Reverend Schon and his family. "He is one of the most prominent clergymen in the Church of England and invaluable to the Church Missionary Society. And his wife, Mrs. Schon, is a wonderful woman and mother."

"I am very grateful," I said, although speaking with a throat full of disappointment was difficult. I didn't have my pendant, my last connection to my African family, and now the joy of returning to England was tempered by not being able to return to Winkfield Place.

All I had left in my heart was hope. Something could still change even before we reached England. Mrs. Forbes could return to Winkfield Place. We could still be a family even without the commander.

As the horse-drawn carriage trotted up to the entrance of Palm Cottage, I gave up on my dream. Bravely, I did not cry as I stepped onto the dirt pathway. I held my head up and made a decision. I would be thankful that at least my new home was in England. But I had to make plans for what I truly wanted.

I was a princess who should live as such, which meant being part of a royal family and being loved by them. None of which was unachievable.

Palm Cottage was a sprawling estate on vast land in the heart of the Kent district. The Reverend Schon and his wife maintained a bustling household. Three children, aged two to thirteen, and an assortment of servants, visitors and permanent guests, of whom I would be one.

With so many people to watch over, I wondered if Mrs. Schon would have time for me. Would she treat me as Mrs.

Forbes had, embracing me thoroughly after knowing me for only a short period? Or would I be just another mouth to feed?

Quickly, I dismissed that last thought. Of course that wouldn't happen. I was Her Majesty's ward.

Still, when I walked through the grand entrance to Palm Cottage, all was a mystery.

I had to put my best foot forward and display my most pleasant demeanor. I had an impression to make.

Reverend Dicker and I were led to a small parlor by a servant who let us know the lady of the house would arrive soon to greet us. After a few minutes, Reverend Schon galloped in. A tall, coarsely built man, he had awkwardly shaped shoulders that appeared crooked beneath his black suit jacket. But he was jovial and enthusiastically greeted me in Yoruba.

Immediately, I assured him in English that I was proficient in both languages.

It was apparent he was anxious to speak with Reverend Dicker. The two men sat at a round table and began catching up on the happenings in Africa.

I plopped down on a lovely sofa with the softest upholstery. With my hands delicately folded in my lap, I thought about introducing myself to Mrs. Schon. Of course, I'd compliment her children and point out how lovely they were and intelligent, too—after an appropriate amount of time. It would go a long way toward getting her to like me.

However, with any plan, something unplanned intrudes. In this case, Mrs. Schon would be further delayed, with good reason (not explained), news delivered by her thirteen-year-old son.

He strolled into the parlor, nodded a greeting to me, and told his father that his mother had sent her apologies. I thought it unusual that Mrs. Schon wasn't prepared to greet us promptly, but there would be an explanation (just not then).

Meanwhile, Reverend Schon suggested his son, Frederick, show me around the grounds.

A red-headed boy, he was the family's eldest and the child closest to my age. He was much taller than me, with odd-looking brownish-red dots on his white-skinned nose and cheeks—freckles, a name I later learned. He was thin as a rail. I had more weight on my bones than he did, and I was practically a waif.

* * *

We hadn't made it any farther than the foyer when the Schons' eldest son opened his mouth. I knew right then we wouldn't get along.

Studying me with squinty eyes and a furrowed brow, he asked, "What kind of girl are you?"

"I am a girl like any other girl," I replied. "And you are impolite."

"I'm not impolite. I'm curious, and if I don't ask questions, how will I learn?"

"I am Negro, which you should know by looking at me, no questions necessary. And according to Reverend Dicker, you've visited Africa with your father on several occasions. Another reason your question is strange. Unless you aren't very observant." I imagined that he pushed his tongue into his cheek, thinking on how he should reply. Or he was too stunned to talk. "And do not be surprised by the way I speak. I have been told I could draw blood with my sharp-edged tongue." No one I knew had told me that, but I liked to believe it was so.

"I agree. I believe you could do just that." He tugged on the lapel of his vest. "You are correct. I have been to Africa. And yes, I know you are African, but you aren't like the Africans I've met in Africa. Are you a missionary?"

"I'm twelve years old. How could I be a missionary?" Then I sighed. How many silly questions would he ask? "I attended the Female Institution in Freetown. It's a church missionary school. So I know about talking to God and his role in our lives."

"You have never practiced the Yoruba religions?"

"I know of them and may have practiced them when I was a little girl, but that was a long time ago." Oh, yes, a small lie, but he did not need to know about the Iroko tree, the magical tree in Freetown, where I had gone to pray for the return of my bluestone necklace. "Do you?"

"Do I what?"

"Practice the Yoruba religions."

Freddie, the name I had decided to call him by, smiled. "Oh, you tease me, yes? I get it. Of course I don't practice Yoruba. But I know a lot about Yorubaland. I'm in training to be a minister like my father." His smile vanished when he said the last part.

"Do you want to be a minister?"

"Why would you ask me that?" His shoulders squared, and his chin poked forward. He seemed offended. "I am proud of my father and would be honored to follow in his footsteps."

His words said one thing, but his expression another. It swam in a pool of doubt. A soft cloud covered his eyes and hid the truth. It circled his head, too, like a plague of wasps. I'd had no idea it was such a sensitive question, asking about him and his father.

Freddie and I never made it out of the foyer. Mrs. Schon joined us with her other children and the entire household (including the reverends). So many people I had trouble keeping the faces and names straight.

In addition to Mrs. Schon and the reverend, there were the children: Freddie (thirteen), Emily (five), and Adele (two). Palm Cottage also was home to two Africans (Darugu, who was eighteen, and me) and another student, I didn't catch the name, who would join us later. There were two servants—Ann Berry and Charlotte Long—and the governess, a second Anne (with an "e") Norris, who all lived in the house, too.

I didn't have time to compliment the younger children, but before I knew it, they had vanished, leaving me with Freddie and his mother.

"Frederick, I know how you are, and I hope you haven't bothered our guest with whatever nonsense is in your head," said Mrs. Schon. "Lately, you can be so rude." She gently patted him on the cheek, squeezing it before moving on.

Dressed in an oversized smock, Mrs. Schon held her stomach, one hand on top of her belly and the other below, as if she'd drop the ball in her belly if she let go. Oh, then it came to me. She was with child. Perhaps that was what had delayed her.

She had a youthful appearance, like a girl. Her smooth white skin wasn't too pale. So she wasn't one to be shy about the sunlight, and she had an abundance of red hair, the same shade as Freddie's, with loose strands curling onto her forehead. She also had freckles on her nose, but not as many as her son.

"Mother, I was not rude," Freddie said after a while, which made me think he'd been stewing over his mother's remark. "But if you'd like me to leave so you can get Sarah settled, I will be in the drawing room, practicing the piano." He bowed deeply.

His mother laughed. "Always a showman, Frederick. Yes,

please leave." She shooed him away, and he was off, down a hallway and around a corner.

"Mrs. Schon, thank you for taking me in," I said, our eyes meeting after Freddie was out of sight.

"Thank you, dear. It is an honor to have the ward of Her Majesty as a guest in our humble home." She walked carefully toward a dramatically long winding staircase.

"Those steps are as steep as the side of a mountain," I said in awe.

"Don't worry. The railing is sturdy, and Darugu and Frederick will carry your trunk. They are strong young men."

"Darugu is strong," said a young girl who had entered from the same hallway where Freddie had disappeared. "But Frederick is too slight to handle the trunk," she added with a teasingly pleasant tone. She turned to me and curtsied. "Miss."

She was stunning. Large brown eyes, cheekbones, distinct, like mine. Brown skin, not as dark as mine, almost gold. She also had specks of gold in her eyes, the same shade as in her skin. She wore her mound of black hair swept up on top of her head. And such an easy smile, I thought.

I was instantly torn between admiration and mistrust. Someone who looked like her was unlikely to be kindhearted.

Mrs. Schon sighed. "Oh, Tilly, I'm so sorry I didn't call you. But she's here. Princess Sarah Forbes Bonetta, this is Matilda Serrano, but we call her Tilly. She is from Cuba and formerly enslaved."

"Miss Sarah." She extended a thin, sculptured hand from a slender wrist. "It is my pleasure to meet you."

Oh my, I thought. She might overshadow me if she lived in this house, too. "Miss Matilda." I ignored the family's nickname for her. "Are you visiting the Schon family?"

"I've been with the Schon family for over a year." She looked at Mrs. Schon. "A year and a half, maybe?"

"About that, dear." Mrs. Schon stopped at the foot of the staircase. "I can climb these steps only twice a day." She turned to me. "We have a large house with many bedrooms and a full house, too. Tilly will show you around, which will give you a chance to get to know each other. You and Tilly will share her bedroom on the second floor."

"Share a room?" I felt dizzy. "She and I will be roommates?"

"Yes. Of course, I checked with the queen, and she agreed. You need to make friends your age or near your age."

Of course Her Majesty agreed. What did she know of my past with roommates and thieves?

Chapter Twenty-three

Palm Cottage, Gillingham, England, 1855

Three weeks after my arrival, I was still adjusting to the unexpected. I had wanted to live with the Forbes family but lived with the Schons. I had thought I'd visit the queen and Princess Alice shortly after my arrival. But I hadn't received an invitation from Her Majesty or her emissary, Mrs. Phipps, and from Princess Alice I received only scribbled notes that never mentioned an interest in my visiting her.

On top of these concerns, I hadn't wanted a roommate but had one.

My last roommate was Rose, and I hadn't recovered from her theft. I had horrible dreams about her, and they were always the same. I would find her with my pendant in an alley in London, maybe in the East End. I'd snatch my property from her loathsome paws and pummel her within an inch of her life.

When I woke up, I was angry, unhappy, and trembling with regret.

I wouldn't say I liked that I'd struck Rose in my dream. I wouldn't do that if I ever saw her again. I'd plead with her to return my necklace. But then, the day after the nightmare, my stomach would ball into knots, and I'd think that I might hit her.

Anger was a constant that flowed through me, interrupted only by sadness and memories of the dead.

It would be risky to show the Schon family that side of me, the sad girl, the angry girl, the stubborn girl. So I embraced my roommate, Matilda. She was sixteen, outwardly friendly, seemingly kind, and not easy to dislike. Although, admittedly, I tried.

Matilda and I had similar interests. She liked to read, write letters, sew, and knit. And even though she was several years older, she played games and ran, skipped, and jumped. It helped soothe some of my ill temper, our common ground. She couldn't sing and hated the piano—two things I loved. But she'd never know that. The most important things to me I would never share with her. They'd always be my secret.

Born in Havana, Cuba, a place I'd never heard of, she didn't talk about what had brought her to England and Reverend Schon's home, and I didn't push her to tell her story. I knew some things in life didn't need to be told.

Freddie and Matilda, or, excuse me, Tilly, behaved oddly around each other, at least to me. They were playful, teasing, argumentative, and acted more like five-year-olds than thirteen- and sixteen-year-olds.

I watched them with a raised eyebrow. Around Matilda, Freddie reminded me of Dayo with the girl he had planned to marry, whose name I couldn't recall. But I could tell Matilda didn't like him that way. She cared most about having the freedom to play. It was as if someone had taken her childhood from her, and she played desperately to get it back.

This I understood. King Gezo had robbed me of my childhood, but I wasn't interested in a return visit. It was full of bad dreams, bloodshed, death, and lost loved ones.

* * *

In Gillingham, Kent, the weather in September was comfortable, with less sticky heat and less wind than in summer. Even I found the cool breezes pleasant. But you couldn't tell that to Mrs. Schon. Her condition controlled her body's temperature, not the weather. She was enormous with child and irritated by the slightest thing.

One afternoon, Freddie and Matilda were immersed in a lively game of hide-and-seek in the main lobby of Palm Cottage, their voices raised to the highest octaves.

"You'll never find me," Matilda exclaimed, giving away her location.

"I can't hear you, Tilly," Freddie replied loudly as he raced through the grand hall. "Where are you?"

"Not how the game is played," Matilda responded with zeal.

Intrigued by the commotion, I stood outside the library and watched, entertained by their riotous behavior.

Mrs. Schon rumbled into the foyer with bright red cheeks pulsing with anger.

"I swear, if you two don't quiet down . . . " She clapped her hands together sharply. The sound echoed from the floor to the ceiling with the power of thunder. "Couldn't you play outdoors? I can't tolerate this much noise on such a blazingly hot day."

Freddie stood still, pausing his search. "Mother, I apologize."

Tilly appeared on the opposite side of the room, smoothing the folds of her dress. "I, too, ma'am, apologize sincerely. I shouldn't even play these games at my age."

"Save your apologies and head outdoors," Mrs. Schon said, moving across the hall in my direction. I tried to step out of her way, but she stopped before me. "That means you, too, Sarah. I swear you've been cooped up in the drawing room since break-fast."

She was not wrong. It was by choice. But I didn't open my mouth to disagree. The fire in her gaze stopped me from objecting. "Yes, ma'am."

"I am heading upstairs, Mrs. Schon," Matilda said suddenly. "I have some letters to write before dinner and need to wash up." She dabbed sweat from her cheeks.

"Oh, Tilly, no," Freddie said, mad as hops. "We were having so much fun, and I was about to win."

"I default. It is your victory," she said. "If you will excuse me." She hurried up the staircase.

"All right, then." Freddie bounced across the hall toward me.

I retreated a step, startled by his exuberance.

"Where are you going, Sarah?" he asked. "My mother has instructed us to head outdoors. So, come along." He took my hand. "Don't try and pull what Tilly just did—you write your letters to the royal household before the sun rises. So that cannot be an excuse."

"Thank you, Frederick." Mrs. Schon exhaled her relief at the anticipated quiet. "On your way out, dear, stop by the kitchen and have Ann bring me a cup of tea in the parlor."

"Yes, ma'am."

Freddie dragged me toward the rear of the house before I could refuse. Then we were in the backyard after a quick stop in the kitchen, where Freddie grabbed two straw baskets and shouted at Ann to bring his mother her tea.

At least, I thought, I'd heard him say please to Ann.

This was the pattern from my first month at Palm Cottage, watching Matilda and Freddie in their one-sided dance, practicing the piano whenever we weren't studying with the governess, and keeping my distance from Mrs. Schon.

Her condition frightened me. Her belly was so round and pronounced, and her temperament so volatile. I wondered how this had happened to her. I didn't know much about marriage or womanhood and nothing about babies.

Some women in the Freetown marketplace had been heavy with child, but I'd never lived in the same house, shared meals, strolled in a garden, or had a woman watch over me with such an ill temperament.

Mrs. Schon may have run an incredibly tight ship with a crowded and busy household, but her mood jumped from sweet as candy to bitter as lemon juice in the blink of an eye. I believe I wasn't the only one who prayed she gave birth to a healthy, happy, beautiful boy or girl—as soon as possible.

* * *

A TYPICAL DAY began with breakfast in the kitchen, and then I'd hurry into the study, where the governess, Miss Norris, taught the morning classes. The courses were like the ones at the Female Institution and included mathematics, English, and geography, except more advanced. Scriptures were in the afternoon.

After these classes, my time was devoted to the arts: piano lessons, singing lessons, and reading Shakespeare's comedies aloud. In the evening, after dinner, I joined Reverend Schon and Freddie in the study to translate scriptures into African languages.

Whatever free time I managed was spent in the library at the piano.

After more than a month (with no invitation from the queen and still only the occasional note from Princess Alice), I needed something more to do than study or even play the piano. I wondered if spending more time with Matilda might help, but she was preoccupied with writing letters to friends and family in Sierra Leone. That left Freddie. Not the worst idea since, lately, he asked fewer questions and was somewhat less rude.

So the next time he invited me to join him for a walk around the property, I said yes.

A hundred yards behind Palm Cottage, on the other side of the garden, was the tree line of a forest to which Freddie was leading me.

"What animals are in those woods?" I tried to sound casual, but my voice trembled.

Freddie cocked an eyebrow. "I don't know. Squirrels—we have red ones, and also birds."

I searched the treetops for hawks, eagles, or vultures, giant birds with pointed beaks that swooped down from the sky and grabbed small animals (and children) with their mighty talons. "That's all? Just birds?"

He shrugged. "Might be some wild boar, but they usually are found deeper into the woods."

"What kind of wild boar?"

He ducked beneath a branch. "I didn't know there was more than one kind, but we aren't going that far, I promise."

It was a warm day. I adjusted the neckline of my dress and hoped for a breeze. The layers of clothing required by British fashion made me extra uncomfortable. "Freddie, can we stop for a moment? I'm burning up."

He pushed aside another thorny bush. "What do you want to be when you leave Palm Cottage?"

"Why do you ask?" I stopped walking and spun slowly left and right, seeking a breeze.

"The way you study people with the same vigor as you study your lessons. Every assignment you are given, every person you meet, you strive to learn everything you can about them—or the lesson. It's as if you believe a perfect student must also be a perfect person."

"Are you complimenting my vigor or ridiculing it? No one is perfect, but if I don't strive to be the best, I won't have a chance at it. As for people, I sense things about them from what they say and how they say it. Doesn't everyone?"

He shook his head as if my logic baffled him. "Do you recall that when we met, I told you I wanted to be a minister, a missionary, like my father? I thought I'd sounded proud, but you doubted me. You sensed something about me I might not have realized about myself."

My heart was beating too fast in my chest. Freddie and I had never spoken to one another this way—all these questions and observations. I didn't like it. "Now it is your vigor I question." I held my hand to my throat. "I am not as warm as I was. We should continue our trek."

"You're right," he said, moving toward another clump of bushes. "I asked you before, what are your plans? Who do you want to be?"

"I don't believe anyone has asked me that question in a long time." I closed my eyes, thought about the places I'd been and the people I'd met, and recalled what I might become one day. "A writer. When I first came to England, I was on a ship, the HMS *Bonetta,* and the cabin boy asked me what I wanted to be one day, and I said a writer like Jane Austen."

Freddie turned and looked at me. He seemed impressed.

"That's unexpected. I would have thought you'd say missionary, like me."

"Why?"

"We're children of the Church Missionary Society, in a way. A minister is raising us in a home of God. So I thought that's what you'd want to do. Marry a man who is a missionary and then go back to Africa to give them the word of God."

"Is that why you want to be a minister? To save Africans?"

He shrugged. "I guess."

I almost forgot about the wild boar and the heat when we started walking again. I was thinking about Freddie's question. What did I want? With each step, I wondered what would happen to me. Who would I marry? Would I want to be a missionary in Africa? I had rejected that idea so many years ago. Had anything changed?

"Were you teasing me about the boar?"

We had reached a place in the woods where the plants were so dense they darkened the sky, and I couldn't see a foot in front of me. I could've been inside a wooden crate, sealed on all sides, with no light slipping through the cracks. "Are we even on Palm Cottage property anymore?"

"We are." Freddie held back a tree branch. "Just a few more feet before we make it to a place no one knows about except me—and then you. You'll know where it is in a few minutes, too."

"That's great, but I'll never find my way without you."

"Then I'll always be with you when you come here," he said.

"Maybe we'll find a path that doesn't include the thorns and the gnarled branches. Those bushes scratched up my hands and arms."

"I hope you'll find my secret place worthy of a few scratches."

I smelled it first, and the delicately sweet aroma danced into my nostrils and lungs, and my mouth watered. "What is this?"

The green and red bushes spread out in front of me for yards. "This is my strawberry patch."

"Strawberries? Is it a fruit?"

He nodded. "I believe so." He strode to a bush and picked a handful of the red, seedy fruit. "Smell it, and then take a very, very small bite. If your tongue swells, throw the rest on the ground."

"Why would my tongue swell? Is it poison?"

He stared at the ground. "My little sister Emily ate one a couple of summers ago, and her tongue swelled, and she almost died."

I shuddered. "Did you bring me here to poison me?"

"Oh, God, no." He rubbed his head, pulling on his red hair, suddenly distressed. "I just thought if I brought you here and you liked them, you wouldn't dislike me so much."

He didn't turn away from me as he spoke. After such a confession, I couldn't look him in the eye.

"You have been rude, and you are loud."

"Rambunctious, my mother says."

"Yes, and I don't care for . . . rambunctiousness."

He laughed. "I don't know if that is a word, but I apologize."

"It's a word."

His eyebrows drew sharply together, and his smile vanished. He looked somewhere between fearful and apologetic. "I know I like to tease and play, sometimes too much. My father told me that you aren't a child like other children. You lived through unimaginable horrors and were shipped back and forth between Africa and England. As his eldest son, he instructed me to make you feel comfortable so you'll think of Palm Cottage as your everlasting home one day."

"Everlasting? Reverend Schon said that?"

Freddie nodded. "I did, too."

I stared at the strawberry in my hand. Then I brought it to my nose and inhaled deeply. It smelled like something I'd eaten before.

"If you've never had one before, please take only a small bite—but if you start to feel sick or your tongue swells, stop."

I raised the strawberry to my lips, but he grabbed my hand, holding me so tightly I couldn't lift my arm to taste the fruit he'd just asked me to eat. "What are you doing?"

"This is a bad idea. What was I thinking? You could get sick like my sister. Christ. Don't eat it."

I pulled my hand free and stuffed the strawberry into my mouth. Red juice stained my fingers, but the taste, sweetness, and tartness combined for the most delicious flavor.

"It's good." I grinned, almost as excited as Freddie appeared to be that I hadn't hit the ground.

"Are you all right?" he asked.

I swallowed and stuck out my tongue. "Is it the same size as before?"

He nodded, but his eyes were hollow pools of fear.

"I'm fine. But the strawberry—I love it—tastes like some fruit I ate in Africa. The miracle berry, except sweeter."

The worry lines etched deeply in his brow began to vanish. "A miracle berry? That's a great name," he said between bites of his strawberry. "The strawberry is my favorite food in the whole world. Although, from now on, we'll call them miracle berries. Is that all right?"

"If you like." I walked a few feet farther, examining the strawberry patch. "Why do you keep your garden a secret? Is it because if your sister finds it, she will eat them?"

"My mother doesn't want to see them." He sighed. "She used to grow strawberries in the backyard, but when my sister took sick, she cut down every strawberry bush in the garden and made everyone in the house swear never to eat another one. But it's hard to give up something you love so much, don't you think?"

"Sometimes, Freddie, we have no choice."

Chapter Twenty-four

St. James's Palace, 1855–1856

Our conversation at the strawberry patch stayed with me for a long while. Whenever I looked at Freddie's sister Emily, I thought about her tongue swelling and Mrs. Schon threatening her other children if she saw them near a strawberry. I felt that Freddie was leaving something out of the story. But it was just a feeling I couldn't pin down, so I had to let it go.

He'd shared a big secret with me—I thought his mother might disown him if she found out about the garden. Freddie hardly knew me and, without thought (so it seemed), had trusted me.

Goose bumps rose on the back of my neck. The conversation had its ups and downs but mostly, it was too comfortable, too easy and pleasant. Why did a good thing bother me so?

It wasn't as if in one afternoon we became friends. I didn't need a friend. I needed people with the power to keep me from being sent back to Africa.

I avoided him for a few months. Not easy since we lived in the same house, but necessary. Instead, while waiting to hear from Her Majesty, I spent more time with my roommate.

Matilda's obsession with writing letters had waned, and she and I found things to do together. We played board games, like chess, backgammon, and checkers. We sewed, knitted, darned, and read scriptures. I told her she'd make a good missionary one day, and she smiled broadly.

But the happenings in the Schon household were insignificant compared to my ultimate concern—it was December, and I hadn't received a summons from Her Majesty since I'd returned to England in July.

By the end of the first week of December, my panic had turned into hysteria. Had the queen's interest in me dwindled? Had she adopted another child from another continent? Someone with a sadder story than mine? That seemed improbable. Since my earliest days in England, my tale of sadness and woe had been famous. I credited Commander Forbes's published journals for spreading my story. Every Englishman and -woman had read about the African princess and the British commander who saved her life. My exploits with the royal family also made the news in 1850 during my first trip to England.

I had done nothing to earn the queen's disfavor. Why hadn't I heard from her?

I stomped my foot. She was the queen of England. Maybe she was busy governing a country. There was nothing I could have done to lead Her Majesty to abandon me. I had to stop my thoughts from careening out of control.

Otherwise, I had little to complain about. Mrs. Schon asked me what color dress I wanted to wear for the Christmas celebrations she was hosting. The queen had generously provided additional funds in my monthly allowance for a new gown. It was an offhand remark, but my chest puffed with pride. If the queen still paid my expenses, I remained in her good graces.

Tiptoeing by the parlor one afternoon, I overheard Reverend Schon and his wife discussing the monthly funds they received for me from Mr. Phipps. There were also gift packages regularly provided to the Schons by Mrs. Phipps with clothing, school supplies, and trinkets, although I couldn't help but long for more—like a summons from Queen Victoria. Not even the letters from Princess Alice mentioned the queen, other than the gold piano Prince Albert had bought for Queen Victoria recently that I could have read about in the newspaper. But no invitation.

Then, as seemed to be the custom with Her Majesty, she surprised me.

"It's here. It's here." Matilda burst into the dining room. "A letter from the queen of England has come."

"Delivered by special messenger in a royal carriage." Freddie bounded into the room behind her.

I sat quietly, pretending to eat my porridge, but I wanted to jump from my seat and shout happily. A letter from Windsor Castle. Finally. The queen wanted to see me.

The new version of Mrs. Schon, since she'd had her baby, entered the dining room with a bright smile and a letter in hand. "Quiet, children. Settle yourselves." She sat at the table across from me. "It is from Mrs. Phipps, not the queen herself. The same Mrs. Phipps sends us packages for Sarah every week. But this letter"—she waved it once—"is an invitation for Sarah to join the royal family, not at Windsor Castle but at St. James's Palace in Westminster. And not for an afternoon, but during the Christmas holidays. Sarah has also been invited to accompany the family to the Christmas pantomime." Mrs. Schon fanned herself as if experiencing heatstroke in the middle of December.

"The Christmas holidays? Oh, my. Will I need new clothes?"

"We must request additional shillings from Mr. Phipps to add to your wardrobe and buy gifts for the queen and the children," she said excitedly. "This will require much planning."

She handed me the letter and rose from the breakfast table. Since giving birth to a baby boy in September, she had become more agile and less agitated. Indeed, she'd become increasingly giddy.

The entire household, including myself, followed Mrs. Schon as she left the dining room and headed toward the opposite end of the house.

She turned sharply, and we plowed into the library behind her.

She paced before the fireplace and appeared incapable of slowing down her feet. Instead, she walked in one direction and then the next, moving toward the bookshelves and the door prior to starting the circle again.

It made me dizzy.

Everyone watched her; Freddie, Emily and Adele, baby Charles, and the entire household.

I held the note from the queen in my hand, staring down at it occasionally before looking back at Mrs. Schon.

"What is the pantomime?" I asked. "Why is everyone so excited about it?"

"You will love it," Freddie said. "I've never been, but my parents went and talked about it for weeks."

"Yes, yes. That's correct, Freddie," Mrs. Schon said, pausing her dance around the library. "The actors, the costumes, and the grandeur of the stage decorations. It's possibly the most important play of the year."

I looked at the note in my hand again. "Is there another letter, Mrs. Schon?"

"Oh, yes. From Mrs. Phipps about a gorgeous dress and other items she also sent by royal carrier." She passed it to me. I skimmed the message, reading to myself.

Dear Mrs. Schon,

I have sent dear Sarah a beautiful dress for when she comes to London. I will give her a scarf with a white fringe, and then we will provide her with a pink bonnet. I think it will do, but to keep her warm, she had better wear an undergarment.

Mrs. (M. A.) Phipps

"Will you be ready, Sarah? This is such an important celebration, and for the queen to include you is lovely," Mrs. Schon said.

"Yes, ma'am. I am ready." So ready, I thought, I could have walked into a carriage that moment and headed straight to Windsor Castle, St. James's Palace, or wherever Her Majesty wanted.

The queen would not catch me sullen, sickly, or without something meaningful to say. I'd started reading newspapers. The *Daily News* was of particular relevance, with pages and pages about the queen, Prince Albert, and their children, of which there would soon be one more. I had missed the birth of five children in my four years in school in Sierra Leone. I had a lot to do to catch up. Alice had kept me up to date on her life. When I saw her, she could tell me what the newspapers hadn't said about the royal family.

No matter. I was ready to reenter their lives.

I had spent four and a half months living less than a day's carriage ride from Her Majesty and her family.

That had been more than long enough.

* * *

THE PANTOMIME WAS a feast for my senses, an inspiring spectacle that entertained and amazed me. There were chase scenes, magic tricks, dazzling lights and acrobats, and outrageous comedy. All things that were very new to me. I sat wide-eyed, my mouth open and my heart pounding at the sights I saw— the colors, the dancing, the laughter, and the makeup. It was brilliant theater.

It must have been apparent to Her Majesty that I'd had the grandest time of my life. Immediately, she extended my stay with the royal family into the new year. After that, I couldn't keep up with how often my name appeared on the queen's calendar—which didn't include my appointments with Princess Alice and the other royal family members.

Once I returned home, I wanted to shout from the top of the winding Palm Cottage staircase. Reverend Schon, his wife, their children, and Queen Victoria's royal family treated me like family. Nothing compared to that.

After the merriment of the pantomime and several days spent in the royal household, I thought the holiday season had exhausted its ability to thrill and astonish. But then Mrs. Schon announced the family's celebration of Twelfth Night, a Christmas tradition.

Freddie and Matilda boasted that the event would be nothing less than exquisite. I wasn't sure I believed them. The holiday season so far had been perfect, and I had no idea what Twelfth Night meant. So I asked Freddie to explain.

He and I sat in his father's study, working on translations, just as we'd done for the past month, three evenings each week. Reverend Schon had recently taken over as chaplain of Melville Hospital in Chatham, leaving Freddie and me to handle the remaining projects.

"What is Twelfth Night?" I asked a few minutes after we were settled.

"January fifth is the last day of the twelve days of Christmas," he said. "It's the day we take down our Christmas trees and decorations, the ivy, the mistletoe, and the like. That's so we avoid any bad luck in the new year." He looked up from the scriptures on the table. "And we sing Christmas carols, and Ann and the staff cook a lavish meal." He put down his pen. "Most importantly, it's a Christian holiday. The family goes to church, and Father blesses the house. Then we eat, sing, and pack up any remaining decorations."

"It sounds like a very busy day," I said. "But it's a Christian holiday, too. Not just a time to eat and make merry."

He resumed his writing. "It's also the Epiphany, the coming of the Three Kings."

"I see," I said, but my expression must've shown my uneasiness. It didn't sound as if it would compare to the pantomime.

"Don't worry. We also get to dress up in our finest clothes. We might even dance."

"I don't dance."

"Maybe you should learn."

"In two days."

He laughed. "By next year, we'll dance together."

"Promise?"

"You can count on it."

On January 5, 1856, the Schon family's home was filled with

friends and relatives. After attending the church service, we returned for the house blessing and then more Christmas decoration packing before a party of twenty was seated in the main dining hall.

Everything was splendid. It was like being with the royal family with the amount of silk, satin, gold trim, lace, flowers, and jewels adorning the table and the beautiful gowns and handsome suits.

I wore a dress with layers of pale-yellow silk and a delicate pink and blue floral spray. The bodice had silk ribbons lined with cotton and whalebone strips and a skirt shaped like a bell. When I entered the dining hall, Freddie stood nearby, and I thought I heard him gasp—I had surprised him in a way I hadn't done before. I felt sure of that.

He looked pretty dashing, too, and grown up, in a flared frock coat with a rounded chest, cinched waist, looser trousers, and high upstanding collars. Thankfully, I did not gasp aloud, but inside, my stomach fluttered. Freddie had changed in the past months. His once skinny arms and thin torso had grown larger, with more muscles and bigger bones to rest them on. If I had a trunk that needed carrying, he could haul it up a winding staircase without help from Darugu.

I didn't want to ogle him for too long and moved my gaze to the table the kitchen had set under Mrs. Schon's direction. It was out of a fairy tale—a gorgeous centerpiece with fruit, flowers, tall vases, lace tablecloth, napkins, and gold candelabras. But the elegance didn't stop there. Of all things, the plates, saucers, and bowls put tears in my eyes and a sob in my throat.

"What color is this shade of blue?" I asked shakily, without addressing anyone in particular.

Freddie replied. "Cobalt blue. It's Wedgwood china, from

something called the horticultural series. It's been in the family for ages but only used on Twelfth Night."

"It's beautiful," I said breathlessly.

"Yes, it is." He stepped close to me and lowered his voice. "See the floral pattern. Daffodils and lilies of the valley."

My throat tightened. The color was as vibrant a blue as my lost pendant. "You said China? It's nowhere near Africa."

"That's correct."

"But the color it's almost the same."

"The same as what, Sarah?"

I turned to him, surprised. "Have I never mentioned my blue pendant?"

"No, you haven't."

I stared at him for a moment. Of course I'd never told him. I didn't talk about Africa. "You're right, I haven't, but I will one day."

"I can tell it's important to you."

"Very important." I smiled, nudging my shoulder into his. "Like your strawberry patch."

He leaned in close and brought his index finger to his lips. "Shh . . . that's our secret."

I nodded, raising my finger to my lips. "Shh . . . agreed."

Chapter Twenty-five

Most of my mornings and afternoons at Palm Cottage were spent studying and translating Bible passages into Yoruba languages. Otherwise, I was in the company of royalty at Windsor Castle, Buckingham Palace, St. James's Palace, or Osborne House.

I lived with bells on my fingers and golden leaves in my hair. I was only thirteen years old, and life was near perfect.

Sadly, a weed must grow in every field of sweet lavender.

During my second or third visit to Windsor Castle in early 1856, I met Harriet Phipps, daughter of Sir Charles Beaumont Phipps and my Mrs. Phipps.

Princess Alice and I were in the Crimson Drawing Room, making feverish plans for the upcoming theater season. Somehow, we got diverted and ended up discussing the polka.

"Whatever would possess me to learn the polka or a Viennese waltz?" I asked, selecting one of the sweets from the tray on the table. "I love to sing and play the piano, but I never thought about dancing." Freddie had mentioned teaching me, but I just assumed a princess danced differently—like royalty.

"It is now time to think about it," she said. "The queen has a new ballroom, and you and I will need to know these dances and be excellent at them."

"Ballroom? Excellent? I've never been to a ball."

"I have, but I didn't do much more than watch the queen and Papa dance. They dance beautifully." She smiled into the air, looking at nothing but the memory. "You know we're coming into an age where we'll be greeting suitors and—"

My head felt light, and I rested a hand on the table to steady myself. "I am not interested in a suitor."

"Don't you wish to marry one day?"

"I read somewhere that most women in England don't marry until they are twenty-two or older."

"But my mother will marry us off as soon as she can. That is the way of Her Majesty, the queen of England."

I laughed. It was good to hear the old joke from Princess Alice.

"I'm glad to see you smile, because I've arranged for us to take dance lessons. I already know most of them, but I figured you lost a few years of social graces in Africa, so it's up to me to catch you up."

"I don't believe the queen will be too worried about me and marriage. She has her hands full with eight children."

"And by the way, Mother has agreed to allow us to go to the opera. Just the two of us." Then she slid her tongue over her upper lip. "The two of us and our escorts, the Reverend Venn and his wife."

"I know them."

"Are they nice? Will they chase after us if we mingle with aristocrats during intermission?" She twisted sideways. "No, don't answer that. It doesn't matter. We will be seated in the front row of the royal box. Everyone will see us, and we'll have to dress extravagantly."

I struggled to contain my enthusiasm. "Are you sure she won't change her mind? Why did she agree?"

Princess Alice held a finger to her lips as if to hush me. "I don't know. Sometimes Her Majesty wants her children to meet someone in public informally. Like a beau."

"A beau? Whatever for? I don't understand." I couldn't explain why this news made me feel so discouraged. Tilly was the same way. All aflutter about suitors and marriages.

"Good afternoon." A woman who could have been our age or much older entered.

"Good afternoon, Harriet. It is good to see you," Princess Alice said without actually looking at her. "Where have you been?"

"I didn't mean to interrupt, ma'am." She glanced at me with as much expression as a block of ice. "My mother and I were with Her Majesty not long ago."

"I wasn't referring to this day. I haven't seen you around for the past few weeks."

"I—" Now she was staring at me.

"Oh, you haven't met." Princess Alice raised her hand in my direction. "Sarah, this is Harriet Phipps. She is the daughter of Sir Charles, my father's financier, and Mrs. Phipps, whom you know well." Then she looked at Harriet. "May I introduce Sarah Forbes Bonetta, an African princess and goddaughter of Her Majesty?"

Harriet curtsied and stared at the floor for several seconds, which gave me a chance to study her. I struggled with her age, but she couldn't have been much older than Alice and me. After all, she was Mrs. Phipps's daughter, and Mrs. Phipps was the queen's age. But assuredly, Harriet's look was that of an older woman.

Her attire was stylish, a silk day dress with a tremendous full skirt in striking colors—bright red interweaved with a gold-threaded pattern against a shimmery pale-yellow fabric. It was fetching, but her chilled expression belied the beauty of her clothing. Her eyes were the color of rain clouds, and the tight skin over her cheeks accentuated a long nose and short chin. It did not match the enticing whoosh of her skirt and the glimmer of the dress's threads.

"Sarah." I heard Princess Alice's voice.

"Oh, yes, Miss Harriet," I said. "It's a pleasure to meet you."

Princess Alice and I shared a glance, and her quick smile clued me in on what she was thinking: Harriet's contradictions were mesmerizing.

"How can I help you, Harriet?" Princess Alice asked.

"The queen would like to see you immediately."

"Let her know I'm visiting with Sarah, if you would."

"I already told her your scheduled guest was inside the castle. But she insisted, and Her Majesty wants to see you right away and alone."

"I am sorry, Sarah. We are scheduled for lunch tomorrow, aren't we? We must finish our conversation on the dancing lessons and the opera season—the Royal Italian Opera House in Covent Garden is spectacular."

"I'll see you tomorrow." I rose, but Princess Alice touched my hand. "Stay. Finish your tea. Harriet will escort you to your carriage. Yes, Harriet?"

"Of course, miss."

* * *

"You don't have to wait on me. I know my way," I said proudly. "I've been here many times before."

"As a guest, you must be escorted, Sarah." I noticed she didn't address me as she had Princess Alice, which I should have ignored but didn't. It bothered me. Few people in the royal household, or anywhere else, treated me like a proper princess. But Harriet's tone dared me to object.

After I finished my tea, we walked from the Crimson Drawing Room toward the foyer in silence until we reached the entrance to the courtyard.

"I will be spending more time with you and Princess Alice. The queen has asked my mother if she would allow me to do so."

"Spend more time with us? For what reason?" I thought it an innocent question, but Harriet's shoulders rose in agitation.

"I imagine the queen wants to ensure you and the princess aren't going off half-cocked."

It wasn't a phrase that a proper British lady should use, that much I knew. "That should not be a concern, Harriet."

"I do not question the queen's orders, nor should you. That may be why I was asked to spend more time with you and the princess. Unfortunately, no matter how often you visit the royal family, someone of your background doesn't have the necessary upbringing to completely absorb the complexities of being a part of the royal household."

We had reached the front doors, and outside, my carriage waited. "Oh, and the next time you visit, you should try and take the train," Harriet said. "Modern transportation is something the queen and Prince Albert respect."

"Do you have a problem with my relationship with Princess Alice?"

"I have no opinion of you. My concern is for the royal family, and I will fulfill the queen's wishes."

I didn't believe her. "You sound as if you have a right to say whatever comes into your mind to me. We've never met before today. I have done nothing that should cause you to show me such disdain. I have been respectful of the royal family and the royal household, but your words make me think I should ignore proper protocol and speak my mind."

She stared at me dumbfounded. Her lips were unable to move for several seconds. I could see the struggle in her wrinkled brow. When she finally spoke, it wasn't pleasant to hear.

"How dare you? My family's history with the royal family goes back generations. Most of the servants who work in Windsor Castle, Buckingham Palace, and St. James's Palace have been in the royal family's service for as long as my family. You are the interloper, Sarah Forbes Bonetta. Not I." She inhaled deeply and pointed toward the carriage. "Your driver awaits."

* * *

HARRIET PHIPPS CONTINUED to be a shadow. Lurking in the halls of Windsor Castle and Buckingham Palace, she spied on Princess Alice and me, reporting to the queen every declaration of rebellion we proposed. But she couldn't take away my joy.

There was a wedding to be planned.

The Princess Royal had agreed to marry the prince of Prussia. The engagement, which could last a year or more, wouldn't be announced to the public until that May, but the nuptials were already the talk of the royal household. Vicky was the first of the royal children to be engaged, and the staff who had watched her grow to womanhood were anxious to celebrate.

I had never thought so much about engagements and weddings before in my life. But with so much excitement in the castle, I couldn't think of anything else. We discussed every detail, Princess Alice and I. We talked about the bride's dress, white silk, embroidered florals, and fresh flowers, and the bridesmaids, who would wear all white with lace veils. The bride's mother would wear black, purple, or red. If in mourning, she wore black.

We discussed every expectation and the disappointments to be avoided: the imaginable and the impossible. But the groom wasn't discussed, except casually.

Of course, he was admired and loved, but he was never at the center of the conversation.

It was the bride.

She was the heart of a wedding. Its very soul.

The only troublesome thing was that this beautiful, awe-inspiring bride never looked like me. So when I dreamed of weddings, the bride would be the Princess Royal, Princess Alice, or even Matilda, but I was never the one reciting the vows.

Although, wouldn't a princess need a prince at that moment? Which made me wonder who my prince might be.

Chapter Twenty-six

Osborne House and Palm Cottage,
Gillingham, England, 1856

Several weeks passed with only a few new adventures for Princess Alice and me. Somehow we were outflanked every time we planned to visit some theater, opera house, or dance hall in London. I blamed Harriet Phipps.

I had no doubt her junkets to the queen had something to do with the cancellations, conflicting appointments, and other barriers we encountered. We did manage a night at Covent Garden Theatre using a private entrance through a large building with a gallery of some sort. We enjoyed a marvelous production seated in the royal box, but a fire destroyed the theater a few nights later. At least we still had the Surrey Gardens Music Hall and festivities, such as a boat race on the River Thames between Cambridge and Oxford University—Cambridge won. We slipped away to watch it with a carriage of escorts, but we eluded Harriet. Other events of importance occurred in the castle. There, there was a Congress of Paris, which led to the signing of the Treaty of Paris, ending the Crimean War.

Harriet Phipps had nothing to do with the Covent Garden fire or the end of a war, she wasn't a witch, but her eagle eye never lost sight of Princess Alice and me.

Even with Harriet spying on us, Alice and I remained our chatty selves, plotting new adventures (whether they came to fruition or not) and preparing for the Princess Royal's wedding announcement.

While strolling through the walled garden at Osborne House, which the Prince Consort had created, we debated who was the true heroine of the Crimean War. And for the first time in my recollection, we didn't agree.

"What do you think of it?" I asked Alice about an excerpt from a letter written by Florence Nightingale in the *Daily Telegraph*.

"As I've stated, she's a woman ahead of her time," she said. "All those poor injured soldiers. You know, my mother and I visited London hospitals during the war—the suffering of those brave men was so tragic. Mrs. Nightingale's work in the midst of battle was a godsend."

"Yes, I cannot disagree. But why aren't she and Mary Seacole of equal standing? Didn't they both serve our injured soldiers heroically during that campaign?" I knew Florence Nightingale was Alice's hero (and Queen Victoria's), but I was a devotee of the Jamaican nurse. A brown-skinned woman had healed as many as Mrs. Nightingale but was shunned.

"I don't think you can compare their contributions. I agree with Her Majesty. Mrs. Seacole shouldn't be placed on a pedestal, not above or equal to Mrs. Nightingale."

"Humph. It's unfair—your mother won't invite Mary Seacole to Windsor Castle. Florence Nightingale has been a guest on several occasions."

"Don't be naive. Seacole ran a brothel!" Alice's face had turned bright red. "That's why the Church of England looks down on her, and the queen supports Miss Nightingale."

"There's no proof. Only hearsay." My voice quaked with rage. "It was a hospital. Have you read her biography? I have.

She was a dedicated healer and risked her life in the Crimean War for British soldiers."

Alice stopped before a section of Prince Albert's garden, gazing at the trees and shrubs her father had planted and tended to. "Don't you think this would do better if it were a flower garden?"

"Why are you changing the subject?"

"I don't wish to argue, and we're very close to a severe argument."

"Are we close or already in the midst of it?"

"Sarah, please."

She was right. My face was warm, my palms damp. An argument? We were on the verge of war. I closed my eyes and tried to recall the pointless question Alice had asked me about her father's plants. "What kind of garden is it meant to be? A tree garden?"

"A nursery is what Papa calls it."

"A nursery for trees and scrubs?" My tone was terse. "Do you know British soldiers have thrown an event to raise money for Mary Seacole? Would they do that if they didn't love and admire her?"

Alice touched the prickly-looking leaves of a plant. "Florence Nightingale can do whatever she wants with her life. Her forte is in how she cares for the sick and injured. She will start a nursing school, which the queen will support."

"Mary Seacole has services to offer as well," I said, my irritation hammered into each syllable.

"Her Majesty disagrees."

"Mrs. Seacole will be the woman history remembers. Not Florence Nightingale."

"We'll just have to see about that," Alice said with a smirk. "How do you know about such things?"

"It's what I read in the newspaper, or perhaps," I started shyly, "overheard in the Queen's Sitting Room."

She raised an eyebrow in concession. We both knew how much we learned by staying quiet and listening while in the Queen's Sitting Room. The scandalous were often loud.

"Other than rumors of improprieties, what words of wisdom has Mary Seacole put in the world?"

"Your sarcasm is unwarranted," I countered. "She said, and I quote: 'I am not ashamed to confess that I love to serve those who need a woman's help. And wherever the need arises—on whatever distant shore—I ask no greater or higher privilege than minister to it.'

"She is Creole and, as I pointed out, brown-skinned. Do you think the divide in Britain over her commitment to saving the lives of British soldiers is partly because of her skin color?"

Alice puckered her lips. "I hadn't considered that. The queen and British aristocrats are adamant about their dislike because of reports of her indiscretions."

"What if they aren't true? What if they are spread mainly because of her skin color? Both she and Florence Nightingale were essentially doing the same work. Why put Mrs. Seacole down as behaving in an unladylike manner?"

Alice tapped her throat with her gloved hand. "I don't know. But can we finish our walk? I can't discuss these heady topics while exerting myself."

"Then I will find someone else to discuss this with." Suddenly, I found myself marching back toward Osborne House, leaving Princess Alice in the garden, alone. I hadn't realized the extent of my anger until I was halfway to the house.

Lately, I felt the eyes of judgment watching me, following me. The public's kind, sweet curiosity for a small African child, a princess, had fallen away. A young Black woman, a Negro, who boldly dressed in fancy clothes, sat in royal boxes, and partied publicly and privately with members of the royal family, wasn't a curiosity. I was a thing to be scrutinized, judged, and criticized. Alice may not have noticed the furrowed brows and whispered insults, but they weren't intended for her to hear. They were meant for me.

Sometimes Princess Alice didn't see me. She only saw what mattered to her. We were so much in the public eye. I wanted her to see some of what I saw. The sneers. The hatred. The jealousy.

I never forgot that she was white-skinned and her mother was Her Majesty, the queen of England. These facts shaped who she was. My skin, the texture of my hair, and my place of birth shaped me.

However, none of it meant my opinions should matter less than hers. After all, we were both princesses.

* * *

AFTER MY LAST visit with Princess Alice at Osborne House and my abrupt departure, I was worried. My stubbornness had led me to disagree with a member of the royal family. Yet I was right—Mary Seacole's reputation was being deliberately sabotaged by groups and individuals I would not name publicly (the Church of England and the queen, by not acknowledging her). But what was I thinking arguing with Alice about it? Risking my standing with the royal family over a woman I'd never met? Let's call it what it was—insanity. I had to repair the damage. But how?

As the days passed, I worried about resolving the disagreement between myself and Princess Alice. But no solution came to mind, and I wandered around Palm Cottage, plagued by deep, unhappy thoughts.

The rain fell heavily on a Saturday afternoon. It was fall, and everything, including my bones, felt wet and cold. This kind of rain usually sent me to bed with shivers, begging for extra blankets, a steaming pot of tea with plenty of sugar, and a bottle of milk.

Instead, I rambled through the kitchen, scouring for sweets, but then I heard the piano. Freddie was playing the new Erard grand piano, one of the finest made. His father had recently purchased it, making it the second piano at Palm Cottage.

I hadn't talked to Freddie in a few days other than to say good morning, afternoon, or evening or converse politely at mealtime. I'd kept to myself, brooding over what had happened with Princess Alice.

But the music enticed me, and soon I stood in the drawing room doorway, listening, not wanting to interrupt. His selection was a piece we both loved to play and hear: the "Emperor" Concerto by Beethoven.

I entered after he'd finished and lifted his fingers from the keyboard.

"You play that piece beautifully, Freddie."

"How long have you been standing there?"

"Only a few minutes, but I heard you playing while I was in the kitchen, hunting for sweets."

He turned fully around on the piano bench. "What did you find?" he asked, eyebrows wiggling.

"Sorry, no chocolate," I replied. The disappointment in my tone was reflected in his expression. We both were obsessive about chocolate. "I did grab some clove rocks and stuffed them into my apron pockets. Would you like some?" I pulled out a handful.

"Please. Bring them over." He turned back to the keyboard. "Sit with me."

I went to the piano, adjusted my skirt, and plopped on the bench beside him. Then I handed him a clove ball, returning the rest to my pocket.

He popped the sweet in his mouth. "Where have you been? I haven't seen you except at meals all week." He looked at me with a frown that didn't match the humor in his eyes. "And even then, you were quiet as a mouse, and that's not like you, Sarah."

"I did something I shouldn't have done, and it's filled my head. It's not serious. Nothing to worry about." I placed a sweet in my mouth. "I've never heard anyone play that concerto better than you."

"You are too kind, Sarah." He glanced at me sideways. "I don't believe you."

"No, I am very serious. Your playing is divine."

"That's not what I mean. What did you do that has filled your head? Whatever it is, it's not nothing."

There wasn't anything Freddie could do to help me. He'd never met Princess Alice. He knew nothing more of the royal family than any ordinary Londoner. Or little more than what I told him. "You're right. It isn't nothing, but it also isn't anything you can assist me with."

"Perhaps not. But it might help to talk about it. I can listen."

He was trying to be a friend. I understood that. In many

ways, he was a friend. I had almost told him about the blue
pendant on Twelfth Night, but my trouble with Alice wasn't
something I wanted to share with him. "I don't wish to talk
about it."

"Very well. Then we won't talk about it." His words were
agreeable, but his tone wasn't. "Then shall we play something
together?"

I studied him for a moment. Between the way he sounded
and the speed at which he had accepted my refusal to discuss
what was bothering me, I knew I had upset him, and I hadn't
meant to. "Don't be angry at me."

"I'm not," he said sharply. "You told me you didn't want to
talk about it, and we aren't talking about it."

"You are outraged." I heaved a sigh. "But I am old enough
to figure out my problems on my own. If I am to be a proper
English lady, pursue adult things, and worry less about playing
games, walks in the forest, and chocolate bars, I must handle
my own affairs."

"You're thirteen, Sarah."

"Or fourteen. Or fifteen. Who knows how old I am, but
I've lived enough life to take care of myself." I popped another
sweet into my mouth, but my voice had gotten shrill. "What
had you asked me? If I wanted to play? Yes, I'd love to."

We were seated shoulder to shoulder on the piano bench. I
shifted slightly to give us room to play whatever he suggested.
But Freddie had leaned away from the keyboard, and his hands
were on his knees. It was as if he was luring me in, waiting for
me to realize I could trust him. He had shared a secret with
me—the strawberry patch. I had promised to share a secret
with him one day. The blue pendant. Except it was such a big
secret. My love of that stone and losing it had hurt so much.

"All right. All right." The words erupted from my throat. "I argued with Princess Alice. Not a brawl, but an angry exchange." I looked at him with tears in my eyes. "What if she hates me and tells the queen to return me to Africa?"

The tears fell freely. My body shook from my sobs.

Freddie wrapped an arm around my shoulders. "Shh. She doesn't hate you. Disagreements between friends happen. Besides, if she does act the way you fear, she is not a friend. Either way, I don't believe the queen would send you away because of something that happened between you and her daughter."

My sniffles were as noisy as my sobs.

He pulled a handkerchief from his pocket and handed it to me.

I looked at him in astonishment. "When did you start carrying a handkerchief?"

"You are a proper English lady. I aspire to be a proper English gentleman."

I laughed and wiped my face.

"Now, shall we play?" Freddie asked. "Whatever you'd like."

I stuffed the handkerchief in my pocket. It would need to be washed. "Yes, I'd love to. But please, I insist. You choose."

Chapter Twenty-seven

Palm Cottage, Gillingham, England, 1857–1858

Freddie had been right.

Alice and I moved past our disagreement within weeks. Although our opinions about Mrs. Nightingale and Mrs. Seacole remained unchanged, we both agreed that they were adult women, and we were young girls looking forward to parties and nights out at the opera house, theater, and music halls. We also promised to never forget a fundamental rule of being a proper English lady: *small talk is preferred over conversation, which can turn into a dreadful discussion.*

My relationship with Princess Alice had returned to normal. We were spending time together as before, but then fate interceded.

I didn't see anyone in the royal family or the Schon household for two months. I had been invited to stay with the Forbes family in Scotland.

Her Majesty and Mrs. Phipps graciously arranged the surprise trip. It was delightful being with my first English "mama," but as much as I enjoyed the time spent with them, I missed the Schon household and, of course, the royal family.

So I was as anxious to return to England as I'd been to visit Mrs. Forbes in Scotland. My enthusiasm doubled when I arrived at Palm Cottage and found an invitation from the queen to the Princess Royal's wedding in January.

I had expected an invitation, but not one posted in the London *Times* and every other newspaper in Britain. Quite a welcome home, I thought with measured delight.

I had hoped to be a bridesmaid. Although, throughout the previous year of chatting about the wedding, there had been no indication from Her Majesty or anyone in the royal household that such an honor would be extended to me.

Nonetheless, it had been a fervent hope I'd kept to myself. But my presence at the ceremony wouldn't be a secret. The queen had ensured the news was spread to every corner of England. The African princess, her goddaughter, rescued by a British naval commander and gifted to the queen of England, would be among the privileged at her first daughter's wedding.

The invitation did require my presence at social events celebrating the coming wedding. There were so many dinner parties, balls, and teas I feared I might grow tired of smiling, dancing, sipping champagne, and elegance—but I didn't.

My life in England had been spent wanting nothing less than the royal treatment, and I was getting it.

Still, I wondered. Why had it been crucial for the newspapers to know I would attend the wedding? Humph. I thought I should ask, and then I thought again. What if the answer was not to my liking? So, instead, I enjoyed the parties.

* * *

THE NEW YEAR began with the marriage of Victoria, Princess Royal, to Prince Frederick William Louis of Prussia on January 25, 1858, in the Chapel Royal, St. James's Palace. It was the grandest of affairs, and I was there. The entire day was splendid and one I would never forget, if only for the pageantry, the wedding gown, the flowers, and the bridesmaids, too, with only a tinge of regret. Maybe more than a tinge, but I was mesmerized by everything and everyone. And the wedding march. Oh, my. Mendelssohn was the queen's favorite composer, and mine, too, that day.

But a few weeks later, there was a change to my living conditions at Palm Cottage.

My roommate was leaving the house.

Matilda Serrano had received news that her family, enslaved in the Caribbean, had escaped and made it to Freetown. She had burst into the drawing room, waving a letter, tears streaming, and stumbling over her words. The household rejoiced. Imagine reuniting with the family you had believed dead and forever taken from you. It was unimaginable to me.

I had to hide my jealousy behind a smile.

I would miss her. She had treated me respectfully, even if my envy of her easy manner and pretty face surfaced occasionally.

Perhaps my smile wasn't that much of a lie, for I would have my own room. But did it still matter after all these years? Should it matter? Hadn't I matured?

After Matilda's belongings were packed and she'd said her tearful goodbyes, I watched the carriage drive off, and my only thought wasn't about a room. I would never feel her joy about returning to Africa for any reason.

Africa was home to the kingdom of Dahomey and King Gezo. Whether a thousand kilometers away or with an ocean between us, I sometimes felt as if all he had to do was reach out and touch me. My fear, which still woke me in the middle of the night, was that he would find me one day.

How was it that at fifteen years old (or thereabouts), I lived one day at a time? It was as if I didn't believe in the future or didn't trust it. I never wanted to get too far ahead of myself.

* * *

BY JULY OF 1858, I had done and seen five times as much with the royal family as I had the year before. However, my busy year at castles and palaces came to a halt in early July.

I was trapped in Palm Cottage. Indeed, anyone within an hour's carriage ride of London was trapped in their homes by the stench of the River Thames. No one dared travel to the city that summer unless they suffered from hysteria.

The newspaper headlines read that the heat, waste, and unspeakable filth had turned London into a Great Stink. But the cause of the smell was a killer, the polluted River Thames, which caused cholera and who knew what more.

"When the Great Stink ends, we should go to London," I said, sitting in the library rereading the *Wonderful Adventures of Mrs. Seacole in Many Lands*.

"If it ever ends." Freddie sat across from me on the uphol-stered bench, reading the *Times*.

"I want to visit the East End. Will you take me?"

He swung around with wide eyes. "I may strike you as an adventurer, but please know I've never been to the East End of London."

"I'm sure you'd make the best escort."

He frowned, closing one eye. "Why the East End?"

"It must be awful for all Londoners, but more dreadful for those who live in the poorest parts of the city. That's the East End, isn't it?"

"Yes, it is, but you don't know anyone in the East End. Why did it come to mind?"

"I did know someone once from the East End. His name was William Bartholomew. He was the cabin boy aboard HMS

Bonetta when I was brought to England for the first time, years before I met you and your family."

"You've never mentioned him."

"He was nothing like you. As I recall, his hair was black, and he was as thin as a reed and missing some of his teeth. But he taught me English and about the sea and ships and introduced me to novels by Austen and Dickens. He was a brave lad and the best cabin boy I've had the pleasure to know."

Freddie's expressive eyes dimmed. He'd heard the sadness in my voice. "What happened to him?"

I sighed. "He drowned." My hands trembled only slightly, and I closed my book. "So, will you take me to the East End in London?"

He still had that look of hesitation in his eyes.

"Oh, Freddie. I know it's rough-and-tumble in the East End, but I can't ask Princess Alice to take me. That would be scandalous. But you can take care of us," I said with a sly smile.

He sat up straight. "I guess I could."

"Of course you can. You've grown into a man with a robust appearance. You are tall and fit, and smart. Your wit alone could get us out of dangerous situations."

He cocked his head and smirked. "I do have a silver tongue."

"Ha ha." I sat forward in my chair. "Silver tongue aside, you would lay down your life for me if I were in danger," I said dramatically. "Therefore, I need no one else to accompany me to the East End but you."

There was a silence, just the sound of footsteps in the distance, someone walking down the hall toward the kitchen. "You are right, Sarah. I would never let any harm come to you. So I guess I am your man."

Chapter Twenty-eight

Windsor Castle, 1859

It was a day of celebration. The former Princess Royal, the German empress and queen of Prussia, had given birth to her first child, a son named Wilhelm II, born on January 27, 1859—a year to the date plus two days since Vicky's nuptials.

The dinner in honor of the queen's first grandson had been earlier that evening, but Princess Alice and I had left the Crimson Drawing Room when the crowd of well-wishers had become too dense and noisy. Eavesdropping was wasted in a room full of loud voices. Everyone could hear the tasty tidbits. And what fun was that?

So our exit went unnoticed, as far as we could tell. No one came after us, which guaranteed freedom for at least an hour.

I went directly to the piano as soon as we slipped into the Queen's Sitting Room. Alice wanted to sing, and I began playing the "Cradle Song" by William Cox Bennett. She had practiced it to serenade her first niece or nephew and sang it exceptionally well, sounding very much like her mother.

We had worked on the song for months, and I could play the piece blindfolded. However, on this day, I had some trouble. I kept striking the wrong keys, but Alice didn't stop singing, so I thought she hadn't noticed or ignored my mistakes.

When we finished the song, she left my side for one of the three gilded mahogany sofas, the one in front of the window, with its straight back and slightly curved arms. She then placed her delicate hands on her lap and gave me the oddest look.

"What's on your mind, Sarah? You seem preoccupied. You never make a mistake playing that piece of music. And the way your fingers struck those notes, it was as if you were fighting the keyboard. So, tell me, what has happened?"

I had never considered myself a piece of glass someone could see through, but Alice could and didn't hesitate to ask me what was wrong. No matter how awkward. "I've been thinking about my future, and marriage, and children."

"And a husband, too, of course, I assume?"

We giggled heartily but recovered our composure in two deep breaths. I rose and joined her on the sofa.

"Marriage does seem to be the topic of the season," Alice said ruefully.

I mirrored her pose, hands in my lap, trying to relax so I could tell her some of what was on my mind. "You'll be engaged soon. You'll meet your future husband any day now. The queen will arrange everything, and you will love him. And your life will be perfect for the next ten, twenty, fifty years." I chewed my lower lip, my nerves exploding. "I've never thought ahead, not that far. My life has been so uncertain. I haven't had choices. Life just happens." I paused and breathed in through my nose. "I'd love to choose and have a real say in my future."

I had broken the rules of polite conversation and, unable to look Alice in the eye, stared at my hands.

Then one of her pale, thin hands covered my dark ones. "I don't know what you mean about choice. I've never had that many myself," she said earnestly. "In polite society, I must always appear genteel, ladylike, demure, and silent when I am in the presence of the queen or any of her loyal subjects. The only time I am free, Sarah, is when I'm with you. Remember when we'd sneak through the castle, lose the guards in the tunnels, and find ourselves lost in the countryside? They have been the most joyful to me."

I could see that she spoke from the heart, and I felt much of what she felt about our time together. But her freedoms beyond our activities together were vastly different from mine; many had been denied to me.

"And for me, too. But when the queen and her doctor had decided I must live in Africa, my bags were packed and I was in Freetown thirty-three days later." I pressed a fingertip to my temple to ward off the headache brewing. "When I begged to come home, it took four years and a threat to my well-being in the form of King Gezo to convince Her Majesty to approve my return."

Staring at me blankly, Princess Alice seemed at a loss for words. I hadn't meant to upset her by speaking so seriously. "But I'm sure your mother wouldn't force you to marry if you objected."

She leaned back on the sofa, glancing up at a portrait of His Royal Highness the duke of Kent, her mother's father, Edward, a doting grandfather, she'd heard, if he had lived.

"My mother will do what a queen must do for her children. The same I imagine I will do for mine." She smiled. "My mother, Her Majesty, the queen of England, knows best." We both chuckled softly.

"Other than that," she continued, "I have no idea what to say. You have experiences I will never have—would never want to have. You have been denied many things that I have been given without a bat of an eye. But there is nothing we can do about the past. Nothing we can change. All I can say to you, Sarah, is that I am sorry."

Suddenly Alice's expression brightened. "For this conversation to go on, we need tea, gingerbread cakes, and perhaps chocolate bars."

I was astonished at her swift change in tone, but what more was there to say? So I followed her lead. "Chocolate. I love those pieces of dark chocolate and gingerbread cake. Let's have them both."

"I completely agree."

Alice rang a handbell, and a servant stepped into the room. Alice gave her instructions, and the servant hurried off.

"Move closer, Sarah. I don't wish to waste time. We must dive right into this matter," she said.

We were already seated next to each other on the sofa, but I complied, and our shoulders touched.

"Before we began that other conversation, were you asking me what I'd do if I didn't like the husband my mother selected for me? If I thought him a boor?" Alice's mischievous eyes searched my face. "I would never disobey the queen."

Alice pulled her lips to one side, making a funny face. "I can see the question in your eyes. Why? It's easy. Because I trust her." Our heads were practically touching. "Ladies of our stature are duty-bound to marry and work to uplift our husbands in whatever endeavors they choose. Isn't that correct?"

I shrugged.

"What is your worry about marriage?"

My fear of uttering the wrong words was my present concern. I didn't wish to disagree and didn't want to argue, but I had to speak some truth. "I'm not sure I'll find someone to marry me and love me the way I want to be loved. Other times, I'm not sure I want to be in love. It requires too much faith."

"My, my. What a dilemma. To love or not to love, that is the question?" She poked me in the arm playfully.

"Who are you, William Shakespeare?" I laughed, poking her back.

"No, I prefer mangling the words of Hamlet."

"But tell me, even trusting your mother as you do, as we all do, would you marry a man you did not love?"

"I would pray for my mother's luck. She fell in love with Papa the first time she saw him. That's what I would want."

I rested my hand on the sofa's armrest. "I wish I knew what love would look like for me."

My words went unheard as the servant entered with the tray of sweets, and we squealed together, "Chocolate!"

Any more serious conversation for the evening was lost to sweets, games, and gaiety. The kind of day spent together Alice and I enjoyed most.

Chapter Twenty-nine

Palm Cottage, Gillingham, and London, England, 1859

A letter arrived at Palm Cottage from Matilda Serrano in March of 1859, and Mrs. Schon read it aloud at the dinner table.

Matilda had married Captain James P. L. Davies, a wealthy African businessman from Lagos and a former lieutenant in the British Navy.

My stomach dropped. How was it that every young woman I knew seemed to be in love, had announced her engagement, or was already married? The Princess Royal, a few others Princess Alice and I knew, and now Matilda. I was in danger at almost sixteen of being an old maid.

I left the table in a hurry when dinner ended, feeling sorry for myself. I was delighted for Matilda. She was happy and had fallen in love with a man of wealth and influence who reunited her with her family. Matilda's life was perfect.

But what about mine?

Matilda had often talked about marriage, children, houses, and love between conversations about books and knitting needles. My favorite topics were novels, party dresses, royal pony cart rides, Shakespeare, the Viennese waltz, and piano music.

It was the duty of a woman of privilege like me to be married. Any respectable English lady would be overjoyed with such a life. But did I want a husband? Or did I doubt I'd find one? Being an African princess in the royal household of Queen Victoria made finding a husband a problematic task.

So no, I was not jealous of Matilda exactly. I was jealous of any girl with a proper suitor and a marriage proposal from a man she'd fallen in love with.

Love was paramount in marriage. This much I had concluded from watching Queen Victoria and Prince Albert.

It was just that I didn't know if I could fall in love. Or find love with a proper husband. What prince could Queen Victoria find for me?

I couldn't shake these thoughts. The pressure of marriage surrounded me. Social gatherings with girls my age or slightly older chatting about husbands, weddings, and children as if they were the only conversations worth having. I understood a proper English lady married with the single purpose of supporting her husband's ambitions, but did we have to talk about them the entire time we were together? Once a woman had married, any interest she might have had for self-fulfillment was discouraged or forbidden outright.

I slept fitfully that night.

The following morning, I sat on the edge of my bed, waiting for the Schon's maid, Ann, who sometimes served as my lady's maid, to help me dress and do my hair. She was the only one who could groom my coarsely knotted hair. Thank goodness for bear's grease and a stiff brush with boar bristles.

Matilda's happy news aside, I hated fretting about my sad state of affairs. Why waste more time on worries that only worsened the more I thought about them?

I had plans for the day and should have been excited about the adventure ahead for Freddie and me. He was the only one I could have fun with other than Princess Alice.

We had an adventure planned in London. Not the East End, we would build up to that, but we were spending the weekend with the Honorable Reverend Henry Venn and his family. Freddie's father had highly praised our translation skills, and we had been invited to help Reverend Venn's assistant with his translations. But I had some additional ideas. Whatever free time we could manage, I wanted to explore London. I was sixteen (or thereabouts), and Freddie was seventeen. We were finally old enough to do more than promenade through Hyde Park with his parents.

We stepped off the train at the Fenchurch Street Railway Station, our first stop, and I was starving. I couldn't wait until we reached Reverend Venn's home to eat. So I convinced Freddie to make a detour. We found a block of street merchants near the station selling everything from chocolate bars to pea soup and puddings—and gingerbread cake, which I craved. I pleaded with him to buy a slice or two.

"Sarah, we will miss the connecting train, and Reverend Venn and his assistant are waiting."

"Freddie Schon, you are so cautious. We will catch the next one and still knock on his door thirty minutes before we are due." I was ready to drag him by his roots but instead latched onto his arm, and I must admit I was surprised.

The long-ago scrawny Freddie had more than a wee bit of muscle. His arm felt like an iron pipe from the Palm Cottage kitchen. "Have you put on some weight in your arms, Freddie? Trying to be as strong as Darugu, perhaps?" I laughed, and he joined me but somewhat reluctantly.

After that, he relented and bought the gingerbread cake. I scarfed it down as daintily as a girl with a ravenous appetite could.

Then a silence came upon us as we boarded a later train to Reverend Venn's home. It continued, other than polite chitchat about his brothers and sisters, his mother and father, and my last visit to Windsor Castle.

By then, we had arrived.

I had met Reverend Venn on several occasions. He had been my escort upon my return trip to Africa in 1851. He also had been present in Mrs. Sass's office along with Abigail's father and another gentleman the day I learned about Rose's disappearance and about King Gezo's attack on Abeokuta.

By early afternoon, we had completed the projects the reverend had for us, and we were free to return to London for a few hours. Of course, we swore to be mindful of where we were in the city. It wasn't the safest place, but it was early in the day, and we'd return before it was too late.

The only problem was that we weren't supposed to go where I wanted to go.

On this particular Saturday afternoon, the American abolitionist and activist Sarah Parker Remond was lecturing. What I'd read about her was fascinating. In addition to wanting to end slavery in America, she was a suffragette—meaning she was in favor of women's right to vote. I told Freddie of her mission with awe in my voice.

"I read about her in the *Times*." I said this as if God Almighty himself sanctioned the newspaper. "She has traveled to Liverpool to campaign against American slavery. Her lectures are popular, and hundreds of people have come to hear her speak."

We walked on a crowded street, and I had to pick up my pace while speaking loudly to ensure Freddie could hear me in the din of the street. "I hear she describes the crimes of brutality and rape Black women face in slavery and urges Britain to denounce the United States for its refusal to end the institution."

I was losing my breath, running and talking, but Freddie moved briskly, not mindful of my shorter legs or my effort to maintain a ladylike demeanor.

"It sounds as though she speaks on subjects some might consider taboo," he said, launching the words over his shoulder.

I grabbed his coat sleeve, stopping him. "The world is larger than London, Freddie Schon. And I can't attend these events with anyone from the royal family. I can't even discuss American politics at Windsor Castle or Buckingham Palace, or Palm Cottage unless we are out for a stroll in the forest. Conversations about slavery, Darwinism, Mary Seacole, and even Dickens's *Little Dorrit* are taboo to the British aristocracy. You are the only one I can talk to about these things."

So many people crowded the sidewalk. Freddie pulled me close to his side, protecting me from the bumps and shoves, but he'd heard me. He just wouldn't respond until he was ready. Freddie was never in a hurry to respond. I think he was learning the risk of saying more than he wanted to say.

So I waited patiently.

"Where is her lecture being held?"

I contained my excitement and didn't grin from ear to ear as I sputtered, "London Tavern, on Bishopsgate Street."

He exhaled.

"It's not only a tavern," Freddie began. "It's a place of business with a lecture room. Did you know that ten or twelve years ago, Frederick Douglass, another American abolitionist, spoke at the London Tavern?" He didn't wait for me to answer. Instead, he took my hand and led me across the busy street. When we reached the sidewalk, I responded.

"No. I was in Africa in Gezo's enslavement camp. But it doesn't surprise me that you would know about Mr. Douglass's visits to London."

He held my hand tighter and stared down at me. "I am only a student of the abolitionist movement, Sarah." He moved his thumb over the top of my hand. "And I started to learn what I know about abolitionists because of you."

"Because I am Negro or because I was once enslaved?"

"My answer may or may not please you, but it is honest. I am learning about abolitionists, civil wars, and England's history in the slave trade because I care for you." He pressed his lips together and leaned forward, his breath on my cheek as he whispered, "One day, I will care because it's the right thing to do, but for now, my reason is you."

I froze momentarily, feeling as if I were tied in ropes as in the Abomey camp. I didn't know why the past leaped into my thoughts. Freddie was not a danger to me. His words were meant to be kind, soothing, and loving.

It was just that my heart couldn't handle his care, kindness, or commitment to learning about the things that should matter to a young Negro woman of intellect.

I felt a sickness in my stomach and pressure in my chest. It was too much. Could his reason for becoming a better man be me? Was that what I heard him say?

I stared into his eyes. He had said "care." He cared about me.

"I am unsure how I feel about your honesty, but when you tell me you care about me, my response is to say that I care about you, too." I squeezed his hand back.

"You look frazzled. Have I shocked you, Sarah? I had thought my feelings were clear."

"Perhaps what I find shocking is that my feelings are the same as yours."

He smiled and hugged me around the shoulder, but an instant later, we were shoved in the back and stumbled forward a step before Freddie righted us.

We were then reminded that we were in the middle of a crowded sidewalk.

I smiled shyly. "Now, how quickly can we get to the London Tavern?"

Chapter Thirty

*I*t had happened. The queen had found a match for Princess Alice: Prince Louis of Hesse.

"He is delightful. Very charming, and we think the same about certain things. The official announcement of our engagement won't happen for another year. And then we won't marry until December of 1861. So there is time to get to know him even better."

"You do sound pleased." I sat next to Alice on the sofa in the Crimson Drawing Room.

"I've heard my mother talk about a December wedding, just before Christmas, the perfect time of year. Mother loves to plan early; Mrs. Phipps and a few others are already involved." She started to sound less cheery.

"Do you love him?"

"I know this question plagues you. I care for him, and the better I know him, I am confident I will learn to love him." Alice squeezed my hand, and I looked at her. Her brow was one deep furrow, her eyelids hooded, her mind working on a puzzle, sorting through the maze until she had an idea. "You'll never find a beau until you have suitors. So that's where our focus should lie."

"My dance card is always full at parties. But none of those young men qualify as a suitor."

"I know you've had doubts about marriage and finding a man you love enough to marry. But you want to be married."

"Well, I don't know if I do or not, but I should, shouldn't I, I suppose?"

"You talk about it as much as any of us."

"I talk about engagements and weddings."

"We all talk about engagements and weddings."

"I never felt the need to speak out loud about myself. Now I do. Your sister is a wife and mother, and you will be a bride soon, too." I took a breath. A sudden urge to share my growing feelings for Freddie overcame me. Alice was a trusted friend, but our lives were different. I was the queen's ward or god-daughter, as some called me, but I was not the daughter of the queen's womb. "There's someone I think I care about, who cares about me, and he may not be of my station, but . . ."

Princess Alice squeezed my hand tighter. "I think I know who it is."

"I don't think so. How could you?" I looked at her with disbelief.

"Of course I already know. It's your Freddie. Frederick Schon."

"What? Why would you say that?" Oh, God. Had I given away my secret without knowing? If so, who else knew? I could deny it. The self-satisfied smirk on Alice's lips seemed permanently affixed, however.

"Come, come, Sarah. You talk about him constantly, or if not constantly, with that dreamy tone in your voice and a spar-kle in your eyes. You have been in love with him for months. I would've mentioned it if you hadn't been so resistant to subjects of the heart. I thought I imagined it. But of course, I don't have a great imagination, so I was right."

"I am not in love with Freddie. We are friends, Alice."

"I don't believe you, but if you say so, then you really need a suitor." She raised a triumphant brow. "And to find a suitor, you need a party. I have an idea."

Her glee silenced me. I waited to hear, holding my breath.

"My birthday is April 25. What if I say that from now on, your birthday is also April 25?"

"Why would you say that when it's not true?"

"You've always told me you don't know your birthday. You celebrate it on the date you first arrived in England. We're going to change that."

"You can't just do something like that, can you?"

She smiled with the lips of a conspirator. "I am the new Princess Royal of Windsor Castle, now that my sister is married. I could make it a law."

"Your mother could make it a law. And you're not the Princess Royal. There can only be one. So I don't believe you can."

She shook my shoulder gently but firmly. "Stop punching holes in my plan. I am submitting a proclamation—April 25, 1860, is Princess Sarah's and Princess Alice's birth date. The two will celebrate their shared seventeenth birthdays with a debutante ball—and a grand reception hall filled with prospective suitors."

"I don't celebrate birthdays, Alice."

"We're going to have a ball for our birthdays. My mother will give us permission, and Mrs. Phipps, and her daughter Harriet, will orchestrate everything. It is last minute, but the royal household knows how to respond quickly, especially when throwing a ball."

Princess Alice could be as stubborn as her mother.

I was speechless.

Alice nudged me in the side. "Now, aren't you glad you learned the Viennese waltz?"

* * *

It snowed on a Wednesday afternoon in March of 1860, and it was too cold outdoors to be anywhere other than in front of a burning fireplace with a cup of hot tea and the smell of a hearty stew winding through the house from the kitchen range.

Freddie and I had finished our tea and had been working on piano duets in the drawing room. That day, we were absorbed by Schubert's Fantasie in F minor, a composition for four hands. Freddie and I were close to conquering it when an urgent summons disrupted the afternoon's serenity. Mrs. Schon had received a telegram from Freetown, Sierra Leone, with news that needed to be shared immediately.

Whatever joy we'd felt about Schubert's music vanished when we entered the library and saw Mrs. Schon's tear-filled eyes.

The Reverend Schon held his wife with one strong arm around her shoulders. The dread and sadness were familiar, like a twisted ankle that constantly ached when it rained.

"Someone is dead," I whispered to Freddie as we stood near the long bookcase in the back of the room.

I was right. Reverend Schon announced the death of Matilda Serrano Davies. Mrs. Schon's tears turned into gut-wrenching sobs. The Schons had known and cared for her long before they met me.

I looked at Freddie and squeezed his hand. "I'm so sorry."

"Tilly's dead. I can't believe it." He didn't let go of my hand.

"Does the letter mention how she died? What happened to her? Oh, poor, poor Tilly. She'd been excited about her family's freedom and traveling to Africa. She loved Africa."

His father replied. "The letter says she passed away in February after a short illness, leaving Captain Davies overwhelmed with grief. I also received a dispatch from Reverend Venn, and it's a tragic situation. I know the reverend and Captain Davies have worked closely over the years on behalf of the Church of England and its missionaries in Africa. It is a blow to those who loved her."

Death never struck gently. What else could it be but tragic? On the contrary, I expected unhappy endings with death at their center. No matter what happens, good or bad, death can show up at any time, but in my experience, it came at the end of a sharp sword or a long rifle.

Matilda's dying after a short illness, with her husband and family at her bedside, seemed oddly like a blessing.

There was no grief or sadness in my heart, just a flutter of loss in my belly. I covered my face with my hands, ashamed I could not feel more.

Freddie, such a lovely soul, wrapped his arms around me. "Don't be sad. Hopefully, she didn't suffer. She was married for such a short time. My heart breaks for her husband and family."

I buried my face against his chest with no intention of raising my head anytime soon. I didn't want him to see my dry eyes.

* * *

MATILDA'S DEATH HAD put a damper on things, but I rebounded as the ball approached. Alice was obsessed with having the most-talked-about event of the season.

It was my first ball, a coming-out ball, a debutante ball (but not exactly, since we would turn seventeen years old instead of eighteen, the year most girls in society made their debut). However, our ball would be the finest ball of the season. April 25, 1860. Except it wasn't my birthday. Or it might be. I didn't know my birth date. But I had agreed with Princess Alice to share her birthday and her ball. So, this year, Princess Alice's birthday and ball belonged to both of us.

With a hairdresser (although I longed for Ann and her boar's-bristle brush) and a lady's maid, a woman named Charlotte, assigned to me, and a private drawing room in Windsor Castle, the anticipation was almost too much to bear.

My nerves were glass and knitting needles. The slightest surprise and I shattered and had to sew myself back together before the next shocking occurrence. My narrow view of what to expect versus the reality of a ball sabotaged my ability to think clearly.

It was going to be a long day, beginning with my hair. The German stylist, a man named Petra, came into the drawing room with an assistant carrying a large trunk. When he opened it, I gasped.

The gadgets, the layers of loose hair—he also had a pair of stilts—confounded me. "What in heaven's name?"

"Have a seat, ma'am, please."

"Oh, very well." I hadn't realized I was standing. But my alarm at the sight of the contents of his trunk had captured my imagination most unpleasantly. I seriously thought about running, but that would have caused a scandal—and I couldn't do that to Princess Alice. She'd worked hard to make this night happen. "What do you intend to do with those things?" I pointed at something Petra had in his trunk I couldn't describe. "Where would that go?"

He rushed to the trunk and shut the lid while giving his assistant a nasty glare. "Not to worry," he said to me. "Your hair is knotty, and the best style must be neat. I think a braided plait that cascades down the back will be most attractive."

I sat on the stool, and he began. It felt as if hours passed with him combing and brushing while I winced and cried out a dozen times—with good reason, for he was clawing into my scalp with a rake. But I didn't put my complaints into words, just groans.

I would have to trust Petra not to make me appear foolish.

In Freetown, I'd taken care of my own hair after Miss Sass and Miss Wilkerson insisted (demanded) I grow it longer. I had been quite comfortable with closely cropped hair, but they said it was unbecoming for a young lady, and Abigail had agreed. She did at least show me how to brush and braid my hair. But since returning to England, the hairstyles and the length of my hair called for attention I couldn't provide. For example, that perfect part down the middle of my head and the low bun, perfectly round, at the nape of my neck, were unachievable with just my two hands. But still, why did Petra require an arsenal?

Another hour or so passed before I heard him take a breath. "I believe we have finished." He and his assistant stepped away from the stool but then walked around me several times, touching a strand of hair here and there, tucking a piece into place in one spot and pulling a strand down in another.

"Very feminine. Very neat," Petra exclaimed.

"May I look?" I asked.

He raised a large mirror, holding it a few feet from my face. It was a complicated braid, and the hair he'd added put extra weight on my neck and back. Nevertheless, it was attractive, and my knotty hair looked smooth and shiny.

Still, I wasn't sure if it was right for me. That's when the lady's maid assigned to me for the day stalked into the room.

I stared at Charlotte with panic in my heart. "How does it look?"

"Immaculate, dear. Very neat. Well done, gentlemen."

It seemed the best I could hope for was "neat." I nodded at Petra. "Thank you."

Petra gathered his things, his trunk, and his assistant and left. Charlotte and I remained, along with the gown I was to wear.

"Are you sure my gown will look as wonderful as those of every other girl at the ball?" I was standing on a platform in my undergarments, ready to be buried in layers of cloth, lace, and manufactured flowers. "Won't my bosoms show?"

"My lady, it is a common ball gown design, and you must enter a ballroom in a stunning dress. This is stunning." Charlotte was a little older and the more mature lady's maid of the royal household. She had helped each of the royal children on at least one occasion. I should have trusted her, but I couldn't help worrying. I didn't want to make a mistake at my first ball that would haunt me for the rest of my days in London. The stares I already received as the African princess in the royal household were enough. I wanted to avoid adding to the list of criticisms.

The African princess. The African princess.

The ball would prove to all of England that I was as worthy of the title of princess as any daughter of Queen Victoria— including her goddaughter, as some called me.

While I mused, Charlotte worked. I glanced in the mirror.

"Isn't the décolletage too low? Should I have a shawl? My arms will be bare." I started shaking.

Charlotte looked dismayed. "You've seen the dress before and tried it on at least four times when the dressmaker visited. Nothing has changed."

"It feels different tonight. Everything is different. The Grand Reception Hall will be crowded with people, and I'll be the only one."

"The only one what, my dear?" asked Charlotte.

"Why is the skirt so heavy? And look at all these layers of puffs and trim, these flowers, ribbons, rosettes, and lace. It may be messy. What do you think?"

Charlotte had been pinning me into the dress, adjusting hems, adding a button where necessary and more things I couldn't dwell on because of my nerves.

But then she stopped. She stood tall and crossed her arms over her chest. The expression on her face wasn't pleasant. "It will be spectacular, trust me, my lady. I would not send you to a ball at Windsor Castle looking foolish."

"Is that a promise, Charlotte?"

"Of course it's a promise." She exhaled a lifetime.

Her eyes spoke loudly. How dare someone, namely me, question her dedication, her loyalty to the queen? "Princess Sarah, what is bothering you so terribly? You doubt everything and everyone around you. This is your day. You are making a grand entrance into British society. Your star has never shone so brightly in the sky as it will on this night."

"But—"

"You are dark-skinned. Yes. A Black girl. You cannot change that, but it should not make you feel less lovely. One of these young men will see you, and his heart will beat faster. His smile will grow broader, and his shoulders will stretch across the sea to touch you with a fingertip."

She turned me around to look in the mirror, and I slowly twirled. The dress against my dark skin was vibrant and beautiful, more so than any dress I'd seen or heard gossiped about.

Charlotte had not lied to me.

"I believe I will give Princess Alice a run tonight."

"So you shall, Princess Sarah."

She wasn't wrong. My dance card was one shy of full, but I was keeping that spot open.

I had danced perfectly for every waltz, polka, and galop I performed. That was what Princess Alice told me at the end of the evening. Afterward, exhausted, we lounged on the settee in her drawing room.

"I think we should have a ball every month," I said boldly.

"You do?" She laughed. "What was your favorite part?"

"I didn't have one part I preferred over another."

"Weren't you surprised when Frederick Schon arrived and invited you to dance?"

I'd been floored, almost unable to breathe, when he walked up to me and asked for a dance, but I was not about to admit that to Alice. "I don't believe I was surprised. Did I look surprised?" Or desperately pleased at being held in his arms? I hoped not. "I didn't know you'd sent him an invitation."

"Oh my, Sarah. Of course I did. I know how you feel about Freddie. He had to be here. Although he didn't stay long."

He'd left after our dance, which I planned to ask him about when I returned home, but to Alice, I voiced curiosity. "I'm not sure why he came only to stay for one dance."

She laughed. "Perhaps it was the only dance that mattered to him."

"You must stop reading Jane Austen, Your Royal Highness," I said in a scolding voice. "She will be your ruin."

She chuckled. "She's a favorite author, dear. But I think it's you who are the romantic."

I didn't think so, not until that night.

* * *

"Can you believe this?" I marched into the Palm Cottage kitchen, waving the day's newspaper. "There is an article in the *Daily Telegraph* that dares speculate on my marriage prospects." My horror was clearly displayed in my outraged tone and trembling hands. "Why would this be news?"

"Please don't read the newspaper at the table, dear," said Mrs. Schon.

I tossed it on the floor and sat. "It's garbage, anyway. I should throw it out." I scanned the faces at dinner, seeking understanding and pausing to catch Freddie's eye, but he avoided my gaze. He had arrived from his school in Canterbury minutes before we sat for dinner. The South Eastern Railway had been running late, he said. But his tardiness was no excuse for being seemingly uninterested in what had upset me. "Freddie, you don't agree?"

"Sorry, I haven't had a chance to read it." He glanced toward the floor. "Maybe later."

"That newspaper reporter knows nothing of my suitors," I exclaimed.

Since the seventeenth-birthday ball I shared with Alice, several young suitors from Britain (and several other countries) had sought my attention. But adding that to my outrage would have sounded vain. Still, imagine an African princess courted with the same zeal as a princess in Her Majesty's court—in a country like England.

I was no fool. My dark skin impeded some suitors. But not

all. Many appreciated my Blackness or ignored it because they were charmed by me.

I sat pouting, wishing Freddie wasn't behaving in such an odd manner. I wanted him to be as aggravated as I was and to show his concern by listening intently to me, whether I was being logical or acting like a lunatic.

Right then, he put his fork down and finally met my gaze. He smiled at me. "Now, what were you saying?"

"I am in a tizzy, and don't tease me."

"Sarah. Frederick. Please eat your dinner, and would someone pick up that newspaper off the floor," said Mrs. Schon, laying down the law in her genteel fashion.

Ann moved from a corner, grabbed the paper, and handed it to Freddie. "Did you drop this, sir?" She knew perfectly well I'd done it, but she was quick-witted and could see Freddie and I were in a dramatic mood. Or I was.

"Ahh, thank you, Ann." He folded the newspaper, placed it in his lap, and picked up his fork. "And yes, Mama. I am hungry." He proceeded to shove food into his mouth. I lowered my head and exhaled my exasperation. Then I ate my dinner, too.

We finished our meal without returning to the topic of the newspaper article, but then Reverend Schon led us to his study to translate another section of the Bible into another African language. During translations, Freddie and I were focused. Always. When we were done, I retreated to the library to read.

"What are you doing up so late?" he asked, entering the library hours later.

"Waiting for you, of course. Where have you been?"

"I was playing cards with some of my friends."

"Your father doesn't mind you gambling?"

"I didn't say I was gambling."

"Or drinking?"

"I'm nearly eighteen, Sarah. I can do as I please."

"Yes and no. Were you behaving in such a way as a future missionary would behave?" I asked teasingly.

"You should hear yourself. There are times when your teasing goes too far."

I was shocked. He wasn't teasing me back. He was angry. "What is wrong with you? I didn't mean anything. What has happened?"

"It is unimportant. Just a situation at school today I should've avoided but didn't."

I put my book down. "Come on, Freddie, tell me."

His jaw tightened, but he pushed out what was on his mind. "I lied. I read the newspaper article—as did half the men in my class."

Freddie attended the King's School in Canterbury, a prestigious public school for boys, and his classmates were the sons of British aristocrats and noblemen. The story about me must have embarrassed him.

"Oh, it was a hideous article," I said, my tone as soothing as I could muster. "The reporter knows nothing about me or my life. It was laughable. I shouldn't have been so upset."

"Don't you know it doesn't matter what the truth is once a story appears in the newspaper?" The words flew as if he were spitting vinegar from his mouth. "Even the tallest tale becomes something people can make fun of once they've read it in a news sheet."

His anger surprised me. "Did you get into a fight about me because of that article?"

"It was the principle of the thing that bothered me. The way these boys assumed everything they read about you was the truth. It annoyed me. That's all."

"Oh, so it could've been about anyone, and you would've had the same reaction." I grinned.

"You are exasperating," he said. "But you were also offended. I saw that at dinner."

"I was, and still am, deep inside. But I am of the age when a suitor would be appropriate."

"Oh, so you are looking forward to the attention of these young men."

"Drat, Freddie. I'm sorry you had a bad day," I said, then quickly added, "I'm sorry I haven't helped by acting oddly. I was as surprised as anyone to see that article in the newspaper."

He looked at me, arms folded, but with less strain in his mouth. "Honestly, I'd rather not think of you as having suitors."

Aha. I'd had a feeling that was it. "Don't worry. No one I met at the ball has captured my serious interest."

"Well, that's good news."

I laughed, and he did, too, after chewing the skin from his lower lip. Then we played backgammon and didn't mention one more word for the rest of the evening about his day at school or the *Daily Telegraph*.

Chapter Thirty-one

*Palm Cottage, Gillingham, England,
and Windsor Castle, 1860*

Following the news of Matilda's death, Freddie and I spent more time together. We missed her in different ways. Freddie mourned her. I hated that he'd lost his first love. I don't think he knew she was his first love, but no matter, he'd lost her, which hurt him. I saw the pain in his face and heard the ache in his voice every time I looked at him, every time he spoke.

"Do you want to talk about her? I will listen if you'd like to."

Freddie and I sat on the back porch, looking at the garden. I was seated in my favorite wicker rocking chair, and he sat with his back to me on the top step of the landing.

"What was it that you said?" he asked.

"Matilda. Do you wish to talk about her?"

"What do you expect me to say?" His words were more demanding than his voice. "I am sorry she is dead. I am sorry she died so close to having everything she wanted from life. It was a tragedy." He rubbed a hand over his eyes, but I couldn't tell if he had wiped away tears or the memory of her. "Think about it. We work hard to get what we want, and when we have it all, poof, it's taken away." He turned, leaned against the column, and looked at me. "I don't have to tell you these things. You've seen horrors no one should ever see. You survived more than I could imagine. You and Matilda are rare women. More courageous and full of life than anyone I've ever met."

It broke my heart to see him hurting, but I listened and tried to understand how a conversation about Matilda was also about me.

"She and I were very different, Freddie. But I understand why you clump us together, I suppose."

He closed his eyes, shaking his head. "Sarah, I didn't mean it that way."

"I guess you wouldn't know anything about Matilda or me if it had not been for the monsters who enslaved us." I had no reason for the anger that suddenly overtook me. But I couldn't stop it from spilling out of me. "Your pity exists because of men like King Gezo and those barbarians who took Matilda's family and enslaved her and them. The world doesn't look at coloreds as human. Even the so-called decent, God-fearing men and women see Blacks as people to be saved from themselves." I took a deep breath, closed my eyes, and counted backward from ten. "Matilda was just a girl like me. She never asked to be a cause. Never wanted to be enslaved. She wanted to live and love, as any woman should have a chance to do. Don't you see, Freddie, she died, and we don't even know how. We know she's no longer on this Earth, but she wasn't only a cause. Do you hear me? She was a girl like me."

I covered my face briefly with my hands. Shame swallowed me as I glared at him. "I am a Black princess, and no matter how dark my skin or the scars I have on my face, I have a right to happiness, just like Matilda, but happiness is something I shouldn't expect. But you do? You do not doubt that happiness is in your future. Do you know what I mean?"

His hand was balled into a fist as he tapped on the hardwood floor of the back porch. It sounded like the rhythm of despair, grief, and anger. He couldn't stop making the sound. "You know, when she first came here years ago, I asked Matilda a thousand questions, and she answered every single one. Then one day, she said, if you're done, let's play, and I never asked her another question.

"I miss her because she was a kind girl. Funny, and I had a crush on her when I was young. Not because she was brown. But because she was my friend."

He cleared his throat and rose from the stoop. "I think the cook is making ice cream today. Shall we go see?" He straightened his vest jacket, tugging it down to align with his trousers. When he reached out his hand to help me from my seat, I accepted it without hesitation and didn't let go until I stood comfortably on my two feet. How quickly my mood changed.

Our intertwined fingers lingered.

We stared into each other's eyes. My heart raced in my chest. It was more than holding hands—his touch was familiar and different at once. I wasn't afraid or hesitant when he didn't let go, and I didn't tear my gaze away from his. We were getting closer to something, something unexpected. No, something inevitable.

But nothing would happen today.

"Ice cream sounds perfect," I said.

He released my hand, and we walked back into Palm Cottage toward the kitchen.

* * *

IT WAS THE first week in May of 1860. Only a couple of months had passed since we'd learned of Matilda's death. The Schon family still grieved. Freddie, too. She'd been close to everyone, his parents and the house staff, and she was my roommate. But I probably knew her the least because I never tried to know her well. I enjoyed her company. There were moments when I called her a friend. But mainly, I had been preoccupied with myself, my worries, my battles, and what I wanted in my life.

But a letter I received that May morning had Matilda's name written all over it—and with a question asked of me that set my temper ablaze.

"What kind of insensitive man would write this three months after his wife's death?" Although I was alone on the back porch of Palm Cottage, I said this out loud, slumped down in the wicker rocking chair. I held the letter in my hand, not having read it carefully but enough to peg Captain James P. L. Davies as an egotistical, heartless human. "How could he?" I said, staring at the scribbling on the paper. "How dare he?"

"What are you raging on about, Sarah?"

I jerked forward in the chair, startled.

It was Freddie, but once I saw his worried face, I didn't wish to launch into a conversation where poor Matilda's name would be bandied about. "Give me a moment," I said.

"Are you injured?" He stepped out of the doorway and walked toward me, looking anxious.

I shook my head. "I'm just so angry I can't breathe. So let me catch my breath." I closed my eyes and placed a hand on my chest.

He watched me as if I'd been struck and lied about it. His impatience showed up next.

"All right, I can see you are breathing," he said. "Now tell me, what's wrong?"

Suddenly, my temper was twice as hot. I waved the letter at

him and shouted, "This! This is what's wrong. The most arrogant, thoughtless, vain correspondence ever put to paper. I honestly can't believe he had the gall to send it to me. And then ask me for my hand in marriage, as if I'd consider such a thing from a stranger. A man who only months ago was married to my roommate, whose grave is still fresh in the ground."

My condemnation of the man who wrote the letter and its contents continued uninterrupted for several minutes as Freddie waited for the anger to run out of me.

When I finally stopped ranting, he tilted his head, his eyes grave. "So Matilda's widowed husband asked you to marry him?" It sounded even more incredible coming out of Freddie's mouth.

"He doesn't know me. We haven't met, and that's not the worst of it. Such disrespect for his deceased wife, a woman he surely knows was acquainted with me." I started rocking back and forth in the chair. "Then what else does he do in this letter? He callously mentions how much money he's contributed to missionaries and CMS schools in Sierra Leone and Lagos—one hundred pounds." I rolled my eyes in frustration. "Am I to be persuaded to wed him because he donated a fortune to schools in Africa?" I pause as a realization strikes me like a boulder from a mountaintop. "My God. He lives in Africa. Africa! I would never live in Africa."

I had begun rocking so fast, I might have broken the chair if not for Freddie's firm hand on the arm, stopping my wild ride. He then moved a chair across the porch closer to the rocker and sat before me.

"Sarah, I want to help if I can." He held my hands between his. "But you need to calm yourself. This kind of hysteria is not healthy. You are in no danger at this moment of walking down a church aisle." His voice was kind, soft, and mildly teasing.

"I'm sorry if my tirade sounded self-centered."

"Not at all. It is rather bold of him and causes me to question his true feelings for Matilda." When he said this, I could hear the lingering grief. "How could he propose to someone he's never met less than three months after Matilda's death?"

"So you see—what a despicable man." My rage flared again.

Freddie cleared his throat. "So I can assume you aren't going to marry him."

I looked at him, stunned. "I'm not marrying him!"

"Then, as soon as you are completely calm, respond to his letter and tell him your answer is no. Then forget about it and him."

I placed both of my hands over my heart. Of course, I hadn't mentioned everything in the letter to Freddie and had no intention of doing so, but still, I asked him, "Should I say anything to anyone else about the letter?"

Freddie gave me a wary look. "I believe the most important task you face is letting Captain Davies know your answer. Anyone else I don't think of as relevant."

I nodded in outward agreement, folded the letter, and held it in my fisted hand. But Captain Davies had mentioned someone in the letter whom Freddie and I both knew quite well. Reverend Henry Venn, one of the most honored men in England for his work with missions and missionaries for the Church of England.

He was relevant.

In the letter, the captain claimed that the reverend had endorsed our engagement. Reverend Venn had encouraged a man

I'd never met and couldn't possibly love to ask for my hand in marriage. Freddie and I had spent hours and hours in Reverend Venn's home. We saw him frequently at Palm Cottage, assisting him with translations.

He was a guest, as I was, at royal gatherings. So why wouldn't he mention that Captain Davies had inquired about me? Why wouldn't he tell me? Why keep it a secret? Just because I was a woman? No. That wasn't it. There was some other reason, but I couldn't imagine what it might be.

* * *

I DIDN'T TELL Princess Alice about the letter. I hadn't told anyone other than Freddie and Captain Davies, who, by a month later, had received my reply politely declining his marriage proposal. I figured the letter would take at least thirty-three days to reach him in Africa. So I was satisfied the incident was behind me.

Meanwhile, Princess Alice had decided that we needed to have an adventure. I disagreed. I was almost thankful when Harriet Phipps happened upon us, but she, too, had lost some of her fire of late and didn't attempt to stop us. Not that she knew where we were headed. Then again, Harriet's lack of interest could be explained. Her Majesty had arranged Alice's engagement, which hadn't been publicly announced, but Harriet had done the planning. The wedding would occur the following year, December 1861, but some days, Harriet seemed panicked. That left Alice as the new arbiter of our fate. And she had plans.

"Stop worrying, Sarah. It is unlike you to be so squeamish about an adventure."

"I can't help it. I don't think we should be here."

After a long carriage ride, we entered a new part of London for both of us: the East End. I had longed to visit the neighborhood where the cabin boy, William, had lived, but it was worse than he'd let on. There was filth, poverty, crowds, noxious fumes, and people with toothless grins and soot-smudged faces. But they held their heads high. I could see in their sunken eyes where William had learned about courage.

We'd taken precautions, dressing in costume to avoid being recognized, but I was nonetheless worried. I wasn't interested in making any more newspaper headlines, but Alice brushed aside my concerns, and the next thing I knew, we were at this café for a lecture by a poetess and model named Christina Rossetti. She had modeled for her brother Dante Gabriel, a member of a group of painters, poets, and photographers called the Pre-Raphaelite Brotherhood.

"Weren't the Pre-Raphaelites the rage five years ago and for five years before that?" I remarked, with hostility in my tone. "And weren't they condemned by Dickens and others for their work and behavior?"

She smiled coyly. "I think that's entirely true."

We were led to our seats at a small table, with another dozen small tables scattered throughout an elegantly decorated room. I looked around at the paintings covering the walls and the stunning, beautifully ornate glass vases on the tables, holding stalks of celery. I was impressed with the café but still wary about why we were there.

"I really am looking forward to hearing her speak. She refuses to marry. Isn't that amazing? She has broken off at least one engagement and declined several proposals. Imagine that."

I nearly gagged. Here I'd just refused a marriage proposal, but I had more than reasons. I had principles. "We shouldn't be here," I said. My nerves were knives twirling in my belly. "Our reputations could be ruined if we're found out."

She leaned forward, elbows planted on the tabletop. "No one will recognize us. We are in costume." Alice grinned. She had made an earnest effort to disguise herself. A tightly wrapped scarf around her head, powder on her face, and rouge on her cheeks. She had also stained her lips red.

On the other hand, I could do little to disguise myself. But I made an effort to appease Alice. I had also covered my head with an elaborately wrapped scarf and wore large earrings.

"We're here, and we'll listen to what Christina Rossetti has to say." Alice gave me a grave look. "I'm getting married eventually, and we won't have many more chances to enjoy our girlhood. So stop complaining, please."

I saw the sadness in her eyes and understood why our adventure was important. It was just that I was jittery after what I'd been through lately. I still couldn't believe Reverend Venn had approved Captain Davies's proposal without thinking to let me know.

I took a deep breath. "I forgot. Your reputation cannot be ruined. You are engaged to a German prince," I said teasingly.

"A minor prince, and I am not engaged officially. Nothing's been announced." Now she stared at me with curiosity. "Are you going to tell me what is going on with you? You never complain like this about an outing."

"I am sorry. I guess I am preoccupied."

I stared at my hands, debating. Should I tell her? Honestly, I was bursting to tell her.

"It's a huge secret, and you can't mention it to anyone. Promise?"

"Yes, I promise. Now tell me."

"I received a letter with a marriage proposal from an African businessman and former officer in the British Navy."

Her eyes nearly popped from her head. She recovered only to lean so far across the table that I feared she'd lie on it. "What's his name? Tell me everything."

I did just that, and as I rambled on, I stumbled headlong into the information about Reverend Henry Venn. "Can you believe he'd do something like that? I would have thought he'd say something to me. Or even Mrs. Schon. What right did he have to participate in making arrangements for my wedding?"

Slowly, Alice straightened her spine and pulled down her shoulders. Then she looked me in the eye with the most severe expression I'd ever seen on her face. "He wouldn't have done such a thing, Sarah. Not unless he'd been instructed to do so. And the only person who has that authority over you is Her Majesty, the queen of England. My mother, Victoria."

"I don't understand. What are you saying? That he acted with the queen's permission? She agreed?"

At that moment, Christina Rossetti stepped onto the raised platform. The small audience applauded, and she began her talk.

I sat stiffly, unable to hear, barely able to see. The only thing in my head was disbelief.

Chapter Thirty-two

London, England, 1860

Sometimes a wasp flies into a hornet's nest.

In October of 1860, I was seventeen (or thereabouts), bold, thoughtful, intelligent, independent, quick-tempered, opinionated, prideful, and worried. I had declined my first marriage proposal, possibly supported by Her Majesty. How much trouble was I in? It had been months since I'd responded to the proposal, and nothing had happened.

I was free, and my life had blossomed.

Freddie and I had taken the train to London one Sunday afternoon and disembarked at our usual stop, the London Paddington Station. We had a leisurely day planned. Tea in a café, holding hands while walking through the park, where we could risk being slightly scandalous. No one recognized him, and when I wasn't with the royal family, I could disappear on a busy London street filled with people from around the globe.

The park near Kensington Palace was a favorite spot. On this day, it shimmered with brilliant colors and a crispness in the air that exhilarated rather than chilled.

"Freddie, I want to talk to you about something," I said as we walked next to each other in perfect rhythm, as if we were playing a duet on the piano.

"You've been quiet most of the way here. I thought there was something on your mind. But I assumed you'd tell me when you were ready."

"How do you always know?"

"Know what?" he asked.

"You always can tell if there is something on my mind. That's all."

He smiled shyly. "So what is it? What's troubling you, Sarah?"

I brought my hand to my lower lip and started tugging at it with my fingertips as if I could pull the words from my mouth. Why was it hard to say three words?

"Sarah?"

"Sorry, yes. I was daydreaming."

"You had something you wanted to share." He took my hand and held it lightly on his forearm.

His soft touch helped the words come. "I think I love you. But, no, that's not right. I do love you. I love you."

"I love you, too," he said hesitantly. Then he stopped me with a hand on my shoulder and narrowed his eyes. "Are you saying you love me because we are like brother and sister?"

"Oh, God, no. The other way."

"Oh, thank God." His voice was a whimper, as if he had dropped his heart on the ground and picked it up, only slightly bruised.

We had stopped walking, and when I looked down, I was surprised to see that we were holding each other's hands and squeezing tightly. We stood close to one another, and it felt like such a wonderful place to stand, close to him. I had confessed my heart, and he had boldly confessed his own.

Had I heard him correctly?

I wouldn't say I liked the burst of doubt that had attacked me. But, like a spider, it had built a web so quickly that I barely noticed I was trapped.

"I need to tell you something. And please do not become angry with me," Freddie said, pulling me to a spot between an English oak and an iron bench. "Listen to me until I finish, will you?"

"Yes."

"I never thought you could care about me the way I cared about you. But, and I believed this sincerely, I had to protect my heart because I kept falling more deeply in love with you."

"What did you do?"

"I courted another girl. But there was nothing real between us. Just a couple of walks in the park. That was all. But I might've led her to believe there was a chance for us one day. Even if I knew better."

My breath caught, and I struggled to stand and listen to Freddie. It was as if my legs wanted to make a run for it, escape, and leave the rest of me alone. "How could you? Why didn't you tell me you were courting another? That would have been a friend's duty. A brother's duty, if that's how you thought I felt about you—as if you were my brother, not my lover."

"Sarah, she was not my lover. You are my love."

The sense of betrayal that had descended upon me lifted. I thought about the *Daily Telegraph* newspaper article about the suitors I had supposedly encouraged. Perhaps he had a right to do what he'd done. And more important, he had told me about it.

Then a commotion flared up a few feet from us—a scrummage erupted between street peddlers. Freddie linked his arm through mine and led us away from the mayhem.

"Sarah, we need to leave now," Freddie said, our arms interlocked.

I needed a moment to gather my wits and pulled away. "It's fine. That ruckus is nothing. I just need a few moments. Can I meet you back at the train station? I know my way."

"Are you angry with me?"

"No, I just need to think on my own for a few moments."

"Sarah, after that newspaper article about you and suitors, I thought you wanted something else. Someone else. Not a minister's son. You love the life of the royals. You thrive on tea parties, balls, and the theater. I thrive on strawberry patches, Sunday sermons, and the *Daily News* and *Times*. I gave up hope of you ever looking at me with eyes of love. But my God, Sarah, I do love you."

"I love you, too. But I must take a walk for a while. I will meet you at the station in an hour."

The crowd had gotten unruly, and I quickly slipped between a group of brawlers who I hoped would cover my departure so that Freddie would have to do as I had asked.

"All right, then," he called. "I will meet you in an hour."

I was surprised he hadn't objected further, but I did need some time and wandered the streets for several blocks until I had to admit I was lost. I asked strangers for directions, but their responses only confused me more. So I gave up. I'd reach the train station sooner or later.

A large group of people were huddled outside the entrance to a small theater, all very excited. I was drawn to them—and the billboard that heralded the afternoon's entertainment: a freedman from America performing his escape from a crate on board a slave ship. "Entertainment" was the word that struck me as I paid my penny for admission.

The audience was deeply moved and cheered loudly when the man stood proudly, chains dropping with a loud clang to the floor, proof he was bound no longer.

I sat back in my seat and exhaled, unaware until that moment that I'd hardly taken a breath during his performance. The crate and his actions were dramatic, but the battle for freedom that began in his heart and soul affected me the most. Memories of the long-ago past flooded my mind—memories of my lost family and friends.

I was suddenly angry for allowing self-pity and sadness to crawl inside my brain. My pact to leave those days behind me was like sand in an hourglass. They were always moving from one upside-down place to the next.

My family in Africa would never be replaced. Love now took on a different hue, not the bright colors of the forest, the river, or the night sky. My ability to love and be loved had shades only of purple and blue.

I rose to my feet and moved as if the man on the stage were chasing me, trying to force me into his crate. I had to flee this place or die. Then I slammed into someone much taller than me and staggered backward until a hand caught my wrist.

"Sarah. Are you all right?"

It was Freddie.

I wrapped my arms around his neck and held him as tightly as possible.

He bent forward to hug me around my waist as his other hand moved gently over my back, caressing me.

"We are in the middle of a theater, Sarah. I think people are staring."

I eased my embrace, pulling slightly away to look into his eyes. "Do you care?"

He smiled an achingly lovely smile. "I do not."

"Thank you for finding me."

"I never left, I just lost sight of you for a while, but I kept asking about a beautiful Negro girl, who might appear lost, but is never the type to admit it."

"Oh, so we're going to argue about my stubbornness?"

"No. I love everything about you, Sarah."

I pulled my arms down to my sides. "What are we going to do about all of this?"

"What if we married? That would be a grand idea. Then we could move to Africa where I could minister on behalf of the Church of England, and you could—"

"Become a missionary? Heavens, no," I said emphatically. But, as if a garden of roses had blossomed over my head, I knew what I wanted from my life. "I want to write novels about adventure and falling in love. That would mean everything to me."

Freddie took my hand and linked it around his forearm. We walked side by side, arm in arm, and talked.

"Are we going to make it back to Palm Cottage tonight?"

He removed his watch from his pocket. "We may have missed the last train."

I focused on keeping the panic in my stomach from rising. "It will be a scandal if we don't come home tonight."

He held both my hands between his large ones. "I have an idea. It is risky, but it's better than sleeping on a stone bench at the train station. We can stay at the home of a friend who lives in the center of London."

His friends welcomed us warmly. We chatted briefly but were exhausted and went to our separate rooms and slept soundly.

The following day, Freddie hurried to the nearest telegraph

station and wired his parents, assuring them we were safe and had spent the night in the home of Mr. and Mrs. Wendell, the parents of one of his classmates.

We had a lovely train ride back home, full of laughter and conversations about making plans, what to do first, and who to tell of our newly confessed love.

Little did we know that, filled with worry, Freddie's parents had contacted the royal family, alerting Her Majesty that their eldest son and her goddaughter were missing.

Then, after the Schons received our telegraph, they immediately informed Windsor Castle through Mrs. Phipps that their son and Sarah had spent the night in London at one of their son's friends' homes. However, they did not know the family and could not vouch for them.

It was indeed a hornet's nest.

Chapter Thirty-three

Windsor Castle, 1860

After my overnight trip with Freddie to London, we'd somehow avoided scandal, and things had calmed down in the Schon and royal households. Everything outwardly seemed as it had been before. Freddie and I spent most evenings together at Palm Cottage, translating scriptures, playing board games, and playing duets on the grand piano. I must admit we were never alone in the house. Mrs. Schon, Reverend Schon, Darugu, and even Ann would be in the same room with us.

After church services on Sunday, we'd still take the train to London and visit the parks. On those occasions Freddie talked about our future. I smiled and listened and tried to imagine a life with him.

But I also spent time with the royal family, and one evening in November, Alice and I were in the princess's bedchamber preparing for a charity ball Alice was hosting in the Grand Reception Hall that night. The ball honored Florence Nightingale's nursing school at St. Thomas Hospital, which was celebrating its one-year anniversary. It was the first such school for nursing in England, perhaps in the world, according to the newspapers, and fervently supported by Princess Alice.

And no, I hadn't given up on my support of Mary Seacole. But a princess was a princess, and a ball was a ball.

We had taken a break from our preparations for oolong tea and biscuits. The lady's maid had stepped aside, too. Our gown fitting could be delayed for a moment.

We sipped tea and chatted about the composers Liszt, Wagner, Brahms, and the concert pianist Clara Schumann. We were close to a battle over which one was the true romantic when somehow the conversation shifted to Harriet Phipps.

Alice and I had different opinions of her.

"She is now a confidante of the queen's," Alice said. "Spying on us is no longer her assignment."

"She still makes me uncomfortable, and I think she still relishes interrupting our plans," I said. "Claiming she is performing her duties at the request of the queen. Conveniently, if you ask me."

"Her Majesty's business is now far more interesting than us."

"Of course it is, but Harriet is our age, and I think she has been jealous of our friendship for some time. She just blamed Her Majesty for the disappointments she caused us. The theater tickets she canceled, the private trips to London she revealed, and the late-night excursions to the castle's kitchen she reported. These were just a few adventures spoiled by Harriet," I said emphatically.

Alice laughed. "Eat another biscuit. It will help make you less disagreeable."

Harriet, a woman with great timing, entered the princess's chamber just then, looking like a pan of boiling water on a hot stove.

I almost saw steam coming from her ears when she swept into the chamber. Of course, there was no steam, but better to imagine that than horns rising from the sides of her head.

"What's wrong, Harriet?" Alice asked the overheated woman.

"You look like the world is collapsing. Therefore, tell me quickly so I can return to my fitting for this gown."

"Yes, ma'am. Of course, ma'am. There have been some changes that—"

"You look divine, Alice," I said, deliberately cutting off Harriet. "The dress is extremely becoming on you. You'll be the talk of the nurses' ball."

"Thank you, Sarah. But you are the next pincushion for our dressmaker," she said teasingly about the woman who had been her seamstress for years. "Pray she doesn't adjust the bodice too much. I can scarcely breathe."

"Hush, Your Highness, and be still, or I might stick you," said the seamstress.

Alice chuckled, and Harriet rustled her skirt. "Ma'am, if you don't mind, I have a message from the queen."

"Oh, yes. You have an urgent matter to relate, yes, Harriet?" Alice said with an apologetic tone. "Please, please proceed."

"Thank you." She curtsied. "The queen has asked that you lead the first dance on the arm of Prince Louis of Hesse."

"I didn't know the prince would be here," Alice said stiffly. "The ball is only hours away. I should have known if he was joining us. I would have planned if I had been aware."

"Yes, ma'am." Harriet stared at the floor, her lower lip stiffening. "A courier arrived late last night and delivered the message to the queen."

"And no one thought to let me know?" Alice's voice had risen an octave, making her dissatisfaction apparent.

I rarely saw her get angry in front of anyone other than me.

The seamstress had moved a few feet away from Alice. I walked over to her and took her hand. "Is there anything I can do? I don't mind taking on more of the hostess duties."

Her lips trembled. "Thank you, dear Sarah."

"It is no trouble," I said. "Besides, the ball is our idea. I know as much as you about the ball and its purpose."

"That won't be necessary, Sarah." This was Harriet, taking her turn to interrupt Alice and me.

"What won't be necessary?" Alice asked. "What do you mean? But of course Sarah can help me. She represents the royal household."

"The queen will host, since Prince Louis will be in attendance. She wants you to spend as much time as possible together."

"Oh, I see," said Alice with a slight shrug and a "there's nothing I can do" expression. "Sarah, why don't you finish with the seamstress?"

Harriet cleared her throat.

"Yes, Harriet. Is there something more?"

"Miss Sarah has a guest waiting."

"A guest? Who? And hours before a ball." I looked from Harriet to Alice in confusion. "Why would someone come to Windsor Castle unbeknownst to me and assume I'd meet him?"

"That is bold," Alice said. "Unless a member of the royal family invited them to the castle to meet you."

I heard Alice. But I was waiting for Harriet to answer my first question. "Who is this person?"

"Captain James P. L. Davies."

* * *

"Miss Bonetta." He bowed. "It is my pleasure."

"Captain Davies." I greeted him politely, but the conversation needed to run its course quickly. I had a ball to attend. "I was not expecting to hear from you after responding to your letter a few months ago."

I watched the smallest wince cross his brow as he stood in the middle of the Green Drawing Room. A tall, broad-shouldered man with a wide forehead, long nose, and full mouth, he was dressed in a black frock coat, straight trousers, a short waistcoat, and a shirt with a stiff collar. The fabrics were the most expensive money could buy; even from a distance I surmised that much. And considering it was November and beastly cold in England but blazing in Africa, he looked remarkably unbothered.

"I wrote that letter with sincerity, truth, and thoughtfulness. But I apologize for whatever distress it might have caused you." His voice was deep, a baritone, but his accent was not African. He spoke as if he had been born and raised a British gentleman. He must have been educated in England or by missionaries.

"You are here to see me, but I have no idea what subject you wish to discuss, sir."

He gestured toward one of the chairs at the center table. "Would you like to sit, miss?"

"No, thank you." I held my distance and remained near the entrance, hoping for a short conversation. A bonus if my stance caused him to feel awkward or distressed or if he had to rush through whatever he'd come to say.

He rested a hand on the back of the chair. "We met some years ago at the Female Institution. You probably don't remember. You were only a child." In two strides, he had moved next to the portrait of Prince Albert in his military uniform that hung on the wall.

"I'm sorry, but I don't remember you. Is that why you traveled here? To reminisce about a meeting only you recall?" I strived to make my voice lighthearted, but from his raised brow, I was failing. "Surely you had something more on your mind."

"You are quite right, Miss Bonetta." He crossed the room, stopping a foot away from me. "I don't know if you know my background. I am an entrepreneur—a man of means. I have traded along the River Niger. I have supported and built schools throughout West Africa, seeking to support avenues of education and advancement for free Africans, from whom I am proud to be descended. My parents were enslaved but rebuilt their lives as free people, well-educated and devout. They raised my siblings and me with the same values they cherished—family, children, faith, and enterprise. We are also committed to status and legacy. I have lived a life I am proud of. I am also a British citizen and a member of the Church of England."

"You should be proud of such a prestigious background and ambitious goals. I'm sure you know my history and how I became Her Majesty's ward or goddaughter, as some call me. I am also a princess of Egbado. So you could say we are of equal stature and lineage." I shrugged a shoulder. "So, again, why are you here?"

"Ah, you will not make this easy for me."

"Why would I do that?"

He tilted his head, and I lifted mine in reply. He hadn't moved, but his presence filled the room and made me feel cornered—a feeling I didn't like.

"I am thirty-two years old, Miss Bonetta. I'm not a boy, and I know my mind. I am here to ask again for your hand in marriage."

It was what I expected him to say, but my ire had risen to a boil. First, it was presumptuous of him to think I'd reconsider such a question. Also, how dare he not believe the response I had given him before? "I already replied to your question with a polite no. Please do not force me to be rude by refusing you to your face, sir."

"I had no choice but to ask again, and if need be, I will continue to ask until your answer is satisfactory."

"Captain, I will repeat what I've already expressed in my written reply. I do not wish to marry you. I don't know you. I don't love you, and you were married to my former roommate, Matilda Serrano. I find your proposal callous and uncaring toward me and her memory. Doubly so since she's been dead less than a year."

His body shifted as if something had struck him in the chest. Then he retreated one step, then two, and soon stood behind the chair again, his left hand resting on the bridge.

"She died February seventh." He adjusted the lapel of his frock coat. "I loved Matilda dearly. But I seek to continue my family's legacy and intend to start a family. Together, you and I would form a powerful union. As staunch supporters of England, the church, and the crown, with influential ties to both, we will be able to lead West Africa into its most prosperous decades."

I turned my back and walked toward the floor-to-ceiling window, its red velvet drapes and gold fringe drawn open. The chill of a cold November day allowed me a moment to lessen the shiver inside my chest. Captain Davies had proposed marriage for children and country. Ambition was the man's soul.

It was daunting to have a man you didn't know, let alone love, request your hand in marriage a second time. "You're asking me to spend the rest of my life with you as if you are purchasing real estate. My answer remains unchanged."

"I'm sorry to hear that. I had hoped you'd reconsider your

decision. It's my understanding that your marriage prospects aren't acceptable to the royal family."

I spun around and faced him, but far too quickly. I stumbled and grabbed the back of a chair, holding on tightly to steady myself. Then I let the panic flow through me.

Oh, God. Was he telling the truth? Did Her Majesty know? Did the queen know about Freddie and me? She couldn't. She mustn't. But if she did, was the night Freddie and I spent together in London the problem? No. That couldn't be it. Captain Davies had proposed before that trip.

"What do you know of the royal family's thoughts on my prospects? Where did you pick up such tripe?" I removed my hand from the chair and placed it on my stomach. "When I marry, I will marry for love. Not for politics or whatever influence you seek. I will not be used for your game of power. Sir, I hope you have not invested too much time or money on this fruitless excursion."

I smoothed my skirt, which was already smooth. He might be intelligent, handsome, and wealthy, but that didn't mean he was the man I should marry. I fancied myself ready to tell him this. But instead, I opted for brevity. "I trust you will have a pleasant trip back to Africa."

I marched out of the drawing room and moved down the long corridor, picking up speed until I was running. Arms bent, hands balled into fists, I punched the cold castle air, getting it out of my way. I didn't stop running until I was outside the princess's bedchamber.

Breathing hard, heart pounding, I leaned a hand on the door and closed my eyes, but only briefly. Then I caught my breath.

I had a party to attend.

Chapter Thirty-four

*Palm Cottage, Gillingham, England,
and Buckingham Palace, 1860*

Besides the dancing and as much merriment as I could muster, the ball succeeded in benefiting the nursing school. I was not foolish enough to believe I wouldn't hear something more of Captain Davies and his proposal, but until that moment came, I would carry on as if it had never happened.

I returned to Palm Cottage two days after the ball and awoke groggy. The fireplace blazed in my bedroom, and I struggled to fight the chill of another frigid November day. But the battle was lost, judging from the ache in my lungs and the cough in my chest. I always had a cold in November, and this year wouldn't disappoint.

I slipped out of bed, wrapped myself into a heavy robe, and stepped into my slippers. I sat on the edge of my bed, shivering and wheezing and dreaming of spring, warm sunlight, fresh flowers, and strawberries.

A knock on my door brought me back to winter.

"Come in."

Ann entered, looking unnerved. "My lady." Her fingers trembled, causing the envelope she held to flutter.

"What is it? What's the matter?"

"A message has arrived from Buckingham Palace. Her Majesty is requesting your presence this afternoon."

My morning chill vanished. I rose to my feet. "Are you sure the request is for *this* afternoon?" An invitation from the queen (by way of Mrs. Phipps) usually arrived three days to a month or more before an appointment.

"May I have the envelope, please?" She handed it to me. I read it not because I didn't trust Ann but because my surprise needed confirmation that my hearing wasn't faulty. But then, my shock was replaced by concern. Had I done something wrong? "Did you inform Mrs. Schon?"

She nodded.

"Thank you. Will you help me dress?" I asked.

"Yes, ma'am."

With Ann's help, I was ready in minutes and hurried downstairs to the dining room and breakfast.

"I trust you slept well." Freddie was seated at the breakfast table, and I sat next to him.

"Yes, I slept well."

He and I had spent the evening before in the library, reading our favorite authors, discussing composers and music, and finally deciding to tell his family about us. We had waited to share the news, which was more than fine with me, but it had been over a month since we'd declared our feelings for each other, and Freddie's impatience was showing. Finally, we had agreed that today would be the day. But with the queen's summons, it was apparent today shouldn't be that day.

Of course, I hadn't mentioned my encounter with Captain Davies to anyone, including Freddie. I had barely discussed it with Alice. So my list of secrets was starting to add up.

I stirred the porridge in my bowl. "I received a message from Her Majesty this morning," I said to Freddie and anyone at the table listening. "She has requested my presence at Buckingham Palace this afternoon."

Freddie looked at me with disappointment in his eyes. He knew it meant a delay in our announcement. "Do you know what it's about?"

"I'm sure it's nothing extraordinary." I wasn't sure at all, but it calmed me to hope. "She likely wants me to play the piano, recite some poetry, or agree to be part of a holiday program. She loves to show me off."

He touched the top of my hand. "After breakfast, would you like to join me on a walk?"

Before I could answer, Mrs. Schon clicked her glass.

"Sarah, you don't have time for a stroll. It will take you a couple of hours to prepare for your trip to Buckingham Palace."

So Freddie and I didn't take a walk or talk before I left, which seemed to be for the best. I had glimpsed a flash of something strange in Mrs. Schon's eyes. She appeared her usual pleasant self, but something about her was unusual. Had she known about the queen's request before the messenger arrived?

Was it possible she knew that there was something between her son and me other than friendship? Or did she understand why the queen had summoned me?

Either way, I had to prepare for a visit to Buckingham Palace.

* * *

WHEN I ARRIVED at the palace, I was directed to the White Room, where Harriet Phipps was waiting for me. I had expected Mrs. Phipps, who always escorted me to the queen's chamber.

"Where is your mother? I trust she is well."

"She is fine." Harriet sat at the center table. "If you would." She gestured for me to join her.

Sitting in the needlepoint armchair next to her, I tugged nervously on the fingertips of my kid leather gloves to take them off. I didn't like being nervous around Harriet. "The message I received was from the queen."

"Her Majesty asked me to meet with you for this discussion."

"Oh." I sat stiffly, my spine rigid. My ungloved fingertips, digging into the palm of my hand, were on the verge of drawing blood. I hadn't expected this, whatever this was, but what I sensed wasn't good. Dread filled my chest. "And what subject did she ask you to discuss with me?"

"Captain Davies. You met with him the evening of the nurses' ball and refused his marriage proposal."

I would have collapsed to the floor if I hadn't been seated. "I don't understand. So Her Majesty knew Captain Davies came to see me in the castle unannounced?"

Harriet raised an index finger of her slim, elegant hand. "Shall we have some tea?"

A servant materialized from the wallpaper and disappeared through a doorway. As my anxiety rose, I calmed myself as best I could, but I could read the writing on the wall.

"On behalf of the queen, Mrs. Phipps met with Reverends Schon and Venn, both of whom have known Captain Davies for many years. She invited him to Windsor Castle to meet with you."

I was shaking. "She did? For what purpose?"

"He asked for your hand in marriage, didn't he?"

"Yes," I whispered.

"Mrs. Phipps's inquiries determined that Captain Davies's

finances and suitability for marriage are unparalleled for any African, not only in Lagos but in Africa and parts of Britain."

My nervousness was overcome by my temper, which was beginning to flare. "My meeting with him the other day was the second time I refused to marry him. His first proposal was in a letter he sent me in May, a few months after his wife's death. Was the queen aware of that proposal, too?"

The tea arrived, and Harriet waited for the servant to leave before she replied. "I do not know about this letter, but, likely, Captain Davies did not act without Her Majesty's permission."

I couldn't lift the teacup. I was fearful I'd throw its contents at the red velvet drapes or in Harriet's face. "None of what you have said changes my answer. I will not marry him. I don't know him. I don't love him. And I'm not being disrespectful to the queen. I am honest, and Her Majesty has always advocated for honesty."

"I'm sorry you feel this way, Sarah. But Her Majesty requires that you accept Captain Davies's proposal."

"I won't marry him, Harriet. You can tell the queen, or I will."

She sipped her tea. "Captain Davies is an important man in Africa, England, and the church. He is a trusted ally of Reverend Venn in Lagos and is committed to Lagos becoming a British colony. He supported its annexation and will be in the lead when Lagos is declared a colony. He is a man of God and a man of means. There is no better combination, making him an ideal husband for you, Sarah."

"Why are you not listening to me?" I felt as if I were speaking to a stone. "I will not marry him. I do not care about his wealth, dealings with the church, or with politics in Lagos."

"Sarah, you are making a mistake."

I should have been mindful of Harriet's warning. She was a confidential attendant of Queen Victoria. But that didn't mean I wouldn't speak my mind.

"What are you saying to me? The queen will not even hear my concerns. I want to be in love with the man I marry. Is that so difficult to understand?"

"Sarah, you must stay calm. This is not something you can debate with the queen. I was sent here to deliver a message, and that message is that you will marry Captain Davies."

"And what happens if I refuse to marry him?"

"I advise you not to ask that question or think that way. On the contrary, Her Majesty has been very generous with you and tolerant of some incidents that could have caused the royal family embarrassment."

"I have not said or done anything inappropriate. I have always been mindful of my position in the royal family."

"Your position in the royal family?" Harriet looked astonished. She reached for her teacup and took a sip.

"Why do you take that tone? My position in the royal family has been clear. I am the queen's goddaughter. Therefore, I have been treated like a princess until this moment."

"You've always had illusions about who and what you are. It's time you released them and dealt with the reality." The teacup was back in place, and Harriet folded her hands neatly in her lap.

"I have said all I have to say, but you should remember, the place you live, the clothes you wear, and the food you eat are provided through the generosity of Her Majesty."

"Is the queen threatening to withdraw her support?"

"I did not say that. But it is true. Her Majesty does pay for your clothing, education, and much more."

I sank into the chair, my body boneless, my heart bleeding into emptiness. "It sounds very much like a threat, Harriet."

"Take it as you will. I am tired of this debate," she said, rising to her feet. "I didn't want to tell you this in anger, but you are too stubborn. If you don't marry Captain Davies, the queen will send you to Brighton to live with two matronly women. You will have no access to the lifestyle you have embraced."

The stunned look on my face couldn't compare to the horrible pain of betrayal in my gut. "So the queen will exile me if I don't marry Captain Davies."

"Exile is a term reserved for nobility. You will be sent away."

At those words, I was surprised I did not collapse. Right then and there.

I was numb. How had this happened? Why had this happened? I needed an answer that Harriet couldn't provide.

"I refuse to leave Buckingham Palace without an audience with the queen. Is she in the Throne Room?"

"Yes, she is."

"Excellent." I swallowed the knot in my throat. "I must see her. Indeed, I will see her, and if you wish to avoid a scandal, you should go to the queen now and let her know I'm on my way."

"You are being childish and a fool."

"We are both children. You are what? Three years older than me, at best? I assure you we both have had childish moments recently. But I will march into the Throne Room with or without permission. I want the queen to tell me to my face that I am exiled." The dryness in my throat turned painful. "And I realize the guards will stop me and throw me in prison." I rose and placed a hand on my hip. "But that would be a scandal none of us would want."

Twenty minutes later, I stood before Her Majesty with my chin lifted and shoulders braced.

First, however, I needed to figure out where to begin. It was not as if I could change a queen's mind easily.

My voice came out a pitiful whisper. "Your Majesty, I cannot marry a man I do not love. I am sorry if this angers you."

"I did not ask you to marry him," Queen Victoria said. "The marriage has been arranged."

"I wish we had talked about it."

"And I wish you hadn't gotten lost in London with Frederick Schon."

It was a blow that hit me in the midsection—that night had been a problem for the queen. "Is that why? But nothing happened."

"That's good for your relationship with God Almighty. But honestly, that was not the reason. On the contrary, it simply hastened the situation. You see, I reached out to Captain Davies months ago. As soon as I heard of his first wife's passing from Reverend Crowther and was told of his outstanding work on behalf of the Church of England, I had Mrs. Phipps investigate him. He is a brilliant man with an excellent reputation. And he will treat you with the utmost care and respect."

"How long ago did Mrs. Phipps contact him about me?" I asked weakly.

"March this year, a month after his wife's passing."

Freddie and I had declared our love for one another, unaware that the queen of England had already determined the rest of my life.

I inhaled and exhaled as if loading a weapon, and my breaths were hard and harsh. And I had something I had to get off my chest. "I've never had a chance to choose, but I am choosing now. I will not marry Captain James P. L. Davies. I am in love with someone else, and if I can't be with him, I'd rather not have a husband."

"You are young. But time creeps by when you are alone and lonely."

"I will make the best of whatever situation I am in, ma'am. As I always have."

"You are a stubborn girl, and I am a stubborn queen." She glanced at the servant who had stood discreetly in a corner. "You will leave immediately for Brighton. I've already arranged for you to take some time away from the Schon family residence. A carriage waits for you in the courtyard. The maid at Palm Cottage will be instructed to pack your belongings, which should arrive in Brighton in a few days. The carriage has a small trunk with some personal items and enough clothing for the next week."

And with that, I was dismissed.

"Your Majesty." I took two steps back, turned, and left the Throne Room.

The numbness I'd felt earlier hung on my back like a wet blanket soaked in truth, suffocating me. Any thought of making my own choices in this life vanished with the queen's solemnly delivered order. Why hadn't I understood before? There was always someone somewhere, a queen or a king, who held my life like a puppeteer, making me dance on the stage with no music or audience to cheer me on.

I climbed into the carriage in the courtyard, lifted my feet onto the seat, and hugged my knees.

"Dear Lord, what is to become of me in Brighton?"

PART FOUR

Lost in the Morning Mist

Chapter Thirty-five

Brighton, England, 1860–1861

My new address was 17 Clifton Hill, Brighton. My new family, the Welches (if you could call them a family), lived in a three-story row house on a block a mile's walk from the sea.

The houses on the street appeared to be the same over and over, like mirrors of one another with no space in between. But Clifton Hill was "a salubrious place that was pleasant, clean, and healthy to live in."

Envisioned as a seaside resort a hundred years previously and the home of King George IV's Royal Pavilion and its gardens, Brighton was a retreat from city life for wealthy Londoners. A precious getaway, but not for me. Clifton Hill was my punishment.

Following my exit from the Throne Room, the queen's order that I be taken to Brighton wasn't carried out as she'd intended. After rummaging through the bag in the carriage, I persuaded the driver to return to Palm Cottage. The reason I gave was that my most necessary garments were missing from the bag. The small lie proved successful.

Upon arrival, I raced into the house and the arms of Mrs. Schon. We wept together, holding on to each other fervently, but my eyes sought Freddie—only to learn he had left the house after hearing of my sentence. The cat had been released from the bag. While packing my belongings, the lady's maid must have spread the news of my exile to Brighton throughout the house.

After crying with Mrs. Schon for what felt like an eternity, I returned to the carriage, and the painful realization of my plight dug a path into my heart.

I stared without seeing and listened without hearing as the clop of the horse's hooves and the melody of the countryside melted into nothingness. Sound had vanished, leaving only disbelief, overcoming my senses.

How had I gotten here? How was it possible? Was it a dream? A very bad dream? I couldn't call it a nightmare—those I reserved for the memory of the dead and missing.

How many different families had taken me in at the bequest of Queen Victoria over the years? If I included the Female Institution of Miss Sass and Miss Wilkerson, four. But of all the places I'd lived and left, not one was a choice given to me.

I wrote "Mama" Schon that evening.

> *I do not feel a particle of love for Captain Davies and have never done so. I prefer another [I wrote, wondering if she knew whom I meant]. I have prayed and asked for guidance, but it doesn't come, and the feelings of perfect indifference to Captain Davies return with greater force.*
>
> *I know that people say he is rich, and marrying him would at once make me independent, and I say, Am I to barter my peace of mind for money?*
>
> *No, never . . .*

For several months, I avoided everyone at 17 Clifton Hill. I stayed in my room, weeping, reading, and writing letters to Mrs. Schon. I wasn't ready to correspond with anyone else.

Mrs. Schon's replies were full of encouragement, support, and how much she missed me. She was very sympathetic but offered no solution to my exile *other* than to ask if I might reconsider my response to Captain Davies's marriage proposal.

I marveled at how she and Her Majesty, with their love for their husbands, couldn't understand or respect my resolve to love the man I married.

And as much as I loved Mama Schon, I also marveled at how it hadn't crossed her mind that the other I preferred was Freddie. Had she ever noticed how we behaved around each other? Or was a romance between the African princess in her charge and her eldest son so unfathomable?

*   *   *

BRIGHTON WAS THE farthest from Windsor Castle and Buckingham Palace I'd ever resided in England, even if it was only a two-hour train ride from London.

With a still-in-progress journey to civilization (as far as I was concerned), Brighton's beachfront, covered with pebbles and not a drop of sand, was the most attractive aspect of the seaside town.

Besides daily long walks on the beach, there was not much to do in Brighton unless you were a fisherman or a real estate tycoon or had access to the Royal Pavilion, which I did not.

In Brighton, real estate agents built communities for the wealthy to retreat from the crowded streets of London. True, a museum had opened, and talk had it that a hospital and an aquarium were on their way, but mostly, I smelled dead fish anytime I stepped outdoors.

Sophie Welch was the head of the Welch household, a sixty-two-year-old woman I pegged as feisty due to her quick wit and appearance. She didn't look her age, having maintained a trim figure and unwrinkled skin, and made regular trips to a fashionable hairdresser.

Her widowed sister, Barbara Simon, wasn't as agreeable. I could tell by the thickness of her eyebrows and her hunched back. At seventy-three, she seemed to be angry at her life—a sad thought, for I had more in common with her than with Sophie Welch.

The other household members included a nephew, William Welch, and two servants, Eliza Brewer and her sister Jane.

The family didn't dine together regularly, sit in a parlor, practice piano (they didn't own a piano), play games in the sitting room, or read in front of the fireplace. Indeed, the living room was small and dusty, and the fireplace needed a chimney sweeper. But, blessedly, the drawing room (or second sitting room, as it was called) was decently furnished.

After a few months of tears and isolation, I realized I was harming my reputation by agonizing openly about my situation. I didn't want the Welch sisters to give the queen any more bad reports about my behavior. I was sure they'd written to Her Majesty (or Mrs. Phipps) about my sulking in my room for weeks on end. That conduct was very unlike that of a proper English lady and certainly not that of a princess.

Moreover, it came to me, why should anyone other than me (and Mama Schon) be aware of how ravaged I'd been by Her Majesty's betrayal?

So, one March morning in 1861, I rose, dressed, brushed my hair, parted in the middle with a low bun at the nape of my neck, and practiced my smile in the mirror.

Then I said to myself: *I can do this.*

From that day forward, I swore the Welch family would have no choice but to give me a good report.

I arrived in the drawing room after what should have been the breakfast hour. The Welch sisters were in the den, sipping tea.

"Oh, my," said Miss Welch, startled by my entrance. "I thought it was my nephew."

"We're waiting on him to return to the house with the newspaper," added Mrs. Simon in her dry, gravelly voice. "How can we keep up with what is happening in the world if we don't read the newspaper?"

"Lady Sarah, will you have some tea?" Miss Welch nodded at Eliza Brewer, her maid and the elder of the Brewer sisters. She curtsied and departed, off to bring me tea, I assumed. "Are you feeling better? You've been under the weather since you arrived."

"I am much better," I lied. "I'm so sorry I haven't been sociable. I've had such a headache. All I could do was lie down. But I'm healed, and you will see more of me."

"For four months, you had a headache?" Mrs. Simon guffawed.

"Barbara," Miss Welch warned. "Sarah, that sounds wonderful. I hope that means you'll join us for services on Sunday. Whatever has been causing your ill health won't stand a chance of a return in the face of our minister's sermon."

"Why overpromise, Sophie?" said Mrs. Simon. "I never miss a Sunday service, and my health has been poorly for five years."

I blinked at the harshness of her tone. I was right. She was an ogre.

"Barbara, you'll frighten Lady Sarah with your crude talk."

I swallowed, removing the disdain from my throat. "I would be delighted to join you both for Sunday service."

The servant returned with tea. I accepted my cup and added sugar and milk. "Thank you. Eliza, correct?"

"Yes, ma'am."

I took a sip. "A lovely cup of tea."

Miss Welch chuckled. "They said you were pleasant and well-mannered. I had hoped I'd see that side of you."

"You do not need to worry. As I said, I am much better. My cold"—I coughed for emphasis—"is almost gone."

"I thought your head hurt," growled Mrs. Simon. "Which is it, your head or a cold? I heard you get sick a lot in the English winter. Being African, not accustomed to the weather. Is that true?"

I glared at her. Her rudeness in spouting that ridiculous British belief about Africans—well, I couldn't hold my tongue. "I've spent the past six years of my life in England with no more colds than anyone else in the Schon household or the royal family. So I'd call that a myth, Mrs. Simon."

"Oh, dear. See what you've done, Barbara. You've upset her." Miss Welch smacked her lips. "Please excuse her, Sarah. She's been temperamental for the past five years."

"That's not true. I've been in mourning."

"Yes, of course, Barbara. I am sorry." She turned to me. "Her husband passed away five years ago." Miss Welch smiled at her sister, eyes full of sorrow and affection.

"He was the love of my life," said Mrs. Simon softly.

With those words, I felt like a fool. I had blamed Mrs. Simon's appearance for her sour disposition, but grief and loneliness shaped her. I'd condemned her because of her looks without knowing who she was. "I'm sorry for your loss," I said. "Sincerely sorry."

Just then, a gray-whiskered man with a bald head, no hat, and wearing thick glasses burst into the room.

"Aunt Sophie! Aunt Barbara!" He looked sweaty, and his cheeks were bright red as if he'd run a mile. "There's sad news from London and the royal family." He held the newspaper like a torch.

I sprang forward, spilling tea over the rim of my cup. "What has happened? Is it the queen? Princess Alice?"

"William, please. We have a houseguest. Your composure." His gaze darted from his aunts to me and back to his aunts until he pushed his glasses up on the bridge of his nose and gazed at me. "The queen and Princess Alice are healthy. It's the queen's mother, the Duchess of Kent. She died last evening."

"March 16, 1861," I murmured. "May her soul rest in peace."

I had met the duchess, but she was rarely at the castle or the palace when I was. My sadness was for those who knew and loved her. I was sure Princess Alice was stricken.

I excused myself from the Welches' drawing room to write my friend Alice a long letter of condolence.

Chapter Thirty-six

Brighton, England, 1861

After six months in Brighton, I cried myself to sleep only every third night or so, but I hadn't changed my mind about Captain Davies and had no intention of doing so. Which meant I had to have a plan to keep my sanity. So I developed a routine.

I wrote four letters every day, one each to Mrs. Phipps, Mrs. Schon, Mrs. Forbes (in Scotland), and Princess Alice. And one more, once a week—to Freddie, of course. So much to say but so little that could be said in writing.

I received several letters a day. The first to arrive was from Mrs. Phipps. Her letters were about the royal household and sometimes mentioned the queen's activities. These friendly and chatty letters kept me abreast of the goings-on in Windsor Castle, Buckingham Palace, and Osborne House. But she never mentioned Captain Davies, for which I was grateful. It was a relief from that sinking feeling rolling around inside me at the sight of his name.

Mrs. Schon wrote about her children, her husband, and the house staff. She also sent me bundles of books and diaries in case I wanted to keep a record of my thoughts. I hungered for her letters, hoping for any mention of Freddie, but her eldest son didn't hold her attention as much as her younger children. Mrs. Forbes's letters were similar. Family, hearth and home, travel, and her thoughts and prayers were with me.

Princess Alice sent me weekly letters that never arrived on the same days as Mrs. Phipps's correspondence, which caused me to suspect they worked in tandem. Their letters never overlapped in terms of topics or gossip. Surprising, but also loving and thoughtful of them.

Alice wrote detailed updates on the workings of Parliament and any signs of a change of heart by Her Majesty regarding me. She did mention Captain Davies, but only as the roadblock keeping me in Brighton. Missing from her letters was any mention of her upcoming marriage in December. I believed that also was meant as a kindness to me.

Each evening, after dinner, I'd write my replies.

Freddie's weekly letters were long and full of hope, promises, and dreams about what awaited us on the other side of my exile. I cherished and hated his letters. What if his dream never came true? What if I could never do as I wanted with him or anyone else unless agreeable to Her Majesty?

The thought scared me and made me angry and sad at once. I felt the ache in my chest. What kind of person lives this way?

Tears sprang into my eyes, hot and quick, because I knew the answer to the question, and it was me—Sarah Forbes Bonetta.

* * *

Prince Albert died in the Blue Room at Windsor Castle on December 14, 1861, at 10:50 p.m. At his bedside were the queen and five of his nine children. He'd been diagnosed with typhoid fever five days earlier by his doctor. Princess Alice had stayed with him day and night, nursing him along with those doctors. It was the only place she would want to be, at his side, taking care of him until his last breath.

I knew this of her from our earliest days as friends.

His passing brought me back to London. I had to offer my condolences to Alice in person. His body was interred in the Royal Vault at St. George's Chapel at Windsor Castle, but no formal funeral was planned, by Queen Victoria's orders.

I stayed in the home of Mrs. Phipps, as she was a member of the royal household, and I had returned to be with the family during these dark days.

When I met with Alice, the weight of Prince Albert's death filled my heart. I was startled by how she looked, like a ghost of her former self. But I wanted her to know I was there if she needed me. So I didn't break down. I showed her strength, hoping it might help, even if only the smallest amount.

Queen Victoria was inconsolable, but Alice also faced a joy-less wedding. It had been set for December 23 but was post-poned. However, she didn't appear to mind when I saw her.

So much pain and sorrow surrounded me. However, despite my grief and concern for my dear Alice and the queen, I couldn't be in London and not see Freddie. But when would seeing him be appropriate in light of the Prince Consort's death?

The day before I was to return to Brighton, I arranged to meet him.

* * *

FREDDIE AND I met at a small café near Park Lane with outdoor seating. It was crowded, waiters rushing in and out of swinging doors, but our table faced the street, and we sat next to each other, our backs to the storefront window as we watched the passersby.

I was glad to see him, but it was so close to Prince Albert's death that I couldn't talk about us. Not right away.

"They were so happy, so in love, always in love. I never

doubted their love." I sighed, sipped my tea, and stared into the bustling streets of London. "Bad things always happen when you love too deeply."

Freddie unbuttoned his frock coat as if the fabric were sticking to his skin. "You can't help who you love."

"I know, but it's frightening. I fear that having no control over love can destroy you." I studied his face, the freckled straight nose that belonged to a boy, the firm jaw and curved lips of the man. Could I live without him?

I thought of Queen Victoria's stricken, soulless eyes. "I don't think she'll recover from losing her husband. You risk so much when you love with such single-mindedness, I think. When the loved one dies or leaves you, the devastation is complete. You might as well leap into the grave with them."

"Sarah, I disagree. The risk to your heart should not determine how you love." He touched my hand, resting on the table. "You are grieving."

"Yes, I am. He was kind to me. He was a gentleman, not a father figure, but a decent God-fearing man who loved his wife and children. I admired him."

"How is Brighton?" he asked, seeing my distress and changing the subject.

"Smelly and boring."

He wiped his mouth with his fingertips. "How long will you stay?"

"I don't know." I shrugged. "Forever? The queen won't change her mind about me marrying Captain Davies, and I won't change my mind about not marrying him. I don't love him. I love you."

He exhaled as if he'd held his breath until that moment. "Then let's leave England and live someplace where you and I can be free to love without the eyes of British society and the queen watching over us."

"I sometimes dream of places we might go—for example, Denmark," I said cheerfully. "Or out west in America. It sounds adventurous and lovely, but with the Civil War and slavery, I took it off the list." I was striving for cheeky, trying to recapture the old playfulness Freddie and I used to do so well. "Have you finished your ministry?"

His features hardened. I had introduced a subject he didn't like. "I had always thought I would follow in my father's footsteps, marry, and live a full life between my home in Britain and my missionary work in Africa."

"Yes, I know."

"Well, there is something about him that even I was unaware of until recently." He smiled at me with pain in his eyes. I touched his cheek. "I've lost God, Sarah, partly because of him." There were tears in his eyes. "Reverend Venn, a man I admired, played a role in Captain Davies's coming to London to ask for your hand in marriage."

I already knew this, but I listened with grave concern at what might come from Freddie's mouth next.

"It's as if the Church of England is a puppeteer when it comes to Africans. The missionaries want to educate you, but they also want to control you. It is as if they are enslavers."

I nodded my head. "Yes, you are right. They pull at me as if I had strings, but I cannot stand the thought of you losing your faith over this. You'll find God. I know this. You shouldn't blame God for what humans do. You know this even more than me." I paused, realizing I'd missed something. "You said it was your father who has made you think this way about God, but you mention only Reverend Venn."

He gripped my hand so hard I winced.

"I'm sorry." He apologized and let go. "My father knew. Do you understand? He knew I cared about you, Sarah. He knew, and still—perhaps because he knew—he supported Reverend Venn's efforts. He encouraged Captain Davies, too. He is as much a contributor to your woes as Reverend Venn. But my father is even more insidious. He introduced Matilda to Davies."

I heard every word, and if Freddie was right . . . "Oh, God." I groaned. "We never had a chance, did we?"

"I won't let go of us." He squeezed my hand. "We will fight them. And we will win. Let's make plans. I'll write to you every day instead of once a week until I find a way for us to be together."

"I would love that, but we also must be practical. How will we survive? Without the queen's money, I am a pauper—and if you show your father how angry you are, he might not support you. How would you finish your education, then?"

"The queen will change her mind if you hold out long enough. My father doesn't know I am aware of what he's done. And I will keep silent for us. So be patient. Write to me every day you can, and I will do the same." He raised my hand to his lips. "Will you do that for us?"

I smiled into his eyes. "Of course, I can and will. I promise."

He leaned in and kissed me on the lips, not a peck, but his lips pressed firmly against mine with tenderness and longing, and I responded. The feel of his mouth set off tiny fires in my fingertips that raced up my arms and then trickled down my spine. My entire body burned as if a thousand flames had touched it.

Sound vanished, and people seated nearby disappeared. All thoughts left me. There was only Freddie and me, our lips touching and hearts pounding in our chests.

Breathing demanded attention, and the kiss ended. I couldn't tell which one of us backed away first. But the feel of him, the warmth of his mouth, lingered on my lips.

I was in an Austen novel. A heroine with the lover she'd sought for fifty thousand words.

Oh, to feel that first kiss again.

Chapter Thirty-seven

Brighton, England, 1862

Harriet Phipps sent me a message four months after Prince Albert's death. She would be in Brighton in a few weeks and wanted to see me. We could meet at a café, or she'd gladly stop by the Welch home if that would be convenient.

Her note didn't say much more. I couldn't imagine what she wanted, except when I thought about it, I did imagine.

The last time we were together in the same room, she had told me the queen would exile me to Brighton. If I didn't do as I was told and marry Caption Davies, I could pack my bags—or better yet, they would be packed for me.

I didn't want to see her.

Standing in the foyer of the house on Clifton Hill, I held her note in my hand, and my blood boiled. Then I considered the matter with a bit of common sense.

Could she want to talk to me about Alice's wedding—seek the participation of an exile in the queen's daughter's ceremony?

The queen had postponed Alice's wedding from December to July, and a hotter month in England didn't exist. So when I had seen Alice following Prince Albert's death, I promised to attend, even if I had to pay for it myself—a bold statement since I had no funds. But I would get there, even if I had to walk.

I wasn't invited to be a part of the bridal party. After all of the business with Captain Davies, I hadn't expected that. Besides, it was to be a small, private affair. Although Her Majesty did permit the bride to wear white, following the nuptials, she was to return to her black mourning attire along with everyone else in the family.

If Alice's wedding was what Harriet wanted to discuss, she could have written me a letter. It was not necessary to see me in person for that conversation.

I closed my eyes and swallowed as much frustration as possible. I had to think of Freddie. We were making plans. If I refused to meet with Harriet, I'd risk a poor conduct report to the queen, and my next punishment might not include so much as a roof over my head.

With the note clenched in my hand, I turned and ran up the stairs to my room to write my reply: Harriet Phipps. I look forward to your visit.

* * *

IT WAS EARLY spring, and I could go outside for long walks, and the sea was only a mile away.

One afternoon, I was walking toward Brighton Beach when I encountered a stately woman, much taller than me, but as dark-skinned as I and dressed in a similar fashion. We both wore promenade gowns. Hers was gray, mine a pin-striped brown, hers with a circular row of ribbon, mine with mixed braid. Our coat sleeves were full and high on the shoulders, and our spoon bonnets were identical. She was a handsome woman, and I moved aside on the sidewalk to let her and her baby carriage (and the anxious-looking nursemaid traipsing behind them) pass, but she stopped.

"Good afternoon, and how wonderful to see you. How are you? Isn't today lovely?"

So many questions, and she'd spoken to me as if we were old acquaintances, but I'd never laid eyes on her before. If I had, I would never have forgotten her. I responded politely, "I am quite well, thank you. How are you?" I glanced down at the baby in the carriage, and to my surprise, the infant was as pale as Freddie. "Your baby is lovely."

"Thank you, his name is Marcus. He is four months old, and there are days when I think my head will explode from loving him so much." She laughed.

"Do you live in Brighton?"

"Only in the spring and summer. London can be horrific and very hectic when the weather is hot and sticky. And with the baby, it's our first; we want to make sure he has the best first year ever."

I heard every word but racked my brain trying to remember where we'd met. But I couldn't and had to risk being impolite. "I don't believe I've seen you before in London. I should introduce myself. I am Sarah Forbes Bonetta."

Her hand went to her mouth for a second. "Oh, my goodness, I'm so sorry. I thought we'd met at one of my husband's parties. I'm very sorry, I assumed you were someone else, but of course I've heard of you. It's a pleasure to meet you, Miss Bonetta."

I nodded a greeting. "And you are?"

"Again, my apologies. I am Penelope Campbell, wife of Sir Thomas Marcus Campbell, a captain in the British Army," she said, smiling proudly. "I swear my son has used up most of the little mind I had left. I hope I wasn't rude, miss."

"Not in the least." I glanced at the baby again and noticed the nursemaid step back, giving us room to chat privately. I had seen only a few married couples of different races, rulers of foreign countries, not citizens of London. So the question I was about to ask her was somewhat scandalous. I lowered my voice. "I'm so sorry, but may I ask . . ."

"I understand," she replied. "My husband is a blond-haired man with blue eyes and white skin. You can see his coloring in our son."

"I'm sorry, I only wondered."

"I'm surprised you haven't met more families like ours. London has quite a population of wealthy Black merchants and women of color who have married the second sons of white aristocrats."

"My upbringing has been, shall I say, influenced by the royal household."

"I imagine."

"Where were you born?"

"I was born in London. My parents, however, are from West Africa and were Saro, formerly enslaved people who settled in Sierra Leone."

Her nursemaid stepped forward. "Excuse me, ma'am, it's almost time for the baby's feeding."

"Oh," I said, "I didn't mean to keep you."

"Do not worry. Shall we exchange calling cards? I would be delighted to see you again, perhaps a visit to our home?"

"Yes, I would like that very much." I rummaged through my bag and handed her my card and took the one offered to me.

"Until we meet again," she said.

"Until then."

But of course, I never saw Penelope again. I didn't contact

her, and she didn't contact me. It would have been nice to know her, her son Marcus, and her husband, a captain in the British Army.

It might have helped me if I had known someone like her.

* * *

THE WELCH SISTERS and their nephew were out of the house on errands on the May afternoon when Harriet Phipps came to Clifton Hill.

I awaited her arrival in my tiny bedroom. My wardrobe by choice inside the Welch home was mostly dark, frumpy dresses, but for Harriet, I wanted to look as if every day in Brighton was a holiday. So I wore a pale-yellow silk dress with a gold-threaded embroidered bodice and a floor-length hoop skirt with an intricate butterfly design in pink and gold. I was finishing up my hair when Eliza knocked on my bedroom door.

"Your guest is here, miss."

I hurried to the top of the staircase but stopped to take a deep breath before descending. I was about to learn what was so crucial that Harriet couldn't write it in a letter. I felt as if tiny birds were flapping their wings in my stomach. But, whatever she had to say, I had to control my fear, my tears, and, decidedly, my temper.

I reached the bottom of the stairs, and there she was. "Good afternoon, Harriet."

Eliza had taken her wrap, which she held over her arm as she led us into the sitting room.

"Thank you, Sarah, for accepting my request to see you," Harriet said as Eliza left to prepare the tea tray.

"You are welcome," I said without inviting her to sit. "What is it that you want?"

"What do you do when you are the only one who can prevent a disaster from occurring?"

"You are speaking in riddles, Harriet. Very unlike you." I pointed her to the sofa, the least-worn piece of furniture in the Welches' drawing room.

"I cannot stay long. So I should get to the point of my visit."

"Please do." I sat next to her on the sofa.

"Sarah, I didn't come with the message you'd like to hear from Her Majesty. However, I'd like you to reconsider your refusal to marry Captain Davies."

I slumped in my seat. "I don't understand why you would come all this way to present me with the proposal I've already refused twice. My answer is unchanged."

"There's a difference you must consider. The queen is not the woman she once was. Her grief over Prince Albert's death is all-consuming. Empathy doesn't exist in this Queen Victoria."

"She loved him," I said. "That kind of love doesn't heal after a loss. It erases part of your soul."

"Yes, it does, and it has. Her Majesty will forget about you in another six months, and you will be here in this house with these women until they die, and then what of you?"

"You're trying to scare me, and it won't work. I'm not afraid of you."

"I am aware of your aspirations, Sarah. It is part of what I do for Her Majesty. I am a watcher. You enjoy the finer things. All of which would be available to you if you marry a wealthy man."

Her words seared through me. "I suffer from pridefulness and a desire for stature, and I've enjoyed being treated like a princess. But that doesn't mean I would marry a man I don't love."

She stood and paced across the small room, pausing to touch the top of a chair or stare at a faded painting on the wall. "How does a girl like you respond to being abandoned in Brighton?" She stopped near the window, gazing out onto the street.

I liked games, but not the one she was playing. "This conversation is going in circles. What did you come to tell me that couldn't be put in a letter?"

Harriet turned from the window and faced me. "Your rebellion is pointless. The queen will never permit you to marry another man, especially not the Schon boy."

My blood froze in my veins. "You know about . . . Her Majesty knows about Freddie? No. What do you mean? What does he have to do with this?"

"He'll never have the means to give you the life you desire." Harriet returned to the sofa and sat next to me. "In Africa, you could live like a queen as the wife of Captain Davies. That should be more important to a woman like you than love. Grow up, Sarah," she said. "You can live in a fairy tale, but you can die in one. It is your choice."

I held a hand to my forehead. The world was spinning in the wrong direction. So many things were going through my mind. How was I sitting and listening to this woman insult me in the same breath she praised me? Why did her words not surprise me? I knew what she meant as soon as the words fell from her lips. Had I fooled myself these past years? I knew love. I understood how it felt to love. Freddie was my friend and the man I loved. I had to hang on to that and not allow Harriet Phipps, of all people, to convince me otherwise.

I would not let it happen. I could not. "If you came here only to deliver the queen's mandates with malice, you should leave." I rose.

"I can't leave, because there is one more thing I must tell you. With the queen's knowledge of your feelings for Frederick Schon, you have put him in danger. I am warning you. She won't allow you to marry him. She will do whatever is necessary to ensure that never happens."

I placed my hands over my stomach. I felt sick. "What more could she do to us? I'm exiled."

"Oh, please, Sarah," Harriet said with a condescending tone. "Think about it. Can you or Frederick afford to have the queen of England as an enemy? Who would hire him to work? How could he support a bride accustomed to luxury? His family can only help him so much. And what can you provide without the queen's support? No more gifts, clothes, travel, or dining at castles or in proper homes. You'll find that even Brighton is better than the streets of Lagos. And yes, you would be returned to Africa penniless."

"The queen is not that kind of woman. This is your wish for me, not hers."

"She has changed. She now lives with great sadness," Harriet said solemnly. "She has no tolerance for disobedience." She sighed. "I should be going. Where is your maid? I want my wrap. Can you ring for her?"

"I'm sorry. She must've gotten distracted preparing our tea." I massaged the tightness in my throat. I felt dizzy and afraid. There was no mistake. Harriet had threatened Freddie and me. "The queen sent you here to scare me. I can't believe that."

"I am the queen's confidante. I deliver messages that can't be written on paper," Harriet said. "Do not risk that young man's future for an ill-fated romance."

Eliza walked into the drawing room, her face flushed, and placed the tray of tea on the table. "I'm so sorry for the delay."

I began to ask what had happened but realized it didn't matter. "No apologies, Eliza. It is fine. However, Harriet has to leave. Could you bring her wrap? Thank you."

Eliza left, and Harriet and I stared at each other.

"Shall I tell the queen you will adhere to her request?"

"Tell her whatever you want."

"Good. Then I will see you at Princess Alice's wedding in July?"

"I believe you are lying. The queen would not do anything to interfere with Freddie's future. His father is a friend of the royal family. She would never hurt him like that." I stood in front of Harriet. "You are wrong to suggest such nonsense."

"I would not come to Brighton for, as you call it, nonsense."

* * *

PRINCESS ALICE MARRIED Prince Louis of Hesse on July 1, 1862.

I was there, but it was a solemn affair—only a small group of guests, as the queen had commanded. It was too soon to celebrate life while her grief for the loss of her husband was as fresh as new rain.

Loss. Grief. Life. I understood those words and their contradictions. I was in a fight for my life and for love. The love I wanted. The life I deserved. And, for the first time, in a sad, ironic twist, I had choices.

Remain in exile for God knew how much longer and risk being abandoned by the queen. No money. No place to live. No friends. I'd be sent back to Africa as a pauper. Or I could continue my campaign to marry for love only, walk away from the royal family, marry the man I adore, and destroy his life in the same breath as I say "I do." Then I thought more about

Harriet's visit and her warning. The queen would never allow it. And if we married, the consequences would be dire.

The last choice. I could accept the marriage proposal of a wealthy African man I didn't love—a man who would treat me like a queen in a land that harbored my nightmares.

The life of a princess was suddenly filled with choices.

Two days after the wedding, I sent a message to Palm Cottage and asked Freddie to meet me at the café in London where we'd kissed in the winter. Now, it was summer.

It didn't take months for me to break our hearts—only a few minutes on a bright, sunny day in the middle of London.

"What are you saying to me, my love? I don't believe you."

"Please don't make me repeat it all. We cannot be together."

His mouth twisted, and his eyes glistened. I saw the pain rise from the vein pulsing in his neck and the air he sucked through his flared nostrils. I'd hurt him, but what choice did I have?

"Don't look at me that way. I'm not saying this to hurt you. I'm saying this to save you. Don't you understand? I will not allow you to be destroyed because you fell in love with me. I love you and your family too much to let that happen."

"I can't believe the queen would harm either one of us if we chose to marry. That's vindictive. And she's not that kind of queen."

"She is the most powerful person in the world, Her Majesty, the queen of England, and she can do whatever she wants, including making it impossible for me to go against her will. She wants me to marry Captain Davies. And I will."

"Sarah, please. We can leave England. Go to America. Out west, I hear Negroes and whites are welcome to live and love."

"You've read too many western serials." I held his hand fiercely in mine.

"I love you, Sarah."

"I love your mother, sisters, and brothers. I love your father, and I love the queen of England. And for Christ's sake, I love you. But I could not live with myself if our love caused your destruction."

"Sarah," he said with tears in his voice.

"Hush." I raised a finger to his lips. "I will never love Captain Davies, but I will marry him."

Chapter Thirty-eight

Brighton, England, 1862

I wrote Captain James P. L. Davies the day after I spoke to Freddie—before I weakened and had a change of heart. Although it would be a race, I could feel the doubt at my fingertips, begging me to stand fast. But that would be foolhardy.

I sat at my desk with my writing slope and paper, pen in hand, thinking about how to begin. It had been over a year and a half since I refused Captain Davies's second proposal. He might have found another to marry. I let that thought run its course for a moment and then smiled.

He'd said it himself in so many words. No one compared to me. I was Queen Victoria's goddaughter, an Egbado princess. The only woman in England, Africa, or anywhere in the world with the status and influence he needed to achieve his ambitions.

My letter was brief.

Dear Captain James P. L. Davies,

I'll marry you, but I want to have the grandest wedding a princess—other than one of Queen Victoria's daughters—could have. I trust you will agree and participate in making that happen.

Yours sincerely . . .
S. F. Bonetta

The queen was next on my list. I sent the note to Mrs. Phipps to deliver to Her Majesty with my news as soon as possible.

The queen replied the following afternoon, in her own hand, expressing how surprised and delighted she was with my decision. She agreed that I should have a grand wedding and offered monetary assistance to ensure it was the event of the season, even if that season was in Brighton.

* * *

CAPTAIN DAVIES ARRIVED in England with his brothers, sisters, and closest friends a week before the ceremony. I wanted to hide in a corner, but that was unlike me. They were strangers, including the man I was to marry. What would I say? What would he say? What demands would he make? After all, he was to be my husband, which meant I must obey.

Those first days were hectic, leaving little time for him and me to get to know each other. Someone was always with us, directing us to turn left, right, forward, backward, sideways, or inside out. Yet whenever I raised my head to look at him, I saw the same man I'd met at Windsor Castle. Tight-lipped and full of vanity, ambition, and purpose. I wondered when I'd see something other than arrogance from Captain Davies. Something I'd not seen or thought to look for.

Mrs. Forbes had arrived from Scotland a few days before the captain and his family landed. She had arranged a reception for us at the Grosvenor Hotel on Buckingham Palace Road. The event was scheduled for the third night after his arrival. When the festivities began, we still hadn't had a chance for even the briefest private conversation. I anticipated this first chat with such dread, I jumped at the sound of silence. I was so distracted I hung on to Mama Forbes as if my life depended on it. I had never felt so childish until we entered the hotel's grand suite, and I looked up from the floor.

The decorations were lavish and as captivating as the colors in the Crimson Drawing Room. The grand suite had been transformed into an English garden. Beautiful floral bouquets blossomed from painted porcelain urns. Delicate roses, baby's breath, daffodils, geraniums, petunias, and dahlias filled the room with an abundance of aromas. However, my gaze lingered on the elaborate buffet, an array of meats, cheeses, apple puddings, sweet biscuits, and gingerbread cakes. So many of my favorite foods and flowers in one place, I gasped with delight.

"Are you pleased, Sarah?" she asked, squeezing my hand.

"I am overwhelmed, Mama. Thank you." I looked around, taking in the faces of the people I knew from London society and the royal household in attendance, from Mrs. Phipps and Harriet to the Schon family, but I didn't see Freddie. I searched with no success, and my heart dropped. He hadn't come. I shouldn't have been surprised. But still, I was.

Halfway through the evening, after a champagne toast and gingerbread cake, I was torn between light-headedness and a lingering disappointment. Freddie's absence had slipped back into my thoughts. Why had I thought he would come? Was I cruel or unfair for inviting him? How could I not want to see him? It might be the last time we set eyes upon each other before I was married. But that was selfish of me. How would seeing Captain Davies and me in the same room make Freddie feel?

Somehow, I had avoided Captain Davies for most of the evening. Now and then, I'd glance in the direction of his deep baritone in conversation with one of his siblings or Reverend Venn, Reverend Crowther, or Reverend Dicker. They were all there. But as had been my habit, I became flustered at the thought of a one-on-one talk. I did not like avoiding anyone, but with him, the greater the delay, the stronger I felt.

My next glance across the room, and I caught Captain Davies watching me.

At some point, he and I would have to be alone. We had to discuss how our arrangement would work. Of course, rules had to be adhered to, didn't they? Plans made that would be agreeable to both of us.

As much as I dreaded the conversation, I also wanted things settled.

I turned away. The talk could wait.

The small orchestra Mrs. Forbes had arranged was a heavenly surprise. When it launched into its third or fourth waltz, Captain Davies' and my eyes met. He abandoned his friends and walked toward me.

Judging from his stride, his squared shoulders, and the rise and fall of his chest, he was going to ask me to dance. It made sense. We were to be married in a few days. We should do one thing together, since we hadn't talked or looked at one another for any measurable length of time.

I dropped my gaze and stared at his boots, marching through the crowd until he reached me. Then I looked directly into his dark eyes.

"Would you like to dance?" he asked, as if I might refuse him. Then he shook off that impulse and extended his hand. "We must dance. No point in leaving it to chance. Agreed?"

"I'd love to. I mean, yes, of course." What else was I to say?

He spun me into the middle of the dance floor as a Mendelssohn composition soared. I said a quick prayer, hoping Captain Davies didn't dance like a clumsy oaf. It turned out he was a masterful dancer. His long fingers spread over the middle of my back, and he held me at the perfect distance. We spun and twirled and gave a stunning performance of the Viennese waltz. I had danced with other boys, but he was more experienced. I hadn't ever felt such security in a man's arms.

The waltz ended. I smiled, trying not to show how impressed I was with his skill as a dancer. "Thank you, sir."

When I looked into his eyes, I saw a wry smile. He knew he was an excellent dancer, but the smile vanished so fast I thought I'd imagined it.

The orchestra struck again, this time with a polka.

"Shall we dance again?"

I cleared the lump in my throat and replied, "Yes. That would be fine."

Our second dance ended. "Thank you, Captain Davies."

"It was my pleasure."

Then, with a step back, I freed myself from his embrace. The moment had ended, and we returned to opposite sides of the room. We had done our bit as the perfect couple. No one would guess we weren't in love and had spent less than an hour together since he arrived from Africa.

But being that close to him hadn't been as bad as I thought. Perhaps the champagne was to blame.

Or the truth was the captain and I were like cut flowers in painted urns, delicate and dramatic on the outside, but inside, we were drowning in dirty water. And neither one of us dared to rise out of the mud and run.

* * *

Queen Victoria had arranged for us to have our pictures taken at a photography studio two days before the wedding.

Photography was Her Majesty's latest obsession, and neither the captain nor I understood much about it. More to the point, I wasn't eager to spend time alone with Captain Davies. But I also wasn't about to refuse the queen.

Merrick and Company, located in Brighton, had made a name for itself. The company's photography studio was famous for producing some of the highest-quality silver prints in England.

Captain Davies and I arrived a few minutes late for our session and were hurried into the studio and posed. I sat on a stool, and the captain stood with his thumb hooked in his vest pocket. I had dressed in one of the gowns from my trousseau—and yes, I had a trousseau, courtesy of Queen Victoria. Captain Davies looked like a proper English gentleman in his frock coat, embroidered vest, straight trousers, and high-collared shirt. And I felt like a grand lady waiting for the photographer.

A man strode into the room and headed toward the strange picture-taking equipment assembled on the other side of the studio. He greeted us with a smile and a nod but then ran in and out of the room, bringing this and that for the photos, I assumed.

Though we had been rushed into position, we now waited, and somehow, the captain and I managed to stumble into a conversation.

"Have you had your photograph taken before, Captain Davies?" I asked, both out of curiosity and because the silence between us bordered on absurdity, which I refused to believe was my fault.

"Would you consider calling me James?" he asked, with a smirk and a wrinkled nose.

I glanced toward the photographer, who continued to bounce in and out of the room. "It is a reasonable question, but I'm not ready for such familiarity between us."

"I intend to call you Sarah beginning today."

"That, of course, is up to you."

"Thank you for allowing me such intimacy."

Something in his tone made me look at him. "Are you making fun of me, Captain?"

"No, I don't make fun of anything or anyone."

My eyes widened with suspicion. "Are you being truthful?"

"I don't lie. Ever."

He sounded sincere, but I'd wait and see. "Well, then. What will happen after the wedding? What do you expect of our wedding night? You've been married before and have experience as a husband. I have no experience." I stopped talking to catch my breath. Then, when he didn't jump in, I continued, "You are in your thirties, and I am nineteen."

"I know."

Good. I had his attention.

Mr. Merrick popped back into view. "I am so sorry for the delay. I require a few more minutes of preparation. My assistant broke a lens." With that, he was gone.

"It appears we can relax and have the chat we haven't been able to get around to," the captain said.

"I had hoped to have time today to talk, but do you think this is the right place?" I gestured at the clutter in the photographer's studio. It overflowed with equipment and stage sets, as if we were behind the curtains at the old Covent Garden Theatre.

"I am confident we will have more than one conversation.

We don't have to discuss every aspect of our lives in the next few minutes. I would hope we never run out of things to discuss. For this is not the last time we will talk."

He had a point, unless I decided I couldn't bear to be around him. "Then I'll begin, if that's all right."

"Perfectly fine."

I cleared my throat. "I am prepared to do my wifely duty, of course. I am a proper English lady."

"I intend to make you comfortable on our wedding night. There will be no need for you to be fearful. I am experienced and intend to treat you with care and respect."

He had responded so matter-of-factly it gave me a chill. "You seem to be enjoying the activities leading up to our marriage," he said. "I am pleased."

"I enjoy weddings."

Then Mr. Merrick returned. "I am all set. We are ready to begin. My apologies." He walked over, studying me. "Miss Bonetta, would you mind turning your head, and if Mr. Davies—"

"It's Captain Davies, sir."

"My apologies." Mr. Merrick bobbed his head. "If Captain Davies would move farther to his left so that the two of you are together."

Per Mr. Merrick's instructions, Captain Davies rested his hand on my shoulder as we adjusted our positions. I stiffened. His touch had caught me off guard. He removed his hand.

"We will take time, Sarah." He wasn't irritated. More resigned. "We will be husband and wife, and I will do my best to make our marriage a pleasant experience for you."

"That's very kind of you, Captain Davies. I'm looking forward . . ." I stopped, unable to finish the sentence. I hadn't imagined much of anything beyond our wedding day. "Yes, except I'm not sure what you mean by pleasant. I am sorry to question you, but I don't know much about you or the rules of matrimony."

"Mr. Merrick," said Captain Davies. "Would you give us a moment, please?"

"Of course, sir. Yes, sir. Right away, sir." Mr. Merrick back-pedaled from the room, bowing the entire time.

"There are some things I should tell you about me, Sarah," Captain Davies said. "I know how to be a good husband and will be one to you."

I raised my eyebrow. "I assume you are referring to your first wife." I had no control over the words coming out of my mouth. "Matilda Serrano. Did you forget I knew her? She was my roommate at Palm Cottage."

"You mean my wife, Matilda Davies, and no, I did not forget. She mentioned you on several occasions."

"Oh, she did?"

Captain Davies linked his hands behind his back and stepped away from the stool and me. "Since you seem curious, I will speak upon my first wife. She was a kind girl, and I cared for her as she cared for me. Her death was the single most tragic event in my life."

Now he cleared his throat, but his breath caught. Something was wrong, and he seemed to shatter like glass. Yet he reassembled with the speed of a gazelle, leaving no trace of the damage that plagued him. Ah. My first encounter with one of his rare skills. He had shown me everything he felt but took it away so fast that I doubted I'd seen anything.

"Sarah, please listen. I will not deceive you, but I choose to keep some things private. As I've told you, I am a man with aspirations. I have accomplished much, but there is much more to do, and I require a woman at my side with the education, influence, and demeanor that will benefit Africa and me.

"In that way, you are the perfect wife. We have not yet formed an attachment to one another, but we will."

"It is possible," I said, matching his tone. "But nothing is guaranteed."

"Your directness is appreciated, but I am confident we will learn to love each other. If that is unattainable, we will respect and support each other and that will be sufficient."

"Is that all?" I said this with a proper sarcastic flair, but then I learned another thing about my future husband—he had little or no sense of humor.

"Children are another subject we should discuss."

Now I'd lost my humor. "Children? Is that something we need to discuss right away?"

"Not at this moment, but soon. Very soon."

This was a subject that sent my heart sputtering. "Agreed. Soon, but not at this moment."

"I am looking forward to our having children. Family is how the Europeans and British sustain and grow power through generations, connected by blood, ambition, and a firm belief in Christianity. We will not survive without them or the church.

"Africa deserves a powerful couple in its corner. England is a mighty nation and can be a mighty partner or foe. You and I represent the African elite who can lead our continent to a glorious future. That is my focus. I trust it will become yours."

What was there to say? Together, we would help keep whatever parts of Africa he deemed necessary wrapped within the powerful embrace of England.

In addition to my connections to the royal family, he also would give me what he believed I wanted—wealth, status, and power—all the best things for a princess who would soon be a bride.

Chapter Thirty-nine

Brighton, England, 1862

I was up before dawn on my wedding day, if I'd slept at all, and Harriet Phipps was with me from the moment I entered my dressing chamber. Indeed, she'd been on hand throughout my wedding preparations. Surprising, to say the least.

As I walked into the room, dizziness or nerves blurred my vision, and I stumbled.

"What is it, Sarah?" Harriet asked.

"My head is spinning. That's all."

She rang the servant's bell. "I'll get you some water. But before it arrives, tell me, are you sure nothing is bothering you?"

"What is bothering me is I don't know the man I'm about to marry, and it's as if I am chained beneath a waterfall and will drown unless I swallow a ton of water."

"Rest assured. You'll have a lifetime to get to know him."

Her words were meant to be comforting, but I only heard the word "lifetime." "If this is to be my life, I ought to make the most of it. Is that what you're saying?"

A maid entered the room with a full pitcher and glasses. "Here, drink some water. You'll be better. It will soothe some of that queasiness."

"Thank you." I took a sip but then chugged half a glass. Within a few minutes, the world stopped spinning so quickly. An hour and a half later, with some coaxing from Harriet and two lady's maids, my hair was done, and my dress slipped over me. But then I faced another problem.

"I cannot hold my breath for God knows how long. The dress is too tight."

"You'll be fine."

"Are you sure? I'm not sure," I said, bordering on hysterics. "It is conceivable that I will choke to death."

"Your bodice is not too tight. Besides, you will only have to wear it for another twelve hours or so." The smile on Harriet's face disturbed me. Was she thinking of my wedding night? Well, I was, too.

"I understand what you're trying to say. I spoke to your mother, and she told me everything."

"About?"

I rolled my eyes. "My wedding night. Wasn't that what you meant by twelve hours, and I'll be out of this dress?"

Her cheeks flushed, I assumed, from embarrassment or perhaps from the effort of holding back a laugh. "And what advice did my mother give you?"

I swallowed, recalling her exact words. "She said a wedding night should be treated with reverence. The consummation of the vows is sacred."

"That sounds like her."

"I also spoke with Mrs. Forbes and Alice after her wedding and was told the same."

Harriet loosened the ties in my bodice. I exhaled.

"My responsibility is to my home and my husband's faithfulness to God, the church, and his continent. Everything is centered on him." As I recited what I'd learned, a chill crept beneath my hoops, skirts, and silk layers. Freddie had slipped into my thoughts, and I wondered if God, seeing my hypocrisy, would punish me for making love to a man I didn't love.

"You have been successful in everything you've attempted, Sarah," Harriet said. "From playing the piano and singing songs to translating the King James Bible into Yoruba. You will be a dutiful wife."

It was an unexpected compliment. Indeed, everything about Harriet's presence was unexpected. "Why are you here, Harriet? What has possessed you to take me on during this time?"

"Her Majesty, of course."

I was confused. "The queen has instructed you to watch over me?"

"The queen has requested I assist in your wedding preparations, and on your wedding day I will be to you as I am to her."

"Which is what? Aren't you Her Majesty's confidante?"

"I was appointed the queen's maid of honor and will be a lady-in-waiting one day. The queen is grieving, but she still has a heart. And you've been challenging, but also someone she's very fond of. I am here to represent her for these days. You should treat it as a gift for your wedding."

"Well, please thank Her Majesty for allowing you to be here," I said, but the irony made me sad. Her Majesty supported a marriage I never wanted. But that is the privilege of a queen.

I was married on Thursday, August 14, 1862, my husband's thirty-fourth birthday, at St. Nicholas Church in Brighton, Sussex, England. The wedding was held at eleven in the morning, the ideal time for weddings. I might not have loved Captain Davies, but I loved our wedding.

* * *

THE PEOPLE OF Brighton were on the edge of their seats on
my wedding day. Even the uninvited lined the block to catch a
glimpse of the African princess and her wealthy African captain.

It was quite an elegant affair. Sixteen bridesmaids, all of
whom I knew from social gatherings with the royal household or Schon family, were separated into four groups. The
first were ladies of color, brown- and black-skinned, in white
dresses with red ribbon trimmings around the neck and across
the chest and bosom. A sash of the same color was fastened
at the waist. Long streams of ribbon reached the ground. All
the bridesmaids wore tarlatan opera cloaks, thrown over their
shoulders, of different colors according to the hue of their
gowns. Some wore bonnets encircled in tulle of the purest
white, the latest fashion. The European bridesmaids wore sun
hats trimmed with apple blossoms and forget-me-nots, and
white lace streamers hung down their backs.

The last group to enter the church included me, the groom,
and five groomsmen of color, followed by six young ladies
ages six to twelve. Forget-me-nots were everywhere, adorning heads, affixed to gowns, and sprinkled throughout the
church. I loved the flower, its smell, its pretty pale petals, and
its name—how romantic. I loved them so much that from that
day on, whenever I was asked about my favorite flower, I always said "forget-me-not."

I was draped in pure white. My dress of glaze silk, with trimmings of the same material, included orange blossoms circling
my brow and a veil of white lace dropping over my shoulders
and bosom. What more could I want from a wedding?

Commander Forbes's brother, a captain in the British Navy,

traveled from Scotland along with Mrs. Forbes. I hadn't thought who might give me away, but when he offered, I could think of no better man. It was as if the commander were with me.

So many emotions gathered and collided to give me a cherished memory. I don't know how, but I saw my father's face. Everywhere I looked, I saw him smiling at me. His face, one I hadn't been able to remember for so long, had appeared to me. I grabbed Captain Forbes's arm and held on to it with all my might.

"Are you well?" he asked.

I didn't look at him. I wanted to keep the dream alive in my mind's eye. "I am fine. I am fine."

The ringing of the church bells marked the end of the service, and eighty of us loaded into our carriages and made the short trip to breakfast. The queen had arranged for us to dine at the West Hill Lodge, the most prestigious accommodation in Brighton.

That was the first day I spent as the wife of Captain James P. L. Davies. A very long, very important day.

* * *

FREDDIE HAD BEEN lurking in my thoughts of late, but in the hours after the wedding, my head was full of forget-me-nots.

By the time I had my first dance as the wife of my new husband, I had thought that Captain James P. L. Davies might be an interesting man to know. Between the post-wedding breakfast toasts, the afternoon tea at the hotel, his speech, and the small dinner with his siblings, Mama Forbes, and the commander's brother, I learned he was an accomplished host, in addition to being a philanthropist (which I had deemed a sign of boastfulness). He also was well-read.

"My brother James is a very talented man, Sarah," said Clifford, the younger brother, who was as sizable a man as Captain Davies but closer to my age. "He's an avid reader, too. Did you realize he is obsessed with Shakespeare and Dickens?"

I put down my teacup. "No, I did not."

"He's also an excellent marksman, which has come in handy a time or two, wouldn't you say, brother?"

"You should talk less about my accomplishments, Clifford. My young bride might misinterpret it. I will go through my hobbies with her later."

"Your wife knows nothing about you. Leave it to your brothers to fill in the void."

Captain Davies chuckled. "I'd rather you didn't."

Clifford's laugh was louder, with a daggerlike twist on the end. "Considering you can shoot the eyes out of an owl from a hundred paces, I should do as you say and shut my trap, eh?"

The tension was growing between the two brothers. The other siblings remained mum rather than jump into the fire. Was I the only one concerned?

"You have quite the well of talents, Captain Davies," I said. But then I added, "James." I had promised him that after the wedding I'd try and use his given name when we were in public. "I am fond of Shakespeare, too. But I haven't read his works as much as I've watched the performances at theaters in London."

"You are an aristocrat, Mrs. Davies." Clifford raised his wineglass.

James side-eyed him a warning but then addressed the others seated near us. "I also have read the King James Bible and the poetry of Nana Asma'u. I do not limit my readings to British or European writers only."

"Oh, here we go. My older brother is not against the ruling government. It's just that he believes in the tribes of Africa. I bet you didn't know that."

Not only didn't I know that; I didn't know what he was talking about. "What does that mean?" I asked.

"It's made up," whispered James's sister, who sat to my right.

"I heard you, Pearl," Clifford said. "Hell, he's going to get in trouble if he—"

"That's enough, Clifford."

That was when I realized his brother might have had too much wine. Captain Davies sounded angry. Not an emotion a gentleman showed in mixed company.

"I'm sorry, Sarah," he said.

"What did your brother mean, if anything? I'm curious."

"It means patriotism, not to the government of the state you live in, but to the tribe, race, or sect with which you share an ancestral origin."

"Oh, I see." But I didn't. What was about to happen was a full-scale argument (perhaps a fight) between the brothers if the topic wasn't dropped. Captain Davies might have had the same thought, for suddenly, he was on his feet, giving a speech.

The only problem was that he wasn't talking about his wedding or his new bride. He was discussing the British colonization of Sierra Leone. The issue sounded political, so I stopped listening. But he held the attention of every man in the room, although the Reverends Venn and Dicker didn't look pleased.

Then he switched from politics and was talking about me. My interest in his words returned.

"My bride deserves all the gifts a man can bestow upon his wife." At this point, I believed he had had twice as much to drink as I had.

I frowned, not angry, but with a puckered face, wondering where the conversation was headed. Then suddenly, Captain Davies took hold of my hand and pulled me to the center of the room, wrapped an arm around my waist, and we were dancing our first dance as husband and wife.

Chapter Forty

Brighton, England, 1862

We didn't arrive at the hotel until late in the evening, entering our suite to find our bags had been not only delivered but unpacked.

It was a glamorous series of rooms. Everywhere shimmered with silk and satin, elegant portraits with gilded frames, fresh forget-me-nots, roses, and geraniums in ivory vases.

A streetlamp's light beamed through the window, spilling onto the floral Persian rugs and illuminating the canopied bed.

I took a step back, trying to reason with the butterflies in my stomach, and repeated to myself—this was my duty. And I would be treated with care and respect: I could do this.

As soon as my hands stopped shaking and my heart stopped threatening to burst, I'd be just fine.

I rang for a servant to bring me my nightgown, hairbrush, and combs. Then I dismissed her. The sooner my husband and I consummated our vows, the sooner I could sleep. It had been a long day.

I entered the bathroom near the suite's parlor, closed the door, and began to undress.

My floor-length nightgown was white, with capped sleeves, an embroidered front, a lace collar and cuffs, and lovely long satin ribbons tied loosely at my throat. Once dressed, I studied my appearance in the mirror. Despite the cumbersome outfit, I looked pretty—no, quite beautiful in the nightgown. However, I examined the gown's ties and adornments and wondered how I would get out of it once I was in bed.

I had no idea and sighed at my failure to figure it out. I'd have to leave it up to Captain Davies.

Still gazing at my image in the mirror, I recalled long ago I'd run past the object that reflected me. I imagined I'd matured enough to feel comfortable looking at the handsome woman with a slender frame, a tiny waist, and beautiful hands with long tapered fingers and narrow wrists.

Over the years, the scars on my face had changed, but only slightly since childhood. My brown eyes were as round and large, with thick black lashes like an owl's. A somewhat broad but regal nose, high cheekbones, and full lips that Freddie said always seemed to pout.

However, this new confidence didn't mean I was ready to leave the bathroom. I took another hour. But when I emerged, the suite had been transformed.

In the middle of the room, on the center table, were a pair of candelabras burning tall thin candles, a vase of red roses, and two table settings with a bottle of champagne, fruit, cheese, bread, and gingerbread cakes. I wondered how Captain Davies knew of my passion for gingerbread cakes.

I'm sure I hadn't mentioned it. He must have noticed at our reception how many slices I had eaten.

Everything was in front of me. The only thing missing was my husband.

The door opened.

"Mrs. Davies, would you do me the honor of joining me for a late supper?" He walked to the center table. I had not moved from the doorway of the bathroom. And my wobbly legs felt as if they wouldn't move anytime soon.

He was dressed in a Hamburg dressing gown (I'd heard about them from a maid at Windsor Castle). It had floral ornaments, bold reds and blues, in a satin fabric of the highest quality. Beneath the robe's hem, I spotted the cuffs of silk pajamas.

We both were prepared for bed.

I had planned to move gracefully to my seat, but I could be clumsy, and as I approached the table, I stumbled. But Captain Davies covered the distance between us with long strides and captured my wrist with a steady hand before I landed on the floor.

"Thank you. A fall would have been embarrassing."

"I'm glad I was here." He pulled out a chair, and I sat as daintily as my nerves allowed. He took the seat across from me.

"Would you like champagne?" he asked.

"I love champagne," I said. Then I added, for no reason, "I also drink the occasional whiskey and sherry, too."

He stood. "The champagne is dry and sparkling, not the sweet wine you might be accustomed to, so often served to ladies with desserts."

"I don't like sweet wines," I replied, wanting to add that I knew the difference between sweet and dry champagne. But why sound boastful?

The pop of the cork made me jump. "Oh, my."

He laughed and filled two glasses, handing one to me.

"May I make a toast?"

"Of course."

He raised his glass. "To my bride, Sarah Forbes Bonetta Davies. May there be many happy days ahead for us to enjoy together."

"Happy days."

We clinked glasses, and I gulped half my champagne. The bubbles got into my nose, and I made the tiniest unladylike sound. Captain Davies's mouth curved into a smile.

"Would you like another?"

"Why not?"

He poured, and then we drank until he stood and reached for me. One more gulp, and I was on my feet, being led toward the bed, our meal forgotten.

I decided to focus on the wallpaper. It reminded me of a spring garden full of tulips, hyacinths, and wood anemones, with butterflies and snails. It was red, lavender, pink, and the most magnificent shade of blue. I thought of the bluestone necklace, my heirloom, lost in Africa so long ago. As I sat on the bed, the heavy gown slipping off my shoulder, I could see them, the people who had cherished it, my father and Dayo; the ones who had saved it, Monife and William; and the one who had stolen it, Rose. I closed my eyes. I had not been able to summon their images for so long—Dayo's boyish face, Monife's sly smile, or William's toothless grin.

"What are you thinking?" Captain Davies asked me.

We sat on the bed side by side, his hands on his knees, my hands in my lap.

The waiting was going to kill me. "What should we do first, Captain Davies?"

"I wondered if you could call me by my first name. I think that would be a good place to begin."

I licked my lips and took a deep breath. "James—what should we do next?"

"May I kiss you?"

"On the cheek or the lips?"

He tilted his head and smirked. I turned my head to hide my smile.

"I think we should kiss on the lips," he whispered.

His breath was warm on the side of my neck.

He placed a hand lightly on my shoulder. The other hand wrapped around my waist, and with both, he pulled me to him and kissed me on the mouth. Then he kept kissing me until I parted my lips and kissed him back. It was a quiet kiss but warm and soft.

Everything that had happened in the past year, my entire life, or the past day had brought me to the edge of this bed, and I didn't mind being kissed. A kiss entirely different from my first kiss, the one I'd shared with Freddie.

I loved Freddie. I didn't love my husband, but his lips on my mouth, throat, breasts, and body made it hard to remember Freddie's kiss.

We kissed for a long time, and after a while, we lay in bed, my beautiful nightgown and his silk pajamas in a heap on the floor. He held me gently, then passionately, until he consumed me, and I opened to him, and we cried out in ecstasy as we consummated our marriage vows.

I did not know my body could feel how he had made it feel. I had thought only love made your body ache with pleasure. Was it possible to have intimacy without love?

Or had something more mysterious and complicated happened between us?

I wanted to ask him if he was as confused as I was. And if he wanted to kiss me again. Or if he wanted to ignite the heat of my body like when he was inside me again. But the air in the room was pulled away from me into the farthest corners of the suite. I lay next to him, holding on to him, hanging on to him as the world shattered. Then he released me. Pushed me away. He seemed to be struggling with himself. He hadn't pushed me hard. It was just that I missed the nearness of him. I felt abandoned.

Something was wrong. I sat upright, pulling the sheet to my throat. "What is it?" I asked.

"I can't."

"Can't what?"

He looked wild-eyed, as though he'd seen a ghost. I had seen ghosts while we kissed, but my ghosts hadn't frightened me—for the first time in a long while. "Are you well, James?"

"I can't." He sat on the edge of the bed, a shudder quaking through his body. When it passed, he stood and stared down at me. "I'm sorry."

What was he apologizing for? "You didn't hurt me. I feel fine."

"I can't. I'm sorry."

I was beginning to panic. If he didn't give me a sentence I could understand, I would scream. "I don't understand. I need to understand. You are scaring me." Now I was shaking and didn't like him looming over me. I scooted away, shot to my feet, and put some distance between us. "What is wrong with you?"

Shaking his head (but not talking, which wasn't helping me), he picked up his dressing gown from the floor. He then tied it around his waist with such force I feared he'd cut himself in half.

"I am so sorry, Sarah. I care for you. I wanted to marry you. I need to be married to you, but"—he pointed at the bed—"this was too soon."

"I don't understand. I am standing before you, naked." I

pointed at the bed. "We consummated our vows! And you are acting like a madman. Wandering about apologizing—telling me it's too soon?" He was stripping the flesh from my body. "If you don't hurry up and make some sense, I will—God, I don't know what I'll do. James. Please."

He slowly grew taller, pulling his backbone into place, broadening his shoulders, and preparing himself for the battle ahead. "I still love her, and I didn't know. I swear I didn't think I'd feel this way."

I raised my hand. "Stop."

"Sarah."

"I said stop. Did you hear me? Stop talking." I pulled a sheet from the bed and held it in front of my nude body. "If you dare say another word, I can't make promises."

Hugging the sheet around me, I closed my eyes. It was almost ironic—each of us was in love with someone we could never have. I almost laughed, except for how foolish I felt—my God. I'd given him my body in a sacred act of marriage. Wasn't that what Mrs. Phipps had said? Was it her or one of the other wives? "So, you still love Matilda, which is fine. Didn't you tell me as much the other day at the photographer's studio? And now, you feel as if you've betrayed her. I understand. We need not do this again."

I nodded toward the bed, feeling oddly on firmer ground. The calm, controlled behavior of the robust and powerful man of prestige and conviction, my dear husband, was a mask that hid a heartbroken man full of messy emotions and longing. He was just like me. Except he was in love with his dead wife, and I was in love with a fairy tale.

"As you've said, Captain Davies, we married because of our duty to Africa. So let us get about that duty. There's another bedroom in the suite. I would request that you find it now, Captain."

* * *

AFTER RIPPING OFF the sheets, I spent most of the night curled up on the mattress, thinking about how I had allowed myself to be tricked by Captain Davies and by my emotions. Sometime during our wedding, I had thought for a moment that maybe I'd like him one day.

Determined to have the best wedding, I had held on to the childish belief that a grand event would make up for everything wrong with the marriage. But, adding insult to the rest of it, the wedding night had been a disaster of proportions only the gods could have imagined—and if I had been smarter, less gullible, less enchanted by a wedding ceremony, I would have paid more attention, I would not have been fooled by him the way I had.

The following day, Captain Davies and I were back at square one in our relationship, except he was my husband, and soon, we had a sea voyage to begin.

At breakfast in the parlor of our hotel suite, I put on the face I'd wear for the next few months. The nothing-has-happened expression, I called it. Bright, shiny eyes, quick small smiles, an unfurrowed brow, and, when necessary, a light laugh, like a whimsical musical chord, something by Haydn, I imagined.

With practice, I could imitate whatever emotion I needed to, to convince anyone who didn't know the truth about us that we were happily married.

Funny, I discovered my new husband was a fine actor, too.

He arrived for breakfast late, smiling and appearing well-rested and pleasant on the morning after our wedding night.

His performance was for the servants, I presumed. I did not require it.

With a plate of food in front of him and the butler fading into the wallpaper, he looked at me.

"We will leave for Freetown tomorrow. Everything has been arranged, and I'm sure you will enjoy the stateroom I have reserved. However, we must remain in Freetown for quite some time, who knows how many months, before continuing on to Lagos."

The objection was on the tip of my tongue. I just needed to control my tone. "I thought we were heading to Lagos from here."

"I received a telegram, and my business interests in Freetown require my guidance," he claimed. "It's a brief detour. You should not be concerned."

"What will I do in Freetown while you work?"

He nodded. "I had a feeling you'd ask that question. So I've arranged for you to teach at the Female Institution."

He had what? How many plans had he made without mentioning them to me, even in passing? "I went to school there."

"And you met me there."

"I don't remember meeting you. I told you that once before." I sipped my coffee and spread jam on my toast. "Is Miss Sass still there?"

"She is, as well as Miss Wilkerson."

"Too bad. I never liked her. But you say I will work at the Female Institution?" I pursed my lips in thought. "Then I will teach my students about cultural things. Music. Singing. Reading novels."

"I believe they already have a curriculum for their female students."

"I'm sure they could use some new classes."

"I'm sure they don't have the supplies you'll need for those courses."

I smirked more than smiled at him. "You are a philanthropist. Can't you buy what the school will need for my classes? Like a piano and sheet music?"

"Aha." He took a bite of a pastry. "Yes. I'm sure I can."

"The Institution will appreciate your generosity."

And I could use a chance to do something I wanted to do with my life.

* * *

I AWOKE TO the smell of fire and smoke, constricting my lungs and burning my eyes. Tears fell freely onto my cheeks, lips, and chin. I don't recall much about the hotel fire besides being carried to safety in Captain Davies's arms through the flames.

I should have thanked him, but the smoke seared my lungs, and all I could do was cough.

The fire broke out the night before we departed for Sierra Leone.

So many of our belongings were lost, our wedding gifts, those that had not been taken to the ship. Some of the damaged or destroyed gifts had come from the queen. Vases, linens, beautiful china—items I had planned to use for the luxury I intended to create in my new home.

I hid my face and wept.

The alarms of fire trucks took away any drowsiness that might have lingered inside me. We stood in the lobby in our robes. I had a blanket wrapped around me, watching for more fire trucks to arrive, but when no more came, I was confused.

Also, only a handful of people in the lobby appeared to have been disturbed by the fire.

I turned to Captain Davies. "Where was the blaze?"

"It appeared to have been set in our parlor."

"In only our suite?"

"That is what the investigators are telling me."

"I don't understand. Someone set our suite on fire. Why? Who would do such a thing?"

"Sarah, you can't be so naïve." Captain Davies's gaze darted around the lobby. He looked like a hunter searching for prey or someone who fitted the crime of a fire starter. "We've drawn a lot of attention in Brighton. Some don't like seeing Black aristocrats doing whatever any aristocrat would do in London."

"I have experienced jealousy, but violence? We could have been killed."

"You haven't been exposed to the base elements of society. As the queen's ward, you were protected from those who saw you as a savage. Or an untrustworthy barbarian." His voice had turned dark and scraped the ground with malice.

I hugged my blanket around me tighter. He used words like "savage" and "barbarian" as if he'd been called such names in his lifetime.

My memory stirred to life. I had been called a savage, a barbarian once, too. But the last time I'd heard "barbarian" was the first time I'd heard it, spoken by a white woman, a missionary in Badagry. Many years ago.

I was around seven years old. I'd never been called a name like that since. But the fire and Captain Davies's words reminded me it could happen again. It had happened again, but instead of words, the culprit had used a match.

Chapter Forty-one

Freetown, Sierra Leone, 1862

We were on board the ship to Sierra Leone the day after the hotel fire. It was a calm voyage, the calmest seas I'd ever experienced traveling between Britain and Africa. I took it as a sign of the rest of my life: peaceful, slow, uncomplicated, with a steady wind in my sails and the song of whales in my ears (and, hopefully, no fires).

Nothing incredible would happen to me from now on. I would end my journey in this life as it had begun on a riverbank in Africa, but with a man I did not love and who could not love me.

I had no room left in my heart for love, anyway. What mattered was how to make Africa bearable. Thankfully, Captain Davies had enough money to give me anything I desired. I'd already gotten him to agree that vacations to London would be frequent and lengthy. And once we traveled to Lagos and I saw the home where we would live there, he also promised that he would make whatever changes I deemed necessary.

My only other concern would be our proximity to Dahomey, even if it were hundreds of miles away, even if King Gezo was dead. Assassinated in '59. His son, Glele, was king now and as ruthless and predatory as his father. The fear of the Dahomey warriors, the Amazons, as the British called them, still haunted me, but my husband was an excellent marksman. Perhaps I would ask him to teach me how to shoot.

We arrived in Freetown thirty-three days after leaving England and moved in with Reverend Venn, who was spending more time in Africa. I was civil around him. He was a minister of God. I would not show him disrespect, but I also avoided him whenever possible. Easier than I thought, because he and Captain Davies spent most of their time together, and since avoiding my husband was also a goal of mine, I killed two birds with one stone.

After a few days of getting acclimated, I began my tenure at the Female Institution.

Nearly a decade before, Miss Julia Sass and Mary Wilkerson had controlled my day-to-day life. Now I was a proper British lady, married to a philanthropist. Maturely, I pushed the events of the past from my mind. Or at least, I tried.

On my first day, I entered the rectory, and Miss Sass swept me up in an embrace.

"My dear, young Sarah. You look like such a lady—all grown up and married. And returning to Africa. You've had such an adventure of life, dear. I am sure the years to come will be even more outstanding."

I wasn't as thrilled to see her as she was to see me, but I liked her, so I behaved. "Thank you. I am thrilled to be here, Miss Sass." She released me then, perhaps hearing the chill in my tone. "You look wonderful, too. Like a young girl. You haven't aged a year."

"I'm not that old, Sarah. I just celebrated my twenty-ninth birthday. Middle-aged, yes, but you were very young when you arrived."

"I guess that is part of the reason I thought of you as older." I sighed, looking forward to changing the subject. "You've spent all these years in Freetown?"

"Yes, I have, and gladly. This is my calling. Missionary work, teaching these young girls, and helping Africa become a continent of educated Christians." She smiled. "But I don't need to explain that to you. You do surprise me, though."

"How's that? Because I'm married to a wealthy man?"

"I always knew you'd find a good husband, but Captain Davies is a hero to the Africans and many missionaries here, too." She moved behind the desk and sat, gesturing for me to sit opposite her. "Do you remember meeting him?"

I shook my head at a question I'd been asked more than once.

"He was with me when you and Abigail stormed in that day. Her father was here, and Reverend Venn, and they frightened you horribly, but unintentionally, talking about King Gezo."

My hand clasped my throat. The memory came at me like a runaway train. "I do remember," I said, looking around the room. "I met him here in this rectory. He was on his knees and said not to worry."

"That was your husband, Captain Davies."

I raised a brow. "Mmm."

"He has watched over you for years in his way."

"What way is that?"

"His financial contributions kept the school open, giving Mary—Miss Wilkerson—and I the funds to run it."

"He is a generous man, or so he and others have told me."

She raised a brow, picking up on my sarcasm, I presumed. "You're a lucky girl, or, excuse me, young woman."

I smiled half-heartedly. Luck was in the eye of the beholder.

"Well, I guess we should get started. I have some lovely ideas for the curriculum. Music. Singing. Novels. Theater."

She looked perplexed. "We don't have supplies for any of those things, Sarah."

"I anticipated as much. I brought some sheet music with me from London to get us started. My husband will donate the funds for the remaining supplies. He's also arranged for a piano to be brought here for the chapel. Later, we will offer piano lessons. Meanwhile, the girls will learn hymns and sing them during services. I'll play at the services until others learn. I'm quite good."

"Oh, dear." She pressed her lips together. "That's divine."

I stood as a figure appeared in the doorway. I had expected to see Miss Wilkerson, but it wasn't her. "Rose Orji. What are you doing here?"

She gulped. "Sarah, I thought you weren't scheduled to come until tomorrow."

"Rose teaches here, too," Miss Sass said brightly. "Arithmetic and sewing."

"And thievery, I imagine." The words slipped from my mouth.

"Now, Sarah," Rose said. "I can explain."

How dare she look so calm? I was shaking with rage. Wasn't she afraid that so many years of anger would travel into fists and I'd pummel her within an inch of her life? My nightmare turned into a premonition. "The only thing I wish to hear from you is an answer to the question, where is my pendant?"

Miss Sass circled the desk and slid in between us. "What are you thinking, young ladies? You are no longer schoolgirls."

I spun toward her. "She stole my bluestone necklace, and I

want it back." I faced Rose. "Do you have it?" My voice roared, but I didn't care. "Answer me!"

Miss Sass shifted her shoulders, making me aware of how close I'd gotten to Rose, who had stood her ground but finally stepped back.

"Yes, I still have it," she said. "And I will bring it to you."

My chest ached. "You will bring it to me?" My voice had climbed to an octave I couldn't even sing. "How dare you take it in the first place?"

Miss Sass shot Rose an expression of disbelief. "You stole her property? Oh, my dear. That's awful. Why did you take it?"

Rose jutted her chin with pride. "It was a gift to the Iroko tree to save my brother's life."

"Really," I grumbled. "I had thought once upon a time that the tree would bring back the dead, but I was a child." I grabbed her arm. "Why would you think it would save him?"

"Because it did. He survived and lives to this day."

My mouth closed. The precious tree hadn't worked for me. "Then you will go to your house to retrieve my necklace."

"It is not in my house. I buried it beneath the magical tree."

* * *

THE BLUESTONE PENDANT, my family's necklace, the heirloom. How strange was fate? I had returned to Africa, a continent I had never wanted to set foot on again, and within days, fortune returned what had been stolen from me.

We had to dig for hours. Captain Davies and Rose's brother helped us find it, wrapped in a heavy piece of burlap. It had weathered rain, mud, insects, and time, but the brilliant shade of blue stone was as beautiful and vibrant as ever.

I would've hugged Rose, but she had stolen it in the first

place. So I couldn't bring myself to do that, but I did tell her I was glad her brother was alive.

It turned out that Tiwa hadn't lied. Rose returned to her family a few nights after her disappearance and they left town together for Lagos and a hospital for her sickly brother. But he'd shown signs of recovery even before they reached Lagos.

My relief at having the necklace in my possession again was boundless. At breakfast the following morning, I spoke to Captain Davies without pretense.

I had lived in a nightmare that had turned into a dream and was capable of showing kindness to anyone, even him.

Our conversations now were polite and oftentimes friendly. We slept in separate rooms, interacting at breakfast mostly, and dined separately for lunch and most dinners without raising suspicion (as far as we knew). The explanation for our separate sleeping arrangements was that Captain Davies's snoring could wake the dead. And that was enough to deter any unwanted glances.

One evening, however, Reverend Venn and his wife had company for dinner. Reverend Crowther and his daughter Abigail, my friend from the Female Institution.

I wrapped her up in my arms within seconds of her entering the house. "Abigail, it is wonderful to see you again."

"Oh, my dear. Isn't this fate? After reading about your wedding in the *Penny Illustrated Paper*, I mentioned you the other day. What a grand affair."

I nodded, smiling politely, but I wasn't interested in discussing my wedding. It felt like old news—no longer a popular topic.

After reintroductions, we enjoyed a splendid dinner of cassava leaf and goat stew served with jollof rice, okra, and yams.

I sat next to Abigail, and we chatted like schoolgirls, catching up on the big moments we'd missed in each other's lives. We hadn't written for reasons I can't explain. Perhaps my guilt about how I'd left Freetown, although she never knew what I was thinking at the time.

Abigail had recently married and hoped to be with child soon. I mostly talked about parties, the theater, and balls at Windsor Castle, the glamorous things I'd left behind in London. I stayed away from the unmentionables—like Freddie and the year and a half I'd spent in exile in Brighton.

Halfway through the meal, however, I started to feel faint. My stomach wasn't behaving correctly. The meal was delicious. I ate the same thing everyone else ate. I had eaten soup from the market for lunch when I went on a short walk between classes at the Female Institution. But something had felt wrong for a couple of weeks.

I excused myself from the dinner table, fearing I would be sick at any moment. My health hadn't been in question for years. The only sickness I'd had was a bad cough and a runny nose. But this was something different.

It took a while, and I did get sick more than once, but after a bit, I felt well enough to return to dinner. I washed up with the intent of rejoining the dinner party, but by then, the ladies were in the library, sipping tea and snacking on sweets.

Abigail sat on the sofa, and I joined her while Mrs. Venn excused herself to handle a matter in the kitchen.

"Are you all right?" Abigail asked. "I noticed you seemed preoccupied and tired at dinner but full in the chest and tummy."

I pinched my cheeks self-consciously. "I have been feeling poorly lately. Suffering from an upset stomach and lightheadedness for a couple of weeks, but it goes away."

Abigail twisted sideways, a broad smile on her face. "Are you with child?"

"Excuse me?"

She lowered her voice. "Are you having a baby?"

"No. That is impossible."

"I don't believe that's true." She smiled. "You've been a married woman for almost two months. You could be with child."

"I don't think so, but I don't know."

Her eyes widened, and the expression of alarm was a bit shocking. "No one talked to you about your time of the month?"

"Yes, Miss Sass had to when I was twelve."

Abigail spent the next few minutes explaining how the time of the month was connected to wedding nights and babies.

"I know these things, but we were together that way only once and never again."

"Now I don't understand."

"We have been man and wife in bed only once, but the marriage was consummated. Still, it is not a marriage of love."

"Captain Davies is a great man, but why would you marry him if you didn't love him?"

I gave her a grim smile. The story was too fresh and painful to tell in detail, but Abigail always had been astute. Most of London might have known a version of why, but I hadn't told a soul. However, Abigail always managed to get the truth out of me, perhaps because she asked the hard questions to my face.

"It was arranged by the queen of England, Reverend Venn, and most likely your father, too. They are all the captain's good friends." I paused. "Captain Davies proposed to me twice before I accepted his offer of marriage. I didn't know him. I didn't love him, but as I have stated, the queen required me to marry him." I didn't intend to go into any deeper detail than that.

"I don't mean to sound unsympathetic, but why refuse to marry a man with the wealth and prestige of Captain Davies? A woman would be foolhardy to refuse such a man. Unless." She studied me with a sideways glance that cut through me. "You were in love with someone else?"

I smiled. "I am. Or was, I don't know anymore. But yes, I was in love with a minister's son. We grew up together and had confessed our love for one another a month before the captain proposed."

"A minister's son? Was he a man of means? A descendant of a nobleman? Of royalty?"

I frowned at her. "What is it, Abigail? What are you implying?"

"He had no money, Sarah. It sounds more like a girl's crush than a man you would marry. How would you have lived? I never imagined you marrying someone like that. You had a tragic beginning, but most of your life since has been charmed. You have lived as a princess for longer than you were enslaved. I can't imagine you with anyone other than Captain Davies. You and he are aristocrats." She laughed. "Now you may be with child, and if you are, you will love that baby more than you've cared for any man who walks the earth. I know I would."

"You don't understand, Abigail. You are in love with your husband and would walk through fire for him."

"One day, you will feel you'd do the same for Captain Davies." She reached for her teacup on the table. "From what I've read in the newspaper, he has already walked through fire to save you."

The night of the hotel fire that only burned in our suite. "Yes, he saved me. But I never read a news report about the fire. I had expected lies. Never a story about my husband as a hero."

Abigail put down her cup. "If you started your marriage without love, you'll find it somewhere down the road. And if you are with child, the baby will bring you closer."

"I'm sorry, but it won't work out. The captain loves his first wife, Matilda. Did you know her?"

Abigail pressed her palms together beneath her chin, looking as if she was about to pray. "I met her once, but they married and left for the Caribbean. By the time they returned, she was ill, and she died shortly after."

"You didn't meet them in Freetown?"

"I spend most of my time in Abeokuta, at my father's mission."

Not that I believed Abigail, but a flutter in my stomach made me wonder. "What if I am pregnant? What will I do?" I covered my mouth with my hands. "I can't have a baby by him."

"When I say he is a great man, I mean it. He saved Lagos last year. The British had put a tyrant in charge of their operations there. His name was Commander Bedingfield. He attempted to force Lagos's native chieftain, King Dosumu, to sign the Treaty of Cession of Lagos to the British government. That commander was ready to attack Lagos to get him to sign it. Captain Davies intervened and wrote a protest letter on behalf of King Dosumu to Queen Victoria—and it worked."

"I am glad about his successes, but I was given no choice but to marry him. His heroism will be rewarded elsewhere, I'm sure."

"He's not that type of man. He is sincerely God-fearing. He's brash but humble. If such a combination exists. No one knows he wrote that letter but my father and Reverend Venn, who hand-delivered it to Her Majesty. He doesn't shout his victories from the mountaintops."

Then she spoke quietly. "Back to the possibility of your pregnancy. When you go to bed tonight, go through the days and weeks and make a chart of what you can remember of the dates of your monthly. If you can't, that's fine, too. Wait another three weeks. If the sickness continues and your breasts become larger and sore, you are with child. And if you are, think of a way to fall in love with your husband. It will make your life and your child's much easier."

Chapter Forty-two

Freetown, Sierra Leone, 1862

Three weeks after my chat with Abigail, my monthly visitor had yet to arrive, which meant I was with child. How had one night led to such an unbelievable situation? But I refused to remain alone in my shocked state for long. It was time to share the news with Captain Davies.

I sat at the breakfast table, stirring the food on my plate with a fork. Unfortunately, Captain Davies was late, and when he finally entered the dining room he was preoccupied. He walked from the buffet to the table three times before finally taking his seat. He hadn't spoken, and although we didn't say much during meals, he always gave me a gentlemanly morning greeting.

"Not like you not to speak," I said with a bit of saltiness. "Good morning, Captain."

"I apologize. Good morning, Sarah." He sat and stared at his plate. "I received disturbing news from Lagos this morning, and it's on my mind." He lifted his head.

"Oh." I didn't ask for any details. We didn't discuss his business dealings. "Well, I need to add to your news."

"In what way?"

"I haven't been well. You may have noticed. And when I mentioned it to Abigail a few weeks ago, she suggested I wait before I became too concerned."

"What is wrong? Are you ill? You should go to the doctor

immediately." He was on his feet, pacing around the breakfast table. I'd never seen him so agitated.

"I would hope what is wrong with me isn't a disease but a condition."

He stopped. "You know what's wrong?"

"I haven't seen my monthly visitor this month, or last month, for that matter. So I understand from Abigail there is a strong likelihood I am with child."

He dropped into his chair as if he'd been wounded.

"I won't know for certain until I visit a doctor. So don't be alarmed. It might be something other than a child."

"I will contact Reverend Venn's doctor, and you will see him today. I will make the arrangements now."

He excused himself and bolted from the table. I honestly couldn't tell if he was thrilled by the prospect of being a father or horrified.

The doctor confirmed my pregnancy later that afternoon.

We were in the parlor after dinner. Reverend Venn and his wife were out to dinner with friends.

"Would you please pour me a sherry?" I asked.

"Of course, Sarah." He brought me a glass and sat on the small sofa next to me.

I didn't know what to say. Where to begin? So I dove off the ledge. "Should we talk about the baby? I know it is unplanned. We aren't living as husband and wife, but we will need to make the best of it."

"Of course," he said, the muscles in his jaw tightening.

"I know it's a shock. To me as well. But I am taking it better than you."

"What do you mean?" He rose and poured himself a sherry.

"I am sorry if I am not behaving as you'd want me to. But . . ." He drained the sherry and poured another.

"I hope you aren't going to drink yourself to death because of it." I swallowed my sherry and extended the glass. "Another, please."

He took my glass and filled it.

"I know our relationship is not ideal, but I would have thought a child would interest you. Children are important if we are to be an elite presence in Lagos, I would think."

"You are right. It shows our commitment to this land, this history. This portion of Africa." He handed me a full glass. "But if you don't believe that . . ."

"Then what? You don't want the baby?"

He laughed. "God, I've wanted a child to love and cherish for my entire life."

My spine bristled. "But not with me?"

He sat in the chair across from me, rubbing his forehead. "That's not it. Or maybe it's part of it. I never told you the truth."

"Oh, yes, you have. On our wedding night, you spoke the truth."

He closed his eyes briefly. "That night was something different, but I wrote a letter to the Schons about Matilda's death and left out the truth about how she'd died."

"Which was?"

"She died in childbirth. She and my son died together within days after our return to Lagos from the Caribbean."

I took a sip of the sherry and put the glass on the table. Women died in childbirth. They died all the time, trying to bring life into the world. God, I hoped I wouldn't die. "I'm sorry, James. I'm sorry for your loss."

"Thank you." Then he was on his feet again, pacing. "She was such a sweet girl. She wanted to give me everything I wanted."

Different from me, I thought, but I held my tongue.

"So I hope you understand why I have acted the way I have," he muttered. "You see, I am afraid. I don't want to lose you or the baby. I couldn't save Matilda and our son, but I will keep the two of you safe and sound. I swear to God."

He might care for me beneath all the pain he was holding inside. He had loved his Matilda dearly but lost her. Now all he could think about was loss.

I chuckled to myself. Wouldn't you know, Captain Davies was a lot like me.

* * *

MY PREGNANCY WAS progressing healthily, I was told. No signs of trouble, according to the doctors whom James sent me to every other week. And yes, I called him James now, almost all the time. I thought it was the least I could do with a growing belly.

He doted on me. Or the baby inside me. From the flowers left in my room every morning to the footbaths and the back rubs, from the daily delivery of fresh herbs and spices, teas, and poultices to the African women who claimed they would ease the pain of my delivery.

None of which I took too seriously. I gathered that the captain's intense interest was not as much for me as for the child.

Matilda could never be replaced. The infant he never knew could be. His continuous acts of charity were tantamount to sainthood, I wrote to Princess Alice, but I also explained there was still no love between us. My letters would go on about my life in Freetown and waiting for the baby to come. But we still had many months before then and before we left Freetown for Lagos, the captain's true home.

My habit of writing daily letters had continued in Freetown. So Mrs. Forbes, Mrs. Phipps, and Mrs. Schon, and through these proxies, the Forbes household and the royal household, including Harriet and Alice, and, most assuredly, Freddie—all were kept up to date on my life in Africa.

After convincing my husband I wasn't an invalid, I kept teaching and having dinners with Abigail, her father, Reverend Venn, and his wife. Then, one November morning, I could tell something had happened when the captain's furrowed brow made more of an entrance to the breakfast room than he did.

We sat at the table, my stomach a bit queasy, as we waited for the maid to bring my oolong tea and plenty of sugar. It helped settle my upset morning stomach.

But the captain couldn't hold whatever was bothering him. "Sarah, I have something to tell you, and I don't want you to be upset."

My tea had arrived, and I was busy spooning mounds of sugar into my cup. "Why don't you tell me first, and then I'll let you know if I'm upset." I put down my spoon, having filled my teacup to the rim with tea.

"The governor has called on all British subjects to return from Abeokuta to Lagos, leaving their property in the hands of the chiefs of Abeokuta. Those chiefs will be answerable to the British government for that property."

"What does that have to do with you and me in Freetown?"

"It's complicated. But we also have been ordered back to Lagos."

"There are many things I don't understand about Africa, James. But I am not a child. I am with child and need to know why we are being told to leave Freetown months earlier than planned."

"It's Glele, the Dahomey king. He is sticking his foot into the mud to create trouble. And that trouble is getting too close to Freetown."

I dropped the spoon I was using to stir my tea. "Dahomey?" The trembling in my hand wouldn't stop.

James was on his feet and at my side. "What can I do?"

"A sherry would be good."

"Are you sure?"

"Don't get prudish with me now. If I don't stop shaking, my bones will break." He poured me a glass and held it to my lips, and I took a sip.

He set the glass down on the table and returned to his seat.

"I should be happy to return to Lagos," I said shakily. "Anything to be farther from Dahomey."

"As residents of Lagos, we are British subjects. All the subjects of Lagos in Africa are being called back to the colony. There is the chance of war among the chiefs of Abeokuta. The burden on the tribes is significant." He sighed, eyes nearly closed in thought. "There have been a number of robberies by Dahomey warriors on trade routes between Freetown and Abeokuta. Dahomey wants war, and the strategy is to deny access to trade routes to force men to fight. The plunder ceases when the war ends. In the meantime, the safety of the traders traveling to Abeokuta cannot be guaranteed. It's too dangerous. And Britain can't afford to get involved in a war between tribes. No matter how it harms the business of merchants."

"And you travel to Abeokuta often."

"Not personally. Not recently, now that you are pregnant. But my business does use the trade routes under attack."

I suddenly felt profoundly exhausted. With my elbows on the table, I rested my head in my palms. Why had I thought that Dahomey would no longer be a threat to me?

"Yes. We must leave. Can we go back to England?"

"Sarah, no."

"Why not? Do you want your baby to be butchered in his sleep by Agojie? The damn Dahomey Amazons? If we stay in Africa, it will happen. I know it will." I hugged my arms over my swelling stomach. "Please, James. Please. I want to go home. To England."

"You are home, Sarah, and you will be safe in Lagos. I promise you." He knelt in front of me. "I swear to God Almighty."

In a week, our bags were packed, and we sent load-bearers ahead with the many gifts, large and small, and keepsakes and furniture that had been shipped to us in anticipation of our furnishing a new home.

I was angry about not returning to England. So James again became Captain Davies to me. It was a punishment that brought me some satisfaction.

After a series of goodbye dinners in and around Freetown, we took a steamer down the coast, arriving in Lagos after a couple of weeks. I worried about Abigail and her father, but she said they were accustomed to living in Dahomey's backyard. The danger was losing the faith of Africans who relied on the mission for medical care and spiritual well-being. Abigail and Miss Sass were the women I would keep in my prayers and close to my heart.

And we were on our way to the Lagos colony and our supposedly permanent residence. Since I'd moved so many times over the years, I couldn't quite wrap my thoughts around the idea of a permanent home, especially if it didn't suit my expectations.

Maybe the thing to do upon arrival was to make sure it did suit me.

Chapter Forty-three

Lagos was a fishing community on the north of Lagos Island, lying in Lagos Lagoon, in a large harbor on the Atlantic coast of Africa in the Gulf of Guinea. James had built his house on Lagos Island.

I had heard his detailed description of the land, water, trees, earth, palm oil, and cocoa plants. I did love chocolate, and wondered if the cocoa plants were a gift he had intended for me, but then I recalled his telling me that he'd been exploring ways to bring the cocoa plant to Africa for years. He'd only met me when I was twelve.

The house was sturdy, resting on a hillside with a view of James's cocoa plants and fields of root vegetables. In addition to being a merchant of wares and fish, he also traded in fresh produce. He had boats at sea filled with goods. We were far enough inland to avoid the constant sounds of the fishermen and large ships that docked in the Lagos harbor. But I still could feel the strength of the water, and the sky had the beautiful fullness I loved while at sea.

"The grounds are lovely, Captain."

He smiled and nodded. "You love a garden, and I thought you could do what you would with it."

"It will need some work."

We stood on the veranda of the rambling two-story house.

It wasn't my home yet. I didn't know if it was brand new, although the smell of fresh paint and lye dominated the scent of the air around me.

"Shall we go inside the house?" Captain Davies walked into the foyer, holding my hand. Then he let go and spread his arms wide.

"Here you are, my dear. Your home." His puffed-up chest and dramatic gesture showed his pride in the estate he'd built for his bride. But I couldn't stop myself from wondering which one.

"Did you build this for Matilda or me?"

He looked like I'd stabbed him with one of my knitting needles. "I'm not being mean. I am curious."

"Sarah, I promised to give you everything. So if you'd prefer to live in another house in Lagos, I will build another house. Matilda never set foot in this one."

His voice hitched as if saying her name hurt his throat. I wanted to take back what I'd said about the house. It was beautiful. But Lagos was where he'd lived with Matilda. I just didn't like the idea of following in her footsteps any more than I already was. "I'm sorry. I was being rude."

He took my hand. "I'm not offended. Let me give you a tour."

It was a tropical house with a deep veranda and overhanging eaves in classic forms. "It's colonial but Victorian, as you can see by the floor plan."

"The rooms are so large, and the windows so high and wide."

"The upstairs?" From the large foyer, with a winding staircase to the second floor, we'd walked through the great room, kitchen, parlor, and a dining room as large as the first floor of the Welches' house in Brighton. From the exhaustion in my ankles and feet, I felt the house was as large as Palm Cottage.

"The only rooms furnished are the dining room and the bedrooms," he said.

"The library has furniture."

"But I thought you might wish to select the decor. So I didn't do too much. Just enough to be comfortable when I was here."

"You lived here."

"We started building the summer after Matilda's death." He cocked his head. "It was a few weeks after I received your letter refusing my first proposal."

"Oh, so you thought I'd marry you, then."

"Yes, I did."

"And I waited a year and a half to change my mind."

"Again, yes. You did."

"Where's my bedroom? My feet are hurting."

"I'll have a bath prepared for you. Sally will take care of it."

"Sally?"

"Yes, she runs the household. Keeps everything shipshape. She's been with my family since I was a boy. You'll meet her soon. She should be around somewhere."

"When will the load-bearers arrive?"

"Sarah, please. You should rest. I have a woman who has been with me since my sister and I were children. She can take care of the house."

"I may have to live in Africa, but I want a proper British home."

I had spoken boldly, but would he give me everything I wanted in exchange for my staying in Africa and giving him children?

"Perhaps a solid gold piano?"

I looked at him to see if I could detect sarcasm. But no, only his strong, straight nose and dark eyes. Hooded and heavily lashed, dark eyes. "I don't need a gold piano. I am a princess, not a queen."

* * *

THE FIRST TIME I met Sally Broderick, I wanted her to like me. Or was it that I wished I'd known her all my life? That would've made it easier between us.

She was warm-hearted and gracious, with a kind face and gnarled fingers. She worked hard, had round cheeks because she enjoyed cooking, and a manner that, if you didn't know her, made you want to. I had high hopes before we first met that she'd not only like me but, perhaps, love me the way she loved the Davies siblings. But she didn't. The tragedy was that I understood why I wasn't her favorite. I also understood I might not be able to change her mind.

Her problem with me, I assumed, was that she loved Matilda more. The idea of it made me dizzy. Why couldn't the dead leave me to live my life in peace?

"I have been a part of the Davies household since I was a young woman," Sally said while we were on the veranda after sunset a week after my arrival. "I was born enslaved but fled with my family to Freetown, and from there, I met James's parents."

"You have a long history with his family. That's beautiful."

"They were enslaved, too, but escaped. His people and mine built a good life in Freetown and then Lagos. We were committed to helping others like us—the formerly enslaved."

"They sound like wonderful people." In the short time that I'd known her, she'd shared these stories with me before, but she liked to repeat them. Or else talking about the past was all she had to say to me.

"They are dead now."

"I know."

"Lost their lives in one of the bad floods that come upon us with as much warning as a clap of thunder."

We were standing, my hands holding the railing to keep the weight off my legs, but my feet ached. I ambled toward my rocking chair.

"Do you mind if we sit?" I asked with a thin smile.

"Please do," she said, but remained standing. "So, now that you are in Africa, what do you plan to do to help Captain Davies with his mission?"

"Help him bring England to Africa. I would love to do that."

"Oh," she said without enthusiasm. "I wondered what you intended to do in the community. Are you planning on teaching at one of the CMS schools? Or other missionary work?"

I winced. "I spent five years translating the King James Bible into Yoruba languages. I believe I have made my missionary contribution for the time being."

Rocking back and forth in the wicker chair, I looked out in the distance on the lagoon and decided to try something to curry her favor. "You have a bond with James, an unbreakable bond. Shared experiences, loves, and losses. I'm sometimes jealous. I don't have that history with him."

"I am proud I helped raise a man like James Davies."

"And you have raised a proud man."

"My lady, may I be direct?"

I stopped rocking, thinking I'd likely gone too far with praising her. "Yes, please do."

"Matilda was a darling child. And she loved James, but I don't prefer her over you. I didn't have a chance to spend much time with her before they sailed to the Caribbean. Upon their return, she was—well, she died. Then Captain Davies asked you to marry him twice. You turned him down twice. But for some reason, unknown to me, he believed you would change your mind, which you did." She smiled. "Despite his weaknesses, and he has one or two, he will overcome his guilt and show you the man he can be to a wife, and he will come to love you. Just as you will come to love him and the baby you carry."

"Guilt?" It was the loudest word I heard in her speech. "He shouldn't feel guilty about Matilda's death. She and his son died in childbirth. It wasn't his fault."

The expression on Sally's face shocked me, but what she said next shocked me more. "It was his fault."

"Sally, that's not true."

"The boat ride from the Caribbean. She was many months with child. He decided to return to Lagos late in her pregnancy. He had business to attend to. He should have waited. So guilt is warranted, but so is forgiveness. And that's what he needs to do. Forgive himself for the choices he made. Then he'll be free. I hoped you would help him find that place in his heart where he could remember forgiveness, but—"

"What? But what?"

"After meeting you, I'm not sure you can help him."

A blunt statement, I thought, offended. "Why? Why do you think I can't help him?"

"Because you had to ask."

* * *

In early May, I felt the first pain in my belly. It circled my abdomen, sending agony down my legs and across my chest at once. By the second day, I thought I wouldn't live to see another, let alone the birth of my child.

My solace came from Sally, who continued to show her indifference toward me without apology. But her passion for James's unborn child could not be questioned. And she was skilled at midwifery.

"It hurts." I clutched my stomach. "Why does it hurt so much?"

"This is only the beginning of the pain, Miss Sarah. You should try and rest between the contractions."

"Rest? My God, how can I rest while this is happening to me? Don't you see? Something is wrong."

"How many babies have you seen born, child?"

"Mrs. Schon had a baby when I was a little girl living in England, and she yelled for a few hours before the baby came. I've been screaming for two days!"

"It's only been one day," Sally said, but I saw signs of worry in her narrowed eyes. "Excuse me. I'll be right back."

Suddenly, Sally was gone. She'd left me in the bedroom. As my eyes darted around the room, barely able to focus on any one thing, I was aware of one missing person. I couldn't recall seeing James for the past day. Since the first pain came, he had disappeared. I started to roll onto my side, but another pain seared across my back, stopping me. My fingers curled into fists, and I screamed at the top of my lungs. I was dying, and there was no one there to watch. If they couldn't help, they might as well bear witness.

"Sarah."

"James?"

His figure, blurred, moved closer. He was with someone, a breathless man.

Despite the pain rattling my bones, I grabbed the sheet to cover myself. "Who is with you? And why are they here?"

"This is a doctor from the Lagos Hospital. Dr. Carson, my wife, Sarah. Princess Sarah. The queen's goddaughter. The queen of England's goddaughter. You must help her. I can't lose her. I can't."

"Captain Davies, give me a moment with her. Please. Let me examine her and see what's happening here."

My husband left me with the white doctor, and I was frightened. "What's wrong with the baby?"

"Do not worry, Mrs. Davies. I am here to examine you."

"My husband went to get you because something's wrong. What is it?" I went to sit up, and another pain hit me so hard that I grabbed the side of the bed and howled.

"That was a hard one, ma'am."

Outside my bedroom door, I could hear the thud of his feet, marching back and forth. I could hear when he paused to listen to the sounds I made when the baby started down the channel of my body. If I'd had some strength, I would have called his name and begged him to come to me. I needed his touch, a gentle stroke on my brow—a loving smile, even. I needed to know someone was thinking of me.

Dr. Carson delivered my baby six hours after he arrived. I don't recall if Sally ever returned until the child was in my arms. I was overjoyed. I was still alive after giving birth to a little girl. I'd been so fearful of death that I wept when James entered the room. I reached out my hand for his touch.

He wrapped his arms around our child and me. "You scared me. We almost lost you."

"But I didn't die," I said in a silly high-pitched voice. "Can you believe it?"

He smiled and sat on the edge of my bed, watching my face to ensure he hadn't hurt me by sitting. "What shall we name her?

I kissed her forehead and inhaled her pure scent deep into my lungs. "You know the Yoruba people have a tradition. They name children as to what their birth was like. I was born with a cord around my neck. Thus, my mother named me Aina."

"I knew some of that."

"Oh, you read Commander Forbes's journals."

"No. You told me."

"I did? I don't remember, but I want to name her Victoria, after the queen. We must make a formal request and also ask if she'll be her godmother. What do you think?"

He stroked the baby's head and looked at me. "I love it, but would you mind if we gave her a middle name—Matilda? She had wanted a baby."

I scooted upright in the bed, wincing, for it hurt so much to move. But I had to be upright to respond to such a thing. Looking into his eyes, I saw what Sally had warned me of. It wasn't that he loved her so much. He had loved her, but his guilt was stronger, and it was the barrier between us. "Fine," I said finally. "Her name will be Victoria Matilda."

Sally walked into the room. "I'm tired," I said to her. "Could you take the baby, please? I need to sleep." Then, as much as it hurt my heart, I handed over my daughter and turned my back on her father. "Good night, Captain Davies."

* * *

SHE WAS PERFECT. A more beautiful baby had never been born. She smelled of life, with the softest skin, the curliest hair, and a flawless shade of brown, and I swear she was laughing from the moment she came into this world.

But how tragic to have a mother who feared her. That was me. So frightened by the thought of motherhood, so frightened by the idea of raising a child, so scared of loving her, and of the knowledge that I would die for her in the blink of an eye—well, I didn't like these feelings.

The obligation to another human was too great. My breasts were her life. She clung to them and cried out for my embrace. I never wanted to run farther and faster from anything in my life. So I decided to stop loving her so much. Victoria Matilda Davies needed to grow up and face reality. Therefore, at three months, I was going to wean her off my breast.

Of course, there was no one I could talk to about these cascading feelings that swallowed me every day, every minute of each day, especially when she cried. And, God help me, when she giggled. Her father would stride into the nursery, planting kisses on her cheeks and her chubby little arms and then a lingering kiss on my forehead.

Since her birth, James and I had behaved differently around each other. It was as if the love we felt for Victoria Matilda was so plentiful it spilled over and landed on us. We embraced love, grabbed and seized it, and hung on to it. We still had our problems. He hadn't let go of his guilt, and I missed England, castles, and strawberry patches. But life wasn't as bleak.

One afternoon Sally came upon me as I stared at my baby girl in her crib, a thing I was apt to do for hours at a time if she was asleep. I had a feeling Sally, bless her soul, could read my mind, and on this day, I learned I was not wrong.

"Would you like me to bring you a cup of tea, ma'am?" We also were getting along better since Victoria Matilda's birth.

"I could use a wet nurse. I thought I would stop nursing Victoria Matilda to spend more time working in the community."

Sally's gaze felt critical.

"What do you think? Is there someone you might know we could make arrangements with?"

"I think I should bring you some tea."

"Oh, Sally. You could discuss the subject with me instead of ignoring it."

"If you want me to give you my opinion, I will."

I wasn't sure I was ready, but I had opened the can. "Yes, please."

"You are afraid of your child because you are afraid of loving her too much. It is not an unusual emotion for a new mother, a first-time mother. It is a lot to deal with, thinking of someone other than yourself every moment of every day. And for you, Sarah, that truly is a new world. So my answer is no. There is no wet nurse in Africa who should do the job you are meant to do."

With that, Sally left me alone with my thoughts, which weren't that complex, for damn it if she wasn't right. It still didn't mean I could do it—be a good mother. The only female I was accustomed to watching over was myself. I wasn't sure I could think of others before I thought of myself.

So again, Sally was right.

Chapter Forty-four

The Lagos Colony, 1866–1877

In 1866, my daughter was three years old and chatty. She didn't talk to me much. She was her father's daughter, and both Sally and I had to fight for her attention. But I swore I would fix it one day.

A sharp-minded girl, Victoria Matilda had a keen sense of who she was and why she mattered. She was the bravest child I'd ever met, other than Monife. She proved her gumption at three by asking me why I never kissed Papa good night but always kissed her. "Don't you think Papa wants kisses, too?"

"I agree, Victoria," James said. "I want kisses, but your mother loves you so much that she doesn't want to use them up on me." His sarcasm didn't go unnoticed by me or our three-year-old.

"Well, I think there are plenty of kisses left after Mama kisses me. But sometimes, Papa, you're not here to get them."

I laughed. "He does work too much, doesn't he, Victoria?"

"Too, too much. If he came home earlier from work, you'd have kisses ready for him."

Seated at the table in the parlor, James dropped his head into his hands. "I see. A plot has been woven, and I embrace the cleverness of your reasoning."

James raised his head and laughed, his eyes sparkling, his gaze only on me.

Sally came into the parlor. "It's time for bed, Victoria Matilda. Come along."

She ran to me, flung her arms around me, and kissed me long and hard on the cheek. Then she skipped off to her father. Hugged him close before saying, "Only one kiss, Papa. Save the rest for Mama."

Sally waved good night, and I shook my head at James and rose. "I guess I'll call it a night as well."

"Are you running away from me? Because of a kiss?"

"James. Come on, we kiss. You kiss me on the forehead, and I kiss you"—I giggled—"in my dreams."

He crossed the room and kissed me on the forehead, but his lips lingered, and he held me around the waist, lifting me off my feet. By then, the kissing was on my lips and my throat, and that was the night we slept together for the first time since our wedding night. And this was the night we started falling in love with each other—and that was quite a surprise.

* * *

A YEAR LATER, it dawned on me. My husband did his best to please me. The sign of his commitment to my happiness extended well beyond the house, too, in which I'd duplicated the decor of every English home I'd ever lived in. However, many things in London didn't exist in the Lagos Colony, and they were missed.

There was no theater, no music halls, no polkas, no singing, and no nursery gardens, but James had an idea along with several other members of the Lagos elite.

The Academy was a social and cultural center that opened in late 1866 with the goal of public enlightenment, dedicated to promoting arts, science, and culture. James was the president, and I created the program. I was also the opening act—the singer, musician, composer—all me.

"Can you believe it happened?" I said to Abigail, who had joined us for dinner. "We have a theater."

"And a newspaper, the first of its kind in Lagos. The *Anglo-African*," James said proudly as if it was his paper. Then, leaning back in his chair, he folded his arms behind his head. "Owned and operated by a Negro man, Robert Campbell."

Abigail giggled, rubbing her stomach. She was several months pregnant and further along than in her recent pregnancies. Her son was a year younger than Victoria Matilda.

"How are you?" I asked.

"Better. Thomas and I are hoping for success," she said. Then she looked from me to James. "What about you two? Aren't you going to have more children? Or am I being too personal?"

"You are being too personal," I said, smiling, but she caught my arched brow. "But yes, I am with child."

"How glorious! I am so excited for you both."

James laughed. "Thank you, Abigail. Sometimes I think everyone in Lagos knows everything there is to know about the Davies household."

"I'm not sure about that," Abigail said. "Don't you have more good news to share, Captain?"

I was confused. "What do you mean? I don't like secrets."

"Captain Davies, will you tell your wife, or should I?"

He poured his drink and nodded for her to proceed.

"The queen has set forth a law—if the Lagos Colony is put in danger by an attack from Dahomey or any foreign entity, Her Majesty's Service, the Royal Navy, has been instructed to provide escorted passage back to England for two citizens of Lagos. And only two."

My nerves shook as if I'd been tossed in the air. "Are they attacking? What is happening? James, why didn't you tell me Lagos was in danger from Dahomey?"

"Because they aren't a threat, not yet. And I would put you and Victoria Matilda on a ship to England before any harm came to you. This is different. Please, go on, Abigail. Sarah will find this of interest." He nodded toward our guest.

"The two to be saved are my father, Reverend Crowther, soon to be named bishop of the church in Africa—"

"Of course he should be saved. That's wonderful news," I said.

"—and the other person to be kept safe at all costs is Her Majesty's ward, Princess Sarah Forbes Bonetta Davies."

My hands covered my face and hid the tears that had come to my eyes. When I had recovered, I removed my hands. "Seriously?"

"Yes, Sarah," said James. "I received the letter today and had intended to share it with you before I remembered Abigail was joining us for dinner."

"Oh, my goodness." I chuckled, wiping my eyes. "The queen is forever thoughtful—and forever cruel. What about her goddaughter? Not me, not the name attributed to me in the newspapers. I was never the queen's goddaughter. But my child is official." I was on my feet, and my voice was loud enough to be heard as far as the lagoon, if not Windsor Castle itself. "She did not include Victoria Matilda? Or my husband?" I pointed a trembling finger at James. "What about you?"

"Darling, please. You're upset."

"Of course I'm upset. She makes this lovely gesture, but she is always shortsighted." I walked over to Abigail, who had been silent too long. "Isn't your father incensed that his family was not included in the gesture?"

"My father is like you. He was upset, but he would never leave us. And your husband would buy a fleet of ships and save half of Africa from Dahomey or whatever blight curses the land. But he wouldn't leave, either." She tilted her head at James. "We love Africa. It is our land. The British are our guests—who believe they are our rulers. They have helped us, but they have also harmed us. If Dahomey comes this far, we will fight them. We will win. And we will carry on."

"Abigail, no better words on the subject have been spoken in my presence. Your children will join you as diplomats," James said. "Now, enough excitement for one evening. Shall we have a glass of sherry?"

I sighed. "That would be lovely."

A few minutes later, we were in the library, glasses of sherry in hand.

"What should we toast?" Abigail asked. "Her Majesty?"

I glanced at James. "No. We are toasting—me."

"Mmm. That sounds like a toast you'd make."

"Ha! But I am toasting James and me, because I am with child."

Abigail covered her heart with her hand. "Bravo." She raised her glass. "To Mr. and Mrs. Davies and their brood."

* * *

IN THE SUMMER of 1867, I lost my second child, a baby girl we named Alice, after the princess, now the Duchess of Hesse.

My grief was tolerable after I lost her—a surprising thought.

I had a little girl whose memory stayed with me, and I cried long and hard, endless tears. I had a husband who sat with me during the worst days, and he wept, too.

But I learned something about myself when Alice was lost. Death wasn't always a fiend, the creature I'd known for many years. This time there were no machetes, no cries of Agojie warriors, and no giant waves crashing against the hull of the ship. Sometimes, when death happens, it's just because.

* * *

THE YEARS CAME and went. There were highs and lows. I gave birth to a son we named Arthur in 1871 and another girl we named Stella in 1873. However, that same year, Reverend Henry Venn, my husband's dear friend and the man who knew my first love, Freddie, met his God. A few months later, I suffered a terrible cold that lasted for several weeks, but I recovered. However, something good did result from my illness. The hospital situation in the Lagos Colony for native Lagosians caught my attention. But I didn't do anything until later.

My eldest daughter, Victoria Matilda, was ten years old and following in her mother's footsteps. A fact I didn't look upon with pride. She wanted to attend school in Britain. It was our first serious disagreement. Her father's support of schools in Lagos and Freetown created legacies. I had attended the Female Institution. Why couldn't she study in Africa? I never mentioned I'd hated almost every moment I spent at the Female Institution, but that was not my point.

No matter how much she frustrated me, perhaps because of our similar personalities, her father was the rock that kept us in place. She was too young to leave home and remained at school in Lagos.

On the other hand, James was secretive, which I discovered in the summer of 1873. The Academy had failed almost a year after it had opened. Something to do with politics was the reason for its quick demise. I paid little attention to particulars. My heart was broken. But James bought me a piano and shipped the children and me off to England for a few months.

I felt better upon our return. But my husband had found a new adventure—charitable—with only a hint of political upheaval.

The Lagos Philanthropic Club had the same members as the Academy. I believed that it aimed to help the young men of Lagos have something better to do with their evenings than become layabouts. The club had opened Phoenix Hall in Tinubu Square. The entertainment focused on African culture, very different from the Academy, but art nonetheless.

The money raised was donated to the Aroloya Church, but the reverend refused it. James wouldn't tell me why, but the club was denounced in the press.

The articles accused it of giving performances with a "great prevalence of licentiousness which hinders the property of families and churches in this place." Yet from what James was willing to share, the only things performed were African stories, plays, and history. Not European. Not British.

Looking at my husband's glum face every evening was boring. So it was my turn to find a project for him instead of the other way around. I talked to Abigail, who knew more about important things in Lagos than I did. And before long, I had a plan.

"I think I'd like to start a hospital where Africans can be treated by doctors who want to treat Africans. Not those thirty beds the Lagos hospital reserves for native people when the rest of the hospitals are filled with Brits." I peered over the top of my whiskey glass, trusting that he'd be intrigued by what I'd said. Perhaps I should let him talk.

"What do you think?" I pressed my lips together to force myself not to say another word until he could reply.

"I think it's a marvelous idea."

I waited for a few beats, then a few more beats. "That's all? It's a marvelous idea? Do you want to help me, or is it something you intend to go off and do yourself?"

He left his wing-backed chair and walked over to me. "I will do whatever you want. I'm glad you're back. I missed you and my children. Next time, I think I'll go with you to England. How does that sound?"

He kissed me on the forehead, and I noticed the exhaustion in his step, his voice, and even his kiss. "I read some things in the newspaper. Is the business safe?"

"It will be, but I don't want you to worry. Let's see what we can accomplish with the hospital. My business isn't going anywhere."

Chapter Forty-five

The Lagos Colony, 1878–1880

If we talked about miracles, the Iroko tree in Freetown was one I could attest to—because of it, my blue pendant hung around my neck that day.

I had not found an Iroko tree in the Lagos Colony. But something here was magical and a sign from the Yoruba gods, and not something the Church of England manifested.

I was not being sacrilegious. God had saved me many times, and I would not deny his power, love, or mercy. Ever. After all, I was a Christian woman.

Nonetheless, the human form of an Iroko tree walked into the Lagos hospital out of the blue. She didn't recognize me. She hadn't seen me since I was maybe seven, almost seven, but I recognized her. I could never forget those wiry limbs, straight back, and the fierceness of a girl who ran like a gazelle.

And those marks on her cheeks. Like mine, they were still there, too.

"Monife."

The woman looked at me, but it took a moment of staring and squinting before her lips curled into a smile. Then her eyes brightened with that gaze of appreciation I recognized, when she saw something she wanted to grab and hold on to.

"If it isn't Aina. Where have you been all these years? I thought you were sliced up and left in a pit."

"And you as well. Or shackled and dropped into a ship's hull."

At that, we were in each other's arms, tears flying, the hug so completely engulfing that I could feel her heart beating against mine.

Monife was alive. After all these years, I'd found someone I'd lost.

I hugged her so tightly I felt her muscles give way. "What happened to you?" I released her to see her face, where tears brimmed in her wide brown eyes.

"I was enslaved and taken to the Americas, but I'm free now."

I caressed her cheek. She was real. "The day you disappeared was when they put you on a ship?"

"Yes. I was too old at twelve to hide. That's why I was so brave that day. I knew they'd catch me." Her eyelids lowered, hiding her emotions for a breath. "I kept getting so close to being caught, I grew tired of the chase. It was time to stop messing about and face my maker. It wasn't the best choice. There were nights and days, long days, dreadful nights when I thought it might have been better to have my head chopped off, but after all these years, I'm still alive. I must have made the right decision. And look at you. My God, you look like a princess and sound like one, too. A British princess."

I laughed. "Do you have time to come with me? We must talk. Do you live here in Lagos? Tell me everything."

"It's a long story, but I do live here. I've been here for a long time, but I needed quiet for a while."

I nodded, understanding. "I've been here for a while, too. I have a husband and children and a house. You can come to my house. Please come to my house. We can have tea."

"Oh, my Lord," she said, eyeing me from head to toe, a brow lifted. "That dress, those shoes, and the bonnet, too. What has happened to you?"

"What can I say? Like yours, it's a long story. I want to tell you everything and hear everything about you." Then I remembered. "Look. I still have it. My blue pendant necklace."

Monife touched the blue stone as I pulled it from underneath my collar, and then she covered her mouth as a fresh stream of tears fell from her eyes. Then I cried more, too. Overdue tears that had been held in my heart and beneath my skin, untouched, for so long. For too long, they'd been buried inside me. Drowning my spirits, holding on to just enough of me to keep me from the joy I deserved.

"I can't believe you still have it." Monife brought the pendant close to her face, as if doing so would bring the scents and sights of its journey to life.

"Of course I do." I nudged her in the arm. "I've lost it a few times, but it finds its way back to me. Like you."

We stood in the corridor, talking, reminiscing, and sharing our lives, for a long time. So long, the sky became dark. We made plans to see each other in a few days when we could talk until dawn if we liked—and then we embraced.

"My oldest and dearest friend." I kissed her cheek. "Promise. We will never lose each other again."

"I promise. Never."

* * *

THERE WAS A freshness in my spirit, a bounce in my step, and a smile that I couldn't stop sharing. Even with my cough and a worried eldest daughter, I liked the feeling of hope.

"Mother. Mother! We must return to the house!" Victoria Matilda shouted. "You've walked far enough. Sally will have my head."

My daughter wasn't a patient caregiver. "You worry too much. I am much better. I intend to reach the lagoon today."

We were taking a walk near the harbor at my insistence. My household was recovering from a lingering cold that had taken out most of its vengeance on me.

"Mother, remember, we have to walk back."

"Are you listening to me or not? I want to reach the lagoon. Then we can turn around. I need to build my strength, which won't happen if I am lazy about these walks."

Victoria Matilda gave a raspy cough.

"The walk is good for you, too. Your cough sounds better. Still bad, but better."

She rolled her eyes. "How about your breathing, Mother? You shouldn't be overtaxing yourself."

"Are you worried more about me or Sally's wrath?"

We both laughed. In the fifteen years since Victoria Matilda's birth, Sally's sweet, gracious manner had been tested by my two youngest children. James had to hire a nanny for Arthur and Stella, a young Egbado girl named Omi. But Sally still raged when it came to my eldest and me.

My chest discomfort caused me to pause, and I leaned against a nearby wood bench.

"I told you we should start back, Mother. How is your breathing?"

"Stop asking me about my breathing. But if you must know, it is like climbing a hillside with a giant gourd on my head. What else would you like me to say? I'm a bit tired. Still, don't worry."

"I'm not worried," she said, and skipped to pick up a handful of pebbles to pitch into the lagoon. One moment she was a young girl approaching womanhood—the next, she was just a girl playing with stones.

I sat on the bench. "Victoria Matilda. Come here."

She plopped down on the bench next to me. "Yes, Mother."

"Why did you want to join me today? Is something on your mind?"

She twisted her mouth to the side, a pouty expression that reminded me of her father, which would mortify him. "Don't get angry," she pleaded.

"Not the best way to start a conversation with me—but go ahead."

"Queen Victoria has invited me to spend the early part of the new year in London at Windsor Castle. And Mother, I want to go. Please. Father said it was up to you."

The queen invited her every year, and every year I said no. My daughter already spent summers in England. She had wanted to go to school in England since she was ten. "It will be too late for the pantomime," I said, "but the castle loves its winter parties."

"Yes, ma'am. You know about them?"

I took her hand and held it. "Of course, I know about all of them. I attended every ball, theater, and opera in London with members of the royal family. Princess Alice, mostly. But it's cold. You'll need a warm wardrobe."

"I can go?" She jumped up in the air so high I thought she'd fly away.

"Yes, you can go." I couldn't explain to my daughter why Monife's return to my life made it easier to say yes to Victoria

Matilda after so many times saying no. I guess I had faith that she wouldn't be lost to me. She would return.

Victoria Matilda hugged my shoulders achingly hard. I had to tell her to release me.

"My friend you've met is spending the weekend. Monife. Remember her? Well, you know she's someone I thought I'd never see again. I want you to have dinner with us—us girls. I want you to get to know her."

"I remember. But she's not from England, is she?"

"No. No. She's never been to England. We met in Africa."

"Oh, Africa. In Freetown when you were at the Female Institution?"

"No. Before."

At that moment, I realized I'd told my daughter very little about my life before I was the African princess in Queen Victoria's castles. That needed to change.

"Look, Mother." Victoria Matilda was up and waving. "It's Sally with the carriage."

"What is she doing here?" I watched her approach with my heart in my throat.

"She's come to fetch us," Victoria Matilda said. "Oh, dear. I bet she's furious."

"No. Something's happened." I rose from the bench and walked toward Sally, who had stepped out of the carriage, but she wasn't moving like her usual self. My heart pounded, and dread blurred my vision. I stopped, staring at only the swish of her skirt. I didn't even notice her expression as she told me what had happened.

"I'm sorry, Miss Sarah, but we just received word. The Grand Duchess of Hesse died. May God have mercy on her soul."

I gasped. Alice was only thirty-five years old. The same as me. My friend. Dead and gone. "What happened? I just received a letter from her the other day. How can she be dead?"

Sally held me as she whispered in my ear, "She died of diphtheria, taking care of her children and her husband, who all came down with the dreaded disease."

"When did she pass?"

"December 14, 1878."

"Oh, my," I sighed. "Her father died on the fourteenth of December in 1861."

* * *

MUSIC WAS ALWAYS playing, always in the back of my mind, the sound of drums in the distance, the nine-note trill of a Mendelssohn concerto at my fingertips. I heard melody and percussion, even in the silences, like waves crashing against the rocks, reminding me of the discord of my life.

As I walked along the peer, staring at the lagoon, I hummed a melody—the Princess Royal's wedding march, of all things—and I thought of those days in England, the other days in Abomey, Freetown, and now, Lagos.

My many homes. My many worlds. So many different lives, too perfect to imagine and too difficult to ignore. But what was life without hardship? What was love without loneliness? Who was I without my past? What would be my legacy?

"What are you thinking about, Sarah?"

My husband walked at my side, holding my hand. "Oh, I'm not sure. Just a jumble of thoughts."

"Tell me. I want to know everything you are thinking."

He surprised me, sounding almost romantic. "If you insist, I'll recite some passages, from the novel I started writing."

"A novel. How wonderful."

I shrugged, feeling shy. "I've wanted to write a novel since I read Jane Austen years ago. And I also write travel journals, like any proper English lady."

"You aren't English. You are African, my love," he said teasingly while smiling down at me.

I turned to face him, looking him in the eye. Eyes I stared into warmly, lovingly, when once upon a time, I thought I'd never be able to feel such affection for him in just a glance. "I know, but I hang on to the pieces I wish to hang on to. Can't I do that?"

"Of course. Now, tell me about your novel."

"I'll recite some of the lines I've rewritten. I am not sure yet what it's about."

"Very well, I'm listening." A soft smile touched his lips.

"Here goes." I adjusted the scarf around my throat. "I've had a mighty love and have been loved mightily."

"Yes, you have." He lifted my hand and planted a kiss on my palm.

"Stop your shenanigans and let me finish." My tone was admonishing, but he knew I wasn't serious.

He held up his hands playfully in surrender. "I'm sorry—no more interruptions. I promise."

"Thank you." I rose onto my tiptoes and kissed him. "I have hated with every bone in my body and wanted to die from sorrow and live forever with joy." Then the coughing began.

James's smile faltered, his expression stern and severe.

It took a moment for me to recover. "There were days I regretted and nights I thought would never end. I have hopes and dreams but have also been jarred from my sleep by nightmares where I am forced to relive the horrors of my life."

The shadow of a bird's wings darkened a patch of sand in front of us. It stirred a memory, something from long ago, like the river outside Okeadon. I coughed again.

"I've made arrangements."

I smacked my lips. "I don't want to go."

"The doctors have said you will be better if you go." He held my face in his hands.

I chewed on my lower lip. "Can the children come with me?"

"I'll visit when I can. But yes, the children are coming with you. Except for Victoria. She wants to spend the summer in London."

"I know. I know. And I told her she could go." Even though a part of me wished I hadn't. I was going to miss her terribly.

"Then it's settled?" He seemed surprised.

"So, off I go—to Funchal, Madeira, for the summer. What will you do without Sally and me around?"

"You can't cook. I will starve without Sally, but she won't let you go without her."

I laughed. "And to think I thought she'd never like me."

PART FIVE

It Ends in the Middle

Chapter Forty-six

Funchal, Madeira Island, Portugal, 1880

From every room, I smell the salt in the ocean's waves and can watch the seagulls swooping and diving over the sand until they disappear into the water. Even my bedroom has a splendid view—a view befitting a princess is what my husband promised. A man who always keeps his word.

"I finished! It's done! Three volumes. It's quite the tale, too."

Of course, I may have yelled, but mostly I am talking to myself, but that's fine. A celebration doesn't need an audience, even in a house full of people.

I clear my throat, which hurts my chest. My cough is a little worse today, but I won't let that interfere with my celebration.

"I finished!" I stack my journals neatly, proud of what I've accomplished.

Sally enters the room, feet scurrying, hands full. "What is wrong?"

I wonder why she appears so nervous. "I'm fine, better than fine, but if you don't mind, I'd like to go for a walk on the beach before lunch. I'm celebrating. I finished the journals."

"That's lovely, Miss Sarah," she says, sounding breathless. "I heard you yell. I was at the bottom of the house and those stairs."

"It's all right. I'm fine. You worry too much."

"I can't help it." She gives me a knowing look as if to remind me in that one glance how much I need to remember about my health.

"I know. You love me." I smile and recline in my chair. "Why is that? You didn't always."

Sally checks the vases for the freshness of the flowers, picks up doilies, and puts them back in the same spot. My question made her nervous. "Come on, Sally. Tell me why? I need an ego boost."

She stops in front of the grand piano. "You're a good girl. That's why. Spoiled. Self-centered. But you suffered and survived. More than most. Less than some."

"Why, thank you. It's the best compliment I've ever received." I attempt to sit up, but my strength isn't what it should be. "Maybe I will save the walk for tomorrow, Sally. I know I've written my letters for today. But I'd like to write a note to Victoria. Would you bring my stationery?"

"Certainly, Madam Sarah."

"I think I will join her in England for the Christmas holidays. The queen invited her again, but I'll join her this year. She's seventeen, and I'm sure she'll marry soon. That young doctor she's seeing is impressive. But before she turns into a married woman, we will have one last mother-daughter adventure. It will be divine."

"A splendid idea." Sally places the items I need on the table.

"I want to tell her about the Iroko tree, too. And everything I can remember about the Egbado people and Okeadon. They said I never remembered my life before England. But the older I am, the more I remember. There's so much I want Victoria Matilda to know about Okeadon. My father and mother. My brothers and sisters. Their history must not die."

The pain comes fast and sharp, closing around my rib cage

like a jagged fist. Each breath is harder than the last. Another cough cracks through me and doesn't dissipate. But the very next thing I feel is Sally's strong fingers massaging the muscles along my spine.

"Thank you," I say after a time.

"Do you wish to go to bed and rest?"

"No. I'm fine. I want to write my daughter that letter. I thought I had put everything in those journals, but my head is filling with memories." I sit in the desk chair, with its rosewood spiral legs and balloon back. "Would you mind fixing me some tea? I have too many thoughts. Oolong tea. And another empty journal."

"Yes, ma'am."

"And gingerbread cake, Sally."

"Yes, ma'am," she says. "Oolong tea, an empty journal, and gingerbread cake."

"Bring the journal first." I lift the pen, but my fingers tremble. It doesn't matter. I'll just try again.

Sally returns to the room, journal in hand. "Here you are, ma'am. But the stove is acting up. Won't have hot water for a few minutes."

"I don't need tea to begin writing in my journal, Sally. I only need to begin."

Chapter Forty-seven

Windsor Castle, 1900

It was Wednesday, November 9, a little before noon. Her mission was to hand-deliver three volumes, although she wished there could have been four, but only three journals had been written by Sarah Forbes Bonetta Davies. Wife, mother, princess, and her eldest daughter's hero.

Windsor Castle was a jungle of tapestries, domed ceilings, and sparkling chandeliers, with a breeze that sailed across the back of her neck with the finesse of a swarm of bees. It also didn't help that the last time Victoria Matilda Davies Randle had visited Queen Victoria, she'd been a wide-eyed teenager. But not like her young daughter, who now clung to her skirt with the fierceness of a warrior. She was like her son, walking ahead, looking around as if he planned to set up shop. He was, like his father, searching for answers among the ruins.

Victoria Matilda was like her mother, who charged from one room into another, daring servants, guards, princesses, and a queen to stop her. Although sometimes Victoria Matilda preferred to sink beneath the carpet-covered floorboards rather than enter any room in the castle without permission.

Bishop Johnson was her escort. He led the way to a waiting room. "Now, what is this room's name?" he asked.

"It's the Green Drawing Room, Bishop," said her son before Victoria Matilda could reply.

It had been an arduous journey from Lagos to London. She'd arrived months ago believing she knew what she intended to do with the journals. First, she had to read them. That took longer than expected because there were days when she couldn't turn a page. Her mother's words warmed her heart so much the most she could do was weep or laugh, or sigh.

The journals had been packed away for twenty years when she received them following Sally's death. The instructions had been simple. "Give Victoria Matilda the journals. Her mother wrote them for her."

Her mother's words touched Victoria Matilda's heart and mind. So much history, her mother's flaws, perfections, loves and hates, challenges, defeats, and victories. After reading the journals, her first instinct was to donate them to England. But that wasn't enough. Her mother's life should be exalted.

The journals had to be in a place connected to the woman she was and the life she led.

A shiver went down her arm and into her young son's clenched fingers, which only tightened inside her palm. Her daughter, eight years old, had released her mother's skirt and skipped ahead, turning this way and that, taking in everything, leaving nothing untouched by her gaze. She was her grandmother's child.

Victoria Matilda, the daughter of a princess and the godchild of a queen, had left a part of herself in Lagos. In England, her stomach clenched, her back stiffened, and her footsteps tapped out the sounds of a tune she recalled from her youth. One of the many songs her mother had sung to her.

Suddenly a door opened and a woman Victoria Matilda recognized entered.

"Her Majesty and Princess Beatrice are ready to receive you now."

"Lady Harriet, it is good to see you again."

"As it is to see you, Victoria Matilda. And your two lovely children." She smiled at them with ageless eyes, glistening. "Bishop, will you wait with them while I escort Mrs. Randle to the sitting room? I will return shortly with tea and sweets."

"Of course."

"Thank you, Bishop." Then Lady Harriet Phipps led the way.

After such a long journey, Victoria Matilda stood before Her Majesty, the queen of England, but with a change of heart. "I have come here to give you these journals. My previous letters expressed my belief that my mother's letters and journals should be in a Royal Archive."

Princess Beatrice glanced at Her Majesty and then at Victoria Matilda. "We've been talking about creating an official archive but haven't started the process yet."

"My mother's story shouldn't be forgotten but celebrated. She is a part of England's history. Still, I have realized that her life's mission was her work in Africa, in Yorubaland, her homeland, her heritage—and her beliefs, opinions, ideas, happiness, and even her grief should be preserved and honored for posterity."

"We agree, Victoria Matilda. That is why we are meeting today, isn't it?" Princess Beatrice glanced at the satchel Victoria Matilda held.

"It was." She pressed her lips together, biting back the nerves that had gripped her. "But I changed my mind walking through these halls, thinking about her and these journals, her life in Africa when she was a child, and those early days with my father." She raised her hand. "My mother belongs to Africa. England was part of her story, but who she became was despite

England. I want Africa to know her, and the journals belong in Africa."

They blinked at her without saying a word.

Victoria Matilda drew a steadying breath and continued, "She hated Africa, and she loved Africa. She loved my father. She loved me, my brother and sister, and her friends Monife, William, and Princess Alice. She had heartbreak and heartache, but one hundred years from now, people will learn from her. People who look like her will know a woman who was an African princess, the ward of Queen Victoria, and the wife of one of the wealthiest African men in Lagos. A mother, a masterful pianist, singer, writer, and a girl who liked to win."

"We agree," Queen Victoria said, surprising Victoria Matilda when she thought Her Majesty might object.

There was nothing more to say about the journals after that. The queen, Princess Beatrice, and Victoria Matilda sipped tea and spent the afternoon sharing memories of Sarah and happier, younger days.

It was Victoria Matilda's last visit with Her Majesty before the queen's death, two months later, but it was the best afternoon she'd ever spent with her godmother.

Her mother, Princess Aina of Okeadon, and Sarah Forbes Bonetta Davies, would have been proud.

The British Cemetery, Funchal, Madeira Island, Portugal, 1880

IN MEMORY OF PRINCESS
SARAH FORBES BONETTA

WIFE OF THE HON J. P. L. DAVIES WHO
DEPARTED THIS LIFE AT MADEIRA

AUGUST 15TH 1880

AGED 37 YEARS

Author's Note

I love research. It allows me to dig into history, cultures, people, and philosophies that assist me in bringing the past to life in a novel.

For *The Other Princess*, I was blessed with two amazing works that served as my guide to digging deeper into the life and times of Aina, renamed Sarah Forbes Bonetta, and Captain James P. L. Davies.

In writing the novel, I did make some adjustments. Most notably to the age of Abigail Crowther, the daughter of Samuel Ajayi Crowther, the first African Anglican bishop of West Africa, who attended the Female Institution in Freetown, Sierra Leone. She attended the school, but I adjusted the years, so she was Sarah's elder at the institution. But the two women did give birth to their first children in 1863 and 1864: Victoria Matilda in 1863, and Abigail Crowther's son Herbert Macaulay, who became a famed Nigerian nationalist, in 1864.

The Other Princess: A Novel of Queen Victoria's Goddaughter is inspired by the life of Sarah Forbes Bonetta, an African princess captured by Dahomey warriors (Agojie, also known as Amazons) led by King Gezo in 1848. She spent two years in captivity before she was spotted by Lieutenant Commander Frederick E. Forbes, who chronicled his experiences in Africa in two journals: *Dahomey and the Dahomans: Being the Journals of Two Missions to King of Dahomey, and Residence at his Capital, in the Year 1849 and 1850*. These journals were published in 1851, following his death.

Other resources used include: *At Her Majesty's Request: An African Princess in Victorian England* by Walter Dean Myers, as a children's book, in 1999; *The Life of James Pinson Labulo Davies: A Colossus of Victorian Lagos* by Adeyemo Elebute, 2013; *The Yoruba from Prehistory to the Present* by Aribidesi Usman and Toyin Falola; and works of the Nigerian Poet Gabriel Okara.

Numerous articles written between 1850 and 1901 about Queen Victoria's "ward or goddaughter" and other historical events in the London *Times*, the *Daily Telegraph*, the (London) *Sun*, and many other British newspapers were invaluable, as were articles, videos, and nonfiction book excerpts from ProQuest, Ancestry.com, and digital libraries such as JSTOR.

I also utilized the Map Room at the Library of Congress in Washington, DC, as well as its online resources for more information on the West Africa of the mid-nineteenth century, the Dahomey and King Gezo (also spelled "Ghezo"), and the history of Freetown.

Note that Sarah's journals are fiction. The letters she wrote that appear in Mr. Myers's and Mr. Elebute's books are the primary source of original materials written by her. Sarah Forbes Bonetta Davies died of tuberculosis on August 15, 1880.

Acknowledgments

I feel humbled and honored to have had the opportunity to write a novel about the life of Sarah Forbes Bonetta Davies. I spent a lot of time with her over the past few years, and she has been a beacon that kept sharing her light throughout this journey.

This story was been a gift in many ways. And I would like to acknowledge those who have been instrumental in helping me at every stage.

First, thank you to my editor, Tessa Woodward. Your commitment to getting this story told is at the heart of this novel's existence. Your zeal in seeking stories that need to be told by voices anxious to write them is commendable. I appreciate the faith and the support you and the William Morrow team have given me. Hooray to the production team, the art department for the dazzling cover, and everyone at William Morrow who has helped this book fly. And I'd very much like to acknowledge my agent, Nalini Akolekar. Thank you for all you do.

It is no joke that it takes a village to get a book written, and for me, I need an entire town of villages in all shapes and sizes. So, let me dive in and thank those shining lights so dear to me.

My beta reader, Nadine Monaco. Your time and devotion, and your keen eye, are a blessing. Eliza Knight is a tireless advocate, and thank you for your friendship. Also, I must recognize Nina Crespo, my go-to brainstorming queen. You always have a way of saying the right thing at the right time with flair. Some of the other village inhabitants I couldn't have written this book without are Sharon Campbell, Leslye Penelope, Nancy Johnson, Ines Johnson, Pintip Dunn, Deborah Evans, and Veronica Forand.

And I like to save the superstar for the final curtain. A huge thank-you to my bestie, Vanessa Riley, author extraordinaire; she is a woman who keeps sisterhood and friendship as her guide.

About the Author

DENNY S. BRYCE is an award-winning and bestselling author of historical fiction, including *Wild Women and the Blues* and *In the Face of the Sun*. She is an adjunct professor in the MFA program at Drexel University, a book critic for NPR, and a freelance writer whose work has been published in *USA Today*, *Harper's Bazaar*, and Frolic Media. She is a member of the Historical Novel Society, Women's Fiction Writers Association, and Tall Poppy Writers. Currently she resides in Savannah, Georgia.